"Tell me who you are."

"Raine Wimbourne," she said on a strangled gasp.

Philippe used his teeth to tug the offending chemise out of his way. "Your real name."

"That is my real name." She shivered, but Philippe possessed enough experience to know it was not from fear.

"You said if I told you my name you would release me," she charged.

"You have not told me why you were playing such a dangerous charade."

"I cannot."

Philippe was busily learning the sweet hollow between her breasts.

"Dear God," she breathed.

Her husky voice was an unwelcome intrusion.

"Stop this and I will tell you the truth."

A DARING PASSION

Rosemary Rogers

MILLS & BOON®
Pure reading pleasure™

First published in Great Britain 2009
by Harlequin Mills & Boon Limited,
Eton House, 18-24 Paradise Road, Richmond, Surrey TW9 1SR

© Rosemary Rogers 2007

ISBN: 978 0 263 87401 3

037-0209

Harlequin Mills & Boon policy is to use papers that are
natural, renewable and recyclable products and made from
wood grown in sustainable forests. The logging and
manufacturing processes conform to the legal environmental
regulations of the country of origin.

Printed and bound in Spain
by Litografia Rosés S.A., Barcelona

New York Times bestselling author **Rosemary Rogers** has written over twenty historical and contemporary romances. Dubbed "the queen of historical romance," she is best known for her passionate and sensual characters, and her Steve-and-Ginny series is a classic with fans. Born in Ceylon, Rosemary now lives in Connecticut.

*Available from Rosemary Rogers
and Mills & Boon®*

A RECKLESS ENCOUNTER
AN HONOURABLE MAN
RETURN TO ME
JEWEL OF MY HEART
SAPPHIRE

For my family

CHAPTER ONE

THE NIGHT WAS FRANKLY miserable. Although the rain that had drenched the Kent countryside over the past two days had at last drizzled to a halt, the air was still thick with moisture and a blanket of fog lay over the slumbering villages and estates.

A miserable night to be certain. At least for decent folk.

It was a perfect night for thieves, scoundrels and dastards.

Too perfect, Josiah Wimbourne was forced to concede as he entered his small cottage and painfully tossed aside his brilliant crimson cape and hat. He should have known the magistrate would be on the alert. The muddy roads and heavy fog would slow even the finest carriage. Such easy pickings were far too great a temptation for any highwayman.

Especially for the notorious Knave of Knightsbridge.

With a grimace Josiah crossed the small kitchen to settle in a chair near the smoldering fire. Only then did he glance toward his shoulder, which was still seeping blood. Damn his stupidity. He was nearing forty years of age. Old enough to know that it was a dead man who underestimated his enemy.

The previous magistrate might have been a blundering fool who was quite willing to turn a blind eye if the price was right, but this new man, Tom Harper, was cut from an entirely different cloth.

In less than a month he had proved to be impervious to

bribes, intimidation and even outright threats. Nothing could sway his sense of duty or determination to uphold the king's law.

Even worse, the blighter possessed an uncanny knack for thinking precisely like a criminal.

Any other magistrate would look at the dismal weather and presume that any brigands would be cozily drinking ale at the local inn, or warming themselves in the arms of a willing whore. But not Harper. He had taken stock of the rutted roads and thick fog and known instinctively that the Knave would be out hunting.

Blast his interfering soul.

Unwittingly a small smile flickered over Josiah's weathered features. Despite the burning pain in his shoulder, and the undeniable realization he was in a precarious position, he could not deny a measure of admiration for the tenacious magistrate.

Since leaving his life in the navy, it was rare to discover an opponent worthy of his skills. Certainly not the Runners, whom his victims occasionally hired to track him down. Or even the militia, which had been called in by the local aristocrats who had wearied of having their elegant guests robbed traveling through Knightsbridge. How could he not respect the damnable cur?

His ridiculous thoughts were cut short as a slight, dour-faced servant entered the kitchen to regard him with a startled frown.

Foster had once been a trained manservant who had worked at some of the finest homes in London. A position he might still be holding today if he had not been caught forging his employer's signature to obtain a number of bank drafts. It didn't matter that he had used the money to assist a floundering orphanage rather than lining his own pocket. He had been found guilty and ordered to the penal colonies.

He had tossed himself from the convict ship and was near death when Josiah had fished him from the waters.

That had been nearly twenty years ago and Josiah had never had cause to regret his impulsive gesture. Foster had proved to possess unwavering loyalty and the skill to teach Josiah the proper manners necessary to pass for a true gentleman.

The fact that Josiah remained a scoundrel beneath his elegant image was entirely his own fault.

Noticing the blood staining his master's shirt, Foster hurried forward. "Good Lord, sir, you've been injured."

"So it would seem, Foster."

"Well, I've given you warning enough, the Lord knows." The servant gave a click of his tongue. "A man of your age should be seated by the fire, not tearing across the countryside as if you were still a strapping lad. Bound to come a cropper in the end. I suppose that demon-spawn beast you claim as a horse gave you a tumble?"

"No, I did not take a tumble, damn your impudence. I am neither a man in his dotage nor a greenhorn unable to control his mount, demon-spawn or not."

"Then what…?" Bending forward to have a closer look at the injury, Foster abruptly caught his breath. "Bloody hell. You've been shot."

"Yes, I did suspect as much." Josiah gave a muttered curse as he pulled his ruined shirt over his head and tossed it to the nearby fire. "Damn Liverpool and his wretched Tories. They take delight in taxing their citizens into abject poverty and then pretend horror when those citizens are forced to live a life of crime to survive."

"Liverpool shot you?"

Josiah gave a short, humorless laugh. "No, you muckworm. It was the magistrate."

"Oh…aye." Moving to the cabinet, Foster wet a cloth and returned to Josiah's side. "Well, let us have a look."

Josiah sucked in a sharp breath as the servant pressed the

cloth to his wound. "Have a care, Foster. It hurts like the very devil."

Foster continued rubbing at his shoulder, indifferent to Josiah's muttered oaths.

"Only a crease, thank the good Lord, but a deep one." He stepped back to regard Josiah with an expression that managed to be even more dour than usual. "You'll be needing stitches."

"I feared as much." Josiah gave a shake of his head. It wasn't his first wound and doubtless wouldn't be his last, but it was damn well inconvenient. "Don't stand there gawking, Foster. Fetch the needle and thread. Oh, and the brandy. If I'm to endure your ham-fisted surgery then I have a feeling I shall want my wits dulled to the point of insensibility."

Without warning Foster was backing away, his hands lifting in dismay. "Fiend seize it. I'm a manservant, not a damnable sawbones. If you need stitching then call for old man Durbin."

"And have him spread the tale of my injury to the entire neighborhood on the first occasion he is in his cups?" Josiah growled. "Don't be more a fool than you have to be."

"What does it matter?" Foster shrugged. "No one takes notice of his drunken babblings."

"I assure you the magistrate will take great interest in any babbling that concerns a wounded gentleman," Josiah confessed, grimacing at his stupidity. "He knows he managed to shoot the Knave of Knightsbridge this eve. You might as well put the noose around my neck and be done with it."

There was a pregnant pause as the servant sorted through the words and at last comprehended the danger of their situation.

"Bloody hell," he breathed, a frown tugging his shaggy gray brows together. "I suspected that the man would prove to be a pain in the arse. Can't abide a gentleman who is forever sticking his nose into the business of others."

Despite his pain, Josiah's lips twitched at his servant's indignant tone. "I believe, my dear Foster, that he perceives it his duty to stick his nose into whatever business happens to be conducted in his district."

"Oh, aye, determined to make a name for himself in London, no doubt. Don't matter how many decent folk he has to hang."

"Or indecent folk, as the case may be."

Foster gave a snort as he tossed the bloody cloth into the sink. He was a simple man. A man who possessed his own unique sense of right and wrong. And nothing could convince him to consider his master a dastardly criminal.

A pity not everyone was so sublimely indifferent to his wicked habits, Josiah acknowledged wryly.

"He ain't nothing to old Royce," Foster groused. "Now, there was a magistrate who knew how to do his duties."

"He also had the decency to accept a friendly bribe when offered," Josiah lightly teased.

"Aye, a man of sense."

"And an unfortunate appetite for cheap gin and cheaper whores that managed to land him in an early grave." Josiah gave a shake of his head, wincing as a pain shot through his shoulder. "We may rue his loss, but it will not alter the fact that our mission has become considerably more dangerous, old friend."

"Mayhap you should lay low for a while."

Josiah attempted to get comfortable on the wooden chair. He wanted nothing more than a hot bath and a soft bed, but he knew that he had to tend to his wound before either was possible.

Which meant convincing his stubborn companion to get on with the bloody business.

"Never fear, Foster, this damnable wound has seen that I will be laying low for several days, if not weeks. And speaking of wounds, you're stalling. I have no intention of bleeding to death because you are too squeamish to stick me with a needle."

Foster gave a shake of his head. "Nay, sir."

"Fine, then fetch the blasted needle and I'll do it myself," Josiah commanded, his patience at a limit.

"Perhaps I may be of assistance?"

Both men stiffened at the sound of the soft, decidedly female voice. Briefly closing his eyes, Josiah wondered why he had ever left his bed that morning. Surely the gray weather and chilled breeze should have warned him to pull the covers over his head and give it up as a loss?

Unable to avoid the inevitable, Josiah slowly turned his head to discover his only child standing in the doorway of the kitchen.

No, not child, he corrected himself. Somehow his Raine had managed to transform herself into a woman while she was being schooled in that damnable French convent.

A remarkably beautiful woman.

As always he was forced to battle a small measure of astonishment.

Although he had been considered a handsome enough fellow in his day, and his long-departed wife had been a pretty maiden, there had been no warning that together they would create a...masterpiece.

There was no other word to describe the young woman standing before him.

Wreathed in the light of the flickering candles, her beauty was luminous, her ivory skin glowing with the perfect sheen of a rare pearl and her dark eyes faintly slanted and surrounded by a lush thicket of lashes that lent an air of smoldering mystery. Her nose was a tiny, straight line that contrasted with the full bow of her mouth. And just beside that lovely mouth was a tiny black mole that seemed deliberately placed to provoke a man's attention.

At the moment her sweet face was still flushed from sleep and her heavy amber curls were pulled into a simple braid that hung nearly to her waist. With her slender body modestly covered by her threadbare robe she should have appeared a dowdy child. Instead she was as radiant and fresh as an angel.

Josiah gave a rueful shake of his head. When Raine had been but twelve years of age it had nearly broken his heart to fulfill his late wife's desire to have her daughter schooled at the same convent that she had attended as a child. To have Raine so far from him seemed an unbearable sacrifice.

But he couldn't deny a small, sensible part of him had been relieved to whisk her from the neighborhood.

Even then she had shown the promise of great beauty, and Josiah had been deeply aware that all too soon the lecherous gazes of the various noblemen would be turning in her direction. They would consider such a delectable morsel within such easy reach an irresistible temptation, and would have spared no expense or effort to lure her into their bed.

No, it had been for the best that she had been locked away from the world's dangers.

Of course, now that she had returned he could not deny that the old troubles had merely shifted to new troubles.

She might have acquired the sort of mature sophistication that would allow her to resist being seduced, but she possessed no connections, no dowry to tempt a nobleman into considering her in a more permanent role. And just as bothersome, her newfound elegance ensured that she no longer mixed easily with the local farmers and merchants.

She had no ready place among the community, and no mother or sisters to provide her companionship.

Heaving a rueful sigh, Josiah held out his hand.

"Well, well. I suppose it was too much to be hoped such commotion would not arouse you, pet. You might as well come in."

Her finely arched brows drew together as she moved toward his chair.

"You have been injured."

"That seems to be the universal agreement," he said, turning his head to regard the silent servant. "Foster, pour me a brandy and then tend to my horse."

"Thank the Lord," the man muttered as he readily moved to pull a bottle of brandy and a glass from the nearby cabinet. Leaving them on the table, he turned for the door.

"Foster," Josiah called softly.

"Aye?"

"Make sure there is no evidence from this night's work. Our stable is bound to receive more than its share of interest over the next few days."

Foster gave a slow nod. "The magistrate won't find so much as a mouse dropping when I am through."

"Magistrate?" Raine demanded as Foster slipped through the door and closed it behind him.

"It's a long and rather tedious story, I fear."

His daughter gave a lift of her brows. "Actually I suspect that it will be quite fascinating."

Josiah grimaced. "Fascinating, perhaps, but at the moment I prefer that you fetch a needle and thread and sew your poor father back together again." His hands tightened on the arms of his chair as he battled a wave of pain. "Unless you intend to stand there and watch me bleed to death?"

She gazed at him for a long moment, not missing the sweat that lightly coated his strained features before she gave a slow nod of her head.

"Very well, Father."

He breathed a sigh of relief as she readily left the room and returned a short time later with her needle and thread in hand. Unlike Foster she had never been a squeamish sort. Indeed, Raine had always possessed more pluck and backbone than any of the lads in the neighborhood. There was not a tree she wouldn't climb, a roof she wouldn't leap from, a lake she wouldn't attempt to swim across.

She also possessed the sort of sharp intelligence that was bound to lead to awkward questions.

The thought had barely passed through his mind when she poured a large shot of brandy directly into the wound and gave a small sound of shock.

"Dear Lord, this is…this is a bullet wound."

Josiah grunted as the brandy seared his wound. "And what would you know of bullet wounds, pet?"

Moving to stand behind his shoulder, Raine carefully began her surgery.

"Father, I want to know what happened."

"You have always been too curious for your own good. A gentleman's private doings are not always a fit tale for female ears."

She gave a small snort. "Since when have you been so particular in regards to my female sensibilities, sir? My entire childhood was spent surrounded by drunken sailors who entertained me with stories that would make a hardened cad blush. And even you taught me more of how to ride and shoot than how to perfect my maidenly skills."

Well, he could hardly argue that. It was true enough that his acquaintances were a rough lot and that too often they treated Raine as if she were a precocious street urchin rather than a well-bred female.

And he had been far more at ease pretending she was a son. After all, what did a sailor know of raising daughters? They were strange and mysterious creatures that no mere male could ever hope to comprehend.

"Ah, but you are no longer a child, pet," he murmured, not without some regret. "Something that even a poor father can no longer deny. You have grown into a beautiful lady. One who should be gracing an elegant ballroom, not rubbing elbows with common seamen in a crumbling cottage."

Her smooth stitching never faltered, but Josiah could sense his daughter's sudden stiffening, as if he had unwittingly struck a nerve.

"A lovely notion, I suppose. Unfortunately my invitations to those elegant ballrooms seem to always go astray, so until one does arrive I shall remain precisely as I am, a forgotten Cinderella."

"Cinderella?"

"A character from a French fairy tale about a silly girl who longs for pretty gowns and a handsome prince."

Josiah hissed a breath between his clenched teeth as the needle slid through his tender skin.

"What is so silly about wanting such things?"

There was a moment of silence before Josiah heard his daughter heave a faint sigh.

"Because they are an impossible dream, and I have enough sense not to waste my time pining for what can never be."

This time Josiah felt as if the needle had been aimed directly at his heart. He turned his head to regard Raine with a troubled frown.

"Raine…"

"No, Father, it does not matter. Truly, it does not." She managed a smile, but it stopped short of the dark beauty of her eyes. "Now, stop attempting to distract me and tell me what has occurred."

Josiah returned his attention to the fire. Damn and blast. He had been a fool to believe for a moment he could hide his secret career beneath his daughter's nose. She was no longer a tiny tot to be easily distracted. Oh, no, she was a woman who was quite ready to use whatever means necessary to get what she wanted.

A woman just like her mother, he thought with a fond sigh.

"I suppose you intend to nag me until you have the whole sordid truth?" he said darkly.

"Would I ever lower myself to nag? Certainly not. I will, however, point out that I am currently in the process of a delicate surgery. I should hate for any mistakes to occur."

Josiah offered her a narrowed glance. "Good God, pet, you can't threaten your own father. It is indecent." He winced as she gave a tug on the thread. "Bloody hell."

"Will you tell me?"

He watched as she tied off the knot and cut the thread, and then with efficient ease wrapped his wound in fresh linen.

"Yes, pet, I will tell you," he reluctantly conceded. What else could he do? The chit wouldn't be satisfied until she had wrung every sordid detail from him. "But not tonight. I am weary and in need of a hot bath and a soft bed. We will speak in the morning."

She moved to stand directly before him, her expression somber. "I have your word? You will give me the truth?"

He gave a slow nod. "Aye, my word."

THE SUN HAD BARELY crested when Raine was out of bed and dressed in a simple blue gown. It wasn't unusual. For the past seven years she had lived in a convent that had taken a dim view of any hint of laziness or self-indulgence, and most mornings she had been awake before the dawn to begin her morning prayers.

Even though she no longer had a strict schedule to guide her days, she found it impossible to acquire the habit of lying in bed for half the day. It might be all that was fashionable to sprawl upon a dozen pillows and sip at chocolate, but she possessed a nature that was far too restless for such a tedious waste of time.

Besides, chocolate always made her break out in a rash.

A faint smile touched her lips as she left her chambers and headed down the hall. Oh yes, she was quite the early riser. Unfortunately, once she had risen she had very little to occupy her time.

Her father might not possess a fortune, but he did keep enough servants to ensure that she had no need to do chores about the cottage. And since she had few acquaintances and fewer friends, she was never overwhelmed with pressing engagements.

Far too often she found herself walking through the countryside, wondering if she would ever feel at home again.

Giving a shake of her head, Raine thrust aside the vague frustration that had plagued her since returning to England. On this morning she had more important matters to occupy her mind.

Halting before her father's door, she quietly pushed it open and stepped inside. As she had expected he was still in his bed, although he was not alone.

Standing beside the bed was a tall, sparse woman with brown hair pulled into a tight knot, and features more handsome than pretty.

Mrs. Stone had come to keep house for Josiah and Raine after her mother's death nearly sixteen years earlier. The housekeeper had herself been widowed and seemed to know precisely how to provide a steadfast support and sense of comfort to the grieving father and daughter.

Over the years she had become as much a part of the family as Foster and their groom, Talbot. Indeed, Raine was certain the cottage would be an unruly muddle without her commanding presence.

Crossing the carpet, Raine halted beside the four-posted bed that commanded most of the narrow chamber. A matching armoire and washstand were the only other pieces of furniture. The walls were plain and the burgundy curtains faded.

The room was not precisely shabby, but there was no mistaking that it had not benefited from the more delicate touches of a woman's hand in many years.

"How is he?" she asked of the housekeeper in soft tones.

Mrs. Stone gave a click of her tongue, a faint frown marring her brow.

"A bit feverish, but he refuses to call for the surgeon. Stubborn fool." Her tart words did not quite cover the concern etched upon her features. "For now all we can do is keep the wound clean and pray."

Raine smiled wryly as she glanced down at her father. He was stubborn, and at times a fool. But she loved him more than anyone else in the world.

"Thank you, Mrs. Stone."

There was a sound from the bed as Josiah opened his eyes to glare at the two women hovering over his bed.

"Do not be whispering over me as if I am already a corpse. I've no intention of cocking my toes up just yet." He gave Mrs. Stone a bleary glare. "And you can keep your prayers to yourself, you old fusspot. God and I have an understanding that needs none of your interference."

Far from offended by her employer's reprimand, Mrs. Stone gave a snort and planted her fists on her hips. The two badgered and teased each other like an old married couple, a fact that did not escape Raine's notice now that she was mature enough to sense the intimate ease between the two.

It did not trouble her. She was pleased to know that her father was not entirely alone.

Indeed, if she were to look deep in her heart she would have to admit that she envied him.

"Oh, aye, an understanding," the housekeeper said darkly. "You dance with the devil and never consider the cost. One day…"

"Enough, woman," Josiah interrupted with a grimace. "Your pious lectures are tedious enough when I am cast to the wind, but they are nigh unbearable when I am stone-cold sober. Be off with you."

With a sniff Mrs. Stone turned and marched from the room, closing the door with enough force to bring a smile to Raine's lips.

"You do know that she is utterly devoted to you?" she scolded her parent gently.

He grunted as he pressed himself higher on the pillows and settled more comfortably on the mattress.

"Of course I know she is devoted. Why else would I keep such an old shrew around?"

Raine rolled her eyes. "You are a shameless scoundrel. How are you feeling?"

He gave a shake of his head, his dark hair, now liberally streaked with silver, falling nearly to his shoulders.

"Weaker than I would like to admit."

Leaning forward, Raine gently pulled aside the binding to study the wound. There was an angry redness around the stitches but no visible sign of infection.

Still, it was no mere scratch to be ignored.

Tragedy could strike all too swiftly when injuries were not properly treated.

"I fear that you may have some fever to the wound. We must call for the surgeon."

There was a short pause before her father heaved a sigh. "No, pet, that we most certainly cannot do."

"Why not?"

"Because the local magistrate is currently searching for a bandit he managed to wound last eve. If he should discover the location of that bandit, he intends to hang him from the nearest gallows."

Raine frowned in confusion. "Why would the magistrate mistake you for a bandit?"

"No doubt because I am one."

The words were said simply, without apology, and with a carelessness that made Raine gape in confusion.

"Are you jesting?"

"No, Raine, this is no jest." He sucked in a deep breath. "I am the Knave of Knightsbridge."

"The Knave of Knightsbridge?"

"Aye. Highwayman *extraordinaire*."

With a sharp movement Raine turned from the bed to pace toward the window. There was a fine view of the Kent countryside with its wide pastures and a charming lake surrounded by a copse of trees. Raine, however, did not take her usual pleasure in the peaceful setting, or even in the pale autumn sunlight that dabbled across the stables and cramped outhouses.

Forgivable, of course. She had just been told that her own father was the notorious brigand whose name was on the lips of every citizen of Knightsbridge.

"I do not understand," she at last said as she paced toward the armoire and then back to the window.

"No, I do not expect that you do."

"Why would you do such a thing? Are we in such desperate straits?"

"Sit down, pet, you are making my head spin with your pacing."

"I cannot think when I am sitting." Her brow creased as she struggled to consider how best to rescue them from such a dreadful situation. "We must sell mother's jewels of course, they should fetch a goodly sum if we were to take them to London. And perhaps we could see about a lodger. We have room in the attic to take in at least two...."

"Raine, there is no need for such sacrifices, I assure you," her father broke in with a firm voice.

"There is every need." Returning to the bed, she glared down at the lean face that was so very dear to her. "I will not have you risking your life. We will find other means to get by."

A fond smile touched his lips. "Raine, please listen to me."

"What?"

"My pockets are not to let. Although I will never claim the wealth of some, we are quite comfortably fixed."

She clenched her hands at her sides, not at all comforted by the knowledge they were so well situated.

Not when her father was dashing about the countryside, risking his reputation and very life, as if he hadn't a care in the world.

"Then…why?"

His expression was uncommonly somber as he reached up to take her hand in his own.

"Because our neighbors are not nearly so fortunate as we are, pet. The king and his cronies have happily emptied the treasury while refusing to honor their debts to the soldiers and widows that depend upon their promised annuities." His grip tightened on her fingers, revealing a smoldering anger that burned in his heart. "Proud men have been forced to become no more than mere beggars in the street, and women sometimes worse, just to keep a roof over their heads. And as for the local orphanage…it has fallen into such disrepair that it will soon be no more than a pile of rubble if something is not done."

The flutters of panic began to ease from her stomach. Not that she was any less worried. It was just that she began to understand what was prompting her father's foolhardy behavior.

Beneath his hardened exterior was a tender heart and fierce need to protect those weaker than himself. It was a gallantry that marked him as a gentleman far more than any empty title or grand estate.

"And so you have taken upon yourself to play the role of Robin Hood?"

He tried to shrug only to wince in pain. "In a manner of speaking."

"And I suppose that Foster is your Friar John, and Mrs. Stone and Talbot your Band of Merry Men?"

A grudging smile touched his lips. "They are aware of my secret identity, but I do not ask that they take a hand in any of my nefarious business. I would never allow them to risk themselves in such a fashion."

"But you are quite willing to risk yourself?" she demanded in fond exasperation.

"There is no risk, I assure you, pet."

She deliberately turned her attention to his wounded shoulder, her brows lifting.

"Oh, no. No risk at all."

He at least possessed the grace to redden at his ridiculous claim. "Well, there is usually no great risk. Last night was a clumsy mishap. One that I have no intention of repeating."

"On that we agree." She lifted his hand to press his fingers to her cheeks. "I admire what you are attempting to do, Father, I truly do, but it is far too dangerous. You could have been captured, or even killed, last eve."

"Nonsense," he said gruffly. "It is a scratch, nothing more. And I can promise I will never again underestimate our new magistrate. He is a clever blighter who seems to possess an uncanny ability to be where he is least wanted. He will not sneak up on me again. From now on I intend to be the predator, not the prey in our little game."

Raine dropped her father's hand as she took a step backward. "Good God, this is not a game, Father."

"Of course it is." His eyes glittered with what might have been…pleasure. As if he actually enjoyed his nefarious role as the Knave of Knightsbridge. "A game of wits that has kept me well occupied and, more important, has provided our neighbors with food and a roof over their heads. They have no one else to depend upon, Raine. Would you have me abandon them, as well?"

"Of course not," she denied.

Although she had lived in France for the past seven years, this tiny community would always be her home. How could she ever stand aside and see them suffering without doing whatever possible to assist? And in truth, she could not deny a fierce pride in her father's brave quest to save them from ruin.

Still, she also could not deny a lingering fear for her father. She had already lost her mother. She could not bear to lose him, as well. He would have to take far greater care if he were to continue his dangerous charade.

Parting her lips to demand his promise that he would not take foolish risks, Raine was interrupted by the unmistakable sound of hoofbeats. She hurried to the window and watched the rider approaching, her heart lodged in her throat.

"Dear heavens."

Her father struggled to sit forward. "Who is it?"

She slowly turned, her eyes wide. "It is the magistrate."

CHAPTER TWO

"BLOODY HELL." WITH A PAINFUL effort Josiah struggled with the heavy covers that were wrapped about him. "Call for Foster and tell him to put the man off until I can get dressed."

"Dressed?" Raine crossed to the bed and firmly pushed her father back into the pillows. It was a testament of his weakened state that he gave up the fight with no more than a low groan. "Have you taken leave of your senses? You are not leaving this bed."

Her father's lean features hardened with frustration. "I must. The magistrate is already suspicious."

"So, let him be suspicious."

"Raine, if he discovers that I am injured he will have me hauled off in chains."

Raine pressed her hands to her knotted stomach. No. Now was not the moment to panic. Not when her father's life hung in the balance.

"Do not fear, Father." She squared her shoulders. "I will deal with the magistrate."

"Raine, no. I do not want you involved in this."

She smiled wryly. "I am already involved, Father. Besides, you are in no condition to stop me. Remain quiet and I will return as soon as I can."

"Raine, I beg of you, do not do this."

Ignoring Josiah's agonized plea, Raine headed firmly toward the door. Her father was willing to risk everything to do what he thought was right.

How could she possibly do any less?

TOM HARPER WAS NOT a modest man.

Although he had been born the son of a vicar who had little to offer his ambitious child, Tom had benefited from a formal education and introduction to gentlemanly manners. When combined with his own natural intelligence and an unwavering drive to succeed, he was assured a comfortable existence.

Comfortable, however, was not enough to satisfy his restless heart. He had traveled to London with every expectation of making a name for himself in the Home Office, and eventually earning himself a seat in the House of Commons.

The fact that it had proved much more difficult than he had anticipated had not dampened his determination. It had, however, made him realize he would have to do something to capture the attention of his superiors.

Which was, of course, the reason he had leapt at the opportunity to become a magistrate in this secluded village.

And why he was standing in the drawing room of the comfortable cottage awaiting the arrival of Josiah Wimbourne.

Hearing the sound of approaching footsteps, he politely turned and smoothed his hands over the material of his plain blue coat. He was careful to dress with a somber simplicity that suited his lean body and pleasant features. It revealed he was a man of means without presuming to rise above his station.

The door opened and Tom battled a flare of surprise as a small blond-haired angel slipped into the room.

He had seen Miss Wimbourne in the village, of course. She could not step foot on High Street without every male in the vicinity dropping whatever he was doing and rushing to catch a glimpse of her.

Even himself.

Not that he would ever expect to capture such an exquisite morsel, he thought ruefully. But he was man enough to enjoy the fantasy.

Moving forward with an innate grace, Miss Wimbourne offered a warm smile that seemed to add a glow to the shabby room. It was odd that the powerful and rich so often tended to have children that were pale and unremarkable, while the rogues of the world could father offspring that possessed such vibrant beauty.

No doubt that was the reason the *ton* was so careful to exclude the riffraff from their society. What insipid debutante could possibly hope to compare with this woman?

Halting directly before him, Miss Wimbourne performed a small curtsy.

"Mr. Harper, what a pleasant surprise."

Tom bowed, his mind rapidly adjusting to this unexpected encounter.

He didn't believe for a moment it was mere happenstance that brought this young maiden to the drawing room.

"Miss Wimbourne, I hope I do not disturb you?" he murmured.

"Not at all. Indeed, I have had a very dull morning and have been wishing for a visitor to distract me." Her dark eyes were wide and guileless, but Tom was not easily fooled. This woman could have every gentleman in the county lined up at her door if she but offered the least encouragement. "I have requested that Mrs. Stone bring tea. Will you have a seat?"

"You are very gracious, but I have actually come to have a word with your father."

"Why, Mr. Harper, how can you be so cruel?"

"I beg your pardon?"

Her breathtaking smile flashed again. This time Tom suspected that it was deliberate.

"I was just indulging my vanity with the thought that you rode all the way from the village to pay me a call, and now I discover that your interest instead lies with my father. A very lowering realization, sir."

"My dear Miss Wimbourne, I am certain you know that there is not a gentleman in the entire county who would not ride far farther than a mere five miles to be granted the privilege of your smile," he said dryly. "Your return to Knightsbridge has created a greater stir than the rumors that the railroad might reach our tiny community."

"Most charming." She waved a hand toward the threadbare settee. "Are you certain you will not be seated?"

"No, thank you." He was too shrewd to become overly comfortable in this maiden's presence. She would charm him into insensibility given half the chance.

Moving to perch on the window seat, Miss Wimbourne tilted her head to one side. "I believe that you have only recently moved to Knightsbridge?"

"Yes, I lived in London until three months ago."

"Ah." She wrinkled her nose. "I am sorry."

"Sorry?"

"You must have done something quite terrible to have been sent to such a remote, tiresome place."

He gave a low chuckle. It was an assumption shared by most of the community. "On the contrary, I requested to come to Knightsbridge."

"Whatever for? It is home to me, but I would think it the last place anyone else would wish to be. Especially a handsome, ambitious gentleman who could be enjoying the delights of London."

In spite of himself, Tom experienced a small heat in the pit of his stomach. The woman was a born temptress.

"Knightsbridge has one thing that London could never offer."

"And what would that be?"

"Actually I should say two things. The first, of course, is the most beautiful woman I have ever laid eyes upon."

"And the second?"

He shrugged. "The Knave of Knightsbridge."

She blinked, as if caught off guard by his blunt confession. "The highwayman?"

"Yes."

"There are no criminals to be had in London?"

"An endless supply, but none with the reputation of the Knave." He eyed her carefully. Since arriving in Knightsbridge he had nurtured a suspicion of the charming Josiah Wimbourne. Unfortunately, possessing a suspicion and possessing evidence were two entirely different matters. After last eve, however, he cherished a hope that his search might be at an end—and not even this beautiful angel was going to be allowed to stand in his way. "Surely you have heard the stories of the dashing rogue?"

"Who has not? Not that I believe a word of them." She gave a dismissive wave of her hand. "What man could possibly appear and disappear like smoke? Or lead entire militias into the bogs? Or so enchant the ladies that they happily hand over their jewels and flatly refuse to give the authorities a description of him? He would have to be one of the fey creatures to possess such unearthly skills."

"No doubt the gossip has greatly exaggerated the bandit's skills, but he has proved to be a most cunning cad who has outwitted every officer who has come against him. It will take a man of considerable cleverness to capture him."

"I believe I begin to understand." She slowly rose to her

feet. "You think to enhance your own reputation by being the one to bring the Knave to the gallows?"

He was caught off guard by her shrewd perception. By God, this was a dangerous woman. And one who was deliberately attempting to distract him.

The question was, why?

"As much as I am enjoying your companionship, Miss Wimbourne, I have many duties awaiting my attention and I must speak with your father. Would you be so kind as to request he attend me?"

"I fear I cannot, Mr. Harper," she replied, smiling. "He is not at home."

Tom stiffened, his instincts on full alert. "Indeed. May I inquire when you expect him to return?"

"Not for several days. He has gone to town to deal with some business interest or another." She gave an innocent bat of her lashes. "No doubt he told me the tedious details, but I must honestly confess I paid him little heed. I have no head for investments and such."

"He is in London?"

"Yes, sir."

Tom clenched his hands at his sides. He would bet his finest pearl stickpin the maiden was lying, but they both knew he could not openly accuse her.

Nor could he insist on searching the cottage for the treacherous bastard, damn the luck.

"For how long?"

"He promised to return within the week, but of course, he does tend to be rather impulsive and he might very well discover something that amuses his fancy and remain longer than he first intended."

"And he left you here alone?"

Her smile never wavered. "I am hardly alone. Both Foster and Talbot are here, as well as Mrs. Stone."

"It still seems odd he would not wish to take his daughter." He paused, allowing his suspicion to be revealed in his expression. The fact that Miss Wimbourne was so determinedly attempting to keep him from her father only confirmed Tom's belief that Josiah was the Knave of Knightsbridge. "Or his favorite mount."

She moved to straighten a candlestick on the mantel, her face serene, but Tom sensed a tension in her slender form. She was not quite so calm as she wanted him to believe.

"Since we have no town house I would only be forced to remain in some hotel while my father was busy with his solicitor, and as for his mount—he traveled post." She abruptly turned back to him with a narrowed gaze. "Is there a reason for your questions, sir?"

He briefly considered confronting her directly. It was amazing how often people blurted out secrets when they were nervous.

Then he gave a small shake of his head. This chit might be young, but she possessed the polished composure of a woman twice her age. She would not be teased or bullied into betraying her father.

No. He would have to hold on to his patience a while longer. Sooner or later he would catch Josiah Wimbourne. It was as inevitable as the sun rising.

"I am by nature a curious man," he murmured.

The dark eyes flashed. "Then you are fortunate in your choice of careers."

"Yes." Sensing he had accomplished all that he could on this morning, Tom offered a shallow bow. "I will keep you no longer. I pray you tell your father that I called upon him?"

"Oh, you may be assured he will be told the moment he returns."

Their gazes locked and held, both of them knowing that the battle between them had just begun.

"Then I bid you good day."

"Good day, sir."

Raine sucked in a deep breath as her guest walked to the door and disappeared.

She knew beyond a doubt that her efforts had been futile. The magistrate may appear a polite, unassuming sort of man, but she hadn't missed the sharp glitter in his pale eyes. Nor the suspicion that had hardened his youthful features.

Mr. Harper was convinced that Josiah Wimbourne was the Knave of Knightsbridge, and her hasty story of Josiah's trip to London had only confirmed his belief.

How long would it be before he checked with the inn to inquire if her father had indeed traveled by post to London? Or even sent word to town to check the various hotels for his presence?

Not more than a day or two, she was certain. And then he would be back insisting on seeing her father.

Dear Lord, she had to do something to distract him.

Something that would force him to second-guess his own certainty in Josiah's guilt.

Pacing across the carpet, Raine came to a slow halt as she was struck with sudden inspiration.

Of course.

It was bold and daring and no doubt dangerous, but it might very well be precisely what was needed.

And she was just the woman to accomplish the outlandish feat.

Two months later

THE SMALL COACHING INN set near the crossroads was no doubt considered by the natives to be a source of pride. It did, after all, boast a fine wooden sign proclaiming it the King's Arms, and a newly thatched roof that offered some protection from the bitter chill of the night air. It could even lay claim to a stable yard, although the snow had piled high enough to make it nearly impassable.

Seated in the comfort of his carriage, Philippe Gautier was singularly unimpressed.

He had traveled too widely to suppose the inn could offer more than watered ale, food boiled to tasteless mush and an infestation of vermin. No matter how cold and miserable the night, he intended to press onward. His carriage was preferable to the hospitality of the King's Arms.

A preference that the innkeeper clearly found galling as he waddled his way through the snow and pulled open the carriage door to offer up the steaming mug of hot cider that Philippe had ordered.

"Here you are, sir." The man shoved the mug in Philippe's hand with a fawning smile on his round, ruddy face. "Nothing like a bit of cider on a cold night."

Philippe pulled back, his austere features frigid with distaste. There was an overwhelming stench of stale tobacco and onions that clung to the man.

"That will be all."

Impervious to Philippe's icy dismissal, the innkeeper cleared his throat even as his gaze covertly took in Philippe's exquisitely tailored greatcoat and Hessians that had been polished to a blinding perfection. The avaricious gaze lingered a moment on the gold signet ring that graced Philippe's slender finger before returning to meet the narrowed green eyes.

"Such a miserable night and only to get worse, I fear." He raised pudgy fingers to smear back his thinning patch of gray hair. "The cook swears that she smells snow in the air, which means it shall be upon us before long. She is uncanny, she is. Never wrong."

Philippe gave a lift of a chiseled brow that perfectly matched his raven locks. He was well aware the man was attempting to frighten him into remaining the night at the inn. The ridiculous imbecile.

"Do you mean to tell me that you possess a cook who is also a witch?" he demanded in a low, silky tone that was only faintly accented.

The innkeeper gave a choked cough. "Oh, nay, sir. Nothing of the sort. She merely has a nose for weather."

"A nose? Like a bloodhound?"

"All perfectly natural, I assure you."

"It does not strike me as perfectly natural." He lifted the mug to drain the cider. The dregs were bitter on his tongue, but it at least provided a warmth to his chilled body. "Indeed, I should think it most unnatural."

"Aye, well." The innkeeper awkwardly cleared his throat. "She is harmless enough, and makes a fine shepherd's pie that will melt in your mouth. Just what is needed on this cold, miserable night."

"I abhor shepherd's pie," Philippe informed the man as he shoved the now-empty mug back into his hands. "And before you begin to bore me with the delights of your boiled-oxtail soup and the perfection of your ale, be assured that nothing could prevail me to remain beneath your roof."

The beefy face flushed with offended pride. "Sir, I must protest…"

"What you must do is close the door before you allow any more of the night air into my carriage," Philippe announced in a voice that brooked no argument. "I grow weary of your chatter. Be off with you."

"As you wish." Offering a stiff bow, the man backed away

just as a large, dark form slipped past him to enter the carriage and shut the door in his flushed face.

Philippe watched as his companion settled himself on the leather seat across from him.

At a glance Carlos Estavan did not seem the sort of man that Philippe Gautier would choose as a trusted friend. While Philippe was a slender, elegant gentleman with a cool, some would say aloof, composure and an aristocratic air, Carlos was broad and dark with the swarthy complexion of his Portuguese ancestors. He also possessed a fiery temperament and the sort of earthy passions that were decidedly absent in Philippe.

The two men had, however, been the closest of companions since Philippe had arrived at his father's estate in Madeira when he had been but a tender lad. At the time Philippe had been devastated by his mother's death and ready to strike out at anyone who crossed his path. Carlos had been the son of a local fisherman and an English maid who worked at Philippe's family estate, and not at all shy about holding his own, even against a nobleman.

Philippe had been beaten senseless, but much to the astonishment of all, he had refused to allow Carlos to be punished. In truth, he had developed a grudging respect for the ill-tamed rascal who would rather risk the pillory than be bested.

It was a friendship that had flourished despite the disparity in their social positions, and Philippe knew there was no one he trusted more in the world.

Which was precisely why he had insisted that Carlos accompany him on this journey to England.

"So you do not possess faith in the cook's uncanny nose?" Carlos demanded, revealing he had been lurking in the shadows to listen to Philippe's conversation with the innkeeper.

"Ridiculous jackass." Philippe settled back in the seat and

pulled his coat about him. Lud, but he had forgotten just how cold and miserable England could be in November. "As if I were not perfectly aware he was attempting to cozen me into spending the night at his shabby inn."

Carlos smiled as he rammed his hands through the long black hair that had been tousled by the stiff breeze.

"Well, you can hardly blame the man. He is stuck in the midst of this dreary landscape with no companionship beyond cows and half-wits. How often do you suppose such a fine and elegant gentleman arrives at his humble establishment? No doubt he was already plotting to have the town crier inform the local citizens that you halted for a mug of cider. Just imagine the bragging he could have done if you were to have actually slept in one of his beds."

"Along with the bedbugs and mice?" Philippe shuddered. "No thank you."

"We have bedded down in worse."

That was true enough. Over the years Philippe and Carlos had bunked down in hovels, fields, and on one unforgettable occasion, in the dank cells of a Brazilian prison.

"Only when promised enough of a fortune to make it worth my while, and never where I am forced to endure such a despicable toadeater," Philippe drawled. "What news from the stables?"

"There have been no strangers pass this way for the past fortnight."

Philippe swallowed a curse. It was, of course, a great deal too much to hope that he would simply stumble across the scoundrel he was seeking, but not to have even the smallest inkling of the dastard's location was straining his already raw nerves.

"No wonder the innkeeper was so desperate for my blunt." He glanced out the frosted window. "How far are we from London?"

"We are still some thirty miles, with many of the roads impassable."

"Devil take it. If we are to have a decent roof over our heads before the night is out then we shall have to dare the main road." Philippe grimaced. He had lived too long in warm climates not to feel the bite of the winter air. "No matter, there will be few travelers about at this time of eve."

"Not with the cook smelling snow in the air."

Philippe narrowed his gaze. "Tell Swann to take the turnpike before I leave you here to grub among the natives."

Lifting the hatch in the top of the carriage, Carlos passed the command on to the groom before resuming his seat with a smile that revealed a flash of perfect white teeth.

"I wouldn't complain at lingering an hour or two. There is a very eager barmaid who was casting her eye in my direction. She would no doubt warm a man on such a cold night."

The carriage swayed from the stable yard and began to pick up its pace as it hit the turnpike. Philippe gave a shake of his head as he resigned himself to a chilly, disagreeable night.

"Good God, do you never think of anything else?" he demanded.

Carlos gave a low chuckle. "That is your trouble, you know, Gautier."

"What? That I do not tup every chit who tosses herself at my feet?"

"That you don't tup any of the chits who toss themselves at your feet. It's no wonder you are so grim and cross. A man needs the comfort of soft arms to keep him in high spirits."

Philippe smiled at the familiar chiding. Unlike Carlos he felt no need to possess a different woman in his bed every night. Oh, he was no saint. And certainly he was no eunuch. He had bedded the most beautiful, the most talented and the most exclusive women throughout Europe.

But his affairs were always discreet and conducted with the same cool precision he approached the rest of his life.

The mere thought of a hasty tumble with some tavern wench was enough to make him shudder in distaste.

"Do you have a point, Carlos?"

Sprawling with indolent ease, Carlos gave a small shrug. "Only that life is meant to be enjoyed."

"I would enjoy life a great deal more if my brother was not languishing in Newgate prison."

The dark, forceful features hardened at the mention of Philippe's younger brother. Not surprising. Carlos held Jean-Pierre in barely concealed contempt, considering him a frivolous dandy who could boast no accomplishments beyond dallying away Philippe's fortune.

Unfortunately Carlos was not entirely wrong. Jean-Pierre was only one year younger than Philippe's one and thirty, but he had been absurdly pampered by their father. As a result, Jean-Pierre had grown into a man of weak character and dissolute habits who cared for nothing beyond his own pleasure.

"Jean-Pierre is always courting some sort of trouble or other, and you are always charging to his rescue," Carlos said dryly. "It is what you do, after all."

"His troubles to this date have involved moneylenders, illegitimate brats and cuckolded husbands, not treason," Philippe felt compelled to point out. "This snare may be one that not even I can untangle."

Carlos remained indifferent. "You will find the means. After all, he is for once not guilty."

"Of course he is not guilty, but how to prove him innocent?" Philippe clenched his hand as he thought of his brother stuck in a rat-infested cell surrounded by cutthroats and lunatics. For all his sins not even Jean-Pierre deserved such a brutal fate. "By God, the authorities must be worthless lobcocks to believe for a moment Jean-Pierre could concoct such a scheme. The fool cares for nothing beyond the cut of his coat, bedding his latest paramour and paying outrageous sums of money on what anyone with even a modest eye for art would consider worthless tripe. Certainly he has not the wits to dabble in politics."

"No one has ever claimed that the king is the most brilliant of gentlemen."

"True enough." Lost in his dark thoughts, it took Philippe a moment to realize that the carriage had inexplicably slowed and was coming to a halt. "What the devil is the matter now?" Yanking open the window, Philippe glanced upward to ensure his groom had not come to some injury, before his narrowed gaze moved to discover the vague outline of a horse and rider standing in the center of the road before them. "Damn."

Pulling in his head, Philippe reached into his pocket to touch the dueling pistol he always carried.

Easily sensing Philippe's sudden tension, Carlos straightened, a dangerous fire burning in his dark eyes. "Trouble?"

"It seems we are about to be introduced to the local bandit."

Far from worried by the news, Carlos slowly smiled. "Entertainment. Good."

Philippe chuckled at his bloodthirsty friend. "Hold, Carlos. I do not wish him dead. At least not yet."

"Why ever not?"

"If anyone is to have noticed the coming and goings on this road it will be the resident highwayman. I wish to question this scoundrel before you put a bullet through his heart."

With a sigh Carlos reached down to flip open the trap door that Philippe had installed in the floor of the carriage, a clever addition that had saved their lives on more than one occasion.

Philippe waited until Carlos had slipped from the carriage, knowing that his cunning friend was plotting to circle around the highwayman and take him from behind. It would be Philippe's task to keep the scoundrel distracted until Carlos was in position.

Keeping the pistol in his pocket, with his finger on the trigger, Philippe waited until the carriage stopped, then stepped out onto the road and walked toward the head of the horses.

"Stand and deliver." The highwayman was gruffly commanding as he waved a small pistol toward the offended groom.

Swann gave a snort of disgust. The groom possessed a rabid dislike for thieves and cutthroats and was always happy to shed the blood of any who crossed his path.

"Get out of my way, you pathetic worm, or I'll rip out your heart and…"

"That will be enough, Swann," Philippe drawled as he stepped toward the middle of the road.

"Bloody hell, I am well able to handle a half-grown rapscallion without your assistance."

"I haven't the least doubt in the world, but it does not seem entirely fair that you should have all the fun." Philippe kept his gaze upon the highwayman, who had shifted the pistol in his direction. Seated upon a dappled gray, the bandit sported a brilliant crimson hat and flowing cape, and he had possessed the sense to wrap a muffler around his lower face. Still, Philippe sensed that beneath the gaudy costume he was a small, nervous sort of man. A cold smile touched his lips. "There is nothing like a bit of target practice to relieve the tedium of a journey."

"Aye, but now you have ruined the gloss on your boots and I shall be the unfortunate soul who will have to spend endless hours polishing them," Swann groused.

"We all have our crosses to bear."

"Some of our crosses are greater than others," the groom muttered.

"That is enough," the highwayman snapped, waving the

gun in a dangerous fashion. "Put your hands in the air before I lodge a bullet in your heart."

"Good God." Philippe gave a sudden laugh at the high-pitched voice. "I believe it is no more than a babe, Swann."

"Young enough to still be sucking his mother's teat. A fine welcome to England, eh?" Swann readily joined in Philippe's amusement. "Being robbed by a brat still wet behind the ears."

The villain sucked in an outraged breath. "I am old enough to pull the trigger, sir."

Overhead the clouds parted to reveal a slash of moonlight that bathed the frozen landscape in a silver mist. The chilled air stirred the crimson cape, making it appear like a river of blood swirling around the slender form.

Philippe's smile never wavered as he moved forward with a slow, deliberate step. A part of him was aware that Carlos was creeping through the shadows, and that Swann was behind him with a loaded pistol tucked out of sight, but his concentration was centered on the pistol pointed at his heart.

"Ah, but being old enough to pull the trigger is considerably different from being willing to pull the trigger," he taunted, his pulse perfectly steady. He had courted danger too often to be unnerved by a half-grown brat who dared to interrupt his journey. "It is no easy thing to take a man's life, not even a man who might very well deserve to be in the grave."

"Stay back," the boy warned.

Philippe took another step and reached up to grasp the bridle of the lad's mount.

"You see?" He was close enough to see the dark eyes of the highwayman widen with sudden fear. "You should never hesitate. Once you actually begin to consider the cost of murder, you are always lost. You must allow instinct to rule if you intend to kill hapless travelers."

"Move back."

"Had you shot when I first appeared I would already be dead on the ground and you would be happily picking through my pockets." He pretended to consider for a moment. "Of course, it's more likely that Swann would already have put a hole in your head, but…you comprehend my meaning."

"I said to move back," the villain commanded.

"Or?"

Without warning there was a loud explosion as the boy did as he had threatened and pulled the trigger of his pistol. The bullet flew harmlessly past Philippe's head and he regarded his adversary with a lift of his brows. By God. He had underestimated the lad's pluck.

"Damnation, the bastard is out of his wits," Swann snapped. "Stand back, sir, while I…"

"You will tend to the horses, Swann. I shall deal with our feral urchin," Philippe commanded as he narrowed his gaze. "A brave, but foolish, gesture, *mon enfant*. Unless you have another loaded pistol hidden about your person?"

The brat threw the pistol at his head. "Damn you."

Philippe ducked and gestured toward the lurking shadow beside the road. The encounter was all very diverting, but he was still hours away from a warm bath and his favorite brandy.

"Carlos."

On cue the large man leaped toward the horse, and before the hapless lad could so much as squeak, Carlos had him plucked from the saddle and tossed across his shoulder.

Philippe recaptured the reins of the horse before it could bolt, his lips twitching as Carlos struggled to keep control of his squirming bundle.

"Forgive me, *amigo,* I had presumed you more than capable of controlling one small imp. Do you need assistance?"

"What I need is a whip to teach this whelp a lesson in manners," the man growled.

"When you have finished toying with him, Carlos, perhaps you would be good enough to put him in the carriage?"

"Are you certain? He's a filthy thing with who knows what sort of nasty diseases." Carlos paused to smack the captive on the bottom. "You kick me again and I shall throttle you."

"I will do more than kick you. I will lodge a bullet in your arse. I will stick a dagger in your heart," the lad swore. "I will kill you both, I swear it."

Philippe grimaced. "Yes, it is a pity to ruin such fine leather with the vile creature. I paid a near fortune to have it imported from Florence, but I will not stand in the frigid air to question a petty criminal."

"Fine, but do not expect me to share the pungent experience," Carlos warned as they walked back down the road. With a heave Carlos tossed the snarling lad into the carriage and reached for the reins that Philippe held. "I intend to test this nag and decide if it is worth keeping or not."

"No." The would-be highwayman struggled with the cape that had wrapped about him and trapped his arms. "You cannot."

"Oh, yes, I can." Carlos narrowed his eyes. "And you will shut your mouth and behave yourself or I'll return and hang you from the nearest tree. *Capisce?*"

"I hope you break your bloody neck," the lad muttered.

"I would cut out his tongue, if I were you." Carlos muttered. "It would be a great improvement."

Philippe ignored his captive's sharp gasp. "Not until I have the information I need. After that…well, you shall be quite welcome to hang him from whichever tree you prefer."

CHAPTER THREE

RAINE WAS FURIOUS as she struggled to free herself from the folds of the damnable cape.

What an impulsive fool she had been.

When she had decided to take on the role of the Knave of Knightsbridge to dupe the magistrate, she had deliberately chosen the back roads and lanes near Knightsbridge to stalk her prey. The pickings were hardly fine, and more than a few nights she was forced to return to the cottage empty-handed, but the dangers were few. And most important, she managed to keep her father from the gallows.

How could Josiah Wimbourne be guilty when he was so visibly seen about the village at the same time the Knave was robbing carriages miles away?

Not that Tom Harper was entirely convinced that Josiah was innocent. But he could hardly arrest the man without some proof.

Today, however, her father had sternly informed her that this would be her last night of playing the dashing Knave. His shoulder had at last healed and the magistrate was temporarily thwarted. He was determined that his daughter would no longer court such risk.

Raine had discovered herself sharply disappointed by his command. Her daring charade had proved to be remarkably exciting as she had dashed about the countryside and collected a small fortune in coins and jewels to be handed over to her neighbors.

She felt as if she were actually accomplishing something important. Something that could give her rather empty life meaning.

An odd sentiment in a young woman, perhaps, but she had never been the sort of maiden to be content with keeping house and pandering to the needs of a man.

With the knowledge that she would soon be returning to her dull existence, Raine had taken a ridiculous gamble and chosen this well-traveled road to make her grand departure as the Knave. Her head had been filled with images of wealthy noblemen dripping in jewels and carrying crates of gold.

Her head should have been filled with the knowledge that such wealthy noblemen never traveled alone, and invariably possessed the sort of servants who were perfectly capable of protecting their masters.

As if to emphasize her stupidity, she was forced to helplessly watch as the dark, irritating Carlos vaulted on top her beloved Maggie and took off down the frozen road. At the same moment the raven-haired gentleman climbed into the carriage and with a low command to the coachman closed the door to lock them together in the shadowed interior.

Gritting her teeth as the carriage jerked to a start, Raine stared at the man seated across from her.

Had they simply met in the street, she had to admit that she would have considered him the most handsome gentleman she had ever laid eyes upon. Not that handsome really suited the elegant male features and startling green eyes, she decided. There was an undeniable beauty in the sweep of his brows, the prominent line of his cheekbones, the aquiline nose and the perfectly chiseled lips.

It was a glacial beauty, however, and Raine abruptly shuddered.

Carlos might be a hot-blooded brute, but she sensed between the two men, this icy fallen angel was by far the more dangerous.

Unnerved by the steady, piercing gaze, Raine halted her struggles with her cape and cleared her throat.

"What do you intend to do with me?" she demanded, careful to keep her voice low. The only bit of luck she had enjoyed this disastrous night was that her captors believed her to be a young boy. It was a belief she intended to encourage. God only knew what would happen if they discovered she was a female. "If you think the magistrate will thank you for…"

"Shut your mouth and do not speak again unless I ask you a direct question," he snapped, his voice as cold as ice. Instinctively, Raine pressed her lips together. There was something unnaturally commanding about the man. "Good, not entirely a simpleton, then." The green eyes narrowed as he leaned close enough to wrap her in the scent of warm, male skin. "I have need of information from you. Answer me truthfully and you might actually escape the hangman's noose."

She swallowed heavily, her heart lodged in her throat. Dear God, what had she gotten herself into?

"What information?" she rasped.

"I wish to know of any strangers you have noted passing this way during the past fortnight."

Raine paused as her mind raced with possibilities. Perhaps if she could pretend to have the knowledge he sought she could distract him long enough to escape. It was a desperate plan, but better than none.

"There are always strangers on the road, guv." She made her voice even rougher. "What yer wishing to know?"

His eyes shimmered with a dangerous light. "A large number of strangers?"

"Oh, aye."

"Odd, I was informed that this road had been nearly impassable for the past week, and that travelers had been few and far between."

Blast. She licked her dry lips, wishing he would back away. His proximity was far too distracting.

"Perhaps there have not been so many strangers as usual," she was forced to concede.

He gave a low, impatient sound. "It will go bad for you if you fib to me, boy. Have you, or have you not, noticed any strangers on the road?"

"There have been a few."

"Any Frenchmen?"

"Well, as to that, there was one gentleman who spoke with a French accent that passed this way last week," she readily agreed.

"Describe him."

She clenched her hands in her lap, fearing the man might actually hear her heart racing.

"He was tall, and thin, with a…large nose and…"

Her words broke off with a gasp as he reached out to grasp her shoulders, giving her a violent shake.

"I warned you not to lie to me."

"No, please," she pleaded, but not in time. Even as she struggled to loosen her arms she felt the flamboyant hat tumbling from her head. One last shake and her long curls were dislodged to fall in a river of gold around her shoulders.

Philippe stiffened at the sight of the glossy curls.

"*Meu Deus*," he breathed, his hand instinctively reaching to rip the heavy muffler that concealed the thin face.

A female. There could be no doubt.

No doubt at all, he thought as his gaze took in the captivating beauty of her countenance.

Never had he seen such pure ivory skin. God, it nearly glowed against the gleaming amber of her hair. Her nose was a pert, straight line and her lips so lush they could make a man hard at the thought of them pressed to his body. But it was her eyes that caught and held his attention.

They were as black as that of a raven's wing and surrounded by a tangle of long lashes. Such dark eyes should have been flat and lackluster, but instead they flashed with a smoldering spirit that Philippe could almost swear was tangible.

Suddenly all the elegant, sophisticated women who had shared his bed seemed to be pale imitations of femininity. Whatever their charms, they could never compare to this chit's vivacious, stunning magnificence.

Philippe gritted his teeth as he grasped her arms even tighter and with one smooth motion pulled her onto the seat next to him. She gave a startled scream, but he never hesitated as he pushed her flat onto her back and trapped her flaying legs between his own.

He was furious. Not the aloof disdain or the cold, calculating anger that he was accustomed to. No, this was a blistering, searing fury that caught him off guard and destroyed his icy composure.

There was no reasonable explanation as to why this woman had stirred such unfamiliar heat, but he found himself unable to battle the sensations that flowed through his body.

"Stop," she panted, struggling to free herself.

Philippe easily controlled her frantic wiggles as he shifted his hands to capture her wrists above her head.

"Damn you to hell, what are you playing at?" he gritted.

"Let go of me."

"Oh, no, my beauty, you are staying precisely where you are until I discover who you are and, more important, who put you up to attacking my carriage."

She should have been terrified. He held her life quite literally in his hands. Instead, she glared at him with a fury of her own.

"You are hurting me."

"Keep struggling and I shall put you across my knee and beat you as you deserve," he warned without compunction.

"Brute," she muttered as she tried to knee him in a most delicate location.

His eyes narrowed. For such a tiny thing she managed to put up a hell of a battle.

"Halt your struggles."

"Sir…" Her words came to a startled end as the buttons on her jacket were tugged open and the heavy material parted to reveal she wore nothing more than a thin chemise beneath.

"*Voce e bonita,*" he whispered at the sight of her curved breast perfectly outlined by the clinging muslin. Without warning there did not seem to be enough air in the carriage.

"*Bastardo,*" she gritted.

His gaze jerked back to her pale face. "You speak Portuguese?"

"I speak any number of languages," she said with a proud disdain.

His gaze narrowed. So the girl was no peasant. A knowledge that did nothing to ease the burning in the pit of his stomach.

"Then choose one of those numerous languages and explain to me what the hell you are doing here."

"Will it halt you from behaving like a lunatic?"

His fingers tightened. "Now."

There was a brief pause before she licked her lips. Philippe ignored the burst of awareness the unconscious gesture sent ricocheting through his body. Those damnable lips would not distract him. Not when he was certain that she was about to tell him a lie.

"This was nothing more than a lark."

"A lark?"

"My friends and I thought it would be amusing to see if

one of us could masquerade as the notorious Knave of Knightsbridge."

"And who, pray, is the Knave of Knightsbridge?" he demanded in a lethally soft voice.

"A highwayman who has become something of a local legend." Her lashes lowered to hide her expressive eyes. "The stories of his tedious escapades are repeated so often that my friends and I decided that we should prove his dastardly deeds were not so difficult to accomplish."

"I see." He studied the delicate features. "And it did not occur to you that this charade might lead to a bullet through your heart? Or at the very least the destruction of your reputation?"

"I realize now it was a stupid folly. But we meant no harm."

Philippe deliberately paused, allowing her a brief moment of hope before dashing it with a sharp laugh.

"You really are quite accomplished, you know."

"I beg your pardon?"

"The lies tumble from your lips with remarkable ease. I can only presume you are a local actress or a reprehensible hoyden who has a talent for falsehoods."

Her lips tightened, her dark eyes flashing in the shadows. "You asked me to explain my presence here and I have done so, now, I insist that you release me."

"Insist?" He gave a lift of his brow. "You are in no position to insist upon anything, *querida*."

"You cannot hold me against my will."

"I can do whatever the hell I please with you." His gaze lowered to the delicate curve of her throat before roaming down to the tantalizing glimpse of her breasts. The urge to taste of that soft flesh hit him with a force that had him clenching his teeth. "An intriguing notion, is it not?"

Her eyes widened as the air filled with a prickling awareness that she could not fail to sense.

"You are no gentleman."

He had never felt less a gentleman than at this moment, he accepted with a flare of unease. The things he longed to do to that soft, slender body were more fitting for a randy dockhand.

Fiercely, he turned his thoughts to more important matters. "No, I am a man who is accustomed to doing precisely as he pleases, and one who will halt at nothing to have his way," he warned. "A knowledge you would do well to bear in mind. I have no compunction in making you suffer if you do not tell me the truth."

A mutinous expression settled on the beautiful features. "You intend to beat me?"

"If necessary."

"Fine. You can beat me all you desire. I will not tell you anything."

Philippe did not doubt her sincerity. She was clearly a chit who possessed none of the usual female sensibilities. A woman prepared to take any outrageous challenge, no matter what the consequences.

A fact that might have inspired his admiration, if her audacious courage had not led her to assault his carriage. He possessed too much pride to easily forgive being treated as a common pigeon waiting to be plucked.

Of course, he had no intention of taking a whip to the ivory skin. It would be a sin against all that was holy. Oh, no. He had a far more pleasant sort of torture in store for this lovely criminal.

"Then I shall have to find another means of persuasion," he said as he lowered his head.

"What do…?" She stiffened in shock as his lips skimmed the line of her jaw. "Oh."

Philippe closed his eyes as the heat and sweet scent of lilacs washed through him. By God, she was wasted as a thief. She could make a fortune as a courtesan.

Meu Deus, at this moment he would pay that fortune.

"Such skin," he whispered, his lips following the long length of her neck. "As perfect as the rarest pearl."

She gave a small jump as he lightly nipped at the pulse racing at the base of her neck.

"No, you must not."

His mouth continued its exploration, discovering the swell of her breasts. "Tell me who you are."

"Raine," she said on a strangled gasp.

Philippe used his teeth to tug the offending chemise out of his way. "Your real name."

"That is my real name." She shivered, but Philippe possessed enough experience to know it was not from fear. "Raine Wimbourne."

"Raine." He pulled back to regard the tight rosebud at the tip of her breast. It was already puckered as if pleading for the touch of his mouth. A plea he had no intention of ignoring. "Yes. It suits you."

"You said if I told you my name you would release me," she charged.

"You have not told me why you were playing such a dangerous charade."

"I cannot."

"Good." Philippe closed his lips over the hardened nipple, his grip tightening on her wrists as she abruptly arched upward in shocked pleasure.

"Dear God," she breathed.

Philippe barely noticed her ready response. This was no calculated seduction, no well-rehearsed lovemaking that was designed to captivate his partner while leaving him satisfied, but unaffected.

Far from it. His blood rushed through his veins and his heart pounded with excitement. The woman must be part fey, he decided as he suckled her with a growing insistence. Only some dastardly magic could have set his body on fire with such shocking need.

Any thought of the inappropriateness of seducing some unknown wench in a near-frigid carriage was lost as Philippe pressed his erection against her hip. He wanted to spread her legs and take her with a fierce, pounding passion. He wanted to be so deep inside her that her moist heat surrounded him completely.

Using his teeth and tongue, he mercilessly teased her sensitive flesh. Her soft moans filled the carriage, her head twisting from side to side as if she were battling her rising tide of desire.

"No, I—" she gave a small gasp "—I will confess all."

Her husky voice was an unwelcome intrusion as Philippe was busily learning the sweet hollow between her breasts.

"Mmm?"

"Stop this and I will tell you the truth."

Philippe muttered a savage curse as he was forced to pull back and study her flushed face. A portion of his mind might remind him that a confession was precisely what he had desired when he had started this business, but the larger part of him wished she had kept her lips closed. Damn, he had never endured such a brutal need for release.

"Explain," he at last managed to mutter.

Her dark eyes were stormy. "I am here because of my father."

Philippe frowned in disbelief. "Your father has forced you to become a highwayman?"

"No, of course not," she denied. "My father *is* the Knave of Knightsbridge."

His gaze flicked over her deliciously rumpled form. "So, you are the daughter of a common criminal," he said, not without some satisfaction.

He would not hesitate to seduce a noblewoman, of course, but her disreputable position did make sure that there would be no complications.

Raine gave a low hiss of fury. "Josiah Wimbourne is no common criminal. He was a hero in the Royal Navy and decorated by the king." Her tiny chin tilted. "More than that he is a wonderful person who has devoted his life to caring for me and for his neighbors."

"You have admitted that he is a highwayman."

"Only because he was desperate to help the poor and the helpless in our village. The people who are forgotten and neglected by everyone but him."

Philippe was unmoved. He would wager his finest vineyards that the heroic Josiah Wimbourne kept the lion's share of his bounty for his own pleasure.

After all, it was obvious the man had no conscience whatsoever.

"I should think more of his efforts if he didn't willingly risk his own daughter's life for his noble deeds," he said coldly.

"I assure you that my father argued fiercely against my taking on his role, but we had no choice." She paused before she grudgingly continued her explanation. "The magistrate was becoming far too suspicious. It was necessary to divert him before he had my father arrested."

"And so you took on the role?"

"Just until my father could return."

He gave a slow shake of his head. *Meu Deus,* what other woman would have endangered herself in such a manner?

This Raine Wimbourne was either incredibly loyal or touched in the head.

"How long have you been doing this?"

"Almost two months."

"And you have yet to be caught?" He gave a lift of his

brows. "Your magistrate must be a simpleton. Unless, of course, you have bartered those considerable charms to encourage him to overlook your criminal activities? They are certainly tempting enough to make even the most intelligent man toss aside his morals."

Something very close to hatred smoldered in her dark eyes. "You are repulsive."

"You did not find me so repulsive a few moments ago," he was swift to remind her. "Indeed, I have never heard sweeter cries of pleasure."

"They were cries of disgust, but then I suppose a man who regularly forces himself on unwilling women finds it difficult to distinguish between the two."

Philippe froze at the deliberate insult. By God, she was a damnable wench. Not a soul would blame him if he *had* forced himself upon her. She was a brazen doxy who had willingly put herself, and her dubious virtue, in danger.

But unlike many gentlemen, he possessed a profound distaste in the thought of bedding an unwilling woman. Why bother when so many were eager to share their bodies? He had done little more than kiss her. And she had enjoyed the experience as well as he had.

He damn well did not appreciate being accused of such infamy.

Pulling back, he glared at her with distaste. "Cover yourself."

With awkward motions she pulled the coat over her slender form and struggled to sit up. Philippe sternly resisted the urge to rip the coat off her and toss it out the window.

What the devil was the matter with him?

"Will you release me now?" she demanded.

Slipping behind his cool composure, he smoothed his greatcoat and forced his mind to return to the reason that he kidnapped the annoying chit in the first place.

"You say you've been acting the highwayman for the past two months?" he demanded.

She gave a startled blink at his abrupt question. "Yes."

"Always this road?"

"No. I usually remain closer to Knightsbridge. It is far less dangerous."

"So this is your first night on the turnpike?"

"Yes."

He fisted his hands. "Damn."

A frown tugged at her brows. "Who are you searching for?"

"That is none of your concern."

Her lips pursed at his aloof reprimand. "Considering you kidnapped me for information on this mysterious person, I would think it very much my business."

"The only thing that is your business is whether I intend to bed you, beat you or take you to the authorities in London, who will not be so easily seduced as your local magistrate."

Her eyes widened in startled disbelief. "You cannot take me to London."

Philippe hid his unease at his impulsive words behind a mask of cool indifference. He hadn't intellectually considered the notion of taking this female to London. Why should he? Not only did she know nothing of the man he was seeking, but this was no time to be distracted by a pretty face and body that would drive a man to insanity.

But now that the words were out of his mouth, Philippe had no urge to take them back. *Why not take her to London?* a devilish voice whispered?

She was clearly in need of a sharp lesson to keep her from endangering herself in such a reckless fashion again. A lesson he sensed would have to be severe enough to overcome that fierce, restless spirit.

And, of course, once he had her suitably settled in his town house he would be at his leisure to explore the strange heat she managed to stir in him. It was…dissatisfying to think of her disappearing before he could actually discover if she could provide the intense pleasure that she promised.

Yes, now that he truly considered the matter, it seemed the most logical of decisions.

Settling back in his seat, he offered her a taunting smile. "And how do you propose to stop me?"

Without warning she scrambled onto the opposite seat, her expressive face revealing precisely what she thought of his options.

"I do not understand why you are doing this. I have told you that I was simply attempting to help those in need. If you possessed any decency at all you would release me."

"If you seek to touch my heart with your sad tale you are far off the mark," he drawled.

"Because you have no heart?"

Philippe smiled coldly. Raine Wimbourne was not the first, nor was she destined to be the last, to learn the truth of him.

"No, *tolo pequena,* I have no heart whatsoever."

CHAPTER FOUR

RAINE KNEW THAT SHE MUST be in shock.

What else could explain her befuddled reaction to this horrid man?

One moment she was furious enough to stick a dagger in his heart, and the next she was quivering with excitement beneath his touch.

Oh, yes. She was honest enough with herself to accept that her body had turned traitor the moment his lips had touched her.

Of course, to be fair, she had to admit that she was singularly untutored when it came to the opposite sex. The convent had been secluded enough that the students never encountered unknown gentlemen. And those who did visit were well into their dotage, and usually priest, as well.

How could she, such an innocent, possibly be expected to remain indifferent to a man who was obviously an expert in the matters of lovemaking?

It was entirely his fault.

Now, however, her temperament had turned firmly back in the direction of a dagger through his heart.

Damn his rotten soul. Was he truly evil enough to carry her off to London and hand her over to the Runners?

She would be tossed into Newgate prison. Perhaps even given to the hangman before a cheering crowd of onlookers.

One glance into the indifferent, painfully perfect countenance assured her that he was more than capable of whatever dastardly deeds might suit his purpose.

A shudder raced through her as she once again turned her thoughts as to how to escape the damnable carriage. Her earlier efforts of distraction had been stunningly unsuccessful, but she could not entirely give up hope of escape.

It simply was not in her nature.

Adjusting the cape to wrap it about her shivering body, she sent her captor a resentful glare.

"If you are to hold me captive, may I at least know your name?"

A shaft of moonlight pooled over the man lounging in the corner of the carriage. In the silver light his dark beauty was almost ethereal. As if he was an angel that had tumbled to earth.

But it was more this man had likely been pushed up from the depths of hell.

"Philippe," he at last retorted.

Raine frowned at the faint accent. It was odd that she could not place it.

"You are not English."

"Actually I am part English," he corrected her smoothly. "My father was half French and half English. My paternal grandmother still resides in Devonshire."

"And your mother?"

Something flared through his cold green eyes. "French."

Her frown deepened. "And yet you speak Portuguese?"

"I have spent most of my life in Madeira, although I do try to spend at least a few months each year in London."

Good Lord, his life seemed complicated. "Which explains your town house."

"Yes."

"I suppose you also possess a home in Paris?" she continued dryly.

If possible his expression became even more glacial. "I possess several homes and estates, but none in France."

"What a grave disappointment that must be for you."

He shrugged. "Not at all."

Raine made a rude noise. How casually he spoke of his various homes and estates. As if they were mere trifles that were due a man of his rank.

Of course, men with his arrogance simply took for granted that they should be blessed with such fortune.

"God, but I hate your sort," she said before wisdom could halt the impulsive words.

There was a startled pause before he gave a lift of his brows. "My sort?"

If she had a trace of sense she would shut her lips and not say another word. The Lord knew that she was in enough trouble as it was. But, she was goaded beyond bearing by the taunting glint in those blasted green eyes.

"Men who believe that because they have a bit of wealth and social position they can go about treating others as if they are no more than rubbish."

If she thought to wound him then she was doomed to disappointment. Her sharp words did nothing more than bring a smile to his lips.

"Well, that is the point of having wealth and social position, is it not?"

"I haven't the faintest notion," she hissed.

"Ah, but I believe there is more to you than meets the eye, Miss Wimbourne. Common sailors' daughters do not possess your polished accent, nor do they speak the several languages you claim to know. Could it be you still have not told me the truth?"

Raine frowned, not quite certain how he had so efficiently turned the conversation back on her.

"I was educated in a French convent. I only recently returned to England."

"And why would a sailor's daughter be schooled in a French convent?"

She tilted her chin at the edge of mockery in his tone. "My mother was the daughter of a successful French sea captain, and it was her wish that I be sent to the same convent that she attended."

"She is no longer alive?"

"No, she died when I was just a child."

"As did mine," he murmured, his voice so low she barely heard the words. Raine stilled as his expression softened with what might have been sorrow, but before she could speak the taunting smile was back with a vengeance. "I suppose it must be difficult for you?"

"Sharing a carriage with you? Yes, extraordinarily difficult."

His gaze flicked over her with a callous assessment. "I meant being trapped among the rustics. You must be a shimmering diamond among the dross. Such beauty and elegance. Do the local farmers and tradesmen come to worship at your feet?"

Horrid, horrid man.

"Are you always so offensive?"

"Only to those who dare to attack my carriage and point a pistol at my heart."

Her hands clenched into tight fists in her lap, but she at least possessed the sense not to strike out. He was no doubt the sort who would strike back, even if she was a woman.

"You cannot know how desperately I wish I *had* put a bullet through your heart."

His smile was suddenly genuine. "Then let this be a lesson to you, *menina pequena,* on the next occasion do not hesitate."

"Have no fear. I will not so much as blink."

An unexpected chuckle filled the carriage, flowing down Raine's spine with a delicious warmth.

"So savage, and not at all what one would expect from an English wench," he murmured in appreciation. "They are usually so dull and bland. But then, what can one expect from such a cold, gray country?"

Raine regarded him warily. She distrusted his heat as much as his ice. Indeed, the heat had proved far more dangerous.

"England is not cold and gray," she protested as she leaned back in her seat. "And its citizens are certainly not dull."

"No?"

"No. Especially not those born in Kent. I will have you know that our motto is *Invicta*."

"Unconquered?" he easily translated.

"Exactly." A sense of pride flowed through Raine. She had always loved her home. The beauty of the rolling hills and fields. The gentle rivers. The lovely villages with their clapboard cottages and timbered halls. And the hardworking men and women who toiled each day to scrape a living from the earth. "We have produced men such as Wat Tyler and Jack Cade, who raised armies to seek justice for their neighbors. And Nelson himself lived in Chatham."

"And now, of course, you have the Knave of Knightsbridge."

"Yes, we do," she said without the least hint of apology.

"And I have his daughter."

There was a rap on the carriage window before Raine could reply, not that she knew what she intended to say.

Philippe turned to lower the window and spoke in a low voice to Carlos, who was riding on Raine's beautiful mare beside the carriage. They spoke too low for Raine to catch the words, but she didn't doubt they were plotting something nefarious.

Despicable pair of cads.

With a smooth motion, Philippe closed the window and returned his attention to her angry countenance.

"I suppose your friend has no compunction about kidnapping a young, defenseless woman, either?" she said bitterly.

He tugged a curtain over the window. "At the moment he still believes you to be a young, defenseless lad. I think it best we keep it that way."

"Why? Does he possess the morals you lack?"

The green eyes narrowed. "Very few, and none when it comes to a beautiful woman who is without the protection of her family. Do I make my meaning clear?"

She swallowed heavily, wishing to heaven this was all just a terrible nightmare that she would wake from.

Unfortunately the large male form consuming far more than his fair share of the carriage was all too real. As was the manner his gaze was straying over her body with increasing frequency.

The fact that his glances were causing the strangest tingles in the pit of her stomach only deepened her anger.

"You call my father a common criminal, but it is you and men like you that are truly evil. I hope someday you get your just rewards."

His lips twisted, as if he were not entirely pleased with his inner thoughts.

"No doubt I shall, but until my villainous end arrives I intend to enjoy myself thoroughly." He stretched out his legs and folded his arms over his chest. "Now, I suggest you attempt to get some rest before we reach town. I doubt you will sleep easily once you are tossed into a damp cell."

With maddening arrogance he closed his eyes, not only ensuring he had the last word, but proving that he wasn't even the least frightened that she might try to harm him, or dare to escape.

She gritted her teeth and spent the remainder of the cold trip fantasizing on the numerous methods of torturing a raven-haired devil.

PHILIPPE PRETENDED SLEEP until they rattled through the outskirts of London and entered Mayfair. He had purchased his house in Grosvenor Square ten years before, when it had become evident his business would mean remaining in England for at least a few months a year.

It was far too large and elegant for a bachelor, but since many noblemen had decided that it was more fashionable to reside in the newer squares of Portman and Cavendish, he had concluded it was too good a bargain to pass up.

His investment instincts were flawless.

His other instincts, at least at the moment, were open to question.

Glancing across the carriage at the tiny woman who was glaring at him with a murderous intent, Philippe suppressed a sigh. Throughout the tedious journey he had been painfully aware of Raine Wimbourne. Even as he had feigned sleep his senses had been assaulted by her presence. The warm scent of lilacs, the soft sound of her breath, the brush of her slender leg against his own.

It was as if she were branding herself deep into his awareness. And there wasn't a damn thing he could do to stop her.

Only a lifetime of rigid discipline had managed to keep him from reaching out and crushing her in his arms.

Feeling the carriage sway as it descended into Brook's Mews, Philippe straightened and buttoned his coat. He had commanded Carlos to tell Swann to take them directly to the stables. Not only did he dislike disturbing the elderly couple who were the only staff that actually resided in the house, but he had no intention of alerting the neighborhood he had kidnapped a young lady.

It was the sort of thing that was bound to disturb the aging nobles.

Once they pulled to a halt he reached across to grasp the cape that flowed over the seat, and with one smooth motion had it pulled over Raine's head.

"Bloody hell, what are you doing?" she rasped.

Stepping out of the carriage, Philippe reached back to grasp his prisoner about the waist and easily tossed her over his shoulder.

"Do you wish the entire neighborhood to see you entering my town house in the middle of the night?" he demanded.

"Oh, certainly not." She futilely attempted to kick him. "I would not wish to ruin my reputation before I am hauled off to prison."

"The night is not yet over, *cara*. Perhaps if you please me enough I will postpone your trip to Newgate."

"Please you? *Please* you?" she echoed in disbelief. "I intend to kill you."

"You are welcome to try." He adjusted her on his shoulder and clamped an arm around her flailing legs. "Now, do be quiet or I will be forced to gag you. Not a bad notion now that I think upon it." He turned to discover his groom approaching him with a furrowed brow. "Ah, Swann, stable the horses and warn the Hibberts that I will only be staying a day or two and have no wish to officially open the house. Whatever staff they have come during the day will have to do."

"And your…companion?" the groom demanded.

Philippe smiled with a surge of anticipation. "I will deal with him."

Swann turned his head to spit on the ground. "You should have him hauled off to the gallows. Or better yet, leave him here with me. I should soon have him ruing his dastardly ways."

"Yes, I am certain you would be very persuasive, however,

I still have use for the brat." He chuckled at the muffled curse that was smothered by the cape and headed toward the door. "When Carlos arrives tell him I will meet him in the library after I have settled my guest."

"Aye, sir."

Carrying his slight burden without trouble, Philippe crossed to the low gate and entered his tidy gardens. Ahead of him the three-storied house built in a mellowed red brickwork slumbered in shadows. It was not the largest house in the square, but there was an aging dignity in the sturdy garrets, the finely carved stonework and wrought iron railings.

He paused long enough to dig the key from his pocket and opened the door to the lower kitchens. From there he used the servants' staircase to make his way to the attics that had once housed the nurseries. If his memory served him right there was a narrow bed among the furnishings, and best of all the windows were too high and narrow to prevent even the most determined escape.

At last reaching his destination, he stepped into the musky apartments and tossed his furious bundle onto the bed.

Leaving her to struggle out of the cumbersome cape, Philippe moved to the nearby fireplace and was rewarded to discover a forgotten candle on the mantel. Once he had the wick blazing, he turned to discover Raine tossing aside the cape and standing to slay him with a murderous glare.

Before she could hurl her venomous insults, he moved forward and offered a faint bow.

"These will be your chambers, my lady," he murmured in taunting tones. "Perhaps not the most elegant room in the house, but no doubt preferable to a cold prison cell?"

Her nose wrinkled at the thick coating of dust. "Barely."

Against his will Philippe discovered himself laughing at

her relentless courage. *Meu Deus,* what other woman would face him so boldly?

Stepping even closer, he surveyed her pale, perfect features. Even attired in the ridiculous jacket and buckskins with her amber hair in tangles, she was still the most beautiful creature he had ever seen.

"Do you never give an inch, Raine?" he said softly.

Her chin tilted upward. "Do you?"

"Never."

Her eyes widened at the husky edge of his voice, but before she could react he had wrapped his arms around her waist and hauled her firmly against his chest. Philippe waited until her lips parted in protest before he claimed them in a rough kiss.

He could sense her shock. Not that it could be any greater than his own, he ruefully told himself. He certainly hadn't intended to grab and kiss her as if he were some bumbling stable lad with his first maid. It was hardly the technique of a practiced seducer.

But there was no denying that there was something about this woman that provoked and bedeviled him in a manner he was finding difficult to ignore.

He desired her. He desired her with a power that was quickly becoming an obsession. But more than that, he was fascinated by her.

She was a unique puzzle he felt compelled to solve.

Outlining her full mouth with the tip of his tongue, he slipped between her lips and tasted the decadent wetness within. His breath was squeezed from his lungs. She tasted as sweet and fresh as the lilacs she smelled of. As sweet as spring.

Just for a moment she stiffened, as if she were about to pull away, and Philippe silently cursed. She was not indifferent to his touch. He was experienced enough to know when a woman returned his desire. She might wish him in hell, but she still wanted him.

Then, with a faint sigh, she was melting into his arms.

A shudder shook through him. It was no more than a kiss, but his entire body clenched with pleasure.

Feeling her grasp at the folds of his greatcoat, Philippe traced his hands up the curve of her spine. She was so delicate. So astonishingly tiny in his hands. It was easy to forget her fragility when she was battling him as if she were as large and intimidating as a dockhand.

With gentle care he smoothed his hands back down to her hips. His lips shifted to spread light kisses over her cheek before he lightly stroked the shell of her ear with his tongue.

She shivered beneath his touch and he felt that strange searing heat race through him. A heat that flowed through his entire body, not just the familiar bits and pieces.

The urge to sweep her into his arms and carry her to the nearby bed was overwhelming.

He wanted to see her spread beneath him. To part her thighs and discover the heart of her pleasure. To thrust himself into her until they were both exhausted and sated.

It was surely what she had been created for?

His arms had already tightened when he gave a low groan.

The devil take it, this was not the time to be indulging in such games. No matter how delightful.

At this moment Carlos was awaiting him in his library, and his brother would be anxiously awaiting word that he had reached London.

He abruptly lifted his head, gazing down at her upturned face with a brooding intensity.

In the flickering candlelight her delicate beauty was enough to steal his breath. The golden curls were a shimmering river as they tumbled about her shoulders, her ivory skin was brushed with a faint flush, and her eyes smoldered with the lingering memory of his kiss.

She looked like a wanton, exotic angel.

Perhaps in another man it might not be so surprising that he had lost all sense. She was lovely enough to tempt a saint.

But he was not just any man, he sternly reminded himself. He was Philippe Gautier. A gentleman who had built a fortune on his ruthless ability to never lose sight of his goals.

Taking a step backward, he sucked in a deep breath. "I have business to tend to. You will remain here until I return," he said in tones that were more abrupt than he intended.

She frowned as her fingers rose to touch lips still reddened from his kiss.

"What are you going to do with me?"

His lips twisted as he turned and moved to the door. "That is the question, is it not?"

Refusing to glance back, Philippe shut the door behind him, and then, taking a chair from the hall, he lodged it beneath the knob.

He paused in the shadows as his gaze lingered on the door. He knew that she was effectively trapped. There was no way out of the room, and even if she tried to scream there would be no one to hear her.

Still, he found himself reluctant to leave. As if she might disappear into a puff of smoke the moment she was out of his sight.

Ridiculous.

He gave himself a shake as he forced his reluctant feet to carry him toward the main staircase and down to the library.

As always he found the house in pristine condition. Despite her advancing years Mrs. Hibbert kept his home constantly prepared for even the most unexpected arrival. There was no musty air or Holland coverings to be found. Instead he was greeted with the smell of fresh beeswax and carpets that were freshly beaten.

It was the sort of loyal service he expected in all his servants.

Entering the library, he was not surprised to discover that a fire had already been lit to glow warmly off the polished oak paneling and to drive the distinct chill from the room. His gaze shifted to take in the sight of Carlos stretched upon one of the leather couches, a large glass of brandy in his hands.

"At last," the younger man complained. "I was beginning to fear that you had been overcome by a half-grown waif." The dark gaze abruptly narrowed as he studied Philippe's tight expression. "Was he more trouble than you expected?"

Philippe crossed the Persian carpet to toss his coat on a wing chair.

"Enough trouble to drive a man to Bedlam," he muttered.

There was a faint pause before he heard Carlos rise to his feet. "What the devil are you up to, Philippe?"

Reluctantly, Philippe turned to meet his friend's curious gaze. "Attempting to rescue my brother from his latest disaster. What else could I possibly have on my mind?"

"You know I speak of the *crianca*. You should have given him a good thrashing, or handed him over to the authorities if you were determined to see him punished. Why would you risk exposing your arrival in London by holding the pathetic creature captive?"

"Because it suits me to do so."

Carlos gave a slow shake of his head. He knew Philippe far too well. "There is something more to the boy than you are revealing. You would never have hauled him to London if he did not have some value."

Philippe shrugged. "He amuses me."

"He…amuses you?" Carlos gave a sudden laugh. "*Meu Deus,* is there something you wish to confess?"

With a frown Philippe moved toward the heavy mahogany desk set near the bay window. For reasons he couldn't name, he had no desire to reveal that the lad was instead a beautiful young woman. Not even to this man whom he considered a brother.

For now she was a secret he intended to keep closely guarded.

"The only thing I wish is to discover if my agents have managed to complete the tasks I set for them," he said as he opened the top drawer to pull out a thick packet. He swiftly untied the string and began to spread out the various documents over the desk. "Ah."

Carlos moved to stand beside him. "What are those?"

Philippe felt his stomach clench as he skimmed through the various papers. Before leaving for England he had sent word to his most trusted agents to begin the investigations to clear his brother's name. Beginning with these papers.

There were promissory notes adding up to an enormous sum, sketched maps of Windsor Castle and the surrounding grounds, lists of guards on duty and a list of drugs that were all lethal.

There were even letters written in French that were supposedly from some cohort that warned Jean-Pierre to murder the king before the end of the year if he expected to collect his reward.

"These are the exact copies of the papers that they found in Jean-Pierre's possession the night he was arrested," he told his companion. He lifted one of the letters to point toward the small etching in the bottom corner. "Here. This is the mark Jean-Pierre noticed."

Carlos frowned. "Looks like a scribble."

"Actually, it's a hieroglyph."

"How can you tell? I thought you hated anything Egyptian."

"Only when it is costing me a large fortune to fund my father's idiotic expeditions," Philippe retorted. "But this particular hieroglyph happens to be very familiar to me. It is the mark of an ancient prince. To be precise it is the mark of the prince that my father unearthed from his tomb nearly twenty years ago."

"Are you certain, Philippe?" Carlos reached to pluck one of the maps from the desk. "These papers are mere copies, and as fine as your henchmen might be, I doubt that any of them would be able to accurately copy something like a hieroglyph."

Philippe smiled. "I hired a trained forger to assist my associates. Believe me, he has a talent for the finest detail. Besides, Jean-Pierre recognized it, as well."

"Which is why we have been searching the roads and posting inns for some mysterious Frenchman from your father's past?" Carlos demanded.

"Precisely."

"Now what?"

Philippe took a moment to consider. It was far too late to accomplish much this evening, but there was one task he needed completed.

"I want you to go to Newgate and get a message to Jean-Pierre that I have arrived in London."

Carlos glanced toward the window. "At this hour?"

"You are weary?"

"Yes, but I was thinking more about the guards. I doubt they will be willing to allow me to visit Jean-Pierre at this hour."

"I do not have a doubt in the world." He reached into the inner pocket of his jacket and tossed his friend his leather purse. There was enough money within to bribe a dozen guards. Besides, he had already managed to use what influence he possessed with the king to ensure that Jean-Pierre was being held in a cell that was separated from the common riff-raff. "When you see him, do not say my name. The guards will be bound to listen and I don't wish them to know that I have arrived. Simply say that you brought his favorite hunter to town. He will know what you mean."

"Fine." Carlos pocketed the money with a grimace. "But, you had best hope that your brother has learned a few lessons in humility while he's been in prison. I promised myself that I would beat him bloody the next time we met."

Philippe clapped his friend on the shoulder. "I promise you can beat him bloody as often as you like once we have him out of Newgate."

"I will hold you to that."

CHAPTER FIVE

ONCE ALONE IN THE BARREN room, Raine wrapped her arms about her trembling body and sternly dismissed the memory of Philippe's kisses.

Why waste her time dwelling on her giddy reaction to his touch? The man was clearly an expert in seduction. He had only to be near for her heart to beat quicker and her skin to tingle with awareness. It was a dark longing that she feared would plague her until she was far away from the hateful man.

She would do better to concentrate on finding some means of escape.

Unfortunately, it did not take long for her to realize that it was a futile exercise.

The door was thick and impossible to budge no matter how she pushed, and the one window was far too narrow for even her slender form. Even worse, the rooms were bare except for a decrepit cradle and small bed.

She had nothing that could possibly be used as a weapon for when her captor returned.

"Welcome to London, Raine Wimbourne," she muttered wryly.

When she had dreamed of this moment, her fantasies had certainly not included being dressed in her father's cast-off clothing and being held prisoner in a musty attic.

Oh, no. She had imagined herself dressed in the finest of

silks as she attended the elegant Season. There would be nights at the theater, opulent balls and exclusive soirees. She would acquire a large collection of friends who would invite her to picnics and luncheons where they could giggle and gossip over tea.

And, of course, there would be gentlemen. Handsome young blades that would be bewitched and bedazzled by her charm. Their dark hair would shimmer in the candlelight and their green eyes would heat with a barely restrained desire and…

Her delightful daydream was abruptly shattered as she realized the face that had risen to her mind.

Damn the irritating man, he haunted her even when he was not in the room.

As if to add to her torment, there was a sudden scrape in the hall and then the door was thrust open to reveal the man who had become her personal nemesis.

She stepped instinctively backward as his large form seemed to consume the room as it had consumed the carriage. He had shed his greatcoat to reveal a tailored charcoal-gray jacket and black breeches that molded to his muscular body with an indecent perfection.

Raine's heart fluttered and she desperately turned her attention to the heavy tray he balanced in his hands and the thick blanket he had tossed over his arm.

A delicious aroma swirled through the air, making Raine's stomach rumble in response, and she narrowed her eyes. She was wise enough to be wary of Greeks bearing gifts.

Especially Greeks who looked like gods.

"I thought you might be hungry," he said as he brushed past her and placed the tray on the floor before spreading the blanket on the bed and sitting on the edge. "I had to make do with what I could pilfer from the kitchen, but there is some smoked ham and cheese, as well as freshly baked bread."

Raine stiffened as she realized that he intended to stay. "You expect us to share dinner?" she demanded.

"Why not?"

Her chin tilted. "In case you have forgotten, I am your prisoner, not your guest."

"I have forgotten nothing." His gaze flicked over her tense form. "But at the moment I am tired and hungry and I have no intention of attacking you. Not unless you ask nicely."

"Must you say such offensive things to me?"

"I do not suppose I must, but it is so terribly enjoyable." His lips abruptly twisted and he lifted a hand to rub the back of his neck as if he truly was weary. "Come, Raine, sit down and eat before you swoon."

It was the realization that he was right that led her cautiously to the bed. She had eaten nothing since early that morning, and she would be a fool to allow herself to be weakened by hunger. The Lord knew that she needed every scrap of strength she could muster.

With grudging reluctance she perched on the edge of the mattress and watched as Philippe filled a plate with the bounty. For the first time Raine noticed the faint dark whiskers that were beginning to shadow his jaw and the hint of bruising beneath his glorious eyes.

Strangely the signs of fatigue did nothing to mar his astonishing beauty. Indeed, they helped to soften the austere perfection, making him appear far more approachable.

A dangerous illusion, she sternly warned herself. This man was a lethal predator that would go to any lengths to achieve his goals.

Taking the plate he offered, Raine began consuming the delicious food. It was only when she had nearly cleared her plate that she sensed Philippe's gaze trained on her.

She lifted her head to discover him gazing at her with an odd smile.

"What?" she demanded defensively.

He reached to take her plate and set it along with his own on the tray.

"I was admiring your appetite. I detest those women who are forever pecking at their food, as if a gentleman would be offended that she might actually eat." The quality of his smile altered, becoming warmer and infinitely more dangerous. "It is enticing to see a woman who enjoys her food."

"Which I suppose means that I am no lady?" she said sharply.

His green eyes watched her with an unnerving intensity. As if he was seeing far more than her defensive frown. As if he was looking straight into her vulnerable heart.

"I meant my words as a compliment. Are you always so prickly?" he murmured.

His voice was low and intimate, sliding down her spine like warm honey. She shivered in response, desperately attempting to ignore the sheer intimacy of the dark room.

"Only when I am being held hostage."

He leaned close enough that his warm breath brushed her cheek. "Would you prefer that I haul you to Newgate?"

"You know I would not."

"Good." He traced a light path from her temple to the edge of her mouth. "Such beauty would not last long among the savages."

She pulled back, her eyes flashing. To be honest, she was beginning to suspect that he had never had any intention of turning her over to the authorities.

"That does not mean I want to remain here with you."

His smile widened. "You have run out of options, *menina pequena*."

"Why?" With an abrupt motion she was on her feet, her

arms wrapped about her waist. "Why can you not simply allow me to leave?"

"And where would you go? Do you truly believe you could wander the dark streets of London alone and not be molested or perhaps even killed?" He gave a shake of his head. "You truly are an innocent."

"I can take care of myself."

He merely laughed at her brave words, rising to his feet in a fluid motion. "If that were true you would not be in my clutches."

"You really are detestable."

"Me?" Something that might have been annoyance flashed through his eyes. "I was not the one to send you out alone in the dark. Or to encourage you to risk that lovely neck by playing such a dangerous charade. If you are determined to blame someone, it should be your father."

"Do not speak of my father. He is a far greater man than you could ever hope to be."

His eyes narrowed. "I, at least, know how to take care of my family."

For some reason his words caught her off guard. "You have a family?"

His annoyance melted as he regarded her with a hint of mockery. "Of course I do. Did you think I just appeared beneath a rock?"

"I assumed you were kicked out of hell."

There was a pause as he walked toward the fireplace and leaned against the mantel. His tall, lean frame appeared casually at ease, but Raine sensed an underlying tension that hummed about him.

"I have a father and a brother."

Raine found herself curious in spite of herself. This man was like none other that she had ever encountered. At times he was as cold and distant as the stars. And then she would catch a glimpse of the man beneath his hard exterior. A man she suspected could be warm and gentle.

"Are they anything like you?"

"Not in the least." A smile touched his lips, but there was an edge of bitterness in his voice. "You would no doubt love them. Everyone else certainly does."

"You sound envious."

"Do I?" He shrugged. "Perhaps I do envy their ability to fritter away their lives without a thought to the consequences of their irresponsible habits. They are charming and witty and utterly committed to their own pleasures at the expense of everyone, including myself."

She studied the austere lines of his countenance. He did not need to tell her that he accepted responsibility for his feckless family. His every feature was etched with the commanding authority that had no doubt been thrust on him at far too early an age.

Raine battled against the grudging respect that flared through her heart. She was a woman who admired loyalty above all things. Especially loyalty to one's family.

"And what are you committed to?" she demanded.

His gaze dropped to study the toe of his boot. As if he was debating precisely how much to share with her. At last his eyes lifted and Raine caught her breath at the fierce glitter in the emerald depths.

"At the moment I am committed to rescuing my brother from yet another tragedy."

"He is in London?"

"Actually he is a resident of Newgate."

Raine did not bother to hide her shock. "Newgate prison? You must be jesting."

"I wish that I were." A muscle twitched at the base of his

jaw. "As irritating as I might occasionally find Jean-Pierre, he does not deserve this particular punishment."

"What did he do?"

"He is accused of treason."

Treason? She unconsciously stepped closer, her eyes wide with disbelief. "And you treat me as a criminal? I have done nothing more than take a handful of coins and jewels."

His lips thinned, the green eyes so cold and hard that they sent a chill over her skin. "For once he is innocent of any crime. He is being used to punish my family by an old and nearly forgotten enemy. An enemy who realized that my brother was the most vulnerable and easily captured in his trap."

It all sounded wildly improbable. A wealthy young gentleman of a good family accused of treason. A nefarious enemy from the past appearing and then mysteriously disappearing. Really, it sounded like something that Shakespeare might have invented.

But she couldn't imagine that Philippe would make up such a tale. Not when it would involve his family in a scandal. His pride was nearly as inflated as his conceit.

"So you are here to rescue him?"

"If you are asking if I intend to charge the prison and set him free, then no. I am here to find some means to prove his innocence."

She gave a short, humorless laugh. "No doubt a trifling matter for a man in your position. You can afford to convince any number of judges of your brother's innocence."

"Perhaps for any other crime, but not treason." With a sudden movement he pushed away from the mantel and paced across the cramped room. "The king has always possessed a terror that he might be betrayed, and he cannot allow anyone to be seen as being forgiven for such a crime. It might give others the notion that he approves of sedition. If I do not find the means of clearing Jean-Pierre he will be sacrificed as an example to all."

Raine bit her lip. Her heart was far too tender not to be touched by the idea of any young man being held in prison and confronting the thought of his own death.

He must be so terrified, so sick at heart, as he was forced to wait for his brother to find some means to free him.

Still, she was not about to forget that this gentleman holding her captive did not possess her own compassion.

"So you are anxious to keep your brother from the hangman?" she said.

He turned to face her. "Of course."

"Just as I was anxious to keep my father from the hangman."

He studied her for a long moment before the hard features slowly softened and that wicked smile began to play at his mouth. With a deliberate motion he moved to stand directly before her.

"Ah, but I have yet to break the law to do so," he murmured. "And more important, I have yet to be foolish enough to allow myself to be captured."

Instinct told her to back away. Even innocent young women understood that it was important to keep a distance between themselves and hardened rakes. Especially when they were already far too attracted to that rake.

Philippe, however, was not alone in possessing his fair share of pride, and the thought of cowering away was enough to make her spine stiffen.

"And what have you done to rescue your brother?" she scoffed. "Kidnapped a harmless woman as you travel to your fancy town house?"

"I have managed to use some of my influence to have Jean-Pierre placed in a private cell and hired a dozen solicitors to keep the trial postponed." His fingers reached to trace down the curve of her neck. Tiny sparks of heat followed the trail of his knowing fingers, sending a rash of alarm through Raine. "And you were kidnapped because I hoped you would have information of my enemy traveling the roads."

She swallowed heavily. "That is not why you kept me."

"No." His eyes lost their icy glitter, warming and darkening to the deepest jade. "That is not why I kept you."

Raine felt as if a spell was being woven around her. And perhaps it was. Why else would the air suddenly feel so thick that it was difficult to breathe? Why else would her wits be so clouded she could barely think? And why else would her body begin to ache in a manner that was indecent?

"Philippe?"

His gaze skimmed over her upturned face, lingering on the uncertain line of her mouth.

"That skin. I have never seen anything like it. So pure and soft."

She unwittingly licked her dry lips, not realizing her mistake until a flare of raw desire rippled over his face.

"We…we were discussing your brother and how you intend to prove his innocence."

Slowly, relentlessly he moved forward, forcing her to back away until at last she found herself flat against the wall. Her breath came in small bursts as the world narrowed to the man looming over her.

"The only certain means of ensuring his innocence is to capture the bastard who contrived the trap. Of course, I must first find him," he said, although it was obvious his mind was on things other than his words.

"Well, he certainly is not in this nursery," she rasped.

"No." His hand once again returned to her throat, as if he truly were fascinated by the feel of her skin. "Actually, it is doubtful he is even in England. I would guess that he made his way back to France the moment my brother was arrested."

"Then should you not be chasing after the villain?"

His head lowered until his lips were brushing her temple. "There are matters here that I must tend to before I can begin any chase. Matters that will have to wait until tomorrow. In the meantime, I can think of a most pleasant means of passing the remainder of the night."

His lips brushed down the curve of her cheek, lingering at the edge of her mouth.

"Wait…" she breathed as her heart thundered. Dear God, her entire body felt as if it were on fire. Her skin prickled with excitement, her stomach twisted in knots and something lower ached with a desire that was directly connected to this man.

And even more terrifying was the realization that she no longer wanted to fight this terrible desire.

The nuns might have drilled into her the stark importance of a woman maintaining her virginity until she was properly married, but Raine was a realist at heart.

She had already accepted that there was no husband and no happily-ever-after in her future. And that was before she had gone missing for God only knew how long, kept in the house of a rake.

There would be no one in her future. At least no one who would care whether or not her innocence was intact.

As if sensing her inner turmoil, Philippe nibbled at the lobe of her ear, his hands lightly running down her arms.

"I can wait no longer, *querida*," he whispered. "You have me mad with need."

Mad. Yes. It was madness, she thought as he scooped her into his arms and carried her the short distance to the bed. Her gaze remained locked on his extraordinary face as she felt herself lowered onto the mattress, and then he was lying next to her, the hardness of his features unexpectedly softened with need.

Her body felt awkward as his arms gathered her close, her

hands not knowing where to go until they at last settled on his shoulders. Thankfully Philippe seemed unaware of her unease as he ran his hands down her back and whispered words of encouragement.

"Yes, Raine, touch me, I need to feel your hands against me."

His hands slid beneath her jacket and began to gently knead her stiff muscles. Slowly she began to relax beneath his touch and his lips brushed down the length of her nose and ever so lightly over her mouth.

She trembled as her lashes drifted downward. "I must be out of my mind."

"No, *meu amor,* this was destined from the moment we met."

Destiny seemed far preferable to simply lust, and as his mouth closed over hers in a searching kiss, she allowed her brief flare of sanity to melt away. Desire, as sweet and warm as the finest liqueur, flowed through her body and her fingers bit deeply into his shoulders.

Hesitantly, she began to return his kiss, a low moan lodging in her throat as he threaded his fingers through the heavy mass of her hair.

His touch was so gentle, almost reverent as he smoothed the tresses from her face. It was at complete odds with the pulsing hardness of the male body that he pressed to hers. She knew enough to realize that he was already prepared to take her, but there was no haste in his seduction.

His lips moved down the line of her jaw, pausing to occasionally take a light nip before he buried his face in the curve of her neck and breathing deeply of her scent.

Oddly, Raine had expected the heat and tension that flowed between them, but she hadn't expected the sense of being… cherished. It undermined any lingering qualms, and she readily welcomed the scorching heat of his mouth as it returned to hers.

With a smooth motion his hands moved to cup her breasts, his thumbs teasing the tight bud of her nipple and making her shudder in reaction.

As if waiting for that telltale response he began tugging at the buttons of her jacket and pulling it aside. Her boots and trousers were just as easily dealt with and, quicker than Raine could ever imagine, she found herself completely naked.

At first she was merely relieved to have the offending garments out of the way. Her skin felt far too sensitive to bear the scratchy wool. But as he paused and pulled back, her eyes lifted to discover him regarding her with such intensity that she was swiftly embarrassed.

She would have covered herself if he hadn't grabbed her arm and pushed it back onto the mattress.

"No, *meu amor,* do not hide from me," he rasped, a hint of color marring the angular line of his cheekbones. "You are so beautiful. So…"

A groan was wrenched from his throat as he impatiently tugged on his cravat and pulled off his jacket. His movements were strangely jerky as he managed to wrestle himself out of his waistcoat and pulled his linen shirt over his head.

Raine caught her breath at the sight of his broad chest faintly dusted with dark hair, but before she could fully appreciate the spectacular sight he was lowering his head and kissing her with a growing urgency.

Still holding her arms pinned to the bed, he allowed his mouth to begin to explore her body with frustrating leisure. He lingered at the base of her throat, planting teasing kisses over the line of her collarbone and then, at last, he found the straining tip of her breast.

Raine released a shaky sigh as the pleasure blistered through her body and curled her toes. Dear God, she hadn't known that anything could feel so wickedly wonderful. The heat of his lips as they suckled her, the rough caress of his tongue and even the gentle tug of his teeth. It was all enough to make her arch upward in a shuddering bliss.

"That's it, Raine," he urged against her skin. "Let me please you."

Raine thought if he pleased her any more she might actually scream. There could surely be nothing better than this?

He taught her that she was mistaken as his hands skimmed down the curves of her body. Wherever they traveled they left behind a shimmer of excitement, like tiny fireworks flaring over her skin.

Her breath caught and held in her throat as his hands reached her legs and gently tugged them apart. Just for a moment she resisted, uncertain what he was demanding.

"Let me touch you," he muttered, his mouth moving to tease the hollow between her breasts. "I want to feel your heat."

Ever so slowly her legs parted and his fingers stroked the inner skin of her thighs. Raine clenched the blanket beneath her as the roaming fingers found her moist parting and stroked between the tender folds.

"Philippe," she gasped.

His head lifted to watch her with eyes that smoldered with such heat that she nearly gasped.

"You are ready for me, *meu amor.* So warm and wet."

Raine blushed as she realized that there was, indeed, an unaccountable dampness between her legs as his clever fingers continued to stroke and tease her. Her embarrassment, however, was no match for the swelling tension that clutched her body.

There was something just out of reach. A beckoning enticement that made her shiver and twist beneath his touch.

"Shh," he murmured, "I will ease what ails you, sweet Raine."

With her eyes squeezed shut she heard the rustle of Philippe removing the last of his clothing, and then shockingly she felt the warm weight of his body as he covered her.

His mouth touched her parted lips as he settled between her thighs, and her arms instinctively lifted to wrap around his neck. She felt the brush of his enlarged shaft against her thigh before it was at her entrance.

She had the briefest moment to consider just what he intended to do before he was pressing into her dampness with a relentless thrust.

Lost in the pleasure, Raine was unprepared for the sharp sting that stabbed through her body, and digging her nails into his back, she gave a muffled gasp.

Philippe stiffened, his head jerking back to regard her with a stunned expression.

"*Meu Deus.* Why did you not tell me?"

"Would it have stopped you?"

A mixture of emotions flickered over his face, all too swiftly for Raine to decipher. Then, with a low hiss, he was slowly pulling himself out of her.

Raine breathed out in relief, only to stiffen in surprise when his head dipped and he began scattering kisses along her throat, over her breast and down her stomach.

Her pain was forgotten as his lips expertly coaxed her passion back to life.

"Oh," she breathed as his tongue dipped into her belly button and then traced ever lower. "Dear heavens…"

"Heaven has nothing to do with this, *meu amor,*" he muttered as he deliberately scraped her sensitive skin with the rough whiskers on his chin. "But I have no strength to deny the devil's temptation. Not on this night."

She had no notion what he meant, but before she could demand he explain, Philippe dipped his head lower and she gave a small scream as she felt his tongue stroke the very heart of her.

Her hands clasped his hair as he licked and teased with a ruthless intent. A part of her was shocked by such intimacy. Good Lord, she did not know this was even a part of making love. Certainly she had never heard it spoken of, even in whispers. It seemed…decadent. But, oh, so wonderful.

A moan escaped her lips as she arched off the bed. That sweet tension was once again clenching her muscles and tugging her toward a pinnacle that she half feared to reach.

"Do not fight it, Raine," he whispered, as if able to read her mind with the ease of a master. "Just relax."

Relax? He had to be out of his wits. Her entire body felt as if it had been wound so tight she would explode.

He shifted, his hands holding tight to her hips as he continued his delicious assault. Raine whimpered as the tension reached a breathless point, and then shattered into a million sparks of pleasure.

"Philippe." She sighed as she floated slowly through the velvet darkness. "That was…that was amazing…."

"That, sweet Raine, was only the beginning."

His body slid upward and once again he was between her legs. She felt the tip of him enter her and the odd lethargy was banished.

Sensing her sudden tension, he lightly kissed her lips before pulling back to regard her with a somber expression.

"Do not fear, I will not hurt you. We will take this as slowly as you need."

Suiting his action to his words, Philippe kept his gaze locked on hers as he gently pushed into her. Raine felt stretched and uncomfortably full, but as he promised there was no pain.

There was a final thrust and he was completely inside her.

He paused, as if waiting for her to adjust to the invasion before he slowly began to move.

At first Raine simply tried to accustom herself to the strange sensations, but as his head lowered and he nuzzled at her breasts she realized that her hips were beginning to lift of their own accord.

He groaned in approval, his steady pace beginning to quicken as that wondrous pleasure spiraled through her.

"Yes, *meu amor,*" he breathed, his hands moving to cup her hips and angle her so he could deepen his penetration.

Raine dug her nails into his shoulders as her breath came in short gasps, the pleasure coalescing into a burst of shocking waves.

Above her, Philippe's features sharpened as he gave one last forceful thrust, and then with a wrenching groan he collapsed on top of her.

In a rather dazed wonderment Raine held on to him with weak arms.

He was inside her. A part of her. As if they were one.

And it was the most astonishing experience of her life.

CHAPTER SIX

PHILIPPE STRUGGLED TO recall how to breathe as he rolled to the side and held Raine in his arms. He was exhausted, his body still shuddering from the intensity of his climax.

Meu Deus, he was one and thirty and fully experienced in the most exotic forms of seduction. But nothing had prepared him for the stunning pleasure, the searing heat and wild abandon that could be found in the awkward caresses of an untried angel.

A distant part of his mind was whispering that he had just taken this woman's innocence. That he debauched and despoiled a virgin. A sin that had had yet to be laid at his doorstep.

That part of his mind, however, was lost beneath the tide of sated bliss that flooded through him.

At last managing to recapture his breath, he gazed down at Raine's flushed countenance as his fingers absently stroked through the halo of gleaming amber curls. The sweet scent of her skin filled his senses and he was quite certain that he would never again smell lilacs without thinking of this precise moment.

"Are you well?" he queried.

A blush of color flowed beneath her skin before she buried her face into his shoulder. "Yes, yes, of course I am."

"Raine." He caught her chin in his fingers and turned her face upward. "Raine, look at me."

There was a pause before the thick fringe of lashes at last lifted to reveal her eyes.

"What?"

"Did I hurt you?"

"No…" She bit off her instinctive denial as his eyes narrowed. "Perhaps a bit."

Philippe felt an uncharacteristic twinge of remorse as he brushed his lips over her forehead. "I am sorry for that. If I had known the truth of your innocence, I would have taken greater care. There was no need for any pain."

A tiny shiver raced through her body. "If I had been thinking clearly enough to tell you that I was a virgin then I would not have… We would not…"

"If you think that I intend to apologize for what just happened then you are wide of the mark, *querida*. I do not even care to know the reason you chose to give your innocence to me." He tightened his arms, savoring the feel of her soft body pressed against him. "For this one night I intend to enjoy what is offered without counting the cost."

His honesty seemed to disarm her as a portion of her blush eased and she gave a lift of her brows.

"Do you usually count the cost?"

"Always."

"Why?"

His lips twisted. It was a question he never allowed himself to ask. Not since he had been fifteen and taken control of his father's crumbling estate. Louis Gautier might be considered by all to be a most charming and gracious gentleman, but he had never possessed the least interest in his land or those servants and tenants who depended upon him. He found digging about in obscure places far more fascinating.

And of course, Jean-Pierre could never be bothered with something so trivial as rotating fields, productive wine vineyards or the cost of transporting goods.

"Because, my sweet Raine, I have a family and enormous

staff who depend upon me to do so." His fingers traced an aimless pattern on her lower back. "I may not be attempting to
save the world by robbing unsuspecting travelers, but I do
have my responsibilities."

Her lips tightened at his deliberate jab, but she was not distracted. "Like your brother."

"Jean-Pierre. Yes, damn his soul. Not only have I traveled
for a fortnight to reach this dismal country, but now it appears
I shall be forced to journey to France."

She blinked at the edge in his voice. "You make it sound
as if it is something terrible. There are a great number of people who would be in raptures at the thought of spending their
days in such a lovely place." Her lips twisted. "Especially if
they possessed the funds to stay at the most elegant châteaus
and palaces in the world."

Philippe stiffened as she unwittingly touched the wound
that festered deep inside him.

"I…dislike France."

Her dark gaze searched his countenance; no doubt she
sensed the coldness that was beginning to chase away the delicious heat that had so briefly held him in its grip.

"But, you said you were born there."

"A perfect reason to hold it in abhorrence, would you not
agree?"

A grudging smile twitched at her lips. "Perhaps to a certain
extent, but not even your birth there can make me think of
France as anything but a wondrous place."

"Then perhaps I shall take you with me when I go," Philippe said before he even knew the words were going to come
out of his mouth. He did not know where they came from, or
what had even prompted the strange compulsion, but once
he recovered from his momentary shock he realized that it
felt…right.

If he were forced to travel through detestable France in search of an unknown enemy from his past, he surely deserved to have some compensation?

Raine widened her eyes in disbelief at his words. "What did you say?"

He deliberately stroked his fingers down the slender curve of her hip. "I will no doubt be occupied with my tasks much of the time, but there will be moments I could slip away to be with you."

"And you think I would be sitting around simply awaiting you to find a moment for me?"

"It is surely better than continuing your rather dangerous occupation as a highwayman," he replied as his roaming hand reached the soft curve of her backside.

"I am not…" She snapped her lips together and gave a shake of her head. "No."

"That is not a word often used in my presence, *querida*."

Her dark eyes flashed with anger. "I will not become your…mistress. And I certainly will not travel to France."

Philippe was genuinely startled. He had never considered himself particularly vain, but after years of having women plotting and scheming to attract his attention he was jaded enough to expect most females to be delighted at the thought of being in his company.

Especially a young woman who was no more than the daughter of a highwayman, no matter what her education.

"And what is it you object to, Raine? Becoming my mistress or traveling to France?"

"Both."

An unexpected flare of anger raced through him. This woman had given him her innocence. He had felt her shudder her climax in his arms. And even now he could feel her body stir beneath his light touch. He had given her the first taste of passion she had ever experienced.

Not to mention the fact he could buy her anything her maidenly heart might desire.

She should be in raptures.

Instead a mulish expression was settled on her features.

"You said that you thought France so wondrous."

"It is, but I must return to my father. He will be worried sick and there is no telling what he may do if I do not appear soon."

Philippe gave a lift of his brows. "You believe you can return home as if nothing has happened?"

"Why should I not? It is not as if…"

"What?"

"It is not as if anything has truly changed."

The anger within him deepened. How dare she pretend that what had occurred between them had been a meaningless mating that would be easily forgotten. There had been enough heat between them to set London on fire.

Just for a moment Philippe wondered why he cared whether or not she had been enraptured by his lovemaking. If the stupid chit preferred to return and live among the rustics as her beauty faded to nothing, then so be it. Certainly she was a distraction he did not need.

But the thought of allowing her to slip from his grasp was unthinkable. Not so long as she could drive him to madness with one glance from those magnificent eyes.

"If you believe that you are a fool," he said, his voice dangerously soft.

Her expression became wary. So, not so stupid, he acknowledged, as he tugged one slender leg over his hip to discover the softness of her inner thigh.

Raine shivered. "I suppose your conceit makes you believe that any woman who has shared your bed must be irrevocably altered?"

Bending downward, he nuzzled her neck. "Something like that."

"Well, I can assure you that I..." Her words trailed to a low groan as he gently slid into her damp heat. "Philippe, what are you doing?"

Philippe slowly began to thrust, his body turning to molten fire.

"Irrevocably altering you," he whispered.

PHILIPPE WAS STILL AWAKE when the sun crested the horizon.

Although he was exhausted, there was an odd sort of peace in holding Raine in his arms as he had watched her sleep. Perhaps because she was one of the few people in the world who was not demanding something from him, he ruefully acknowledged.

Nothing but her freedom, an unwelcome voice whispered in the back of his mind.

It was a voice that was easily dismissed.

He did not doubt for a moment that once he had Raine in France and surrounded by luxury, she would soon forget any desire to return home.

Bending his head, Philippe brushed his lips over hers until her lashes lifted to reveal a sleepy pair of eyes.

"Good morning, *querida*."

She frowned in confusion. "What is the time?"

He smiled. "Far too early to be awake, but I have several appointments that I must keep. I will try to return by luncheon so that I can bring you a tray. Do you have anything you particularly wish?"

Her eyes widened. "You intend to leave me locked in this room all morning?"

He gently tucked an unruly curl behind her ear. "I cannot take you with me and I do not yet trust that you will not run amok in London the moment my back is turned. Besides, you had a late night. It will do you good to rest."

"I do not want to rest." Her hands lifted to press against his chest. "I want to return home."

A chill inched down his spine at her words. "Your home is now with me, Raine. It will behoove you to remember that."

"My father..."

He swooped down to halt her words with a fierce kiss. She would learn that her place was with him. Pulling back, he regarded her with a narrowed gaze.

"Your father was a careless, some might claim a worthless, protector for you. I shall take a great deal more care of you."

That stubborn expression settled on her pale features. "I am perfectly capable of taking care of myself, and the last thing I desire is a...a protector. Especially if it is you."

The anger that only she could manage to stir flared through him before Philippe was sternly dampening the emotion. She was like an untamed filly that would only respond to a firm, steady hand.

His hand.

He allowed his gaze to sweep over her sleep-flushed features, his fingers running over her bare skin with a blatant brand of possession.

"You were not so reluctant last eve to put yourself in my care. In fact, you did so on several occasions with quite delicious results."

A delightful blush stained her cheeks. "Must you be so crude?"

"There is nothing crude in speaking of your passionate nature, *menina pequena*. You are a woman who needs the attentions of a man. A man who will not allow you to run roughshod over him." He smiled into her dark eyes. "A man that can surround you in the luxury your beauty deserves."

"A man like you, I suppose?" she said tartly.

He chuckled softly. "For now."

"You know nothing of me or my needs."

"On the contrary, I know you intimately. And I intend to know you more intimately still." He allowed himself one last lingering kiss before pulling the blanket off his naked body and tucking it firmly around Raine. "But alas not now. I must be on my way."

She huddled beneath the blanket, her eyes flashing fire. "I will never be your mistress."

He rolled off the bed and smiled mockingly down at her. "My dear Miss Wimbourne, you already are."

With utter indifference to his lack of clothing he walked across the room and slipped through the door. He began to move down the hall before he paused and returned to shift a chair so that it was blocking the door. Only then did he return to his proper chambers and swiftly prepare himself for the day.

An hour later found him in a murky alley as he leaned against an unremarkable carriage. Within the carriage was a gentleman that Philippe had met on several occasions, but had never seen. Not that unusual since their association was one of highest delicacy.

No one beyond Carlos knew that Philippe was commissioned by His Majesty, King George IV, to keep an eye on his various enemies, and even on occasion his closest friends. It was a bargain that worked well since Philippe's business led him throughout Europe and beyond to the Americas. He was the last sort of gentleman anyone would suspect of sneaking through houses in the dead of night, or stealing the private papers of the most influential politicians in the world.

And of course for Philippe, it meant a tidy fortune in rewards and the gratitude of a king.

No, not a bad bargain at all.

"Our friend understands your concern and will do all in his power to ensure that Jean-Pierre is kept safe and as comfortable as possible," the man in the carriage was saying through the narrow opening of the window. "There can be no question of a pardon, however. Not while it is rumored he is a part of a conspiracy against the Crown."

Philippe appeared casual even as he kept a careful watch on his surroundings. "All I ask is to be given an opportunity to prove his innocence."

"I will ensure there are enough delays and complications to give you time. But it cannot last forever."

It was as much as Philippe could hope for. "I understand and I thank you."

"One more thing, Gautier."

"Yes?"

"You asked for any rumors concerning a Frenchman who revealed an interest in your family."

"You have something for me?"

"There have been rumors from the Cock and Bull down near the dock that such a Frenchie was overheard boasting that an ancient Egyptian curse was about to be unleashed upon those who dared to betray him."

Philippe clenched his hands at his sides. *Meu Deus.* It had to be the man. If he could get his hands upon him...

"Is he still there now?"

"Highly doubtful, but you might wish to visit the taproom and discover if there is anything more to learn." The window began to rise, indicating the end of the meeting before it paused. "Gautier, don't go alone. The patrons of the Cock and Bull are not the finest of our London natives. They'll slit your throat for a farthing."

"I will take care," Philippe promised, his icy determination edging his voice.

"Good. Our friend has not forgotten the services you have done for him."

"Nor have I."

The man gave a soft laugh before the window closed and the carriage began driving away.

RAINE SQUEEZED HER EYES closed as Philippe left the room wearing nothing more than a wicked smile. Not that it helped matters. She did not doubt that every hard line and angle of his body was irrevocably branded into her memory.

She listened as the door closed and then heard the unmistakable sound of a chair being scooted and wedged beneath the knob.

Just for a moment she considered pulling the blanket over her head and returning to sleep. Obviously she was trapped in the room and nothing could be gained from pacing the floor and cursing the man who held her captive.

In the end, however, she forced herself to leave the dubious warmth of the bed and dressed herself in her borrowed jacket and breeches.

If she remained in bed she did not doubt her dreams would be plagued by Philippe. The few minutes of rest that she did manage to snatch had included vivid memories of the annoying man and the skillful way he had coaxed her body to a fever pitch.

Not that such dreams were entirely bad, she had to concede. She did not regret the night of passion nearly so much as she should. In truth, she found it difficult to dredge up any regret. Her introduction to passion had been…glorious.

His touch had been so tender, so utterly devoted to giving her the greatest pleasure. She doubted that many other women could boast finding such delight when losing their virginity.

But that did not mean she intended to give in to Philippe's casual assumption that she become his mistress.

Good Lord, she would never place herself at the whim of any man. Let alone a man with Philippe's arrogance. No matter how much she might ache for his touch, he would be utterly impossible to live with.

At least for a woman of her temperament.

Besides, she had not lied when she said she was desperate to return to her father. By now Josiah would be frantic with worry. Perhaps frantic enough to do something entirely foolish.

Squaring her shoulders, she turned to push the narrow bed against the far wall. Once it was in place she stepped onto the mattress until she could see out of the narrow window.

Below her there was nothing more than the kitchen garden and a low wall that marked the alley. Nothing that offered any hope.

Not until she glimpsed a young man strolling down the alley attired in rough clothing. No doubt one of the endless flood of poor lads who were hired to clean cisterns or deliver coal or haul away rubbish.

Fumbling with the lock, Raine managed to push open the window far enough to stick her head through.

"You. You there," she called loud enough to capture the man's attention. "Stop."

Grudgingly slowing his pace, the man turned his head toward the house. "What yer want?" He stumbled to a halt as he caught sight of Raine leaning from the window. "Blimey."

Raine was not at all above using her effect on the opposite sex for her own purpose. Why not? It was not as if she had an overabundance of options at the moment.

"Please come closer. I need your help."

"Me?" The lean face was coated in dust, but there was no mistaking the sudden wariness. "Oh, ay. This is some sort of swindle. You lure me close and then conk me over the noggin. Well, I ain't no pigeon."

"No, please. I assure you that there is no trick."

"Then wot yer doing up there?"

Raine swallowed a hysterical urge to laugh. The poor man would never believe her if she told her the truth.

"Do you know who owns this house?" she instead hedged.

"'Course I do." The man removed his battered hat to scratch at his head. Raine hid a grimace at the sight of his matted brown hair. "Some toff by the name of Gautier. A foreign gent who ain't have no wife or sisters. So wot you doing there?"

Philippe Gautier.

Yes. It somehow suited him.

She swiftly searched her mind for some feasible lie. Something that would convince the man to risk entering the house to rescue her.

"I arrived with Monsieur Gautier last evening, but I fear I have made a dreadful mistake. I wish to return to my father, but…"

She deliberately allowed her words to trail away with a dismal sniff.

The man instinctively moved to the wall. "But wot?"

"I have been locked in. I need you to sneak into the house and remove the chair that is blocking the door."

"Nay. I ain't in no hurry to have some gent put a lead ball through me heart."

"Monsieur Gautier is not here, nor does he intend to return for hours. You will be perfectly safe." The man continued to regard her with suspicion. Raine gritted her teeth. "And I promise to reward you for your efforts."

At the promise of a reward the man crawled over the wall to stand directly beneath the window. "Let me see, then."

"See?"

"Are ye daft, give me a peek."

"Fine." Raine cursed beneath her breath as she turned her head to frantically search the room. Her gaze landed on

Philippe's discarded clothing still piled on the floor, and scrambling off the bed, she grabbed his superfine jacket. Hastily she searched the pockets until she pulled out a tiny antique locket that was hidden in the inner lining. It was a decidedly odd piece of jewelry for a man to be carrying, but at the moment Raine's only concern was that it was clearly made of a fine gold. Tossing aside the jacket, she climbed back on the bed. "Here." She held her hand out the window to reveal the necklace. "'Tis worth more than you can earn in a month."

The mud-brown eyes narrowed as a nasty smile twisted his lips. "True enough, but I was thinking on a more intimate sort of reward, if yer know what I mean."

Raine shuddered in revulsion. She would remain locked in the nursery for the rest of her life before she allowed the man to so much as touch her.

Thankfully she possessed enough faith in her ability to outwit most men. They were so tediously predictable in underestimating women.

"Of course." She forced a smile to her lips. "I assure you I can be very, very generous."

He gave a last leer before he was disappearing into the shadows of the house. Raine leaped off the bed and hastily stuffed her hair beneath the crimson hat and wrapped her cape about her.

There were a few minutes of panic as she waited for her rescuer to arrive. For all she knew Philippe was still somewhere within the town house. Or if not him, then at least his servants. And with her current streak of ill luck she would not be the least surprised to have her brief chance of escape snapped from beneath her nose.

At last, after what seemed an eternity, she heard the unmistakable sound of footsteps and then the scrape of the chair being moved.

Not waiting for her rather grimy Galahad, Raine pushed open the door and darted past his lanky body. She ignored his muttered curse and was oblivious to the fact that he was following closely in her wake. Her entire concentration was centered on making her way down the hall and the narrow stairs without being caught.

Only when she was slipping out of a back door into the garden did she breathe a faint sigh of relief.

It was a relief that was short-lived as a bony hand reached out to grasp her arm in a tight grip.

"This way." The man tugged her toward the back wall.

Raine allowed herself to be led through the gate, but she dug in her heels when he attempted to pull her down the alley.

"No." She wrenched her arm free. "My horse is in the stables."

"Blimey, yer going to get us sent to the gallows," the man muttered, but he did not try to halt her as she crossed to the stables and cautiously peered through the door.

Raine carefully scanned the shadowed interior of the stables, not daring to move until she was certain that the building was empty.

She didn't know where the cantankerous Swann or lethal Carlos might be hidden, and at the moment she didn't care.

"No one here, thank God," she whispered as she entered the door and moved toward the stalls.

"Aye," the man behind her rasped. "All alone."

A pair of arms abruptly grasped her shoulders and pushed her face-first against one of the stalls.

"I believe I'll have a taste of me reward." His foul breath brushed her cheek as one of his hands impatiently ran over her jacket. "I've never had me a woman dressed as a man."

Raine resisted the urge to fight his rough touch. Instead she searched the stall for a weapon as she tried to distract her attacker.

"There is no need to rush," she said in what she hoped was seductive tones. "There is no one near."

"Aye, I heard that fancy women like it slowlike."

Raine spotted a shovel set in the near corner of the stall. "Oh, yes, very slow," she urged as her arm slipped over the gate.

She grimly shut out the feel of the man's hand as it slipped beneath her jacket. He could do what he liked as long as he remained distracted while she curled her fingers around the handle of the shovel.

His free hand shifted from her shoulder to the waistband of her breeches. Sending up a silent prayer, she tightened her grip on the shovel and, half turning in his arms, she swung the shovel over her shoulder.

It was an awkward swing and it was more luck than skill that allowed her to strike the odious man directly on the temple. He dropped to the floor with a crash and spinning about, Raine was pleased to discover he was dead to the world.

Or perhaps just dead, a tiny voice whispered in the back of her mind as she noticed the deep gash on the side of his head was seeping a worrisome amount of blood.

She bit her lip as guilt stabbed through her. Lud, she had never intended to mortally wound the man. She had only been determined to knock him senseless.

Her stomach briefly heaved before she was sternly squaring her shoulders. The man had been attempting to force himself on her. She would not regret taking whatever means necessary to halt him.

Swallowing her nausea, Raine forced herself to step over his body and moved down the line of stalls. She was too close now to hesitate, she told herself sternly.

Finding her mare at the very back of the stables, Raine reached out her hand to open the gate. It was only then that she realized she still clutched the golden locket in her hand.

She gazed down at it blindly, wondering how the devil she had managed to hang on to it during her struggle.

For a moment she considered dropping it on the floor. She needed no tangible reminders of the past hours. The Lord knew that it was going to be difficult enough to rid her dreams of her brief time in London.

Besides, the necklace had been tucked in a hidden pocket, as if it held a great deal of value to Philippe. Surely a value that was sentimental rather than monetary.

Perhaps a reminder of a lost love who had broken his heart.

With a grim smile, she closed her hand around the locket.

Soon she would be on her horse and leaving London and Philippe Gautier far behind.

The damnable man would discover not to trifle with Miss Raine Wimbourne.

CHAPTER SEVEN

As ARRANGED, SWANN WAS waiting with Philippe's carriage near St. Paul's. Commanding his groom to take them to the Cock and Bull near the docks, Philippe climbed in to discover Carlos sprawled in the corner, fast asleep.

Philippe did not disturb his companion as he settled on the leather seat. He needed to consider what he had been told and what his next steps should be.

Unfortunately his treacherous thoughts refused to obey his stern commands. Rather than focusing on his brother and the man who was determined to destroy him, his mind was instead consumed with the thought of a small, pale face and pair of flashing dark eyes that made him smolder with desire.

Raine was no doubt furious with him, he wryly conceded. She possessed far too much pride and spirit to easily accept her captivity.

Still, he did not doubt that he would soon be able to coax her from her ill humor. Perhaps he would stop by a jewelers on the way back to his house. A sparkling bauble always managed to smooth even the most ruffled feathers.

He was just at the point of debating between diamond earrings and a ruby bracelet when Carlos stirred and opened his eyes to narrow slits.

"Judging by the smell of the streets I can assume we are not returning to Mayfair for a hot bath and hearty breakfast?"

"We are headed to the docks."

"Ah, what could be finer than strolling the docks on an empty stomach?"

Philippe smiled. "I have been informed that there was a Frenchman who was recently boasting of his intent to release an Egyptian curse at a pub known as the Cock and Bull."

Carlos was abruptly straightening as he regarded Philippe with a hint of surprise.

"Egypt again."

"Precisely."

"A strange choice of words, but not any real evidence," Carlos warned.

Philippe had already determined that a handful of drunken words spoken in a seedy pub were not enough to clear his brother.

"No, no tangible evidence, but it gives me a place to begin my search for the damnable villain."

Carlos considered for a long moment before glancing out the window. "From what I know of the Cock and Bull you won't find many willing to speak to a man of your pedigree. Sailors in the whole have little use for fribbles and fops."

Philippe gave a lift of his brows. "Why else do you suppose I brought you along?"

Carlos flashed his white teeth. "I assumed it was for the charm of my company." The carriage began to slow and Carlos bent to grasp the bag he had tossed on the floor. He rummaged through it until he pulled out a threadbare wool coat and battered hat. Pulling them on, he was pushing open the door before the carriage came to a full halt. "Remain here, I will find someone who can help us."

Philippe reached out to grasp his arm before his friend could disembark. "Take care, Carlos. If you are seen it will be known that I am in London."

"No one will recognize me, *amigo*. Not unless I wish them to."

Philippe abruptly grimaced. "Must you smell like rotting fish?"

"That, *amigo*, is the smell of money to men on the dock," Carlos informed him as he vaulted to the street and turned to send Philippe one last glance. "Try not to kidnap any of the pickpockets while I am gone. I think one filthy urchin a week is enough."

Philippe chuckled as his friend disappeared into the back of the nearest building.

Ah, if Carlos only knew…

Leaning back in his seat Philippe once again found his thoughts turning to Raine Wimbourne. He had yet to discover the reason she affected him with such a strange power. And in truth, he was not certain if he wished to consider it too deeply.

For now she made him feel something beyond duty and endless responsibility, and that was enough.

Lost in thought, Philippe paid no heed to the passing time and it came as something of a surprise when the door to the carriage was opened and Carlos stuck his head inside.

"I have brought someone I believe may be of assistance," he said before he stepped back and helped a short, squat woman with a plain face and voluminous gown into the carriage. "This is Dolly."

"Dolly?" With a vague sense of confusion Philippe helped the woman to take a seat opposite him. Carlos had said the name as if he should recognize the woman. Stupid, considering he possessed a distinct distaste in rubbing elbows with commoners. Then a niggling memory tugged at the edge of his mind. Of course. He regarded the rather plain woman with a renewed interest. "Ah, Dolly. I am pleased to make your acquaintance."

The woman flushed with pleasure. "Get on with you, sir. As if a fancy gent such as yerself would be pleased to meet a mere fishwife."

He smiled wryly. As a businessman he made it a priority to keep track of any unusual happenings that might threaten or disrupt his fleet of ships that traveled throughout the world. There wasn't a major port that did not have at least a few agents on his payroll.

He had heard of this woman and her crafty ability to hide reluctant lads from the nefarious press-gangs. It was rumored that she went so far as to hide the hapless boys beneath the folds of her skirts when necessary.

Philippe admired ingenuity in anyone, whether they were male or female.

"Ah, but you are not a mere fishwife," he murmured. "Your reputation is known far and wide."

A twinkle entered the rather muddy-brown eyes. "Let us hope not too far and wide, eh, sir?"

"Indeed."

She briskly squared her shoulders. "Now, yer handsome friend was saying that you were in need of information?"

"Yes. I will be happy to pay."

"Well, don't be thinking I'm too good to be taking yer blunt. 'Tis always needed in this place."

"I would not have it any other way."

Philippe slid his hand into his jacket to retrieve the purse he had received from Carlos earlier that morning. At the same moment he smoothed over the hidden pocket he always had sewn into his jackets. His heart gave a stutter as he realized that he had forgotten to collect his mother's locket from the jacket that he had left in the nursery.

It was an unheard-of slip.

He had carried the locket every day of his life since he had found it in his mother's possessions when he was just ten. Never in the past twenty-one years had he ever forgotten it.

Which made the fact that he had done so this morning seem far more significant than it perhaps should be.

"Sir? Is anything the matter?" Dolly demanded with a growing frown.

"No." Philippe gave a determined shake of his head and pressed several coins into her hand. "Nothing is the matter."

Wise enough not to pry, Dolly efficiently tucked away the coins. "Then let us get to brass tacks before someone takes more than a passing interest in such a fine carriage. Carlos said that yer looking for a Frenchman."

"Unfortunately, that is true."

"I have heard that you possess an unnatural dislike of your countrymen," the woman said, proving that she not only knew his identity, but his reputation. Good. It would make certain she would not be foolish enough to reveal this secret meeting. No one who had heard the rumors of his ruthless character would ever dare to cross his will. "Not that I can blame you. Nasty creatures, the French."

"'Tis not so much dislike as indifference. I may have been born in France, but my home is in Madeira."

"And so you owe yer loyalty to the House of Bragnaca?"

He gave a faint shrug. "I am a businessman. My loyalty belongs to whoever is likely to offer me the most profit."

She gave a sudden laugh. "A gent with intelligence. A rare combination. I shall keep my eye on you, sir. I've a sense you'll be going far."

"No doubt straight to hell," Philippe said dryly.

"Oh, aye. In time." She did not seem particularly concerned about his imminent trip to the fiery depths of the netherworld, but then neither was Philippe. "Now, about this Frenchman. He was at the Cock and Bull near three weeks ago."

Philippe leaned forward. "What did he look like?"

"A small, slight man with gray hair that was thin on top. He was dressed in plain, good wool and carried an ebony cane. There was a scar here…" Dolly lifted her hand to point at the edge of her right brow. "It ran down his cheek."

Philippe froze as the memory of a stranger who had so unexpectedly arrived at their estate in Madeira rose to mind. Philippe had been young, no more than eleven or twelve when the man had forced his way past the servants and began to storm through the house, demanding the return of his property. Watching from the staircase, Philippe had listened as the demented stranger had threatened to kill Louis Gautier if he did not give him the precious artifacts discovered in the tomb of the Egyptian prince. Whether or not he would have carried out the threat went unknown as Louis had pulled a dagger from his boot and sliced the stranger from his brow to the edge of his mouth.

A terrible wound that exactly matched the scar that Dolly described.

A cold flare of satisfaction raced through him. "That is the man I seek. Did you catch a name?"

"One of the sailors called him Seurat."

"Seurat." He tested the unfamiliar name. Louis had sworn over the years that he had no notion who the stranger might be, or why he had been so determined to claim the artifacts as his own, but he had never quite given up his fear that the madman might return. A fear that was obviously well founded. "Was anyone with him?"

"Nay. He came by himself."

"Did he speak to anyone in particular?"

Dolly gave a firm shake of her head. "Sat in a corner and drank his self senseless three nights running. Occasionally he would talk to himself loud enough to disturb the other customers."

Damn. Philippe clenched his teeth. He had hoped that there might be someone in London who could give him a clue to Seurat's eventual destination.

"Have you seen him since?"

"Nay. He has not been near the docks."

It was what Philippe had expected. The villain would hardly be considerate enough to hang about to be captured. Still, he could not deny a flare of disappointment.

"Thank you, Dolly. I will remember your assistance."

The woman gave a nod of her head as she rose and awkwardly climbed out of the carriage. Once on the street she turned back to regard Philippe with a somber expression.

"Sir?"

"Yes?"

"Most folk around here have some sort of trouble or sickness, but this Seurat…"

"What about him?"

"He was sicker than most."

Philippe frowned. "He has an illness?"

"Up here." She tapped a finger to her temple. "There is something queer in his attic. He's a dangerous man. A desperate man."

"I will keep that in mind," he murmured.

She gave a brisk nod before she walked away and Carlos took her place. Entering the carriage, the large man took his seat and banged the roof to send Swann on his way.

"Well?" he demanded with a hint of impatience.

Philippe shrugged. "Not much more than a name. Seurat. And the fact he has not been seen near the docks for the past three weeks."

"You think it his true name?"

"He was foxed when he uttered it, so yes, I think it probable that is his true name."

Carlos crossed his arms over his chest. "Then the hunt is on."

RAINE KEPT TO THE LESS traveled streets as she made her way from London, inwardly cursing her father's crimson cape and hat that drew far too much attention.

Thankfully it was still too early in the day for any members of society to be about, and the horde of servants, tradesmen and merchants who clogged the streets were far too busy to have time for more than a startled glance before hurrying on their way.

Eventually, she managed to fumble her way through the maze of neighborhoods until she was on the road home. A stroke of fortune, since she had begun to fear she was going to devote the entire day to going in circles.

Her brief spate of good luck, however, turned once she was past Blackheath. Without any buildings to block the biting wind and occasional snowflakes, she soon discovered she was not dressed nearly warmly enough. Even riding low to the saddle she was frozen to the very bone within a few moments.

Her discomfort only intensified over the next two hours as her stomach began to cramp with hunger and a pain began to throb behind her temples. Even worse, she discovered that her night of illicit passion had made her tender in places that a young lady should not be tender.

All in all it was proving to be an unpleasant journey, she decided grimly.

Lowering her head, Raine forced herself to keep going forward. She did not know when Philippe would return to his town house, but she wanted to make sure she was far, far away before he discovered that she had escaped.

As morning passed and a gray afternoon arrived, Raine began to recognize her surroundings. She was still a goodly distance from Knightsbridge, but she was close enough to be recognized.

She turned off the main road and instead took a small cart path that would eventually lead to her father's cottage. Only a handful of farmers and crofters ever traveled through the remote fields. She should be safe enough.

A reasonable thought, although one that should never have passed through her mind, since the minute it did she could hear the sound of masculine voices just around the bend.

More out of caution than actual fear, Raine slowed her mare and turned off the road into the overgrown garden of a decrepit cottage. She hid her horse behind a fallen outbuilding and returned to peer through an overgrown hedgerow.

What she discovered made her heart lodge in her throat.

The magistrate and another man were standing beside the road as they studied something in a nearby ditch.

For a moment she debated simply hiding in the bush until the men concluded their business and moved along. She certainly could not afford to be caught wearing such condemning attire. But, even as common sense urged her to slip deeper into the hedgerow, her curiosity had her scooting toward a nearby tree and silently climbing the lowest limb so she could more easily overhear the men's conversation.

Holding her breath, she watched as the magistrate planted his hands on his hips and regarded his companion with a stern expression.

"You are certain this is where Wimbourne said that he would leave the bag?" he demanded.

Raine gripped the tree branch with frozen fingers, her heart beating so loud she was afraid that it might be heard.

"Aye." The second man took off his hat to scratch his head and Raine recognized him as Alfred Timms, a loud and coarse man who worked for the local blacksmith. "He said that there was a big party up at the squire's place on Tuesday and that there were certain to be some easy pluckings to be had. Then he told Widow Hamilton to send her lad here to collect the bag so that they wouldn't be tossed from their cottage."

"You have disappointed me before, Timms," the magistrate warned. "I will not be happy if I am stuck waiting for hours for a highwayman who never appears."

"'T'aint my fault. The man has been real cageylike for the past few weeks."

"More than cagey." The magistrate was clearly frustrated. "He has been a damnable magician. He must have someone working with him. No doubt that Foster. He would do anything to help his master avoid the gallows."

Timms shrugged. "As to that I can't say. I only know what I overhear."

The magistrate took a step forward to abruptly grasp his companion's coat. "Then pray that you heard correctly. I have not charged you with stealing from the church coffers because you swore you could hand me the Knave of Knightsbridge. You will find yourself bound for the colonies if he is not captured within a fortnight."

His threat delivered, the magistrate marched to his waiting horse and hoisted himself into the saddle. He galloped down the road without once glancing back.

"Bloody bastard." Timms made a rude gesture toward the retreating man before awkwardly climbing on his own horse and heading back toward Knightsbridge at a much slower pace.

Raine sucked in a shaky breath as she considered what she had learned.

The magistrate was plotting a scheme to trap her father. And the detestable Timms was willing to hand Josiah Wimbourne to the gallows to save his own sorry neck.

Blast. After all her efforts, her father was still in danger.

She had to warn him. She had to…

"If you intend to take up residence in my favorite tree I suppose I should invite you in for a bit of tea. It must be thirsty business to perch up there for such a length of time."

Raine squawked as the female voice drifted from directly beneath her. Instinct alone had her clutching the branch to keep her from tumbling to the ground and breaking her fool head.

Managing to regain her balance, Raine glanced down to discover a small woman with silver hair pulled into a long braid and a thin face that was lined from age. A thick cloak that was decorated with an odd fringe of feathers was pulled around her frail body.

Raine didn't recognize her. She was certainly not the sort of woman someone would forget.

Which, of course, only made the awkward situation all the more embarrassing.

"Oh…I… Forgive me," she at last stammered.

The woman tilted her head to one side, seeming to take the sight of a strange female perched in her tree with unusual calm.

"What is there to forgive? I allow the birds and squirrels to make free use of the trees. Why should I not offer the same for a young lady hiding from the magistrate?"

Raine bit her lip. Blast. The woman had not only seen her dressed in the garb of the Knave of Knightsbridge, but now she realized that the magistrate was near.

Even the slowest wits would suspect that something nefarious was occurring.

"Hiding?" Raine tried to choke out a small laugh as she stiffly climbed down the tree and brushed the bits of bark from her rumpled cape. "No, indeed. I was…"

"No, no, you cannot lie to me, my dear," the woman firmly interrupted, peering into Raine's wary expression. "I have been waiting for you, you see."

"Waiting for me?" Raine frowned, her hands stilling in surprise. "I believe you must be confused."

The woman gave a soft laugh. "Most people certainly think so. They call me Mad Matilda."

Raine gave a choked noise. She had, of course, heard of Mad Matilda. Who had not? The poor woman was blamed for every drought or sudden illness or lost child in the neighborhood.

"The witch?"

The thin features tightened. "If I were a witch why would I be living in a cottage with a roof that leaks and chimneys that smoke? And just look at that garden wall." She pointed a gnarled finger toward the wall that was now little more than a pile of rocks. "Why, it is a disgrace. Do you think I would allow it to fall into such disrepair if I could boil a lizard or two and have it all in perfect order? No, lass, I am not a witch."

Raine found herself laughing at the woman's exasperated words. She had never really considered the matter, but it did make sense that if a woman could conjure magic, she would live in a great deal more comfort.

"But you said you were expecting me."

"Aye, I will admit that I do have the Eye," the woman said. "Those who don't understand the power would call it magic, but it is no more than a talent. Like being able to sing or dance."

Raine thought she should be uneasy at being so close to the woman. Even if she was not a witch, there was still something distinctly odd about her. But she experienced no fear or apprehension. Instead, there was an unshakable curiosity growing within her.

"I...see."

With a small smile the woman reached out to take her hand and tugged her toward the decrepit cottage.

"Come, come. It is too cold to be out here in the wind."

Raine hesitated only a moment before she allowed herself

to be urged forward. The woman might be a bit batty, but she didn't seem to be dangerous.

Remaining on the road, however, might prove to be very dangerous.

Who knew where the magistrate might be lurking? Or even the treacherous Timms?

The last thing she needed was to stumble across either one while she was wearing her father's costume. She would be locked in chains before she could utter her first lie. And no doubt her father would soon join her.

No, it would be far better to give them time to return to the village before she took off blindly down the road.

Besides, a few moments out of the freezing wind sounded like heaven.

They made their way along the broken flagstones, then entered the small cottage. Raine half expected to discover it littered with strange objects, dead animals and boiling pots. What she found instead was a small but cozy kitchen that was scrubbed clean and boasting nothing more frightening than solid oak furnishings and a china tea set.

Oh, there were a handful of herbs and plants that were strung from the open timbered ceiling to dry, and several jars of various ointments along one cabinet. But, nothing that couldn't be found in Raine's own home.

Matilda tossed aside her cloak as she bustled toward the kitchen and began to fuss with a tray that was set on a low table. Raine could not stop a small smile. The supposed witch looked like an elderly nanny in her prim gray gown with fine lace sewn into the neck and cuffs.

"Join me by the fire," she commanded, waiting for Raine to settle in one of the cushioned chairs before handing her a plate that was piled high with food. "Here we are, then."

Raine gave a startled blink. The plate was overflowing

with tiny sandwiches. Some with thinly sliced ham, some with cucumber and some with smoked salmon. And then there were tiny wedges of cakes of all sorts.

"Good heavens."

The woman settled in a seat opposite from Raine, a sparkle in her pale blue eyes.

"My talent is not quite good enough to determine which sandwiches and cakes you prefer, so I thought it best to provide a variety."

"It is a feast."

"And you are starved," she said, more as a statement of fact than question. "Eat, lass."

Raine did not need a second urging. Her stomach had been aching for the past two hours and the food was frankly delicious.

She managed to consume all of the sandwiches and two of the cakes before she at last set the plate aside and heaved a deep sigh.

This was heaven, she decided as the heat cloaked around her and her tense muscles began to relax.

"That was delicious, thank you," she murmured.

"Would you like to try some of the seed cake? It is one of my better efforts, if I do say so myself."

"I could not possibly eat another morsel," Raine protested.

Matilda settled back in her seat, a smile curving her lips. "I must say it is nice to have some company."

"I fear I cannot remain long. My father must be very worried about me."

"Aye, he is, but first I must tell you what I have seen."

Raine was not certain what to expect. "Are you going to read my palm?"

"No." The woman gave a dismissive wave of her hand. "I have no need for such gypsy tricks. I see what I see."

"And what do you see?"

"Crossroads."

Well, that was nicely ambiguous. Precisely what any fortune-teller might utter.

"Oh?"

"Yes." Matilda gave a wise nod of her head. "You stand upon them. Down one path are security and a life of comfort. Down the other are turmoil and danger and great happiness."

Raine gave a lift of her brows, willing to play along. "That seems rather confusing. Should the great happiness not be included with the security and comfort?"

"No, the happiness comes from following your heart." Without warning the woman leaned forward to touch the locket that Raine had slipped around her neck as she had raced from London.

A sharp fear flared through Raine as she jumped to her feet. No. She had put Philippe behind her. Whatever insanity had briefly brought him into her life was over and done with.

She would never, ever see him again.

"I must go," she muttered as she turned for the door.

From behind she heard Matilda give a click of her tongue. "You may leave, lass, but you cannot hide from destiny," she warned.

Raine did not bother to turn around as she fled from the cottage.

CHAPTER EIGHT

JOSIAH TUGGED AT HIS freshly starched cravat as he went in search of his elusive daughter. It was amazing that in a cottage so small the stubborn chit could manage to elude him with such ease.

She always had an ample supply of excuses, of course.

The cottage had to be scrubbed and polished until it gleamed. She needed to visit the local dressmaker. Mrs. Stone needed help in the kitchen. Foster needed to be coached on his role during this night's charade.

Perhaps reasonable explanations, but Josiah was quite certain that his daughter was deliberately attempting to avoid him.

The question was why?

At last he discovered her in the dining room as she inspected the table that had been formally set with their best china and silver.

"Raine?" he said softly.

She gave a small gasp as she jerked around. Almost as if she had expected to discover a monster creeping up on her.

It was an edgy unease that had smoldered around her since she had returned to the cottage four days ago.

With an obvious effort Raine forced a smile to her face as she smoothed her hands over the gown she had just received from the dressmaker.

She looked stunning. The pale gold silk was modestly cut, but the shimmering material brought out the faint ivory of her skin and added a luster to her golden curls, which were pulled into a complicated knot on top of her head.

In the candlelight she appeared ethereal. Like a glimmering angel dropped to earth.

The poor magistrate would be so befuddled he would be fortunate not to spill his soup in his lap and choke on his pheasant, Josiah thought wryly. Which, of course, was precisely the point.

"Good Lord, you startled me, Father," she gently chastised.

He moved forward, his gaze carefully watching her tense expression. "That seems to happen a great deal lately."

"Whatever do you mean?"

"I mean, that since you so mysteriously disappeared, you have been decidedly tense," Josiah charged. "You jump at every shadow."

She turned toward the nearby mantel and adjusted the candelabra that needed no adjustment.

"There was nothing mysterious about it, Father. I thought the magistrate was watching the road and found an abandoned cottage to hide in for the night."

"Yes, so you have said." Disbelief was thick in his voice.

He did not know what had happened during those terrible hours that Raine went missing, but he did know that it was more than simply hiding in an abandoned cottage.

Unfortunately, he had no means to force the truth from his stubborn daughter. Whatever had put those shadows in her eyes was a secret she intended to keep well hidden.

"Actually, I am glad you are here." Squaring her shoulders, she briskly turned to face him. "I wish to go over our plans for tonight."

Josiah gave a slow shake of his head. He could not deny a measure of concern when Raine had revealed the conversation she had overheard between Harper and Timms. The damnable magistrate was determined to prove Josiah was the Knave of Knightsbridge and nothing seemed capable of distracting him.

But while he agreed with Raine that something needed to be done, he was far from convinced that her current scheme was anything more than sheer madness.

"I do not like this."

"Yes, you have made that abundantly clear, Father," she murmured with a forced patience, "but we have no choice. We must do something to convince the magistrate once and for all that you are not the Knave of Knightsbridge."

"I was a fool to ever begin this folly and an even greater fool for allowing you to become a part of it." He gave a pained shake of his head. "If anything happened to you…"

"Nothing is going to happen to me."

"That is precisely the sort of arrogance that has landed me in this situation," he said sternly. "At least one of us should have enough wits to stay away from the gallows, and since it is far too late for me, I fear it will have to be you, pet."

Her beautiful eyes darkened with a mutinous determination as she reached out to grasp his arm. "No one is going to the gallows. Not even if I have to tie the magistrate to a tree and leave him for the vultures."

Josiah hid a faint smile as he recognized that expression. He should. He saw it in the mirror often enough. Usually right before he was about to do something stupid.

"No one admires your courage and loyalty more than I, pet, but not when it puts you in danger," he said softly.

"What is the danger?" She tilted her chin, clearly determined to go through with the plan regardless of his protests. "The magistrate will be here enjoying a delightful dinner and the pleasure of your very fine cigars while I quietly play the pianoforte in the drawing room. A perfectly respectable evening while the Knave is blatantly hunting carriages near the squire's house."

"Raine…"

The sound of the front door being opened interrupted his words, and Josiah was forced to swallow a curse as Raine stepped away and turned to make her way across the room.

"Remember, Father, that Foster must be within sight the entire evening."

PINNING A STIFF SMILE to her lips, Raine left the room and headed toward the small foyer. Behind her she could sense her father's frustration and a twinge of guilt tugged at her heart. She knew that he had been concerned since her abrupt return to the cottage after vanishing for more than a day. Hardly surprising. As he had so accurately accused, she was restless and on edge, and inclined to discover herself standing in the center of a room staring at nothing. Even worse, she could not banish the vague sensation that she was standing in the midst of a brewing storm, just waiting for the lightning to strike her.

Not at all the sort of thing to reassure a concerned parent.

But, while she hated to deceive her father, she knew that the truth was not likely to ease his concerns. Just the opposite, in fact. Josiah Wimbourne was proud enough to decide to track down Philippe and challenge him to a duel if he ever discovered what had occurred.

It was the last thing Raine desired.

Especially now that they had the additional burden of knowing that the magistrate was still convinced that Josiah was the Knave of Knightsbridge.

With an effort she turned her thoughts to the evening ahead. She did not have the time or luxury of brooding about what was done and over with. Not when her daring scheme would demand every particle of her concentration.

Standing in the shadows, Raine watched as Foster escorted the magistrate into the foyer and took his coat and hat with a crisp formality. Although it had been years since Foster had earned his living in the grand homes of London, he maintained his ability to slip into the role of the proper servant with remarkable ease.

Thomas Harper smoothed his hands over his plain blue jacket, his eyes covertly studying Foster and then his surroundings. His expression was unreadable, but Raine sensed that his searching glance missed very little.

No doubt he was hoping to discover a pilfered chest of coins hidden beneath the ormolu table.

Raine deliberately tugged her bodice another half inch lower before stepping from the shadows. There had to be some means of distracting the damnable man.

"Mr. Harper, how kind of you to join us," she said as she performed an elegant curtsy.

From beneath her lashes she watched as the gentleman swept his gaze over her slender form, lingering a long moment on the swell of her breasts.

"The pleasure is all mine," he murmured, polite enough to have his attention fully on her face as she straightened.

A part of her regretted the need to deceive Thomas Harper. He was a good and decent man who was simply doing his duty. Perhaps under different circumstances they might even have become friends.

Unfortunately, her loyalty to her father ensured they would be enemies. At least for this night.

Placing her hand on his extended arm, Raine led her companion toward the drawing room.

"I hope you do not mind if we dine informally? Father and I live so quietly that we have become quite dull, some might claim dismal, in our habits."

"No dinner with you present, Miss Wimbourne, could ever be considered dismal," he said smoothly.

Raine smiled, inwardly appreciating his understated charm. He was a man who effortlessly inspired a sense of trust in others. If he had not become a magistrate he would no doubt have made a perfect criminal.

"Such flattery will quite turn my head, sir," she said lightly.

"It would be nice to think so." His lips twisted in a faint smile. "Unfortunately, I am quite certain that the only head to be turned tonight will be my own. A knowledge that should trouble me, of course, but when in the presence of such beauty I find it difficult to recall why."

She gave a lift of her brows. "Do you have any Irish blood in you, Mr. Harper?"

He gave a startled laugh. "Perhaps a drop or two," he conceded as they stepped into the small drawing room.

"Then you will appreciate a fine whiskey." Josiah stepped forward to press a small glass into Harper's hand.

Raine stepped back for a better view of the two gentlemen. She knew it would be like watching two master fencers as they each battled to best the other.

Harper took a sip of the whiskey. "Ah, fine, indeed."

Josiah leaned against the faded paneling. "And entirely legal, I assure you."

If the magistrate was caught off guard by the direct attack he was able to hide it behind a bland smile.

"My interest does not lie in smugglers."

Josiah gave a lift of his whiskey glass. "I hope your interest lies in chess. Raine has no patience for the game and poor Foster simply cannot manage to offer any competition."

"I cannot claim to be a master, but I do enjoy the game," Harper slowly confessed, no doubt searching for some hidden trap.

"Good, then we shall match our wits after dinner," Josiah said.

Hearing her cue, Raine stepped forward to wrap her arm through her father's. "Do not allow him to bully you into a match you do not wish, Mr. Harper. My father has even less compassion than the ancient gladiators when mauling his opponent."

Josiah gave a lift of his brows. "What is the use in playing if it is not for blood?"

"You see?" Raine gave a mournful shake of her head. "I urge you to deny him the pleasure, sir. He possesses no shame and will boast of his conquest throughout the village."

Harper sipped his whiskey, his expression hardening as Raine and her father deliberately riled his pride. No matter what his duty he could not turn away from a direct challenge.

"If it is a conquest," he said.

Josiah smiled. "Ah, a man of courage."

"Let us say a man who enjoys matching his wits against another," Harper corrected.

"My favorite sort," Josiah murmured.

Harper drained his glass before setting it aside. "Mine, as well."

Raine gave a slow shake of her head as the two men regarded each other in a silent battle of wills. Rather like two dogs vying for dominance.

She rolled her eyes as she reached for the bell to indicate they were prepared for dinner.

God save her from arrogant men.

DINNER MANAGED TO PASS without incident.

The food was plain but cooked to perfection, and Josiah was at his most charming as he entertained them with stories of his years on the high seas.

Harper contributed his own tales of his career in London,

his self-effacing humor making Raine chuckle even as her stomach constricted with nerves.

At last the final dishes were whisked away and Foster entered with a tray of port and the inevitable box of cigars.

Raine rose to her feet with a smile. "I shall leave you to your cigars and chess match." She waved her hand as the gentlemen began to scoot back their chairs. "No, please do not get up." She flashed a smile toward their guest. "Mr. Harper, I shall be in the drawing room for the next hour or two. You need only call for me if you are in need of rescue."

The young gentleman gave a nod of his head, but there was a glow in his eyes that revealed he had no intention of calling for rescue.

"I will keep that in mind," he murmured.

Josiah sent her a triumphant glance as Foster began to set the chessboard on a small table beside the fireplace.

"Good night, love," he murmured. "I shall see you in the morning."

She performed a small curtsy before leaving the room and making her way up the stairs to the drawing room. Once there she closed the door and moved to seat herself on the small pianoforte and began picking out an absent tune. The sound of the instrument would be muted but unmistakable in the dining room.

Precisely what she needed to convince Mr. Harper she was nicely occupied while the Knave of Knightsbridge rampaged through the neighborhood.

It was less than a quarter of an hour later when Mrs. Stone slipped into the room and silently slid onto the bench beside Raine. In concert, Raine lifted her fingers from the keys and the housekeeper began to play the light tune.

The woman possessed little skill, but it was enough that she could pick out a few keys and keep the music floating through the house.

Raine rose to her feet and, ignoring Mrs. Stone's worried gaze, she moved toward the back of the room and out the door. From there she could easily make her way down to the kitchens and out the back of the cottage.

She resisted the urge to peek into the window of the dining room and instead firmly crossed through the garden toward the stables. Her father would keep the magistrate well occupied for the next few hours. And the sooner she was on the road the better.

Entering the stables, she found her mare already saddled and a small satchel near the door. Foster was nothing if not efficient, and with a minimum of fuss Raine managed to pull off her gown and was tugging on her father's gaudy attire.

As she buttoned the crimson jacket her fingers briefly faltered. She had not seen the garment since she had returned from London. She had not wanted to see it. Now she found herself recalling just how easily Philippe had slipped the jacket from her body. Dear heavens, his hands had been so tender, as if she were the most fragile object in the world.

A small sound rose to her throat as the vivid memories rushed through her mind. The scent of Philippe's warm skin. The sound of his soft voice as he whispered in her ear. The manner in which his beautiful features softened when he touched her.

She gave a sharp shake of her head. No, she could not be distracted. Not now. Her father needed her full attention. She could not fail him.

Ignoring the odd ache that clutched at her heart, Raine finished dressing and led her mare from the stables. It was not until she was some distance from the cottage that she at last mounted her horse and settled into a comfortable pace.

The night was cold and the wind swiftly had her clenching her teeth to keep them from chattering as she headed directly toward the narrow path where she had overheard Mr. Harper and Timms plotting. They would be expecting the Knave of Knightsbridge to arrive with his treasure, and she knew that the magistrate would have men waiting to capture his foe. All she need do was to be seen in the vicinity before making a swift retreat.

Surely that would convince the stubborn man once and for all that her father and poor Foster had nothing to do with the flamboyant bandit?

Sending up a silent prayer that nothing went wrong on this night, Raine slowed her horse and edged toward the side of the path. Bathed in the light of the full moon, she knew her crimson cape would be easily visible. She needed to be prepared to flee at the first hint of danger.

She had nearly reached the spot where her father had promised to leave his bounty for the poor widow when Raine heard the unmistakable sound of a sneeze coming from the trees.

With a smile of relief she abruptly whirled her mare around and began pounding back down the path.

From behind she heard a sudden shout and the crash of men rushing to gather their horses to follow her.

"That's the Knave, don't lose him," a voice growled in annoyance.

Raine never bothered to turn her head as she leaned low over the pommel and urged her mount to an even greater pace. She had already carefully plotted her exact route, and as she rounded a large corner she turned onto a hidden path without missing a beat.

Once she was certain that she was out of sight she slowed to a walk and urged her horse behind a tree. In just a few moments three horsemen thundered past as she breathed a sigh of relief.

If her pursuers were worth anything at all they would double back once they realized that they had lost their prey. By then, however, she intended to have disappeared into the darkness.

Slowly counting to one hundred, she urged her mare back onto the dirt track and made her way toward a nearby gate. She would circle around the village and then the vicarage before approaching the cottage from the back. The last thing she desired was to stumble into her pursuers if they decided to go in search of the magistrate.

She picked her way carefully through a small meadow and entered the heavy copse of trees. The moonlight thankfully kept her from knocking her head on a low-lying branch or breaking her poor mare's leg in a rabbit hole.

By the time she reached the edge of the road her heart had slowed its frantic beat and her breathing had almost returned to normal. Oddly, however, her blood continued to rush through her with tingles of excitement.

She breathed deeply of the crisp night air and tilted back her head to study the near-full moon.

The danger had passed, and for the moment she could simply enjoy the feeling of being free.

And that was what she felt, she realized with a tiny flare of shock.

Away from the confines of the cramped cottage and the local tabbies that watched every maiden with the avid hope that they might create some delicious scandal, she could be herself. A woman who enjoyed midnight rides and the thrill of danger. A woman with the power to save her father from the gallows.

Life in a tiny village had always been a stifling existence for Raine. She possessed too much restless energy to easily submit to the rigid structures that confined her, but now that she had actually tasted such liberty it was nearly unbearable.

Dear Lord, she wanted to thunder down the nearby road and simply keep going.

Of course, the realistic part of her mind assured her that she was being ridiculous. Where would she go? How would she live?

Besides, no matter how far she fled it would not really change anything. She would still be a young woman without the means or the opportunity to break free of the chains that held her.

Blowing out a sigh, Raine shrugged off her strange mood and carefully studied the dark road. By now her pursuers should be back at the village, or even at the cottage warning the magistrate that the Knave had escaped their trap. All she had left to do was remain out of their sight for the next hour or so and then she could return to her chambers with no one the wiser.

Once she was certain she was alone, she urged her mare forward. She would not risk breaking her neck or her beloved mare's leg by stumbling about in the woods.

She had traveled less than a mile when she noticed the unmistakable outlines of a carriage that had halted alongside the road ahead of her. With a frown she slowed as she studied the unexpected sight.

Oh, it was not uncommon for a carriage to have some difficulty or another. Such rough roads tended to lame horses, break wheels and even snap axles. The local inn made a fine living from those poor travelers who had been forced to stay the night while their conveyance was repaired.

As she watched, the driver walked around the carriage as if he were searching for what had caused the trouble. Beside him was a bent form that was heavily shrouded by a thick cape.

An elderly woman and her servant, Raine concluded, hesitating as she unconsciously chewed on her lower lip.

Wisdom demanded that she turn around and find a new path to take her toward her home. She could not possibly offer any help when she was dressed as a notorious highwayman. Besides, the elegance of the carriage and the perfectly

matched team assured her that the woman possessed enough
wealth to smooth whatever troubles might come her way.

On the point of turning off the road, Raine was suddenly
struck by a most tempting notion.

She had come out tonight merely to convince the magistrate
of her father's innocence. She was to be a fleeting decoy, nothing more. Her father had been most emphatic on that point.

But now that she considered the matter, she realized that the
poor widow would not find the coins she had expected to be
hidden for her in the ditch. What if she were turned out into the
cold if something were not done? What if she had nowhere to
go, nothing to eat and no one to care that she was suffering?

Surely the elderly matron in the fancy carriage, who obviously possessed all the luxuries in life, should be encouraged
to do her Christian duty and help another?

And shouldn't the Knave of Knightsbridge be the one to
encourage her?

Ignoring her tiny stab of guilt at the thought of terrifying
the aging woman, Raine reached into her pocket to pull out
her father's dueling pistol. She had no intention of actually
harming the woman, she reminded herself. And it would only
take a few moments to collect her coins and pretty baubles.

With a press of her heels, she urged her mount forward, not
halting until she was nearly upon the two strangers.

"Forgive me, but I must ask you not to move," she rasped
in low tones. "Do not fear, I promise I will not harm you if
you do as I say."

There was a moment's hesitation before the elderly woman
slowly turned. Then surprisingly, the woman was reaching up
to push back the hood of her cloak.

"Unfortunately, I cannot promise the same, *querida,*"
drawled an all too familiar voice.

CHAPTER NINE

PHILIPPE REALIZED THAT THE cold, vicious fury that had plagued him since he returned to discover Raine gone was oddly melting away as he regarded her pale, shocked face.

Oh, he was still angry. His pride had been wounded by the knowledge that while he was planning an erotic interlude, she had been devising a means to escape him.

And beyond that had been a sharp, unwelcome dread. As if her disappearance had lost him more than a potential mistress.

But now that she was once again in his grasp, the chill began to ease from his heart, as if her mere presence was enough to return that warmth he craved.

"Do not bother to flee, Raine," he warned in silky tones. "If I am forced to chase after you yet again, I shall be very annoyed. You do not desire that."

Her gaze tracked Swann as he straightened and moved to stand in the center of the road. He had not yet pulled his pistol, but the threat that he would stop at nothing to keep her from fleeing was etched in every line of his bulky form.

Her expression tightened as she returned her attention to Philippe. "What are you doing here?"

A faint smile touched his lips. "Obviously awaiting you."

"But…"

"Carlos," he called, summoning his companion, who had been hidden in the bushes across the road. "Please assist Miss Wimbourne from her mount and put her in the carriage."

"No," she managed to squeak before Carlos had his hands tightly around her waist and was plucking her from her horse.

Despite her diminutive size she managed to land a kick to Carlos's knee and was attempting to rake her nails down his face when Philippe stepped forward and grasped her wrist in a firm grip.

"Raine, if you try to battle me, it will be very much the worse for you," he warned.

Her dark eyes flashed with a frustrated fury, and something else. Fear?

"What could be worse than being in your clutches again?"

"My clutches?" Philippe instinctively eased his grip, his thumb rubbing an absent path over the thundering pulse in her wrist. "You make me sound like a villain from a Gothic novel."

"An apt comparison, considering your habit of lurking in the dark to kidnap poor, helpless women. What else could you be but a villain?"

Philippe gave a short laugh. "You poor and helpless? A pit of vipers holds less danger than you. Besides, you left me little option. My lover belongs in my bed, not risking her beautiful neck with such reckless abandon."

Her breath caught and a fiery blush stained her cheeks. "Do not say that."

"What? That you are my lover? It is true enough." There was a bite to his tone. He did not like her denying their relationship. His gaze shifted to the silent Carlos. "Put her in the carriage and let us be on our way."

Carlos gave a lift of his brows, his expression faintly mocking. The man seemed to find a great deal of amusement in the fact that Philippe's little urchin had proved to be a woman. And even more amusement in the fact that Philippe had been nothing short of desperate to track her down.

That amusement might have worried Philippe at any other

time. It meant that Carlos thought he possessed some secret information that Philippe did not. But at the moment he was more interested in keeping an eye on Raine as Carlos bundled her into the carriage.

She would never meekly submit to her fate. She would battle him until he could make it clear that she was utterly and completely his.

Waiting until Carlos stepped back, Philippe climbed into the carriage and settled at her side. He closed the door and Swann swiftly had them moving down the frozen road.

Scooting along the leather seat, Raine pressed herself into the corner and glared at him.

"What are you going to do with me?"

He stretched out his legs and folded his arms over his chest. Now that he had Raine close he found the tension that had been plaguing him for days beginning to ease from his muscles.

No, that was not entirely true. There was still a faint hum that tingled through his body, but now it was the sort of tension a man enjoyed. The sort of tension that was entirely due to having a beautiful, desirable woman at his side.

And she *was* beautiful, despite her ridiculous attire.

His eyes lingered on her pale face. He had almost convinced himself that it was mere fantasy that made the memory of her delicate features and faintly slanted eyes so fascinating. That she could not possibly be as lovely as he recalled.

But he had imagined nothing.

She was breathtaking. Still, he was beginning to sense that it was that fiery spirit behind the beauty that was what truly had captivated his interest.

Beauty was easily discovered, but courage and loyalty, and unwavering determination to care for those she loved were far more rare.

Her eyes flashed with annoyance as he continued his intimate survey in silence.

"I asked what you intend to do with me," she gritted.

"I have considered several possibilities," he at last murmured. "Putting you over my knee and beating some sense into you was my first choice, followed closely by locking you in the nearest dungeon for your safety and my own sanity."

She gave a loud sniff. "You need not bother with the dungeon. I am perfectly capable of taking care of myself and I would say it was years too late to hope for your sanity."

There was just enough challenge in the tilt of her chin that Philippe could not resist temptation. With a smooth motion he turned on the seat and, reaching out, he tore the crimson hat from her amber curls. He opened the side window and tossed the hat out of the carriage before following it with her ridiculous cape.

Momentarily stunned by his audacity, it took a moment for Raine to react. As his fingers began unbuttoning the heavy jacket, however, she slapped at his hands.

"Stop that. What are you doing?"

Never pausing, he continued to tug the jacket open. "Your days as the Knave of Knightsbridge are officially over, *querida*."

She struggled against him, but she was no match for his strength. With a last tug the jacket was off and he threw it out of the carriage. Turning back, he stilled as an odd flare of pleasure raced through him at the sight of the golden locket that lay nestled against her ivory skin.

He should be furious at the knowledge she had not only stolen his mother's locket, but now possessed the audacity to wear it. That tiny piece of jewelry meant more to him than all his fortune rolled together.

Instead of fury, however, he experienced a purely male sense of satisfaction.

The gold glittered against her skin as if it were his brand of ownership. And perhaps it was.

After all, she could easily have hocked it for a tidy sum, or given it to the hordes of poor who seemed to depend upon her father's charity. Instead she wore it beneath her clothing as if it were a precious secret she desired close to her heart.

"Whether or not I choose to play the role of the Knave of Knightsbridge is not your decision to make, *Monsieur Gautier,*" she hissed as she shivered beneath his heated gaze.

Philippe briefly paused as he realized she had somehow discovered his identity. Not that it truly mattered. He could hardly keep her with him without revealing who he was. But it was a reminder that it would be difficult to hide anything from this woman.

"Ah, but it is." He pulled off the cloak he had used as his disguise and wrapped it about her shivering form. A pity to cover up the beauty revealed by her thin shift and corset, but he would not have her catching a chill. "I have captured you and on this occasion you will not escape me."

She gave a toss of her head, only the thin fingers clutching the edges of the cloak revealing she was not nearly so fearless as she would have him believe.

"I would not be so certain of that if I were you."

Philippe ignored her threat. They both knew it was empty. Instead he absently toyed with a golden curl that lay against her cheek.

"Just as a point of interest, how did you free yourself from the nursery? I know that none of my servants released you."

"Do you threaten to lock them in a dungeon, as well?"

"That has not yet been necessary." He gave a tug on the curl. "Tell me, Raine. How did you escape me?"

Her lips tightened as she met his relentless gaze. "There

was a man passing in the alley," she grudgingly confessed. "I convinced him to come into the house and unlock the door."

His hand grasped her chin as he regarded her with furious disbelief. He was thankful he had never suspected just how foolish she had been. His nightmares would have driven him mad.

"You called a strange man into a house where you were all but alone?" he gritted. "Do you not have any sense at all? *Meu Deus.* Do you know what could have happened?"

She licked her lips as her gaze abruptly dropped. "I...I escaped."

His heart gave a painful squeeze. "Raine, look at me."

Slowly she obeyed. "What?"

"Did he hurt you? Tell me."

"He tried, but..."

"I will kill him," he said with lethal softness. "I will track him down and kill him."

"No. It was nothing, truly I was not harmed."

"You took a foolish risk." Instinctively, he shifted to wrap his arms about her. "It is a habit you will no longer indulge in."

She was wise enough not to try and battle his hold. "How did you find me?"

"I already knew that you lived near Knightsbridge and discovering your cottage was hardly difficult."

"I suppose, but that does not explain how you knew that I would be out tonight as the Knave."

"I was watching the cottage when you left the stables. It was a simple matter to have Carlos track you and then set up this little ploy."

She pulled back with a frown. "Do you often dress as an old woman?"

His lips twitched. In truth he kept a number of disguises hidden throughout his various carriages. Not to mention a dozen different weapons, trap doors and a few bottles of smuggled brandy.

His carriages were custom-made and cost a fortune to build.

"On occasion."

"Why?"

"Perhaps some day I will tell you, but not now."

Her eyes narrowed, but wisely she did not attempt to force a confession from him.

"So Carlos was following me the whole time?" she instead demanded.

"Yes. He was rather caught off guard when you deliberately stumbled into such an obvious trap. I can only assume that you were intentionally attempting to capture their attention before leading them on a merry chase?"

She shrugged. "The magistrate is currently playing chess with my father."

Fiercely aware of just how tiny and fragile she was, he tightened his arms around her. He breathed deeply of her sweet lilac scent. Damn her father. He did not deserve this woman as his daughter.

"So once again you risk your own life to save his sorry neck?"

She stiffened. "Do not speak ill of my father."

"He is not worthy of you."

"And you are?"

He slowly smiled. It no longer mattered whether or not he was worthy of Raine Wimbourne. She had captured his attention and he would not release her until he had managed to rid himself of his strange fascination.

"I at least intend to take much greater care of you," he softly promised. "You will want for nothing while you are with me."

She sucked in a sharp breath. "You cannot just take me with you."

"Who is to stop me?"

"Why are you doing this to me, Philippe?"

His fingers drifted down the curve of her throat. "That is, *querida,* a particularly stupid question. You know precisely why I am doing this."

"Because you want me in your bed?"

"Because you belong in my bed," he corrected. "You know that as well as I."

Her chin tilted. "If that was what I believed I would not have fled."

Philippe smothered his instinctive flare of annoyance. She was too proud to easily submit to the will of another. Even if it was what she most desired.

And she did want him. He had not imagined her ready response to his touch, or the soft moans of pleasure that had filled the small nursery.

His fingers lingered at the base of her throat, measuring the flutter of her pulse.

"Then it will be my duty and very great pleasure to convince you otherwise," he murmured.

He felt her shiver beneath his touch, but with a visible effort she gave a shake of her head.

"It cannot believe you would go to this trouble simply to have a woman in your bed." Her eyes narrowed. "You are just the sort of gentleman that most dim-witted females would tumble over themselves to be with."

Philippe laughed softly. "I am uncertain if that is a compliment or an insult, but possessing my natural share of vanity I shall take it as a tribute to my male charms."

"Or perhaps to your obvious fortune," she said tartly.

"A cruel blow, *querida.*" He moved so swiftly that Raine did not even have time to squeak before he had her pinned in the corner and his face buried in the curve of her neck. "Perhaps we should discover just what my...best assets truly are."

Her lips parted to protest, and his head shifted to capture them in a deep kiss. His tongue stroked into the moist temptation of her mouth as his hand cupped the back of her head. A groan was wrenched from his throat as that sweet heat poured through him like warm honey.

Meu Deus. This was what he had been seeking. This was why he had been furious when he had discovered she had disappeared. This was why he had postponed his trip to France. This was why he had ignored his servants' bemusement as he had devoted two days to skulking around the small Knightsbridge cottage like a man demented.

He could not allow this woman to slip from his grasp.

His lips devoured hers, his desire so sharp and intense he found himself struggling not to rip aside the offending cloak so he could feel the satin skin beneath.

He had thought to teach her a lesson. To prove to both of them that she was far from indifferent to his touch. But even as he felt her soften against him and her hands clutch at his arms in response, he realized the danger of such a lesson.

Raine Wimbourne was perhaps the only person in the world who possessed the power to shatter his ruthless control. She could make him forget everything but the pleasure of having her near. It was a power that he had no intention of revealing to anyone. Least of all this woman trembling in his arms.

With an effort he eased his kiss, giving her lower lip a light nip as he pulled back to study her flushed countenance.

"So what is your conclusion?" he asked, his heart beating so fast he feared she might hear it in the thick silence. "Is it only my wealth that charms the ladies?"

Her dark eyes held a hint of bemusement. Precisely the sort of bemusement a man wanted to see after kissing a woman senseless. Then astonishingly she was giving a shake of her head and her expression was hardening with determination.

"Tell me why you came after me, Philippe," she demanded.

His lips twisted as he accepted that she possessed much of the same grim determination as he did. It was bound to make their relationship...interesting, to say the least.

"Because, I have need of you," he said, knowing a distraction was in order.

She pulled back and Philippe reluctantly let her go. For the moment he needed his wits about him. Something that was impossible when her soft body was pressed to his.

"Need of me?" Her expression was wary. "What does that mean?"

"I must travel to France to discover a man known as Seurat. I cannot risk having him realize that I suspect him. Since no one knows that I have yet traveled to London, I only need a reason for being in Paris, a city I am known to despise. You will offer me that reason." His gaze skimmed her beautiful face. "What man would not be willing to toss aside all prejudices and responsibilities to be with the young, innocent maiden he has lured from a local convent?"

She was shaking her head in denial before he ever finished. "No."

"Yes, *querida*."

"Philippe, please." The hands that had lingered on his upper arms clutched him with a surprising force. "You must return me to my father. He will be worried about me."

"You may write him a note from Dover to reassure him you are well if you desire. Of course, I will insist upon seeing it before it is sent." He smiled without humor. "You will not be allowed to mention me or our destination."

Her hands abruptly dropped to curl into tight fists in her lap. "You will take me against my will?"

"If I must."

"I will only escape again."

"No, you will not leave my side."

"Do you intend to shackle me to you?"

His lips twitched at the delicious thought of having her shackled and at his mercy.

"An intriguing possibility, but unnecessary."

"You surely cannot be so arrogant as to believe you can seduce me into remaining?"

"An even more intriguing possibility, and one I do not doubt would be most effective, but once again unnecessary," he drawled.

She made a frustrated sound and a shudder shook her body as if she were struggling not to throttle him.

"If you have something to say, then say it, Philippe."

"Very well." He leaned close enough that their noses were nearly touching. "If you so much as think about straying from my side without my permission, I will personally promise the local magistrate that I will testify that your father is the Knave of Knightsbridge."

There was a moment of shocked silence before Raine was at last provoked into doing what she had obviously longed to do since entering the carriage.

Pulling back her arm, she aimed her blow directly at his nose. It was not the feminine slap of most outraged ladies. Oh, no, this was a closed-fist punch that was intended to do as much harm as possible.

With an easy motion, Philippe grasped her wrist and halted the swinging arm. Keeping his grip on her wrist, he forced her hand back to her lap.

"Take care, *menina pequena,*" he warned.

"You...bastard," she hissed.

His gaze narrowed. "I am not the one who chooses to endanger my family by prancing about the countryside and robbing innocent travelers."

"I told you that my father only seeks to help those in need."

"Innocent fool, do you truly think that is his only reason?"

She stiffened at his soft question. "If you mean to imply that my father keeps any of the money for himself..."

"No, his greed is not for silver or gold, but for the adoration of his neighbors."

The dark eyes widened in disbelief. Clearly, she had never considered the possibility that her father was anything but the altruistic champion that she imagined him to be.

"That is ridiculous."

Philippe gave a lift of his brow. "Is it? Can you tell me that he does not fully enjoy his role as the local Robin Hood? That he does not take pleasure in being the beloved savior of his neighbors? That he does not linger at the local inn while the people boast of his bravery?"

Her gaze dropped at his charge, but there was a mulish set to her features. She was nothing if not loyal. A character trait he greatly admired upon most occasions. At the moment, however, he struggled not to shake some sense into her.

"My father cares about others."

"Perhaps that is how it all began, but he would never have continued once you were put in danger if it were not for his own vanity."

She slowly lifted her head, her dark eyes wary. "Whatever my father's reasons, they are considerably more noble than a man who kidnaps a proper maiden and holds her against her will."

Philippe smiled wryly. "Cast me as the villain if you must, Raine. But you belong to me now. And unlike your father, I know how to take care of my own."

THE INN THAT WAS SITUATED on Kings Road in Dover was small but scrupulously clean and possessed an unmistakable charm. Built in the oldest part of town, the inn had a fine view of the church of St. James and the beautiful white cliffs. It was also tucked close enough to Market Place that the narrow streets clattered with the sounds of heavy traffic at an indecently early hour.

With a groan Raine pulled the covers over her head. It had been the middle of the night when they had arrived at the inn and Raine had been so exhausted that she had not even bothered to protest when Philippe had led her up the narrow flight of stairs to her chambers.

Why waste her efforts on a losing battle? For the moment he held the upper hand and they both knew it.

She would do anything to protect her father.

Even allow herself to be kidnapped and hauled off to France by an arrogant lecher.

With a heavy sigh at the realization she would never get back to sleep with the noise outside her window, Raine tossed aside her covers and sat at the edge of the mattress.

Astonishingly she was alone in the room.

A few hours before Philippe had escorted her to the door and, after ensuring the room was clean and the windows properly bolted, had moved through the connecting door to his own chambers.

Raine had fully expected the man to insist on sharing her bed. He had, after all, made it clear that he wanted her as his mistress. And if she were perfectly honest with herself, she could not deny that during their brief kiss she had done little to convince him that she would be unwilling.

Damn the man. He was determined to destroy her life, and yet for the briefest moment when she had realized who it was standing next to that broken-down carriage, she had felt more than shock or even fear. She had felt…joy.

And to make matters worse, he had only to pull her into

his arms and she had melted like one of those simpering misses she had always detested.

If he truly set out to seduce her, how could she possibly resist?

Her gaze shifted toward the connecting door that was thankfully shut tight. She was uncertain why Philippe had left her alone in her bed, but he must have a reason.

Some devious reason.

Lost in thought, Raine gave a small squeak when there was a sudden knock on the door leading to the outer hall.

Scrambling from the bed, she wrapped Philippe's heavy cloak about her and futilely attempted to smooth her tangled curls. For the moment she had only her shift, her breeches and a pair of old boots to her name.

She smiled wryly as she headed for the door. Perhaps Philippe had an entire wardrobe of female clothing stashed in his carriage.

He seemed to possess everything else.

Pausing at the door, she leaned against the thick wood. "Who is it?"

"Mattie," a voice called. "I have yer breakfast."

Raine's stomach growled at the mere mention of food, and with swift motions she had the lock pulled back and the door opened.

The plump maid with a round face and thick knot of fuzzy brown curls entered the room carrying a heavy tray.

"Where do you want it, then?" she demanded, her arms obviously straining beneath the load.

"On the table is fine."

Raine followed the maid to the small table beside the window, her eyes widening as the woman whipped off the linen cover to reveal half a dozen plates filled with eggs, ham, toast, kidneys, fresh fruit and tea.

"Good heavens, this is far too much," she breathed.

The maid straightened, a faint twinkle in her brown eyes. "Well, yer husband was very insistent that you have plenty of choices. He said as how you were a bit finicky. Cook said if there were anything in particular you wanted you need only send word to the kitchen."

Husband? A queer sensation clutched at her heart before Raine was sternly dismissing it. It was nothing more than relief that Philippe had not punished her with the shame of allowing the entire inn to think of her as nothing more than a light-skirt.

"This all looks quite delicious. Please give my compliments to Cook," she said.

A pleased smile touched the round face. "Oh, aye, Ma'am. I was also to tell you that Mr. Savoy commanded a bath be brought up after you have finished yer breakfast, if that be what you wish?"

Mr. Savoy? She could only presume that was Philippe.

"Yes, indeed. A bath would be most welcome." She gave a faint grimace. "As would a change of clothes."

"Oh, but…"

Raine gave a lift of her brows as the maid abruptly cut off her words with a flustered expression.

"What is it, Mattie?"

"I'm not certain if it is a surprise or not."

At once consumed with curiosity, Raine stretched her lips into a reassuring smile.

"Do not fear, Mattie, there are no secrets between me and my…my husband."

Clearly bursting with the desire to reveal her secret, Mattie leaned close.

"Well, I overheard Mr. Savoy say to Mr. Hill, the innkeeper, you know, as how he sent word ahead to have a num-

ber of new gowns be prepared for you. Then Mr. Hill says to
Mrs. Hill that yer husband had spent a near fortune to make
sure the dressmakers worked day and night so they should be
delivered by this afternoon."

Raine abruptly turned to stare blindly out the window as a
mixture of emotions charged through her.

On one hand she was furious that Philippe would be so certain
he would manage in his horrid kidnapping scheme. To actually
have ordered her a new wardrobe? It went beyond arrogance.

On the other hand, she could not deny a ridiculous sense
of pleasure that he had even considered the fact she would
require clothing. In her limited experience men rarely paid
heed to a woman's comfort. Even her own father had to be
reminded that she occasionally had needs beyond food and a
roof over her head.

Of course, he could hardly haul her around Paris in her
shift, she reminded herself sternly.

"I cannot wait for them to arrive," she muttered.

"Such a thoughtful and generous husband." Mattie sighed.

"He does seem to think of everything."

"And so handsome."

Indecently, wickedly handsome, Raine silently agreed.

And so very, very dangerous.

CHAPTER TEN

RAINE TOOK FULL ADVANTAGE of the vast breakfast and even lingered in the hot bath far longer than was her habit. Why not? She was not the sort of woman to curl up in a corner and weep at her iniquitous fate. Or to create an unpleasant scene that would only embarrass her.

She would eventually find some means to force Philippe to set her free. Until then she might as well enjoy the few luxuries that came her way.

What other rational choice was there?

Once the tray and bath had been cleared away, however, Raine found herself pacing the room with a growing sense of restlessness.

During her years at the convent she had rarely had a free moment. There were always classes and duties and chores that had to be completed. And since returning home she at least had the beauty of the woods and meadows to roam through when her boredom threatened to overcome her.

With a sudden motion she reached for the heavy cloak and wrapped it snugly around her. When they had first arrived at the inn she had noted a small kitchen garden at one side of the building. There would be no room for a proper stroll, but at least she could get some fresh air.

Her decision made, she moved to the door and pulled it open. She never made it over the threshold, however, before the tall, dark form of Carlos was blocking her path.

Stiffening in surprise, she regarded the unwelcome man with a lift of her brows.

"Please move aside," she declared in a tone that demanded obedience.

The gentleman merely smiled as he leaned one broad shoulder against the doorjamb. "You must remain in your rooms. It is not safe to be out."

Raine narrowed her gaze. The man was indecently handsome, of course. His dark Latin looks were combined with a sultry passion that seemed to smolder in the air around him. Precisely the sort of gentleman that made a woman think of warm, exotic gardens and illicit love affairs.

But what Raine was thinking at the moment was that she wanted to blacken his eye.

"I am only going to the small garden."

He slowly smiled, his large bulk as efficient as a brick wall in keeping her from freedom.

"You will go nowhere until Philippe can accompany you," he said, his accent only faintly noticeable. Philippe was not the only one who spent time in England, she thought inanely.

Anger flared through her as she glared into his dark eyes. "Philippe may be capable of blackmailing me into remaining with him, but even he cannot halt me from taking a simple stroll. Move out of my way."

The brilliant white smile merely widened as Carlos grasped her shoulders and firmly moved her backward. Then, before she could recover herself, he was closing the door in her face.

"I am sorry, *anjo*," he called through the heavy wood even as she heard him turn a key in the lock.

Sorry?

Oh, he would be sorry.

Him and his overbearing, infuriating master.

She turned and marched toward the connecting door and entered the second chamber like a gathering storm cloud.

Her only thought was confronting Philippe and demanding to know why he insisted on keeping her locked in her rooms as if she were some wild animal.

It seemed worthy goal, until she reached the middle of the room and realized that Philippe was just stepping from the bath that had been situated by the fireplace.

"Oh," she gasped, abruptly turning her back on his nude body. "Good Lord."

His soft laugh feathered over her skin. "There is no need for such shock, *meu amor*. You are welcome to enter my chambers at any time you please. Especially if I happen to be without my clothes."

Heat burned her cheeks. Which was rather ridiculous. God knew that she had spent an inordinate amount of time fantasizing about the feel of that hard body pressed against her own.

"Please cover yourself," she said.

"So shy," he teased. There was a rustle of movement and then Philippe moved behind her to lightly touch her shoulder. "You may turn around now."

"You are decent?"

His hand boldly stroked up the curve of her neck. "I am rarely decent, but my body parts are adequately covered, which I presume is what you mean?"

She hastily stepped from the temptation of his touch and turned to confront him. Her heart gave a sharp jolt as she took in the sight of the thick brocade robe that covered his still-damp skin and the tousled wetness of his raven curls.

As promised, he was covered, but there was nothing decent about him.

He looked like a Byzantine god that had stepped from the past.

A wickedly seductive Byzantine god.

No, Raine, stop this nonsense. She had come here to make it clear she would not be treated like a prisoner. Not to flutter and swoon as if she hadn't the least measure of sense.

Ignoring the rapid beat of her heart and the strange flush that heated her skin, she tilted her chin to a determined angle.

"I wished a breath of fresh air but your…guard dog refused to allow me to leave my rooms. I presume that you were the one to give the command that I was to be a prisoner?"

He prowled forward until he was once again standing far too close. "I am not certain that Carlos would appreciate the comparison to a mere dog. I believe he considers himself a far more dangerous predator."

She took two steps back. "Did you or did you not tell Carlos that I was to remain in my rooms?"

He took three steps forward. "Yes."

Raine sucked in a sharp breath as his tantalizing heat and scent wrapped around her.

"Do you truly believe that after having gone through the effort of playing the role of the Knave of Knightsbridge to deceive the magistrate that I would now risk sending my father to the gallows to escape you?" she demanded.

"I am annoyingly aware of your loyalty to your father," he said, a strange edge in his voice. "I requested that Carlos prevent you from leaving your rooms because I have no wish for you to be seen by someone who might recognize you."

She frowned. "My circle of acquaintances does not extend beyond Knightsbridge. There is no one in Dover who could possibly recognize me."

"Perhaps not, but there is also the matter of your safety." His hand lifted to gently stroke a golden curl that lay against her throat. "Although Dover is not a particularly large hamlet, it is a port city and therefore has more than its usual share of pirates, profiteers and cutthroats. Not to mention the usual assortment of rakes and rogues."

"Which you, of course, would know all about," she muttered.

Something that might have been surprise rippled over his chiseled features. As if he was not accustomed to being labeled as a rake. Which seemed quite absurd. He was obviously a most accomplished seducer.

"I do, at least, understand men and how they react to a woman as beautiful as you." His hand shifted to cup her cheek. "You would create a near riot if you walked about the inn without a proper escort."

Raine's knees went weak at his gentle touch. "I...I suppose you think to distract me with such stupid flattery?"

His eyes darkened, and without warning Raine discovered herself against the wall with his body pressed hard to hers.

"It is not flattery, *meu amor.*" He buried his face in the curve of her neck, his hot breath sending a shock of need racing through her blood. "And if I desired to distract you I could find a far more pleasurable means of doing so."

She lifted her hands to his chest. She had intended to push him away, but his robe had managed to loosen, and when she felt the satin heat of his skin she forgot all the numerous reasons this was such a ghastly notion.

"Philippe..."

His tongue stroked over the rapid pulse at the base of her throat, sending a violent shudder through her.

"Did you miss me last night?" he demanded.

"Miss you?"

He nuzzled his way up to her ear. "You have no notion just how great an effort it took to leave you all alone in that soft bed," he muttered.

"Why did you?"

"You were exhausted. And if I recall your mood was rather foul."

Her head tilted back as his lips traced the line of her jaw. Oh, Lord…this was dangerous. So terribly dangerous. How could she recall that she was furious with him when her body was melting with pleasure?

"Well, you might as well become accustomed to my foul mood," she forced herself to mutter. "Being kidnapped and blackmailed tends to sour a woman's disposition."

His hands skimmed down her sides, moving to jerk open the cloak. "Perhaps I can improve it."

"Not bloody likely," she breathed, but she made no effort to halt him as his lips moved to capture hers in a kiss that made her head spin.

Over the past few days she had managed to convince herself that she had merely imagined the power of his touch. Her night with him, after all, had been her first real taste of passion. What woman would not remember it as being far more spectacular than it truly was?

But now she was forced to admit that she had imagined nothing. His lips were just as warm, just as deliciously experienced as she recalled. And the dark wave of longing just as irresistible.

His fingers had found the ribbons of her shift when there was a sudden pounding on the door. They both froze, Philippe muttering a string of Portuguese curses.

"Go away," he at last called.

"The clothes have arrived, sir," came the muffled reply. "You said as how you wanted them brought up straight away."

For a moment the leanly beautiful face tightened, and Raine was certain he would send away the intruder. Then, with a sigh he pulled back and tucked the cloak around her with a wry smile.

"So I did. I must have been out of my wits," he said.

Brushing his lips over her forehead, Philippe turned and moved to pull open the door. He had barely managed to step aside when the innkeeper, along with two burly grooms, entered, all three of the men burdened with a vast number of boxes.

"You may place them on the bed," Philippe commanded.

"Aye, sir."

With a minimum of fuss the various packages were spread over the bed and Philippe was handing each man a coin as they offered a bow and left the room.

Raine barely noticed their departure as she absently crossed toward the bed and reached out to touch a silver ribbon tied around one of the elegant boxes.

"These…" Her throat seemed to close and she was forced to clear her throat.

Philippe moved to stand beside her. "What is it, Raine?"

"These are all for me?"

He brushed the back of his fingers down her cheek. "Why do you not open them and discover for yourself?"

She hesitated a long moment as she studied the vast pile of packages. They were beautiful with their bows and ribbons. A shimmering enticement for a maiden who hadn't received a gift since she was six years old.

Oh, her father would occasionally offer her a handful of coins to spend as she wished. And Mrs. Stone always knitted her mittens for Christmas. But this…

It was a temptation she simply could not resist.

Ignoring the tiny voice in the back of her mind that whispered the road to ruination was no doubt littered with such lovely temptations, Raine reached for the closest box and tugged aside the silver bow to pluck off the lid.

Her breath caught as she pulled out the velvet evening gown that was a beautiful shade of bronze with embroidered lace around the scooped neckline and the full hem. Included in the box was a pair of matching bronze gloves, a pair of delicate slippers and an ivory shawl with gold thread.

It was a stunningly beautiful gown. The sort of gown that she could never have dreamed of possessing.

With an odd sense of unreality, she began to open the remaining boxes. There were more evening gowns in silk and Turkish satin, as well as morning gowns, carriage gowns, a lovely velvet cape lined with fur, several bonnets, gloves and pretty kidskin boots. He had even thought to provide several shifts, corsets and stockings.

A gentleman who clearly was accustomed to procuring garments for women, she wryly thought.

Still, whatever his nefarious past, she had to admit that he had exquisite taste. The clothes were magnificent and thankfully not at all what she had been expecting.

These were gowns that belonged to a lady, not a common tart.

Unwittingly, she reached out to stroke her hand over a delectable satin gown in a pale shade of lavender.

Perhaps sensing her confusion, Philippe reached out to grasp her chin and forced her to meet his searching gaze.

"You do not like them?"

"They are beautiful, as you well know, but not precisely what one would expect for a mistress."

His lips curled. "Ah, but you are not just any mistress. You are to play the role of the innocent maiden fresh from the convent, not the usual Cyprian."

For some stupid reason Raine found herself disappointed. Why?

Because his words forced her to recall that the clothes were not truly a gift? That they hadn't been chosen to please her or even to spare her the embarrassment of appearing like a Jezebel? That they were nothing more than a part of the charade she was to play?

"Yes, of course," she muttered.

Philippe narrowed his gaze and his fingers tightened on her chin.

"Raine, what the devil is the matter with you? I thought you would be pleased with the gowns."

"Why should I not be? The daughter of a common sailor could hardly dare dream of such luxuries," she murmured, uncertain why she was becoming so upset but unable to halt the surge of emotions.

"Raine…"

"Of course I am not just the daughter of a sailor any longer, am I?" She gave a short, humorless laugh. "Now I am a mistress to a rich and powerful man."

A dangerous expression settled on Philippe's face, and without warning his hands landed heavily on her shoulders. Her lips parted to protest at the same moment he pushed her backward and she hit the wall. Her breath was jerked from her lungs, more from surprise than from the actual impact, and she glared into the lean, beautiful face with astonishment.

"You have yet to be much of a mistress, *querida*," he growled. "In fact, you have been decidedly slack in your duties. But that is all about to change. I intend to teach you what precisely is required for your position."

Raine swallowed heavily. She was not afraid of Philippe Gautier. At least, not physically afraid. But, there was no missing the air of barely restrained hunger that smoldered in the green eyes. Or the fierce determination that was etched in his face.

"Philippe…no," she breathed.

A thin, cruel smile curved his lips as he lowered his head to stroke his cheek over her curls.

"Your first lesson, *meu amor,* is that you never, ever tell me no," he said in a low, rasping voice. "A mistress is always pleased to accommodate her lover, no matter what his request."

Raine was wise enough not to struggle against his hold. When you were cornered by a dangerous predator you did not continue to bait him.

A pity that she had not been a tad wiser before she had provoked the man.

Of course, she had been in no mood to be wise.

She had been…what?

Restless and hurt and in need of something.

A shiver raced through her body as she instinctively responded to his proximity.

Good Lord. It could not have been deliberate, could it? She could not have unwittingly hoped to stir his passions? She could not be so desperate to feel wanted and needed, that she would inflame him into making love to her?

Disturbed by the mere thought, Raine pressed her hands to his chest.

"You make a mistress sound like nothing more than a slave. Is that what you prefer? A toadie to pander to your every whim?"

His fingers eased their punishing grip to stray down her body. His touch was light, but it left a trail of fire in its wake.

"Pandering to my every whim?" he whispered directly into her ear. "Now, that is a most delicious notion."

She trembled even as she struggled to deny the sensations already coursing through her body.

"I will be no man's slave."

He merely laughed as he tugged open the cloak and his arms encircled her waist.

"You belong to me, Raine Wimbourne." He gave her earlobe a nip before his lips stroked down the line of her jaw. "There is nowhere you can run, nowhere you can hide that I would not find you."

The hands that had been pushing him away now clutched at the lapels of his robe to keep her knees from buckling.

There was sheer male possession in his touch, in his low

voice. It should be infuriating her, not making her heart flutter with excitement.

"Do you always consider your mistresses as possessions?" she forced herself to demand.

His lips nuzzled the corner of her mouth. "There has never been another like you."

Her pounding heart came to a perfect halt.

"What do you mean?"

Philippe pulled back to regard her with a brooding expression. "I wish that I knew," he muttered. "This obsession is not at all convenient. Unfortunately there seems to be nothing to be done but to allow this madness to run its course."

She stiffened at his less than flattering words. "So I am an inconvenient madness?"

Something rippled over the breathtaking features before he covered her mouth with a stark, relentless kiss. At the same moment he was wrenching the cloak from her body.

Raine shivered, but not from the cold as he ripped off the straps of her shift and, with practiced efficiency, had it pooled about her ankles.

It happened so swiftly that Raine had barely registered the startling realization that she was naked when his hands were skimming up the curve of her waist and cupping the fullness of her breasts.

She gave a small gasp that was swallowed by his devouring kiss. His thumbs rubbed over her hardening nipples, teasing them with a tender urgency that soon had her entire body pulsing with an aching need.

Bloody hell. It was just as wondrous as she remembered. Just as magical.

Philippe had called it obsession. And perhaps that was what it was. A hot, searing obsession that could easily consume her.

Her eyes fluttered closed as his mouth shifted to brand hot, restless kisses over her face.

"Meu amor," he rasped against her skin, "I need to be inside you. I need to feel your heat."

A distant part of her urged her to deny his demand. He had already blackmailed her into remaining with him regardless of her own desires. To give into this heady passion would only place her more firmly in his power.

That part of her, however sensible, was unfortunately no match for the sharp ache lodged deep within her.

Her hands clutched at his arms as his head lowered to stroke his tongue down the length of her neck. He nuzzled her pounding pulse before his head was dipping even lower and his lips covered the tip of her throbbing nipple.

Raine moaned at the dizzying sensations. It seemed entirely unfair that any man should have the ability to make her melt with such longing. To quiver with a need that was nearly overwhelming.

Especially one she should hate with her last breath.

He suckled her with a tender urgency that was tightening her muscles and making her legs weak. A low growl rumbled in his throat as his hands skated down her heated skin and grasped her hips. Then, without warning, he was turning her around so that she faced the wall.

Caught off guard she swiveled her head to regard him over her shoulder. "Philippe?"

The lean features were tight and bathed with a damp perspiration, as if he were struggling against a mighty force.

"Shh, *meu amor.*" He tossed aside his robe and pressed his body to her back, burying his face in the curve of her neck. "I promise I will please you."

"But…"

Her words came to a choked halt as his fingers slid down

the gentle swell of her stomach and then through her blond curls to discover the dampness between her legs.

"You should never have run from me, *menina pequena*." He gave a punishing nip on the curve of her shoulder while his finger slid inside her and began to stroke with a slow insistence. "You belong in my arms. In my bed."

Her head fell back against his shoulder. A delicious pressure was beginning to build within her. Later she would tell him that she belonged to no man. That she was a woman who would always hold her independence dear.

But that would be later, she thought as she felt his hard shaft pressing between her legs. With gentle care he parted her and then with one slow thrust he was buried deep inside her.

Raine sighed as her eyes slid closed.

Yes, it would all have to be much later.

THEY ENDED UP IN Raine's bed.

After he had thrust himself to a shuddering release, Philippe had been too intent on continuing his delicious seduction to bother clearing his own bed of the various piles of clothing. It had been far simpler to carry Raine into the connecting chamber and tumble her onto the bed before she could recall that she was supposed to be furious with him.

Now he held her tightly pressed to his body as he attempted to recover from the intense bout of lovemaking.

Meu Deus. He was a sophisticated man of the world, a man who could claim the most beautiful and talented of lovers. And yet, none but this woman could make him ache for her touch, drown him in heat just by being near.

A satisfied smile touched his lips as he breathed deeply of her sweet scent.

"You fit in my arms as if you were made for me," he murmured, his hands trailing down the arch of her back. "And perhaps you were. Perhaps you were born to be my mistress."

She leaned back to glare into his face, the dreamy expression that had softened her beautiful features swiftly hardening with annoyance.

"Do you even realize how bloody arrogant you are?" she snapped. "I might only be the daughter of a poor sailor, but I have worth beyond becoming some man's mistress."

Philippe gave her bare bottom a pat. "There are many women who would consider becoming my mistress a worthy goal. Certainly I have never lacked for willing females."

Her dark eyes narrowed. "Willing perhaps, but none of them were true ladies."

Damn, but the woman was a prickly thing.

"I assure you that being a lady has nothing to do with who your parents might be, or whether or not you are my mistress. I have known any number of so-called ladies, not to mention gentlemen, who were not fit for the title."

She gave a deliberate lift of her brows. "Do you mean, gentlemen like those who would kidnap an innocent young lady?"

He shrugged aside her insult. "You may not possess the proper blood, but you have something most ladies will never be able to claim."

"And what is that?"

"Loyalty. There is only one other woman I know who would risk everything for those she loved."

A portion of her annoyance eased as she regarded him with a hint of curiosity. "Who?"

"My mother." He brushed his fingers over the golden locket about her neck. "She was a woman who was willing to sacrifice her life to save others."

There was a brief silence as she studied his countenance. "How did she die?"

Philippe felt his muscles stiffen. He never discussed his mother. Not with anyone. But, for some reason he wanted Raine to know of the woman who had molded his life despite the fact he could not even recall her face.

"When the Revolution hit Paris my father insisted that we travel to his estate in Portugal, and then eventually we moved to his home upon Madeira. He could not, however, persuade the rest of my mother's family to abandon their homes. In the end most of them faced the guillotine."

Her breath caught at his stark words. "How horrid. No wonder you dislike France."

"I lost fourteen members of my family," he said in clipped tones that belied the cold fury that gnawed deep in his soul.

She frowned. "But your mother survived?"

"She survived, but she never forgave herself for allowing her family to be slaughtered."

"She could not have prevented their deaths."

His lips twisted. "Grief is rarely reasonable."

Her dark eyes softened in a manner that revealed she was all too familiar with grief.

"No. No, I suppose not."

Philippe's gaze lowered to the locket that he had found among his mother's belongings. They had been condemned to the attics after her death, as if his father was determined to banish her memory. Or perhaps it was his guilt he hoped to banish.

Whatever the reason, Philippe had spent hours searching through the large trunks, needing to find some means of bonding to the woman who had given birth to him. A bond that was sharply absent from his feckless, irresponsible father and brother.

At last lifting his head, he discovered Raine regarding him with a searching gaze.

"Once it appeared the worse of the terror was at an end my mother insisted on returning to Paris and searching for any members of her family who might still be alive," he forced himself to continue. "It was the only way that she could make amends with her troubled conscience."

"She went alone?" Raine demanded in surprise.

Philippe's lips twisted with an age-old disdain. "My father was not going to risk his neck on a fool's errand, as he called it. Although, he is always quick enough to risk it when he thinks it might bring him a bit of fame among his fellow collectors."

Her eyes darkened, as if she sensed the part of him that held his father to blame for his mother's death.

"I see."

He gave a restless shrug. "My mother arrived in Paris, but during her search of the various prisons for information of her parents she contracted influenza. She died within the week."

"How old were you?"

"I had just turned four."

Without warning her hand reached up to touch his cheek with gentle fingers. "So you have no memory of her?"

A strange, unfamiliar sensation made Philippe's heart jerk sharply against his chest. He had enjoyed the touch of a woman more times than he could recall. In passion, in pleading, in anger. But never once in sympathy.

"No."

She gave a small sigh. "It is difficult to lose your mother. Especially if you are very young."

"As you know from experience."

"Yes." A hint of sadness rippled over her lovely face. "But I was fortunate to have my father."

He made a sound in his throat. "Your father…"

Her hand shifted to press against his lips, a frown tugging at her brows. "No, Philippe, not a word against my father."

This time Philippe fully recognized the sensations that streaked through his body. He was naked in bed with a woman who made his heart pound and his blood run hot. Enough chatter.

"I agree," he said softly.

Her brows lifted. "You do?"

His hand stroked down the satin skin of her hip. "There are far more pleasurable means of passing the time than arguing over your father."

Philippe heard her breath catch at his bold caress, but she instantly battled against her ready response.

"You promised I could write to my father. He will be worried."

With a smooth motion he rolled on top of her slender form, his own body already hard with need.

"And so you shall," he murmured as he nuzzled at the small hollow below her ear. "But first I have another lesson in the art of being a proper mistress." Taking her hand in his own, Philippe pulled it down to his throbbing shaft. A moan shook his body as her fingers closed hesitantly around him. "Oh, yes, *meu amor*. Do not stop. *Meu Deus,* do not stop."

CHAPTER ELEVEN

As NIGHT SLOWLY DESCENDED, the fog swirled over the docks and at last gathered its strength to blanket Dover in a silver dampness.

Still, Philippe waited until most of the good citizens had returned to their homes and were huddled by their fires before he at last commanded their belongings to be loaded in the carriage.

It took only a few moments for them to arrive at the docks, but the carriage never slowed as they traveled past the looming ships and instead turned toward a rarely used road that wound its way out of the city and then turned back toward the water.

Within a very short time the carriage was shrouded by the fog and there was nothing to be heard but the clatter of the horses' hoofs and the soft lap of water against the rocks. They might have been alone in the world, he thought as he glanced toward the woman at his side.

In truth, it was a pity they were not.

Tonight Raine was warmly dressed in one of her new gowns with the heavy cloak around her and the hood pulled to hide her face in shadows. It was impossible to determine more than a vague hint of her slender curves, and yet he instantly felt a familiar flare of possessive pleasure rush through him.

She could be wrapped as tightly as an Egyptian mummy and he would still recognize her. The warm, sweet scent of her skin. The unconscious elegance of her movements.

He would not mind disappearing into the fog for the next few months, just so long as Raine were there with him.

Unfortunately, the world refused to vanish into the mist and all too soon the carriage was slowing to a halt.

With a faint sigh of regret, Philippe assisted Raine onto the road, commanding her to wait for him. Then he cautiously made his way down a steep trail toward the nearby water.

He was halfway down the path when he caught the faint scent of a cheroot that had recently been snuffed out.

Coming to a stop, he leaned against the large rock that jutted from the ground and folded his arms over his chest.

"Good evening, Captain Miles," he drawled.

There was a brief pause before a string of muttered curses filled the air and a short, stocky man with a battered countenance and rough wool clothing stepped from behind the rock.

"How the bloody hell did you know I was there?" Miles growled. "'Tis unnatural."

Philippe merely smiled as his gaze shifted to the two shallow rowboats that were waiting on the beach.

"Any troubles?"

"There were a few officers who were snooping about earlier, but I had Ranford give them something to chase. No doubt they are halfway to London by now. 'Course, there are always more of the bloody demons lurking about." There was an awkward pause as the captain turned his head to study the frail figure that waited at the top of the path. "Yer companion won't be attracting any unwanted attention, will she?"

Philippe chuckled as he recalled his heated skirmish with Raine when he warned her that she would have to obey his every command without question, and without hesitation, if they were to slip past the port authorities unnoticed.

"No, I can assure you that she will be as quiet as a mouse."

Miles turned his head to spit on the ground. "Christ, the

day any woman is as quiet as a mouse is the day hell will
freeze over. Never can keep their mouths from flapping."

"This one will, I assure you."

Miles spit again. "Mayhaps, but I don't like this, I don't
mind telling you. 'T'aint right to have a female on the ship.
Bad luck. Everyone knows that."

Philippe leaned forward, his expression cold and lethal
enough to make the hardened seaman stumble backward.

"Captain, this woman is my guest and she will be coming
with us, make no mistake about that." His eyes narrowed. "And
if I suspect for even one moment that you or one of your crew
has treated her with anything less than absolute respect, you
will find yourself swimming home. Do I make myself clear?"

Miles swallowed heavily. "Quite clear, sir."

"Good." Philippe straightened, squashing the ridiculous urge
to beat the man bloody. "Did you search the docks as I asked?"

Clearly relieved at the change of subject, Miles gave a
jerky nod of his head.

"Aye."

"Did you discover anything?"

"Only a handful of rumors that a Frenchman was roaming
the local pubs trying to bribe his way aboard a ship. No one
managed to catch his name."

"What of a description?"

"They all said the same thing. A thin man with a shabby
coat and a habit of muttering to himself."

Philippe frowned. "That's not much to go on."

Miles shrugged. "They thought him touched in the noodle
and ran him off whenever they could. They did say they thought
he had managed to leave port a day or two before we arrived."

It was what Philippe had been expecting, but that did not
prevent a stab of frustration. He was weary of being one step
behind Seurat. He wanted the villain in his grasp.

"Did they know where he was staying?"

"Hiding among the rubbish, most likely."

"But it was certain that he was headed to France?"

"Aye."

"Very well." Philippe gave a nod toward the waiting carriage. "Have your men load our belongings into the boat. We will leave as soon as Carlos arrives."

Miles lifted a hand and two men appeared from the shadows near the shore. Together the men moved up the path and began collecting the heavy trunks strapped to the back of the carriage.

Philippe was just about to follow them when there was a sound to his side and Carlos abruptly appeared near the rock.

"Ah, speak of the devil," Philippe said, his gaze flicking over his companion's dark clothes. Carlos had left the inn directly after luncheon to prowl through the various taprooms to discover what news could be had of France. Even with the monarchy restored it remained a restless, unpredictable place. "What news?"

"By all accounts the atmosphere is tense," Carlos retorted. "Charles remains in power and determined to return France to the true Royalists. There are no demonstrations in the streets yet, but the populous is agitated."

Philippe smiled wryly. "When is France not agitated? It possesses a need to keep itself in turmoil."

"True enough."

"Is it safe to travel?"

"Beyond the occasional mobs and demands for the end to the Bourbon rule."

"As safe as France can ever be," Philippe said dryly.

"Precisely. What of Seurat?"

Philippe grimaced. "Every trail leads to France."

"I was afraid you would say that." Carlos shoved his hands

into his pockets and turned his head toward the slender form still poised at the top of the bluff. "You are truly taking her with us?"

"Why should I not?"

Carlos slowly smiled. "I have never known you to go to such a bother over any woman. Let alone one that you are forced to hold against her will."

"She...intrigues me."

"That much is obvious." Carlos gave a lift of his brows. "But you do realize she might very well jeopardize your plans? If she manages to reach the French authorities and claim she was forced to Paris against her will..."

"She would never risk her father's neck," Philippe replied, overriding the dire warning. "Not even to rescue herself from my evil clutches."

Carlos gave a choked laugh. "Evil clutches?"

"Her words, not mine."

"Charming." Carlos paused before giving a casual shrug. "She is a beauty when she isn't dressed as a dirty little urchin. *Anjo.*"

Philippe narrowed his gaze, clenching his fists. *Meu Deus.* There was something almost savage in the flare of fierce possessiveness that raced through him.

"You tread dangerous ground, *amigo.*"

Carlos met his warning gaze squarely, his own expression unreadable.

"Not nearly as dangerous as the ground you tread. Take care that you do not land yourself in a bog." He reached out to slap Philippe on the shoulder before stepping back. "I wish to make sure our tracks are covered. I will meet you at the ship."

Philippe gave a faint shake of his head at his strange behavior. He never allowed a wench to dictate his emotions. Not ever. Certainly not to the point of planting his fist into the face of his closest friend.

Hell and damnation.

"Be careful," he commanded, not sure if he was warning his friend or himself.

RAINE SHIVERED AS SHE STOOD at the edge of the small bluff. It was not from the cold breeze. The thick cloak managed to ward off most of the chill. Or even the fog that danced eerily through the bushes. One could not be English and not become accustomed to foggy nights.

It could not even be blamed on the realization that she was about to be hauled to France by a man who thought of her as nothing more than a convenient body in his bed.

If she were to be entirely honest with herself, there was a small, treacherous part of her that relished the daring adventure. Her tedious days trapped alone in the small cottage could hardly compare with traveling through France in a luxury she could only dream of. And an even more treacherous part was growing addicted to the sweet passion that Philippe could stir within her.

No, the source of her shivering could be directly blamed on the small boats that were obviously waiting to haul her across the choppy waters.

Intent on her dark broodings, Raine did not notice Philippe's approach until he was standing directly before her. She gave a small jerk as he reached out to take her hand.

"Come, Raine. It is time we were on our way."

She pulled free of his grasp, her teeth digging into her lower lip.

"We are going in—" she pointed toward the small rowboats "—that?"

He tilted his head to one side. In the misty fog his features appeared even more unearthly beautiful. As if he were a mystical creature that was not quite real.

"Only for a short distance. My yacht awaits us out of sight of the shore."

She frowned at his casual tone. "Why is it not docked at the port?"

"I did warn you that I have no desire for anyone to know of my brief stay in England. A difficult task when my ship is docked at Dover port."

Her teeth bit deeply enough into her lip that she could taste blood. "Oh."

A frown touched his wide brow. "What is the matter?"

"I…I do not wish to go."

"*Meu Deus.* You are not going to dig in your heels now," he growled, his countenance hard with annoyance. "Or is your word worth nothing?"

Her chin tilted at the deliberate insult. "Considering that my word was given under threat of blackmail, I hardly think you are in the position to be questioning the honor of anyone, *Monsieur Gautier.*"

"Perhaps not, but I am happily in the position to force you to my will, *meu amor.* So long as I can trust your word, then you will be allowed a certain measure of freedom. The moment you break that trust you will discover yourself a true prisoner." He gripped her chin and tilted up her face to meet his glittering gaze. "Now, do you get into the boat of your own will or need I tie and gag you?"

She jerked from his touch, relieved as her surge of anger seared away the ridiculous fear.

"You beast," she hissed. "Brute. Bully."

With a startling speed he had her by the upper arms and was yanking her to his chest. "You have not even had a taste of how brutish I can truly be."

She tilted back her head to glare into his tight features. "Fine, beat me then if it will make you feel better."

For a moment the fingers tightened on her arms. Then he was giving a slow shake of his head.

"What the devil is this, Raine?"

"Good God, what do you think it is? I do not want to go to France. I do not want to leave my father. I do not want…" She stopped to lick her oddly dry lips.

He eased his grip and lifted a hand to cup her cheek. "What? What do you not want?"

Raine heaved a sigh. "I do not want to get into that boat."

A silence fell as he regarded her with a searching gaze. "Are you afraid of the water, *querida?*"

"I cannot swim."

"But you have made the crossing before," he said.

She gave a shudder as her attention returned to the row-boats. "On a decent ship that did not appear as if it would overturn at the first stiff breeze," she retorted, her eyes narrowing as his lips began to twitch. "Do not dare laugh at me. 'Tis not funny."

His hand shifted to tug on a stray curl that dangled beside her ear. "Why did you not simply tell me that you were afraid to get into the boat instead of making such a fuss?"

Raine gave a restless shrug. She was not about to admit that she had been embarrassed to confess the truth. Or that she took pleasure in his belief that she was bold and daring and not at all the usual sort of female who had vapors at every opportunity.

"Does it matter why?" she demanded. "I do not doubt you intend to force me onto the boat regardless of any protest I might make."

He swooped down to drop a light kiss on the tip of her nose.

"We must get to the yacht, Raine. And since you have already admitted that you cannot swim, I see little choice but to take a boat."

Her lips thinned at his patronizing tone. "There are many

choices, Philippe. You could take the boat and I could return to the inn."

Something flashed in his green eyes. Something dark and primitive. Then, without warning, he was scooping her off her feet and cradling her next to his chest.

"Ah, no, *meu amor*," he rasped as he moved down the steep path. "We are in this together."

She instinctively threw her arms around his neck. "Philippe, put me down."

He gazed deep into her wide eyes. "I have you, Raine. I will not allow anything to happen to you while you are in my care."

PHILIPPE KEPT HIS WORD. He maintained his tight grip on Raine throughout the short, unfortunately unsteady voyage to his yacht.

Not that he truly had many options, he wryly told himself. Raine had clung to him like a limpet with her face buried in his chest and her fingers digging painfully into his shoulders. It would have taken a good deal more effort to dislodge her than to simply keep her cradled close to his body.

Besides, the last thing he needed on his hands was a hysterical woman.

Once aboard his luxurious yacht she noticeably relaxed, and after carrying her into his private cabin, he tucked her into bed before returning topside and calling for his secretary, who he had left onboard during his brief stay in London. Juan was far more than a mere servant, as were most of the staff who traveled with him, and his skills would be necessary before they arrived in Calais.

It was near two hours later when he at last was able to make his way to his bed and stretch out beside the slumbering Raine. They would be docking in Calais well before dawn, but he was not yet prepared to approach the Custom House. There would be time enough for a short rest, he decided, as he gathered Raine close and allowed his tense muscles to relax.

Surprisingly, he slept deeply and the sun was well over the horizon by the time he had shaved and attired himself in a pair of black breeches and dark jade coat. Pulling on his caped greatcoat, he made his way up the narrow stairs and crossed to stand at the polished railings.

As always the wharf was bustling with a variety of passengers, common sailors and crowds of spectators. There were also the inevitable runners who waited anxiously to whisk an unwary passenger to whatever nearby inn employed them.

His gaze skimmed the throng, searching for anyone who might be displaying an unusual interest in the sleek yacht, before shifting toward the looming Custom House and the towering lighthouse that had been erected to mark the return of Louis XVIII from exile. It was claimed that his footprint could still be found on the beach if one cared enough to go in search of it.

Philippe did not.

One French despot was much like another as far as he was concerned.

Beyond the Custom House, the town of Calais was separated by an iron gate. It was a drab stone town with narrow streets that were usually dirty and clogged with traffic. Not that it mattered to Philippe. Carlos had slipped from the yacht well before dawn and would have a carriage waiting for them. He intended to begin the trek to Paris as soon as he had dealt with the tedious formalities. And more important, once the word began to spread that Philippe Gautier had returned to France and in the company of a mysterious young woman.

As if on cue, Raine appeared at his side, once again wrapped in the heavy cloak with the hood pulled to hide her face in the shadows. Her caution was perhaps understandable, but that didn't halt the surge of annoyance that rippled through him.

He had never possessed a lover who was ashamed to acknowledge her liaison with him. *Meu Deus.* They usually made certain that it was known throughout whatever city they happened to be in. A fact that had always bothered him until now.

Resisting the childish urge to brush the hood from her head, Philippe leaned against the railing and offered her a faint smile.

"You see, *querida,* I have kept my promise. You have arrived safely."

"Why have we docked here?" she demanded.

Philippe gave a lift of his brows. "Why should we not?"

She gave an impatient click of her tongue. "I shall have to go through Customs. In case you have forgotten, I did not precisely prepare for a trip to the Continent. I do not have my papers."

"Really, Raine, must you continue to underestimate me?" he drawled, reaching beneath his coat to pull out the folded papers that Juan had provided. "I would not bring you to France without your passport."

With a wary expression, she reached to take the packet and pulled it open.

"Mademoiselle Marie Beauvoir?"

"Most recently a dedicated student at the convent in Turin. That is until our paths crossed and I convinced you to travel with me to Paris."

She sucked in a sharp breath. "This is forged."

His lips twisted at her shocked disbelief. The chit had spent God knew how many nights terrorizing travelers along the roads of Knightsbridge. Now she balked at a handful of fake documents?

"I should not say that too loudly, *querida,*" he warned. "Not unless you wish to be hauled before the Custom officials."

She studied him with a narrowed gaze. "Good Lord, are you a smuggler?"

He gave a short laugh. "Not as a rule."

"You must be involved in some sort of illegal activities. You are far too adept at concealing your identity and slipping past authorities for an honest gentleman."

Philippe abruptly straightened from the railing. "A businessman must possess many skills."

"Fah."

"Come along, *meu amor.*" Taking her arm, he led her across the deck. Now was not the moment to confess the truth to her. "Our baggage has already been unloaded. Let us be done with this tedious task."

IT WAS JUST AS TEDIOUS as Philippe had feared. There was nothing more ghastly than a petty autocrat who thought his tiny bit of power gave him license to bother and bedevil anyone who was unfortunate enough to cross his path.

When they were at last done, Philippe left his secretary and a burly crewman to deal with the luggage, as well as to protect Raine, while he traveled into Calais to meet with Carlos.

As they had arranged, Carlos was waiting in front of a small inn complete with a gleaming carriage and a pair of gray horses to pull it. There was also a beautiful black stallion that jerked against his reins with an obvious evil temper.

Philippe smiled with appreciation. He liked his horses with an unruly spirit. Oddly enough, he was discovering that was precisely how he liked his women.

"Well done, Carlos," he said as he ran a searching gaze over the carriage. It was precisely what he had requested. Sturdy, well sprung and the best that money could purchase. "Were there any troubles?"

Leaning against a low iron fence, Carlos gave a shrug. He

was attired in the sort of plain clothes that any common laborer would wear. The sort that would allow him to blend easily with the crowd. At least until one managed to catch a glimpse of the dark, feral countenance.

"Nothing that a bottle of brandy and a willing woman would not cure."

"In good time." Philippe glanced toward the large bay that was tied a short distance down the street. "You intend to ride ahead?"

Carlos gave a short nod. "Unless you wish me to travel with you?"

"No, I will have Paolo and Juan with me. They should be capable of dealing with any unexpected difficulties."

"You will take the road through Abbeville?"

"Yes." Philippe pulled out his pocket watch and grimaced at the realization that the morning was nearly gone. "Do not expect us before Monday. Even with good roads and fresh post-horses we will be forced to halt at least two nights upon the road."

Carlos pulled a knit hat over his dark curls before stepping forward and grasping Philippe's shoulder. "Take care. We only suspect that Seurat is in Paris. For all we know he could be lurking anywhere."

"I will be on my guard," Philippe promised.

"Good." Carlos stepped back, clearly anxious to be on his way. No doubt he already had a notion of where to discover that brandy and willing woman he desired. "I will join you at Montmartre."

CHAPTER TWELVE

THE CARRIAGE WAS WITHOUT fault, of course. The interior was spacious with soft leather seats and wide windows that offered a fine view of the passing scenery. Best of all, there was a ceramic foot-warmer that offered a welcome relief to the chilled air.

For all its comfort, however, Raine found herself more often than not alone in the elegant equipage.

Philippe seemed to prefer riding the beautiful black stallion that Carlos had purchased before leaving Calais.

Which suited her just fine, she sternly told herself. It was enough that he insisted that they have a private chamber to eat their meals together at the various posting inns and, of course, that they share a chamber each night.

A hot blush stained her cheeks as the memory of those nights flooded through her mind. Lud, but she had never dreamed that a man could possess the ability to make her forget everything but the pleasure of his touch.

With an effort, Raine turned her attention to the passing scenery. It was well worth her attention. For miles the rolling hills were covered with a thick forest that was untouched and pristine. There were occasional farms that boasted orchards and vineyards, and sleepy villages that seemed to huddle beneath the biting cold.

Unfortunately among the beauty was also the inevitable

sight of ragged peasants who peered desperately from tumbled cottages or simply trudged down the road with their heads bent in obvious despair.

Her ready sympathy was stirred by the dreadful plight of so many, but without even the smallest coin in her possession she could do nothing but watch them with a heavy heart.

It was late afternoon when they passed through Chaumont and entered Montmartre.

The village sprawled along the slopes of a hill that offered a stunning view of Paris, as well as the open countryside of Saint Denis.

The streets were narrow and steeply inclined as they wound their way past a tumble of shops and gardens and pretty cottages.

Expecting to continue on to the capital, Raine was caught off guard when the carriage began to slow as they approached a two-storied stucco house with a red-tiled roof and shuttered windows. The front of the house abutted a narrow street, but the carriage pulled through a gate and into a large garden before it at last came to a halt.

Within moments the door to the carriage was being pulled open and Philippe was assisting her down to the flagstone path.

She shivered as the wind tugged at her heavy cloak and tumbled the hood from her head.

"What is this place?" she demanded as she eyed the large cottage. There was an ageless charm to the house and the overgrown garden, but it seemed far too plain and bourgeois for a man of Philippe's standing.

"It belongs to my brother." A thin smile touched his lips. "Or rather I suppose it belongs to me, since I was the one who was expected to hand over the funds to pay for it. Not to mention the wages for the small staff. It is not the most luxurious of my homes, I fear."

Raine rolled her eyes. It was far larger than her father's cottage and worth a small fortune to most people.

"Oh, certainly not. Why, I daresay, there are no more than four bedchambers and only two drawing rooms. How could anyone endure such cramped quarters?"

A dark brow arched. "A trial, indeed. Still, we will not be here for long."

She turned to regard his perfect countenance. "You said that you had no homes in France."

"I consider this my brother's home, not mine."

"Just how many homes do you and your family own?"

"A fair number. I have always found that property is a sensible investment. Especially property that is bound to increase in value over the years." He pointed toward the vast tumble of Paris below them. "Do you see how the city is expanding? This area will soon be overrun by Paris and the land will most certainly triple in worth."

"Of course it will," she muttered.

He turned back to her with a narrowed gaze. "You sound disapproving."

Raine gave a restless shrug, not at all certain why she felt the continual need to provoke this gentleman. Perhaps it was because the only time he revealed he possessed the same emotions as the lesser mortals was when he was making love to her.

"I cannot help but wonder if you ever make a decision that does not offer you some profit."

"You think I should make decisions that will make me a pauper?" he taunted.

"Do you ever do anything just because it pleases you?" she prodded.

That aloof coldness she so detested hardened his features. "As it so happens, making a profit does please me."

"And you are never impulsive? Never impetuous?"

His green eyes glittered like chips of emerald beneath the pale winter sun. "*Impulsive* is merely a pretty word for those who are rash and irresponsible. Not all of us have the luxury of ignoring our duties."

A pang of guilt shot through Raine's tender heart. This man had not only lost his mother when he was still but a babe, but he had been forced to bear the entire weight of his feckless family. Perhaps it was not so surprising he wrapped himself in a cloak of impenetrable solitude.

"Do you resent your father and brother?" she asked before she could stop the words.

"What I resent is being kept in the freezing air while you indulge in your ridiculous inquisition. I, for one, would prefer to spend my time in a warm bath."

Without waiting for her response, Philippe was striding toward the back door, his posture rigid and his shoulders tight with annoyance.

Raine heaved a sigh before trailing behind him.

She had desired an adventure that would lead her far from the dull tedium of her life.

She would have to be far more careful of what she wished for in the future.

PHILIPPE'S MOOD WAS STILL dark when he left the cottage to make his way to Paris later that evening.

It was unlike him to allow himself to be goaded by another's opinion of him. Especially a mere chit's opinion. After all, most people thought of him as a coldhearted bastard who took no pleasure in the world beyond making a profit.

And in some respects they would not be wrong.

But the notion that Raine found him lacking because he could not behave as some frivolous, worthless dandy made his gut twist with anger.

For God's sake, her father might very well send them both to the gallows with his reckless behavior, and yet she clearly loved him with an unwavering loyalty. Is that what she desired? A man who would risk her life for a mere lark?

Not that it mattered what she preferred, he acknowledged with a flare of determination. For the moment she belonged to him. And nothing would change that until *he* decided it was over.

Weaving his mount through the heavy traffic, Philippe at last arrived at the Palais-Royal. He shook his head at the rather grim shoddiness that was beginning to claim the once majestic buildings and halted his horse before the Grand Vefour.

Although Paris would always have its share of cafés and coffeehouses, the elegant restaurants that were beginning to sprout up around the city had captured the approval of even the most discerning Parisians.

It was at this particular restaurant that Philippe had been assured he would discover Lord Frankford, a minor English diplomat who would never possess the skill or drive to make his name among the great politicians. He did, however, have one remarkable talent.

There would not be a scrap of gossip in all the city that had escaped his attention.

Entering the restaurant, Philippe handed his coat and hat to the uniformed waiter and allowed his gaze to roam over the smoky interior.

Like most of the aging buildings there remained remnants of the Ancient Régime. Not that Philippe disliked the elegance of the painted walls and ceilings, or the mirrors that reflected the various diners. It was certainly preferable to the dark, damp and congested taprooms in England.

It took only a few moments to spot his prey seated at a corner table, and ignoring the speculative glances of the other guests, Philippe made his way through the room to take a seat opposite the rotund gentleman with a rapidly balding head and ruddy features of a true Englishman.

Glancing up from his plate of oysters, Frankford widened his eyes in shock.

"Good God. Is that you, Gautier?"

"For my sins," Philippe drawled. "I hope you are well, Frankford?"

The man took a deep sip of his Bordeaux. "Well enough."

"And your wife?"

"Thankfully in England for the time being." Frankford gave a grunt as he wiped his mouth with a linen napkin. "I have found marriage much easier to bear when we reside in different countries."

Philippe smiled. "A sentiment shared by many men, which is precisely why I have never bothered to wed."

"Always knew you were an intelligent chap." Frankford settled back in his chair and folded his arms over his remarkably large belly. "Still, never thought to see you here. The last time I invited you to visit you claimed the entire city should be burned to the ground."

"I still believe that it could be greatly improved by a match and bit of kindling, but there are occasions when one cannot avoid traveling through the area."

"So you are not remaining?" Frankford demanded.

"That depends." Philippe stretched out his legs as his gaze casually turned toward the nearby window. "I believe I might be convinced to linger a few days."

"Ah, you have stumbled into some sweet business deal, have you not?" Frankford sighed in resignation. "I swear, I do not know how you do it. You must be some damnable Midas."

Philippe returned his attention to the round countenance. "Actually, my business is of a more personal nature."

"You don't say." There was a moment of puzzlement before Frankford was giving a choked cough. "By God, you do not mean a woman?"

Philippe arched his brows. "Why does that surprise you?"

"I have never known you to chase after the skirts. And why should you?" Frankford shook his head. "Lud, I've never seen so many women making fools of themselves as when you first arrived in London. An embarrassing spectacle, if you ask me."

It had been a damn sight more than embarrassing, Philippe silently conceded. He had nearly been stampeded each time he left his home, and he had swiftly discovered there was no more ruthless enemy than a mother intent on marrying her daughter to a fortune.

Thankfully all but the most persistent were at last frightened off by the realization that no amount of flattery, coercion or even downright treachery would force him to offer for the drab females being tossed at his feet.

"This one is thankfully different," he assured his companion.

Frankford chuckled in a knowing manner. "Ah, of course. Well, Paris is renowned for its courtesans. Beautiful and talented, if you know what I mean. I have tasted a few and I can tell you they are well worth the cost." The man patted his belly. "Perhaps when you tire of her I will give her a tumble or two myself."

Philippe found himself battling the urge to reach across the table and smash his fist into the fat face. Hell and damnation, what was the matter with him? The sole reason Raine was with him was to convince others he was too distracted by his current lover to concern himself with his brother. Or at least, that was one of the reasons, he acknowledged as he felt himself grow hard at the mere thought of her slender body.

He would ruin it all if he did not take care.

"She is no courtesan." He gave a causal shrug. "At least not yet. I managed to stumble across her fresh from the convent."

Frankford gave a startled blink. "An innocent?"

"They do have their charm."

"Indeed, they do." Frankford smiled slyly. "She is beautiful, I suppose?"

"As lovely as an angel."

"Well, well. I hope she does not have any pesky family that might be searching for her? That is the trouble with innocents. There always seems to be some angry brother or father trying to keep one from enjoying such delights."

Philippe briefly thought of Josiah Wimbourne. He hoped to hell the man was suffering agonies at the loss of Raine. It would teach the bastard to take better care of his daughter.

"It hardly matters. I shall not be remaining long in Paris. I must be off to England by the end of the month."

A wariness rippled over the florid countenance. "Ah, yes. I suppose you have heard of your brother's troubles?"

"I received a rather frantic letter that spoke of dire difficulties and impending doom."

"You do not appear to be overly concerned."

Philippe gave a dismissive wave of his hand. "My brother is always facing some sort of impending doom or another. If I raced to his side every time he begged for my assistance, I should never get anything accomplished."

Frankford shifted with obvious discomfort. "I hate to be the bearer of bad tidings, Gautier, but I do believe it is a bit more serious on this occasion. The last I heard he had taken up residence in Newgate."

"It will do Jean-Pierre no harm to spend a few days in prison. Perhaps it will teach him a long-overdue lesson in responsibility. Nothing else has been able to do so."

Frankford gave a short, disbelieving laugh. "Good God, Gautier. You are a coldhearted devil."

"I have already contacted my solicitors. I do not doubt by

the time I arrive the entire mess will have been straightened out." Philippe's tone was soft, but there was an edge that warned his patience was at an end.

"Yes, well, I suppose you know your business best," Frankford hastily said.

"Indeed, I do." Philippe was forced to pause as a waiter arrived with a large plate of pheasant drenched in a thick mushroom sauce. Once they were alone he turned the conversation in the direction he desired. "And speaking of business, my father has requested that I contact an old friend of his while I am in Paris. A Monsieur Mirabeau."

Already tackling the pheasant with an obvious relish, Frankford gave a small grunt.

"Can't say that I've seen him for some months. Word is that he has become a damnable hermit."

"Does he live near Paris?"

"So far as I know he still possesses his estate near Fontainebleau."

"Thank you." Rising to his feet, Philippe dug into his pocket to pull out a handful of coins that he dropped on the table. "This should cover your meal."

"Oh, I say. Very good of you, Gautier," Frankford said.

"Think nothing of it. Give my regards to Lady Frankford."

Frankford grimaced. "Not bloody likely."

Collecting his coat and hat, Philippe left the restaurant and was swiftly making his way back to Montmartre.

He had managed to discover the information he needed.

Tomorrow he would begin the hunt for Seurat.

THE CARRIAGE RATTLED down the rue de Seine before turning onto a narrow street that was lined with ancient hotels that had been transformed into apartments, shops, warehouses and even public baths.

Just ahead an aging building was being slowly demolished to offer a new thoroughfare. The tumble of bricks and broken pillars only added to the air of escalating shabbiness in the once-elegant neighborhood.

"It is all changing," Raine muttered with a hint of sadness. She had been only fourteen when the nuns had brought a handful of students to Paris, but she had remembered it with delight.

Philippe was seated at her side attired in dark breeches and jacket. The severity of his clothing only served to emphasize his aloof, pale beauty.

"Hardly surprising. With every new ruler comes the necessity of altering the city to reflect their power."

Her lips tightened as she caught sight of a couple of ragged urchins huddled near the street.

"A pity that they do not feel an equal duty to care for their people. It is a sin to allow their citizens to suffer," she muttered.

Philippe remained leaning back in his seat, his expression unreadable.

"There will always be the poor and destitute, *querida*. If nothing else the Revolution proved that not even those who boast of equality and the distribution of wealth can alter the fate of the lower classes. They succeeded in nothing more than causing a bloodbath that killed as many of their own as their supposed enemies."

She narrowed her gaze at his smooth tone. "So you do not feel that those with wealth should assist those in need?"

"I employ a great number of servants and tenants and laborers, Raine. I pay them a decent wage and ensure that they have an adequate pension. Because of me they have a very comfortable life. What more would you have of me?"

She bit back her instinctive words. The annoying man did have a point. From the small amount she had been able to determine about Philippe, his empire extended from Portugal to

Brazil to England. He employed thousands of people and invested in countless farms, vineyards, shipping companies and factories. It was a far cry more than she did to help others.

"Who is this gentleman we are to visit?" she demanded in a blatant attempt to change the conversation.

His lips twitched, but he readily followed her lead. "Monsieur Mirabeau. He is an old acquaintance of my father."

"And you believe that he might know something of this man you are hunting?"

His features tightened. "Let us hope."

Raine smoothed her hands over the pale ivory of her gown. She had matched the dress with a gold Spenser and a bonnet with a thick veil that hid her face.

"I still do not comprehend what you hope to accomplish by coming to Paris. If this man is in the city, will he not simply flee when he discovers your presence?"

"That is a possibility, but if he does not yet realize that I am following his trail, then he will more likely believe that it is safer to slink back to his lair and wait for me to leave."

Raine studied his grim expression. "There is more than that."

Philippe gave a lift of his brows. "I beg your pardon?"

"You are hoping to draw him out," she said slowly. "You think he will attempt to strike at you."

A ripple of surprise crossed his features, as if he were caught off guard by her perception.

"I will admit that it has crossed my mind that by having me so near and seemingly unaware of my danger, it might prove to be a temptation too difficult to resist. If he is prodded into attacking me, then I should be capable of trapping him."

She stiffened at his nonchalant manner. Had there ever been a man born who did not take some delight in risking his blasted neck?

"And what if you are hurt? Or, God forbid, killed?"

Philippe regarded her with an odd smile. "Do not fear, *meu amor,* Carlos has been instructed to see that you are protected and returned to the care of your father. He will not fail you."

For some reason his promise only aggravated her further. "Bloody hell, I do not need Carlos or any other man to protect me."

"Then why are you in such a twit?" He reached out to stroke a light finger down the bare skin of her throat. "It could not be that you are concerned for my welfare, could it, *querida?*"

She jerked from his touch. It was enough that he knew her treacherous body would respond to his lightest caress. She was not about to let him realize that he was ruthlessly forcing his way into her heart.

"Your arrogance is beyond belief," she charged.

His green eyes glittered. "Why will you not admit that you do not want to see me harmed?"

"If I do not wish to see you harmed, it is simply because when someone finally does put a bullet into you, I intend to be the one pulling the trigger."

Philippe merely laughed. "Ah, my bloodthirsty beauty. You say such charming things. Is it any wonder you have managed to beguile me?"

"Beguile?" An unwelcome pain raced through her. "Not likely."

"You surely have not forgotten last night?"

She shivered against her will. Of course she had not forgotten last night. How the devil could she? The man had devoted hours to his tender assault. It had almost seemed as if he were determined to brand himself on her very soul as he had made her scream over and over in pleasure.

Thankfully, she was no fool. She understood the shallow emptiness of mere desire.

"Lust is not at all the same as beguilement."

He lowered his head to brush his lips just below her ear. "It feels remarkably similar to me."

"No." Her hands fisted in her lap as she willed herself not to respond. "A man can experience lust for any woman who might cross his path. Beguilement implies that she is somehow special."

Pulling back, he studied her pale features barely visible behind the veil.

"And you wish me to assure you that you are special to me?"

She turned her head to gaze out the window. "Do not, Philippe."

"Raine? What is—"

"We appear to be halting," she abruptly interrupted, studying the white building with a portico framing the door.

"This is our destination," Philippe said, his hand reaching out to grasp her chin and forcing her to meet his narrowed gaze. "We will finish this later."

He gave her no opportunity to respond as he shoved open the door to the carriage and assisted her down. Taking her hand, he placed it firmly on his arm and led her into the building.

Raine barely managed a swift glance around what appeared to be a literary salon when a lovely woman with glossy blond hair and a curvaceous form tightly encased in a brilliant crimson gown was making her way to stand directly before Philippe. She was stunningly beautiful with the sort of china-doll features and wide blue eyes that Raine had always envied.

She hated the woman on sight.

"Ah, Monsieur Gautier." She held out her hand for Philippe to lift it to his lips. "How pleased I am to welcome you to my small salon."

Philippe straightened, a smile curving his lips. "Madame Tulles."

"I received your letter requesting to view my library. I believe you will discover some books of interest. If you will follow me?"

Philippe gave a nod and the woman turned to lead them past the low sofas and marble tables that were scattered throughout the large room. A handful of men were seated in a corner speaking in hushed tones, but none spared more than a fleeting glance toward them.

They entered a narrow hall and continued down to the last door before the woman came to a halt and turned to flash Philippe an intimate smile.

"He is waiting for you," she told him in French.

"*Merci,* Juliana," he murmured softly.

"Is there anything else you need?"

"Only a bit of privacy."

"That I can promise." They exchanged a glance that revealed they were far more than strangers. "I hope once your business is completed you will have time for pleasure. My door is always open to you, Philippe."

With a last lingering smile the woman turned to walk back down the hall, leaving behind a cloud of expensive perfume.

Raine found her teeth gritted as she glared at the man standing at her side.

"Juliana?" she demanded.

"She is an old friend."

Raine doubted that friendship had anything to do with their relationship. "Did she beguile you, as well?"

A smug smile curved his lips. "You sound almost jealous, *meu amor.*"

She did sound jealous. Probably because the mere thought of Philippe with the sophisticated blonde was enough to make her want to slap the woman. And then Philippe for good measure.

Damn, the irritating man. What was he doing to her?

"Can we just get this over with?" she demanded as she folded her arms over her oddly tight stomach. "Or are we to spend the entire day standing in this hall?"

CHAPTER THIRTEEN

PHILIPPE RESISTED THE URGE to laugh as he reached to push open the nearby door. As a rule he disliked jealous women. The last thing he desired was a clinging female who believed that she possessed some claim upon him.

But the sight of Raine's taut expression and the tense annoyance that shimmered about her slender body pleased him in a manner that he did not quite understand.

In truth it made him long to press her into the corner and prove that whatever Juliana's undoubted charm, it was her own fiery spirit that made him ache with need.

With a shake of his head at his odd mood, Philippe stepped into the small, book-lined room. The scent of aging leather and wood smoke greeted him as he crossed over the threshold. And, as Juliana had promised, there was a thin, gray-haired gentleman seated near the fireplace, his lined countenance set in an expression of peevish annoyance.

Not that he had expected anything else. His gaze slid to where Carlos leaned negligently against the heavy mahogany desk. Not many would dare to defy the large, always dangerous man.

Pausing to settle Raine in a chair beside the door, Philippe moved forward to offer a shallow bow.

"Monsieur Mirabeau?"

The man scowled with annoyance. "*Oui.*"

"Thank you for agreeing to meet with me."

"There was no agreement." A gnarled hand banged on the arm of his chair. "Your…henchman simply arrived at my door and commanded that I accompany him. Since he is considerably larger and some years younger than myself I had no choice but to be dragged to this place."

Philippe crossed to the desk and returned with a small glass of cognac. "Perhaps this will help ease any discomfort you might have suffered." He offered it to the gentleman, who promptly swallowed the golden spirits in one gulp.

Setting aside the glass, Mirabeau glared at Philippe. "What I desire is an explanation of this outrage."

"First I believe introductions are in order," Philippe said smoothly. "Carlos you have already met." He motioned his hand toward the silent Raine. "This is Mademoiselle Beauvoir. And I am Philippe Gautier."

A silence shrouded the room before Mirabeau struggled to his feet.

"You are Louis's son?"

"Yes."

"Mon Dieu." He gave a shake of his silver head. "Why did you not simply send me a note? I would have been happy to meet with you."

"I would prefer that no one realize that we have spoken."

"Why?"

Philippe met the watery-blue gaze with a grim expression. "I want you to tell me everything you know of a man named Seurat."

"Seurat?" The elderly man muttered a string of curses. "Do not speak of that loathsome wretch."

A flare of sharp satisfaction raced through Philippe. Thank God. He could not deny that deep part of him had feared he had been chasing shadows while Jean-Pierre faced the gallows.

"So you recognize the name?"

"How could I not?" The elderly man abruptly turned to stare into the fire, a fine tremor shaking his frail body. "He has plagued and bedeviled me for years."

Philippe frowned at the husky confession. "What has he done?"

"Nothing that can be proved." Mirabeau held his hands toward the flames. "The windows of my home have been broken on countless occasions, my collection of Grecian friezes was destroyed while they were on display at the Tuileries, even my carriage has been run off the road."

"And you believe it is the work of Seurat?"

"I have seen him," Mirabeau rasped. "Standing in the shadows. Always in the shadows."

Meu Deus. To have tormented this poor old man for years. The bastard was clearly insane.

"What connection does he have to my family?" he demanded.

"I...cannot say."

Philippe reached out to grasp the man's thin shoulder and tugged him around to meet his fierce glare. He might feel pity for Mirabeau, but his brother's life hung in the balance.

"Do not play games with me, *monsieur,*" he warned in silky tones.

"Your father has sworn me to silence."

"As usual my father is not here to clean up the mess he has created. You will tell me everything you know before my brother is sent to the gallows. Do you understand?"

The wrinkled face paled. "So the rumors are true? He has been arrested?"

"He faces the hangman unless I can find Seurat and force him to confess that Jean-Pierre is innocent."

Mirabeau licked his thin lips. "*Mon Dieu,* this is a disaster," he muttered. "I warned Louis. I told him that he was courting trouble to betray Seurat, but he would not listen to me."

Philippe's hand dropped as he frowned in sudden confusion. "Betray Seurat? What the hell are you rambling about?"

Clearly shaken, Mirabeau returned to his chair and dropped onto the cushions.

"We were in Egypt."

"Who?"

"Your father and I." He shrugged. "I believe that Stafford was there, as well. And, of course, the ridiculous army of servants you must hire when you travel through the desert."

Philippe returned to the desk to pour himself a measure of the cognac. He had a sense that he was going to have need of the potent spirit before the interview was done.

"Do you speak of the occasion when my father discovered the Egyptian tomb?" he demanded as he returned to stand before the seated gentleman.

"Oui."

"And Seurat was there, as well?"

"Your father had hired him as a guide. He was French but he had lived in Egypt for years." Mirabeau gave a short, humorless laugh. "We were warned that he was…unstable, but he was reputed to be the best guide in the entire country."

"And my father would demand the best," Philippe said dryly. At least Louis would demand the best so long as Philippe was footing the bill.

"As you say," Mirabeau agreed.

"I presume that you managed to find your way through the desert?"

"We made camp in sight of the pyramids. Your father suspected that there were many more tombs spread beneath the endless sea of sand. And he was right."

"You found the tombs?"

He shrugged. "A few, but they had all been disturbed centuries before."

"Grave robbers?"

Mirabeau gave a sharp nod. "In most cases we found nothing more than scattered bones and broken pottery. Certainly not the rich bounty we had been hoping for."

Philippe smiled wryly. "Nor the glory my father so desires."

"Precisely."

There was a brief silence as Philippe mulled over the grudging confession. He was far more interested in what Mirabeau was attempting to avoid revealing than what he was saying.

"Obviously you did at last discover a tomb that could offer a bounty beyond your dreams," he said. Even he could rarely view his father's Egyptian collection without catching his breath in wonder.

It was more than the golden relics and gem-encrusted jewelry. There was quite simply an ageless beauty to be discovered among the statues and vases and exotically decorated sarcophagi.

"In a manner of speaking," Mirabeau said vaguely.

Philippe hissed out an impatient breath. He did not have the time for this nonsense.

"Enough of your hedging. Simply tell me what happened," he commanded.

The pale eyes flashed with annoyance at Philippe's biting tone, but thankfully he seemed to realize that he would eventually have to admit the truth of what had occurred in the desert of Egypt.

"Your father was becoming infuriated by our lack of success. He had devoted all his resources to this trip and he swore he would not return without something to show for his investment," he muttered. "That was when he began to notice that Seurat was sneaking away from the camp late at night and not returning until early the next morning."

"Did my father confront him?"

"*Non.* He suspected that Seurat was performing his own dig. And that the servant had managed to stumble over a find."

Philippe stilled, his instincts tingling as he realized he was about to learn the truth his father had kept long hidden.

"One far richer than your own?"

Mirabeau released a soft sigh. "It was…astonishing. I have never seen such treasures. A prince's tomb entirely intact. You cannot imagine how rare and wonderful that is."

"Wonderful enough to steal it from Seurat?"

With an effort Mirabeau struggled from the chair, his face flushed with outrage. "It was not stealing. Seurat was a paid servant who was there to be our guide. He should have come to us the moment he suspected he had uncovered a tomb. That was his duty."

Philippe heard Raine gasp behind him, but he never allowed his gaze to shift from Mirabeau. He had always suspected there had been some nefarious dealings during his father's trip to Egypt. Not only had Louis been strangely reluctant to speak of his spectacular discovery, but he kept his bounty under tight lock and key rather than flaunting it for all the world to see.

"And instead he intended to plunder the goods beneath your very noses?"

Mirabeau's flush darkened. "Ungrateful wretch."

"What did my father do?"

"What any gentleman would do. He claimed the find as his own and we divided the profits accordingly."

There was another strangled sound from Raine. She clearly did not appreciate the notion of *droit de signor.*

"And what was Seurat's profit?"

"The usual for a paid servant."

"No doubt Seurat was not entirely satisfied with his share?"

Mirabeau shuddered at the memory. "To be honest, the man was as mad as the locals had warned us. He tried to stab your father before we at last were forced to drive him from the camp." Another shudder racked the thin body. "Before he left he swore that he would see us all destroyed."

If Seurat was mad then it was the most dangerous sort of madness, Philippe acknowledged. He was willing to wait and plot for years before striking.

"You said that you have seen him in Paris?" he demanded abruptly.

Mirabeau gave a short nod. "*Oui.*"

"Do you know where he resides?"

"He moves and lives among the peasants." Mirabeau made a disgusted sound. "I have hired countless men to try to track him with no luck."

Philippe did not allow the words to disturb him. Mirabeau could hardly be expected to have experience in trailing a determined scoundrel. Philippe, on the other hand, possessed years of practice.

"Does he have any family?"

Mirabeau lifted a hand to run it wearily over his thinning hair. "I…do not know."

Philippe reluctantly accepted that the elderly gentleman was looking distinctly wilted. Clearly, his days of trotting about the world in the wake of Louis Gautier had taken their toll on the poor old sod.

"Is there anything else you can tell me of the man?" he asked as he motioned toward the silent Carlos.

Mirabeau rose to his feet and heaved a deep sigh. "Only that he will not be satisfied until we are all ruined."

"Thank you, *monsieur.*" Philippe shook the man's hand before stepping back. "Carlos will see that you are returned to your home."

"You will halt Seurat?" Mirabeau demanded, genuine fear laced through his voice. "You will ensure that we are safe?"

"I will do whatever necessary to find Seurat and put an end to his vengeance," Philippe swore softly.

A relieved smile touched the elder man's lips. "Bless you, my son. Bless you."

THE CARRIAGE WAS SHROUDED in silence as it wound its way through the frozen streets back to Montmartre.

Philippe was no doubt scheming the best means of tracking down his prey, Raine acknowledged. There was certainly a grim set to his countenance that warned his thoughts were not pleasant.

She, on the other hand, was pondering Monsieur Mirabeau's unexpected revelations.

Dear heavens. She had already suspected from Philippe's rare comments that Louis Gautier was a selfish and self-absorbed gentleman. Certainly he had readily handed the responsibility of his family over to his son while he indulged his obsession with his various collections. He did not even seem concerned for Jean-Pierre despite his dire predicament.

Still, it was shocking to realize how he had treated poor Seurat. Perhaps the servant had been wrong to seek out his own treasure while in the employ of Monsieur Gautier, but that surely did not give anyone the right to simply take it from him?

If nothing else he should have received the largest share of the bounty.

It was little wonder he had gone a bit mad.

The silence remained intact until the carriage slowed to traverse the steep, narrow streets of Montmartre. Shifting on the leather seat, Philippe turned to regard her with a searching gaze.

"You are very quiet, *querida*. What is going through that mind of yours?"

Raine hesitated for a long moment. She had come to

know Philippe well enough to realize that he was far too fond of considering his word as law. There were very few who were brave enough, or perhaps foolish enough, to dare imply he might be mistaken in any manner.

She was not, however, a woman who kept her opinions to herself. Not even when it obviously would be the wisest choice.

"Do you wish the truth?" she asked instead.

"I would not have asked if I did not wish the truth."

"Very well." She unconsciously squared her shoulders. "I was thinking that Seurat must be a lonely and sad man."

He was seated close enough that she could feel his large body stiffen. "He is clearly demented and a danger to others."

"You do not believe that he might have a legitimate reason for feeling betrayed by your family?" she demanded in low tones.

"He was being employed by my father when he stumbled across the tomb. As Mirabeau pointed out it, was within my father's right to claim it as his own."

His tone held that arrogant edge that made Raine grit her teeth. "Within his rights?"

"Yes."

"Which only means that your father possessed the wealth and power necessary to enforce his will," she muttered.

His smile was derisive. "That is the way it has been, and always will be."

Raine balled her hands in her lap. It was that or slapping the cold, aloof expression from Philippe's handsome face. There were times when he could be so blasted superior.

"But Seurat was the one to find the tomb."

"It was my father who financed the excavation. Anything discovered belonged to him."

"So because Seurat was a mere servant he was allowed nothing?"

A dangerous glitter darkened his green eyes. "He was no doubt paid for his services. He was a fool to expect more."

She gave a slow shake of her head. "Good God, Philippe, do you have compassion for no one?"

Without warning he reached out to jerk the bonnet from her head before his fingers were grasping her chin in a firm grip. He leaned close enough for her to feel the heat of his breath sweep over her lips.

"Certainly not for a man who has plotted revenge upon my family for years. A man who has schemed to have my brother hanging from the gallows."

Raine was forced to swallow the lump in her throat. She did not fear Philippe, but there was no mistaking the anger that smoldered just beneath his cold composure.

"I do not condone his…madness, but that does not mean he is undeserving of some pity," she managed to point out.

"Pity is a weakness that has never troubled me."

Well, that she easily believed. He had wrapped himself in an impervious cloak of icy indifference toward all but a handful of people he allowed himself to care about.

"Pity is not a weakness."

His lips twisted. "Tell me, Raine, when the magistrate eventually comes to haul your father to prison, will you feel pity for the man just attempting to do his job? Or will you shoot him in the heart?"

Her breath caught at his brutal question. She had laid herself open for the attack, but that did not stop her from flinching.

"I…do not know," she confessed in a husky voice. "I suppose I will always attempt to protect those I love."

"As will I," he said grimly.

She sucked in a deep breath. She could not explain why it was important to her that Philippe be swayed from his determination to destroy Seurat. The situation had nothing to do with her. But, something deep inside her wanted to reach past his brittle exterior to the vulnerable man beneath.

Her expression softened as she reached up to lightly touch his arm. "Philippe, has it occurred to you that if you could find Seurat and somehow offer him a portion of what he feels is due to him that he might willingly end his vengeance against your family? Would that not be preferable to be always fearing he is in the shadows stalking you?"

If anything his expression only hardened at her reasonable words. "When I am finished with Seurat, none of us will ever again have to worry about the bastard. That much I promise."

"But…"

"Enough, Raine," he rasped, a muscle twitching at the edge of his jaw. "I will deal with Seurat as I see fit. Do not presume to lecture me as if I am a child."

She pulled away from his lingering touch, her own temper flaring. "I hardly consider offering reasonable advice the same as lecturing."

"If I desired your advice I would ask for it, *querida*. That is certainly not the reason that I brought you to Paris."

A sharp, ridiculous pain raced through her. Why did she think that she could reason with this man? He obviously considered her opinion beneath his consideration.

"Of course not," she said bitterly. "I am merely the means for you to lure your prey. And of course, a convenient body in your bed."

A sense of prickling danger filled the carriage as he gave a short, humorless laugh.

"Not even a fool would ever consider you convenient."

Raine ignored the lethal softness of his tone and the relentless expression that tightened his features. She had been forcibly reminded of her shameful position in his life and she wanted to strike out at him. To punish him for not giving a bloody damn for her own feelings.

"Then release me," she charged. "I have served my purpose. Send me back to England and be done with it."

His green eyes flamed with an unfathomable emotion as his arms abruptly wrapped about her and he hauled her onto his lap.

Philippe felt his control snap as her words sent a flare of possessive fury raging through his body.

It was enough that she chided him as if he were a witless idiot. That she thought to badger him to feel sympathy for the man determined to destroy his family. But to actually demand that he release her...

"Never. You are mine, Raine. Nothing will change that."

Her mouth parted in protest, but Philippe swooped down to cover her lips in a possessive kiss. He wanted to brand her. To prove to her once and for all that there was no escape for either of them.

Sweeping his tongue into her mouth, he tasted her sweet freshness. *Meu Deus,* he needed to be inside her. He needed to have her spread beneath him so that he could claim her in the most primitive means of all.

With exquisite timing the carriage rolled to a halt in the gardens of his brother's cottage and, keeping Raine cradled to his chest, Philippe vaulted from the carriage and headed directly toward the kitchen door.

He ignored the raised brows of the elderly cook and housemaids that swiftly scurried out of his path. Unlike Raine he felt no need to hide their intimate liaison. Especially not from a handful of servants.

Using the servants' staircase, Philippe climbed to the upper floor that contained the rooms he shared with Raine. Once in the bedchamber, he kicked the door shut and slowly allowed her to slide to her feet.

Her dark eyes smoldered as she glared at him with an anger that matched his own.

"I am not a bundle of rubbish to be hauled about, sir," she stated, her cheeks flushed. "I am perfectly capable of walking where I wish to go."

"But you might not have wished to walk where *I* wanted you to go," he pointed out. "I have simply ensured there was no tedious argument."

Her chin tilted. "Only a bully must use his superior strength to win an argument."

His gaze blazed over her stiff body, lingering on the frantic pulse at the base of her throat. He had made love to her a dozen times over the past days. He had tasted every inch of her ivory skin, he had tutored her in pleasuring him with her hands and mouth, he had listened to her sweet cries of fulfillment as he plunged them both to climax.

He knew the curves of her body more intimately than his own.

This was the point that he began to find his lovers a bore. No matter how hot a passion might flame it was destined to burn out. Usually as fast as it had sparked.

He should be packing her bags and sending her on her way.

Instead his entire body was throbbing with a hunger that he was beginning to fear would never be assuaged by any other woman.

Hell and damnation.

Unable to stop himself, Philippe reached out with a slow, deliberate gesture. He held her gaze as he put his hands on her pretty Spenser and with a sharp motion ripped it open. The buttons popped loose and fell to the wooden floor.

Raine made a strangled noise as he pulled the ruined jacket from her body and then treated the pale ivory gown to the same savage treatment. The ripping of the fragile silk sounded unnaturally loud in the silent room. For a moment Raine remained frozen in shock and Philippe allowed his avid gaze to drink in the sight of her alabaster beauty.

So fragile. So perfect.

Then she was reaching out to smack his chest with a closed fist. "You demon. Have you gone mad?" she rasped.

He ignored her futile attack as his hands busily set about ridding her of the boned corset and thin chemise.

"If I have gone mad you've no one to blame but yourself," he drawled wickedly, his blood running hot as he regarded her dressed in nothing more than her stockings and dainty slippers. "You have bewitched me to the point that no other woman will satisfy me. Now you must bear the repercussions of your feminine wiles."

"You blame me for your outrageous behavior?" She glared at him, although Philippe did not miss the shiver that shook her body. Whatever this strange obsession, he was not alone in it. "Now I know you are out of your wits."

Philippe chuckled as his fingers blazed a trail down the delicate curve of her back. He could feel her flesh quiver beneath his bold exploration.

"And who else would I blame, *meu amor?*" he whispered close to her ear. "'Twas you that threw yourself in my path. You who tempted me with your sinful beauty. You who have inflamed my desires until they are like a sickness that I cannot cure."

"I have told you the cure." Her eyes flashing, she demanded, "Release me. Let me go."

"I possess the cure," he said just before he covered her mouth in a savage, biting kiss.

Raine flinched in surprise at his punishing onslaught, but she made no effort to pull away. Instead her fingers curled into the lapels of his jacket as if to keep herself upright.

Philippe splayed his hand at the curve of her back to press her against the throbbing hardness of his erection while his other hand cupped the back of her head as he devoured her mouth with the hunger that raged through him.

"Philippe," she whispered in surprise as he suddenly swung her into his arms, and carried her to the nearby bed.

"Shh." He put her down on the bed, the pale sunlight angling across her body as he wrestled his way out of his clothes. "I need to be within you."

She watched him with darkened eyes, her hair tumbled from its tidy knot to spread across the crisp white pillow. He gave a low groan as he moved to cover her body with his.

He knew that a part of her continued to resent her captivity at his hands. Her independent spirit would always rebel at the least touch of the leash. And yet, she belonged to him. Every last satin inch of her.

"So soft," he muttered. "So sweet."

He brushed his fingers across her small breasts and felt her nipples harden in response. She answered his touch with a readiness that clouded his mind with urgent need.

She moaned and lifted her hands to roughly shove them into his hair. He kissed her, feeling her lips tremble and then finally part in capitulation.

Philippe wanted more. Needed more. With a wild heat he framed her face as he kissed her with a gentle ravishment. He stroked his tongue deep into her mouth, he nipped at her lips, he muttered rough demands that made her quiver beneath him.

He felt her yielding as she roughly kissed him back and arched her body in silent demand. He gave a low growl as his lips explored her female temptation. Her breasts and the puckered tips of her nipples. She squirmed beneath his relentless quest, her fingers clutching at his hair as his mouth skimmed over her slender belly.

Philippe chuckled as he nuzzled the curve of her hip. He had made love to her in every position imaginable, and yet she remained oddly shy when he wished to pleasure her in such an intimate manner.

"Open for me," he whispered.

"No…Philippe."

"Open, *meu amor.* I want to taste you."

With a relentless pressure he pulled her thighs apart, ignoring the sharp tugs on his hair as he pressed his mouth against her. Dragging his tongue through the honey-sweetness he teased and stroked with a practiced skill.

Just for a moment she battled against the pleasure coursing through her body. Then with a moan her hips lifted to press against his tormenting mouth. He waited until her breath was coming in soft pants before he slid back up her body. Covering her lips in a fierce kiss, he tilted his hips and entered her with a sharp thrust.

His fingers threaded through her satin curls as he pumped again and again, his ragged breathing echoing through the room until he at last felt the small pulses of her release that massaged his thick shaft. With a grunt of satisfaction he plunged into her one last time and poured his pleasure into her throbbing body.

CHAPTER FOURTEEN

SHADOWS HAD BEGUN TO ENTER the bedchamber when Raine stirred from her sleep. With her eyes still closed she absorbed the feel of Philippe cradled close behind her, his arm curved over her waist and his hand cupping her breast with a possessive grasp. Even more shocking, she realized that his flesh was still deeply embedded within her.

Sensing the moment she awakened, Philippe shifted to trail his lips over the curve of her shoulder. His fingers toyed with her breast until her nipple was hard.

She wanted to protest. What sort of woman so eagerly responded to the touch of a man holding her captive? A man who saw her as nothing more than an object?

Unfortunately her body refused to listen to the voice of caution that warned she was courting disaster. Instead her eyes slid closed in aching need as he slowly began to rock himself inside her, his hand slipping down the length of her body to stroke the tiny nub of her pleasure.

He whispered soft words in her ear, refusing to increase his slow steady pace until her entire body cried out for the fulfillment he promised.

"Philippe," she rasped, her fingernails digging into his forearm as he tormented her. "Please."

"Do you want me, *meu amor?*" he demanded. She remained stubbornly silent and he gave the lobe of her ear a sharp nip even as he halted his delicious thrusts. "Say it, Raine. Tell me you want me."

She nearly screamed in frustration. He had taken her freedom, her body and an increasingly dangerous part of her heart. Did he have to take her pride, as well?

It seemed that he did as he continued to hold himself still within her.

"Damn you," she muttered. "Yes."

"Say the words, *meu amor.* I want to hear them on your lips."

"I want you," she breathed, the words so low that they barely stirred the air.

Philippe moaned as he buried his face in the curve of her neck and began to drive himself into her with a raw, powerful force that had her swiftly arching in a shattering explosion.

She sighed deeply as he gently pulled from her, and then with a gentle care turned her onto her back so he could study her with his thoughtful gaze.

"I will never have enough of you," he murmured softly. "Never."

Raine ignored the treacherous warmth that flooded her heart. For the moment he was obsessed with her body. Why that should be so she hadn't the faintest clue. But she did know that sooner or later he would tire of her. It was as inevitable as the sun rising. She would be the worst sort of fool to believe he could truly desire her to remain at his side.

Opening her mouth to offer a pert retort, Raine was halted by the embarrassing sound of her stomach rumbling in hunger.

A blush touched her cheeks as Philippe chuckled and stroked a familiar hand over her belly.

"I see that I have not yet managed to sate all of your hungers, you greedy angel," he said as he brushed a kiss over her forehead.

"You were the one to keep me from my luncheon," she reminded him in tart tones.

His smile was smug, not at all repentant for having kept her in bed half the day.

"So I did. Something easily rectified." He rolled off the bed and reached for his robe. "Remain here and I shall return in a moment."

Raine lay back on the pillows, watching as he tied the robe and moved with predatory grace toward the door.

He was a wondrous creature. A lion that stalked through the world and took what he wanted with a ferocious will. And for now he wanted her.

Bloody hell, her entire body still tingled with the force and pleasure of his touch. She always felt sated when she left his arms. But today, there had been a raw edge of savagery in his lovemaking that left her feeling oddly disoriented.

It was as if he had been determined to…what? To prove to both of them that she did belong to him? To ensure that she would never be able to forget his touch? To steal what was left of her battered heart?

What the devil did he want from her?

PHILIPPE HAD FILLED A TRAY with delicately roasted pheasant, broiled potatoes, peas in a cream sauce and a delicate pudding that was Raine's favorite.

Returning to the bedchamber, he set the tray next to Raine and settled on the bed to watch her eat with a strange sensation in the pit of his stomach.

He had a dozen tasks that needed his attention. Not the least of which was meeting Carlos, who no doubt was already awaiting him in the garden. But still he lingered, his gaze watching her every delicate movement, his senses drinking in the scent and feel of her.

It was ridiculous. Absurd.

His lust was sated, his body pleasantly weary from the

force of his climaxes. And yet still, there was a part of him that felt restless, unsatisfied. As if he were seeking something from this woman that he could not name.

At last he forced his lethargic muscles to stir, and he pulled on a pair of dark breeches and a rough wool coat that was more suited to a dockhand than a gentleman of means.

Setting aside the empty tray, Raine lay back on the pillows and watched him with those beautiful dark eyes. "Where are you going?"

Philippe's groin tightened as his gaze swept over the fragile ivory features and the glossy amber curls spread across the pillows. The urge to rip off his clothes and return to the soft delight of her arms raged through him.

Meu Deus. The woman had cast a spell over him. That could be the only reasonable explanation.

"I do have duties that cannot be fulfilled by lying in bed with you, *menina pequena,*" he said harshly. More for his own sake than hers. He was beginning to fear that he could forget everything—his responsibilities, his family, even his precious vineyards—to be with this tiny slip of a girl.

She flinched at his words, even as her chin predictably tilted in a blunt challenge.

"Go then, sir. Go and do not return. It matters not to me."

His anger fled as swiftly as it had risen, and with a self-mocking shake of his head Philippe moved to plant a fleeting kiss on her delectable lips.

"Seurat will have heard that I arrived in Paris by now, and unless he is considerably more stupid than I suspect, he will have managed to discover I am staying at this cottage."

She frowned. "You think he will come here?"

"Not directly, but I do not doubt he has been sniffing around in the hopes of learning if I am a danger to his nefarious plans." A cold smile touched his mouth. "I had Carlos hire a number of young lads to keep an eye on the cottage from a distance and come to him if they noted any strangers lurking about the place."

"And did they?"

"He left a message waiting for me in the kitchen."

Her frown deepened. "What do you intend to do?"

"That depends on what information Carlos has for me. I shall hopefully return before dawn."

With one last kiss Philippe left the bedchamber and headed out of the cottage to cross the garden.

Dusk had already arrived, bringing with it an icy chill that sent the few citizens scurrying down the streets to the comfort of waiting fires. Philippe ignored the cold as he entered the cramped stables and waited for Carlos to detach himself from the shadows.

His friend was wearing the same rough clothing as himself, with the addition of a woolen cloak that he kept pulled around his large body as he glared at Philippe.

"Damn, I thought you intended to keep me waiting in this frozen garden for the entire night," he groused.

Philippe shrugged. "I received your message only a short time ago."

"And were obviously in no hurry to answer my summons." Carlos studied him with a sardonic gaze. "Since when do you allow yourself to be distracted from your goal by a quick tumble?"

"Take care, Carlos. No one is allowed to show Miss Wimbourne disrespect."

"What do you care? She is nothing more than a…"

With a blur of movement, Philippe had crossed the short distance and had his friend backed to the wall.

"I will not warn you again."

"Be at ease, Philippe." Carlos held his hands up in a gesture of peace, his eyes narrowed. "I am merely curious as to why this woman is so different than the others."

Well, that was the question, was it not? Thankfully it was a question that he refused to contemplate at the moment.

"That is none of your concern," he muttered.

Carlos gave a lift of his brows. "If you say so."

Philippe grimaced as he stepped back and realized just how close he had come to planting his fist in his friend's face. *Meu Deus,* he was truly losing his mind.

"Tell me what you discovered," he demanded. "Was Seurat seen?"

"Yes, but the man is surprisingly cunning."

"What do you mean?"

"He disguised himself as an elderly priest who seemed to be wandering aimlessly through the village. If the lads had not been watching for him he would easily have escaped notice."

"Did you manage to catch sight of him?" Philippe demanded, wanting more than the word of a handful of boys who were anxious to be paid for their work.

"*Sim.* He hid behind the stables for nearly two hours before he at last slipped away."

"Would you recognize him again?"

Carlos shrugged. "It would be difficult. He managed to keep his hat pulled low and most of his face was covered by a thick scarf. I can say little more than that he was a small man with a faint limp."

Philippe did not miss the hint of smugness in his friend's countenance. The man may not be able to recognize Seurat, but he did know something.

"What else did you discover?" he demanded.

"I followed him to Saint-Marcel. He must have rooms in the neighborhood."

A flare of satisfaction raced through Philippe. He could always depend upon Carlos. No matter what he might ask of him.

"Saint-Marcel," he said softly. "A nasty place."

Carlos gave a slow nod, his expression somber. "Even nastier than usual. The mobs are growing restless and discontent beneath their new king. It is only a matter of time before the city erupts into riots."

Philippe grimaced. He had sensed the same dark pulse that throbbed beneath the frantic gaiety of the streets. Despite the revolution and efforts to halt corruption, the disparity between the wealthy and masses of poor and immigrants remained unaltered.

For the moment the soldiers managed to keep the peace, but it would take only a spark to kindle the waiting bonfire.

"I intend to be far away by then. After I am gone they can tear the bloody city to the ground stone by stone as far as I am concerned." Moving toward the horses that Carlos already had saddled, he vaulted on top of the black stallion. "Show me where you last had sight of Seurat."

Carlos readily mounted his own horse and glanced toward Philippe. "Are we going alone?"

Philippe took a moment before giving a decisive nod of his head. "Yes. We do not want to startle him into flight. If we are careful I can have my hands around his throat before he ever realizes we are near."

"Do not forget we desire him alive," Carlos warned.

"Only until my brother is free. After that the man will learn what it is to threaten a Gautier. Let us go."

AS USUAL THE STREETS OF Paris were clogged with pleasure-seekers strolling past the crowded cafés, the arcades and the theaters. The air was filled with the sound of their chatter and the incessant calls of the street vendors.

And that was not all the air was filled with, Philippe acknowledged as he wrinkled his nose at the pervasive smells of food and sewage and decay that were rampant in any vast city.

It was little wonder that he far preferred his pristine estate on the cliffs of Madeira.

A sense of longing for the untamed beauty of his home washed through Philippe. What would Raine think of the rolling hills that were covered with his vineyards? Or the tiny villages where the fishermen anchored their small boats and their wives waited on the shores for their return?

Would she be bored by the solitude as his father and brother were? Or would she sense the subtle charm that had enchanted him since he was a child?

"Philippe, you might wish to take heed." Carlos abruptly broke into his musings, his voice dry. "This place is seething with pickpockets and cutthroats. You will not do Jean-Pierre much good if you end up floating in the Seine."

Philippe stiffened as he realized that he had, indeed, been careless. Even a moment of inattention in such a neighborhood could lead to disaster.

Still, he was not about to admit as much to his friend. Not when Carlos was bound to suspect that his thoughts had once again been consumed with Raine Wimbourne.

"I have traveled such streets before, Carlos."

His friend's dark eyes smoldered with a wicked amusement. "*Sim,* but never when your thoughts seem to be so… distracted."

"You do enjoy living dangerously, *amigo.*"

"What other way is there to live?"

Philippe gave a rueful chuckle as he slowed his mount. "Are we near?"

"He disappeared two streets down. There was a narrow alley that he entered."

They continued down the dark street at a cautious pace,

Philippe vibrantly aware of the numerous whores and thieves who watched them with a desperate hunger. If he and Carlos did not look like they might kill anyone foolish enough to approach them, he did not doubt that they would already be dead in the gutter.

"It is a wonder that Seurat has not had his throat slit living in such a neighborhood," he muttered, unable to conceive how a small, lame man could have survived even a day.

Carlos shrugged, his gaze carefully shifting for the least hint of danger. "Even the most hardened criminals tend to fear madmen. They are too unpredictable."

"He cannot be entirely mad," Philippe pointed out. "He has managed to concoct a devilish trap for my brother, not to mention terrifying poor Mirabeau until he is near a collapse."

"Not all those who are insane chew on the carpeting and crow at the sunrise. There are many who possess remarkable intelligence."

Philippe had to grudgingly agree. History was littered with brilliant madmen. Some who had occasionally ruled the world.

Still, Seurat was no demented genius. He was a pathetic worm who had allowed his obsession with revenge to lead him to his own downfall.

"Is this the alley?" he demanded as he brought his mount to a halt.

"*Sim.*" Carlos began to urge his horse into the narrow path, only to give a grunt of surprise when Philippe reached out to grasp his reins. "What the…?"

"I do not like this," Philippe said softly, his eyes searching the dark shadows. There was an unmistakable prickling that crawled over his skin. It was a sensation that had warned him of danger on more occasions than he could recall.

Carlos smoothly reached beneath his coat to withdraw a small pistol. "Did you see something?"

"No." Philippe reached for his own weapon. "But it is too quiet. Every alley we have passed has been filled with whores and drunken peasants. Why would this one be empty?"

"You are right," Carlos breathed. "It is a trap."

Philippe had already begun to turn his horse away when there was a bright flash and then a deafening sound of an explosion from the darkness. A gunshot, he realized just as something slammed into his arm and sent him tumbling from his stallion.

Hell and damnation, he had been hit.

It was his last thought as his skull connected with the filthy pavement and blackness engulfed his mind.

CHAPTER FIFTEEN

RAINE WAS DRYING HER HAIR by the fire in her chamber when the sound of footsteps and muffled voices had her rising to her feet. A small trickle of unease inched down her spine as she moved to open the door that connected her room with Philippe's.

Philippe was a gentleman who moved with a careful, calculated grace. Indeed, there had been several occasions that he had managed to slip up on her without a sound. He would never enter the house with such noise unless there was something wrong.

As she entering the master bedchamber, her unease became sharp disbelief as she watched Carlos carry in an unconscious Philippe and lay him on the bed. The rotund housekeeper, Madame LaSalle, was muttering beneath her breath as she turned to make her way from the room.

With a swift motion, Raine had moved to lightly grasp the servant's arm. "What has happened?"

The older woman gave a click of her tongue. "Monsieur Gautier has been shot. I must fetch hot water and towels at once."

Shot? Raine barely noticed as the housekeeper scurried to the door, her own feet carrying her toward the bed. Halting next to Carlos, she gazed down at Philippe, her heart freezing in horror as she caught sight of the dark blood spattered over his pale cheek and staining his jacket.

"Philippe," she whispered softly, her hand reaching out to touch the tousled dark curls. "Good Lord."

"Does anyone in this household ever sleep?" Carlos muttered as he firmly moved Raine back from the bed and set about cutting the thick jacket from the motionless Philippe.

She licked her dry lips as she pressed a hand to her stomach. "Is he…?"

"Dead? No, he will live." With a ruthless efficiency he had cut through the fabric of the jacket and the linen shirt beneath to expose an ugly wound on Philippe's upper arm. "The bullet passed cleanly."

Raine battled her instinctive flare of panic at the sight of the torn flesh. Instead she forced her gaze to move to Philippe's pale, lifeless countenance.

"Then why is he not awake?" she demanded.

"He fell from his horse when he was shot and hit his head on the pavement."

"We must send for a doctor."

"There is no need, *anjo*." Carlos turned his head to flash a wry smile. "His thick skull has taken worse blows than this and he survived with his wits intact. Besides, it will be a blessing if he remains unconscious until I am done cleaning the wound."

Raine bit her lip as she wrapped her arms about her waist. "How did this happen?"

Carlos shrugged. "We were following the trail of Seurat. Regrettably he was one step ahead of us yet again."

A surprising anger flooded through Raine. Was there ever a man born who did not believe that he was utterly impervious to danger?

First her father. And now Philippe. Really, it was enough to make any sensible woman long to slap some sense into them.

"The fool," she muttered. "The stubborn, idiotic fool."

Carlos did not bother to argue as he pressed a clean hand-kerchief to the wound. Raine watched him in silence until at last Madame LaSalle returned with a heavy tray that she placed on the table next to the bed.

"Here we are." She straightened and struggled to catch her breath. "Hot water, towels and a bottle of brandy. And I am making a nice, rich broth for when the *monsieur* awakens."

Carlos ignored the servant as he reached for the brandy and poured a large measure into the wound. Raine winced in sympathy despite the fact that Philippe did not so much as twitch beneath the rough treatment, and she turned her attention to the woman silently inching her way toward the door.

"Thank you, Madame LaSalle," she said with a smile. "You have been very kind."

The round face flushed with pleasure at Raine's soft words. Raine had swiftly discovered that the housekeeper, despite her rather prickly nature, possessed a tender heart and a motherly ferocity when it came to protecting the young maids in her care.

She also possessed a girlish delight in the least display of appreciation for her services.

"Oh, it is nothing." She reached out a plump hand to pat Raine's cheek. "Now, you don't be wearing yourself to the bone; there is barely enough of you as it is. If you need some-one to sit with the master, you call for one of the maids."

"Yes, I will," Raine promised.

"And leave that tray where it is," she sternly commanded. "I will collect it in the morning."

Raine watched as the woman left the room,, before return-ing to stand beside the bed. Thankfully Carlos had finished cleaning the wound and was wrapping a linen bandage around Philippe's arm.

Keeping his gaze on his task, the handsome devil allowed a faint smile to curve his lips.

"You seem to have made a staunch friend in the old tartar."

Raine stiffened. "And why should I not? She happens to be a lovely woman."

His smile widened at her prickly tone. "And what of the maids? Are they lovely, as well?"

"They are good girls who work hard to help their families survive."

"Ah." He finished his bandaging and turned his unnervingly perceptive gaze in her direction. "Is that why you were in the kitchen this morning helping them learn to read?"

Raine felt a blush staining her cheeks. "What do you care if I happen to enjoy the company of servants?"

Carlos tilted his head to one side, the firelight slanting over his dark skin and rich black hair. There was no doubt he possessed the sort of smoldering good looks that would make any woman a bit weak in the knees.

At the moment, however, Raine seemed to have her hands quite filled with handsome, arrogant, impossible men.

"I am just curious as to why you would have made an effort to befriend such women," he said. "Most ladies in your position consider servants beneath their notice."

"My position?" Raine gave a short, humorless laugh. "I am the daughter of a common sailor and currently living with a man who is not my husband."

He gave a lift of his dark brows, his expression thoughtful. "Your connection to Philippe could give you a great deal of power and position, *anjo,* if you would choose to grasp it."

"And what, pray tell, would I do with such nonsense in Knightsbridge?"

"You intend to remain forever in the tiny village?"

Raine abruptly turned from his relentless regard. She did not want him to see the discomfort that must be sketched across her face.

The truth was that she was stubbornly refusing to contemplate the future. However anxious she was to see her father and reassure him that she was not harmed, she had no notion what would happen when she returned to the small village. Would there be a scandal surrounding her sudden absence? Would she be shunned and treated as a harlot?

And more important, could she possibly bear to return to her dull, uneventful life?

"It is my home," she at last said with a small sigh.

"I do not doubt that Philippe will be very generous when you part," Carlos said softly. "You could live anywhere you choose."

Raine clenched her fists as she whirled back to glare at the odious man. Was he making a deliberate attempt to insult her?

"You think that I would take money from him?"

He studied her for a long moment. "Why should you not? He can easily afford to share."

"How dare you—"

Her angry words were broken off as Philippe stirred on the bed, his lashes lifting to reveal dazed green eyes.

"Carlos?" he called out.

Swiftly, Carlos was reaching to grasp Philippe's arm. There was no mistaking his concern.

"I am here, *amigo*."

"Seurat?"

"He managed to take a shot at you before disappearing into the shadows."

Philippe grimaced in frustration. "Hell and damnation."

"He will not get far," Carlos promised. "I will have the neighborhood watched night and day until we manage to capture him."

Philippe gave a pained nod, his lashes fluttering downward before he was visibly struggling against the clinging darkness.

"Raine..." he croaked.

Raine resisted the urge to toss herself forward. She did not want to feel this aching need to touch his damp countenance and offer him comfort. Not when it revealed the susceptibility of her heart.

Carlos placed a firm hand against Philippe's shoulder. "It is late, *amigo*. You need to rest."

"Why is she not here?" Philippe weakly struggled to lift himself from the pillows. "Where has she gone?"

"Philippe, you must remain still or you will open your wound."

"I need to find Raine. She cannot leave…"

"She is right here," Carlos soothed, turning to Raine with an impatient glare. "Come."

Still, Raine hesitated. For a change Philippe was in no position to force his will upon her. She was quite at liberty to return to her chambers and ignore his demands. It was a tempting thought, but even as it teased at her mind Philippe turned his head and captured her with pain-filled eyes.

"Raine?"

With a faint sigh at her own stupidity, Raine discovered her feet moving her forward. "I am here."

His hand shot out to grasp her fingers in a tight grip. "Where have you been?" he demanded with an edge of his customary arrogance. "Why are you not in bed?"

"You have been injured, Philippe," she said. "You must rest."

He gave a tug on her fingers. "I will rest as soon as you join me."

Good Lord, he was impossible even when he was hovering on the edge of unconsciousness. "Philippe, I will be right here."

"I want you next to me."

"For all your undoubted talents you are in no shape to have a beautiful woman in your bed," Carlos protested sternly. "Be content with your brandy until you have regained your strength."

"No."

"Philippe…"

Philippe gave his friend a steely glare. "She will leave. She will slip away while I am unable to stop her."

Carlos slid a dark glance toward the silent Raine. "I will not allow her to slip away, that I promise."

"You cannot halt her. Only I can."

"Good heavens, Philippe," Raine muttered. "Where the devil do you imagine I'll go?"

"Perhaps it would be best to humor him for the moment," Carlos unexpectedly commanded. "If you were to join him, then perhaps he would relax and cease his struggles."

As usual no one appeared to be the least interested in what she desired. If Philippe wanted her in bed then it was seemingly her duty to crawl in next to him.

"He is your friend, you join him," Raine snapped.

Carlos's lips twitched. "I somehow doubt that my presence would offer quite the comfort as your own."

About to respond, Raine was distracted by the feel of Philippe running a caressing thumb over her knuckles. She reluctantly turned her head to discover the injured man regarding her with a brooding expression.

"*Querida,* I merely want you near. Is that so much to ask?"

Their gazes battled for a silent moment and then Raine heaved a deep sigh. Bloody hell. The night was bound to be a long and painful one for Philippe, and if he continued to thrash about he might very well bring on an infection. Goodness only knew how long they would be trapped in Paris if that occurred.

Surely it was only sensible to give in to his wishes and be done with it?

"Fine," she muttered, climbing onto the bed and allowing Philippe to tug her close to his side. She glared up at Carlos, who was regarding them with an enigmatic smile on his lips. "Satisfied now?"

His dark eyes flared over her slender frame. "I could be more satisfied," he murmured.

There was a low sound from Philippe. "Go get some sleep, Carlos," he ordered. "Tomorrow we return to our search for Seurat."

Carlos studied Raine for a moment before he gave a mocking dip of his head and left the room.

Once alone, Philippe shifted until he had his good arm beneath Raine's shoulders and her head tucked beneath his chin.

"Do not think to bewitch Carlos, *meu amor,*" he whispered softly. "No man shall ever have you but me."

PHILIPPE WAS STILL DEEPLY asleep when Raine awoke the next morning. A mere glance was enough to assure her that his face was not flushed with fever and that the bleeding had stopped.

With care not to disturb him, she slipped from his clinging arms and returned to her own chambers. A half an hour later, she was scrubbed clean and attired in a pale lemon gown with matching ribbons threaded through her curls.

Leaving her room, Raine ignored the nagging urge to return to Philippe. She was not about to hover over him, wringing her hands like some besotted fool. Philippe, not to mention the entire household, was bound to jump to the conclusion that she actually cared if he lived or died. It was horrible enough to secretly accept that she did.

Instead she firmly headed down to the kitchen, and seating herself at the table, she accepted the hot, buttered croissants that Madame LaSalle placed before her.

"How is the *monsieur* on this morning?" the housekeeper inquired in her halting English. Although Raine spoke perfect French, the older woman was anxious to improve her accent.

"He is still sleeping at the moment, but I believe he is healing." Raine nibbled at a croissant. "No doubt when he awakens he will be prepared for some of your excellent chicken broth."

"You are a good girl." The servant patted Raine's cheek before moving to begin kneading a large mound of dough. "I must say that I do not like this shooting of the *monsieur*. It is not so good."

Raine grimaced. "No, I am not fond of it myself."

"Why should he be in such a nasty neighborhood? There is nothing to be found there but unfortunate souls who delight in trouble." She gave a shake of her head. "Monsieur must be a man who seeks out the danger, *non?*"

Raine suspected that Philippe's fascination for danger went well beyond Seurat and nasty neighborhoods. He possessed the sort of skills that suggested he was either a master criminal, or an agent for some government.

"Yes, I do believe that he must enjoy a certain amount of danger."

"So different from his brother." Madame LaSalle heaved a sigh as she sprinkled flour on the dough. "A pity."

Raine pushed aside her plate. Ah, an opportunity to learn more about Philippe and his family. It would be intriguing to know precisely what others thought of them.

"You know Jean-Pierre well?" she asked casually.

A sudden smile curved the servant's lips. Clearly, Jean-Pierre was a favorite of hers.

"But of course. He often comes to stay. He—" she struggled to translate her words "—how do you say—gathers the art?"

"He is an art collector," Raine helpfully supplied.

"That is it. He comes to Paris and buys such lovely pictures and things. Always such exquisite taste."

Raine hid her grimace. She had seen enough of Jean-Pierre's art collection around the cottage to suspect he possessed more enthusiasm than actual skill in choosing his art.

"Well, I do not doubt that it is at least expensive taste," she muttered.

Madame LaSalle turned to regard Raine with pinched lips. Her loyalty to Jean-Pierre clearly made her blind to his faults.

"Such things are always expensive."

"Yes, they are. Which makes it an odd choice of a career for a second son."

"I do not understand."

Raine shrugged. "As we have both agreed it is ghastly expensive to collect art. It would seem that Jean-Pierre would be better served to have chosen a career in the church or the military that would allow him a measure of independence from his family."

The servant appeared horrified by the mere thought of her beloved Jean-Pierre soiling his hands with good, honest work.

"Monsieur Gautier would never be happy in such employment. He is a man who is meant to be surrounded by beauty."

Raine gave a faint shake of her head. Good Lord. Philippe had not exaggerated the burdens that he was forced to bear. A mother dead when he was just a babe, an unscrupulous father who had all but abandoned him and a charming rapscallion of a brother. It was a wonder he had not long ago washed his hands of his family.

"So long as he need not concern himself with providing the funds to support such beauty," she pointed out.

"Why should he?" Madame LaSalle shrugged. "His brother is a wealthy man, *non?*"

Raine bit back her sharp words. Philippe had seemingly accepted the burden of caring for his family. It was not her place to protest Jean-Pierre's lack of responsibility.

"Jean-Pierre travels here often?" she instead demanded.

Madame LaSalle returned to her kneading. "Not so often as we would wish. Such an elegant man. So charming and kind to the servants. And such a favorite of the ladies. He is a true Frenchman."

Not overly impressed with the seeming qualities of a true Frenchman, Raine was suddenly distracted by a loud thump that came from above. With a jerky motion she was on her feet and heading toward the door.

"Bloody hell, someone should take a horsewhip to that stubborn fool." She stomped up the stairs and shoved open the door. Philippe was seated on the edge of the bed fully dressed except for the boots he was struggling to pull on with only one hand. "Whatever are you doing?"

He sent her a dry smile. "I am attempting to put on my boots. Unfortunately I do not appear to be having much success."

Raine gave a shake of her head. Although he had somehow managed to comb his hair and even shave, there was a pallor to his skin and dark circles beneath his eyes. He was still in pain and weakened from his wound, even if he was too much of an idiot to admit it.

"Which would be a rather obvious indication that you are not recovered enough to be putting on your boots," she said tartly.

"All I need is a bit of assistance." He continued with his tugging on the boot. "Where is Carlos?"

"Philippe, you cannot be serious." Without thinking, she moved to stand directly before him. "You must stay in bed."

He lifted his head to reveal a wicked smile, his hand running an intimate caress along the line of her hip.

"A tempting offer, *meu amor,* and one that I will be more than willing to accept once I have Seurat in my grasp."

She hastily stepped back, her skin tingling from the heat of his hand. How the devil did he manage to stir her senses with the merest touch?

"You cannot even put on your boots, how do you intend to travel to Paris and capture Seurat?"

A determination settled on his pale features as he grimly set about wrestling his boots onto his feet. Then, smoothly rising, he backed her to the wall. He planted his hands on either side of her shoulders and allowed his body to lean heavily against hers.

"One day, Raine, you will realize that it is a mistake to underestimate me," he murmured.

Raine swallowed the sudden lump in her throat as she glared into his mocking eyes. Her heart was pounding and her knees were weak, but she was not about to give him the pleasure of revealing her reaction to his proximity. He was quite arrogant enough.

"Fine. Dash about Paris all you desire. But when you become ill do not expect me to tend to you."

"Of course you will tend to me." He smiled as his hand trailed over the curve of her cheek. "You are far too tenderhearted to allow anyone to suffer, no matter how much they might deserve such a fate."

"You think you know me so well?"

"Not nearly as well as I intend to, *meu amor*." He studied her with a brooding gaze. "You withhold far too much of yourself from me, but eventually I will wear down your barriers. I intend to have all of you."

The lump in her throat seemed to double in size. "Why?"

"Why?"

"You have me in your bed. What more do you want?"

"Everything." His head lowered to scatter tiny kisses over her upturned face. "Your body…your heart…your soul."

A cold chill inched down Raine's spine. This man had already taken far too much from her. Any more and he would surely destroy her.

"No," she breathed in denial.

"Yes." His tone was fierce as he abruptly cradled her face in his hands and glared into her wide eyes. "Every silken, beautiful, irritating inch of you will be mine."

"Until you decide to toss me aside."

"Is that what troubles you? Do you wish me to promise I will keep you always?"

Her heart gave a sharp, uncomfortable jerk before she was steeling herself against his potent appeal.

"You must have been wounded more grievously than I feared if you believe such nonsense," she accused. "For God's sake, the only reason I am here at all is because you threatened to harm my father. Or have you managed to forget your disgraceful part in this charade?"

"I have forgotten nothing." A smile slowly curved his lips. "Certainly not the manner in which you moan with pleasure in my arms, or how you whisper my name in your sleep."

Her breath caught in her throat. "I do not whisper your name in my sleep."

Philippe chuckled softly, his entire body aching with the need to finish what he had started. Unfortunately he had already wasted too much time. He could not risk Seurat slipping away before he could capture him.

"Do not worry, *meu amor*," he whispered in her ear, "so long as it is my name you are whispering you have nothing to fear."

She opened her lips to offer a cutting reply and he effectively silenced her with a deep, possessive kiss. His hands tightened on her face before he forced himself to reluctantly step away.

Once he had ended the threat to his brother, he could devote his entire attention to Raine. Until then he could not allow himself to become distracted from his duty.

Unable to resist one last light kiss on her lips, Philippe turned to gather his coat and gloves before leaving the room and making his way from the cottage. His arm ached and he suspected that it would not be long before his strength gave out. He could only hope that Seurat would be considerate enough to remain waiting in the alley to be captured.

Gathering his horse from the stables, Philippe headed for Paris, shivering as he was forced to slow his mount to a careful trot. The drizzling rain from the night before had frozen to leave the streets slick with ice. His arm was painful enough. He didn't need a broken neck.

The trip was cold and tedious and more than once he damned himself for not having remained tucked in his bed with Raine in his arms. Seurat was going to pay for every frustrating moment Philippe spent looking for him rather than enjoying the pleasures of his mistress.

Despite the inhospitable weather the streets of Paris were clogged with traffic. There was the usual clutter of public cabriolets, gentlemen heading toward the gambling houses, ladies intent on reaching the Arcades, and the King's Guard, which made a show of protecting the local citizens.

Philippe was cursing beneath his breath before he at last managed to locate the filthy alley where they had last seen Seurat. Perhaps unfairly, his foul mood was not noticeably improved when Carlos appeared from the shadows.

The younger man was attired in his usual rough woolen clothing with a cap pulled low on his head. He was also looking annoyingly hale and hearty, Philippe noted as he dismounted and struggled to keep his knees from buckling.

"I should have known you would not have the sense to remain in bed," Carlos said.

Philippe deliberately met his dark gaze. He may have been disoriented and less than lucid last eve, but he had not forgotten Carlos's overly familiar manner toward Raine.

"Actually, the notion did cross my mind," he drawled, his

lips curling into a sardonic smile. "My bed seemed uncommonly comfortable this morning."

"I would imagine any bed would be uncommonly comfortable with Raine in it," Carlos retorted, his arms folded over his chest.

Philippe clenched his hands at his sides. For a moment their gazes silently battled.

"You tread dangerous ground, *amigo*," he warned softly.

Carlos shrugged. "I am not blind. She is a beautiful woman."

"She is mine."

"For the moment."

Philippe had never been a jealous or possessive man, but there was no mistaking the searing fury that raced through his blood. Carlos might be a brother to him, but he would beat the hell out of him if he did not retreat.

"This is no game, Carlos." His voice was low and lethal. "I will kill any man who touches her."

Carlos leaned negligently against the side of the building, his expression indifferent.

"You know that you cannot threaten me, Philippe. I shall always do what I desire."

"And what do you desire?"

The dark gaze momentarily shifted to the pathetic souls that struggled down the cramped street as Carlos considered his answer.

"I have become…fond of Raine. I would not stand aside and allow her to be harmed."

Philippe frowned at the unmistakable implication. "You think I intend to harm her?"

His friend's features hardened. "She is not like the other women you have seduced. She has not willingly traded her honor to acquire a wealthy protector."

Philippe clenched his teeth together. He needed no reminders that he had been forced to blackmail Raine into his bed. Or that his hold on her was tenuous at best.

"What is your point?"

"If you hope to keep her, you will have to win her heart."

Philippe gave a short, humorless laugh. The woman should already be desperately in love with him. He had swept her from the choking confines of her tedious village. He had draped her in satin and silk. He had tutored her in the arts of passion.

And, God knew that he had used every skill in his seduction arsenal to wring those sweet words from her lips.

What other innocent would still be battling against him?

"A task easier said than done," he rasped. "She continues to keep me at a distance."

"She does not trust you."

"And you believe that she trusts you? You did, after all, assist me in kidnapping her."

Carlos slowly smiled. "I have not yet forced her to my bed."

"Enough." Philippe grimly thrust aside his overwhelming urge to throttle his friend. For the moment he needed Carlos alive and well. "This discussion will be finished later. For now we will concentrate on Seurat. Have you managed to find his apartments?"

In the blink of an eye, Carlos had straightened and his expression was somber. Like Philippe, he possessed the ability to put aside all distractions when he was on the hunt.

"I have searched the buildings on either side of the alley, but there is no one willing to admit to knowing Seurat."

"Dammit." With an effort, Philippe moved down the narrow alley, his gaze flicking over the rubbish and filth. "He must have deliberately allowed himself to be seen near the cottage so that we would follow him into his trap."

"He is clever," Carlos grudgingly conceded. "And dangerous."

"He cannot hide forever." With a frown, Philippe bent down to study the ground, his fingers touching the rough ridge of the hoofprint that had been left in the frozen mud.

Carlos sensed his sudden tension and crouched beside him. "What is it?"

"How many of the local residents do you suppose possess horses?" Philippe demanded.

"Any horse in this neighborhood is in the cook pot."

"My thoughts exactly."

Carlos gave a lift of his brows. "Shall we follow the trail?"

Philippe straightened with a nod. "It seems the only course of action open to us at the moment."

In silence they gathered their mounts and carefully set about following the lone hoofprints left in the alley. It could very well be a wild-goose chase, but as Philippe had already noted they did not seem to have a large number of choices. For the moment Seurat had managed to slip back into the shadows.

They followed the northward trail through the back alleys, occasionally forced to halt and clear away rubbish before being able to continue on.

"It appears he spent some time here," Carlos murmured as they studied the trampled mud. "The question is why."

Philippe agreed. They were at the corner of a busy cross-road that catered to various hotels and lodging houses, some of which possessed the stables necessary for Seurat to keep his horse. Was he forced to halt here and hide? Was he waiting for someone?

The various notions floated through his mind as Philippe absently kicked aside the nasty rubbish that lined the nearby buildings. He was cold, weary, and plagued with a chafing need to return to Montmartre. Not just because he desired a hot bath and a few hours of rest, but because he wanted to see Raine.

It was ridiculous. He had left her only a few hours ago, but already he needed to assure himself that she was waiting for him at the cottage, where she belonged. And just as important, he needed to know that she was safe.

The nagging urge was as irritating as it was unexpected, but there was no denying it.

On the point of calling an end to the futile search, Philippe hesitated as the toe of his boot pushed aside a broken crate to reveal a black jacket. He bent down to inspect it more closely and saw a priest's collar hidden beneath it.

"This is intriguing," he murmured.

"That looks like the jacket Seurat was wearing when I caught sight of him," Carlos said with a frown. "But why would he leave his clothing here?"

Philippe considered for a long moment. "Perhaps he is well enough known in these streets that he could not risk being seen attired as a priest."

"Which would mean that he must be close." Carlos glanced about the surrounding streets before giving a rueful grimace. "Still, it will take days to search all the buildings. If Seurat possesses any wits at all, he will disappear before he can be cornered."

CHAPTER SIXTEEN

PHILIPPE COULDN'T ARGUE with Carlos's logic. There were far too many shabby apartments and hotel rooms to easily narrow their search. With only the two of them it would take forever.

With a sigh, Philippe leaned against a nearby building and absently rubbed his aching arm.

"We have a few acquaintances that can assist us," he said, his thoughts turning over his numerous contacts within the city. His years of espionage did have its benefits. "With some help we should be able to keep a careful watch on the neighborhood. If Seurat attempts to flee, he will be followed."

"We have only a vague description that could fit any number of gentlemen that live in this area. How will they possibly know if it is Seurat or not?"

"Do you have a better plan?" Philippe demanded dryly.

Carlos gave a shake of his head. "Not at the moment."

"Then let us find Belfleur." Philippe straightened from the wall and headed down the street. "He has an entire network of thugs and pickpockets that work these streets. They will be capable of determining the local citizens from the visitors."

It took only a few moments to press through the thick traffic toward the small shop tucked between a coffeehouse and a gambling club. Philippe left Carlos to keep an eye on their horses, as well as the passing crowds, as he stepped over the threshold.

The shop was filled with a strange jumble of items from lacy handkerchiefs to silver candlesticks to small pieces of jewelry locked behind glass cases. Belfleur insisted that they were all purchased from honest citizens who had fallen upon hard times, but there were few who did not know that most of his possessions came from his small army of thieves.

What most did *not* know was that Belfleur had been a guiding force in the rebellion against Napoléon's rule, and that he had often used his considerable resources to assist Philippe in gathering information on the lingering Bonapartists. Not that the short, pudgy man with a shock of silver hair allowed the least hint of recognition to touch his face as he hurried forward.

"Monsieur, welcome to my humble store," he purred with a deep bow. "Please tell me how I can be of service."

Philippe cast a rather contemptuous glance about the shop, noting the two ladies sorting through a basket of handkerchiefs and the younger gentleman who was clearly in Belfleur's employ.

"I seek a gift for a beautiful lady."

"Of course." Belfleur smiled as he rubbed his hands together. "We have many lovely items, as you can see."

"I am searching for something far more special than these triflings."

"Ah. A gentleman of discerning taste. I possess several items in the back that might capture your interest. If you will follow me?"

He waved a hand toward a curtain at the back of the room, covertly signaling to the younger man to keep an eye on the two other customers. In silence Philippe allowed himself to be herded through the curtain and down a short hall. Belfleur halted at a door and retrieved a key from his pocket. Together they entered the small room that held the more valuable jewels.

Absently, Philippe crossed to study the necklaces that were

laid out on the swath of black velvet. There was a delicate silver collar with diamond teardrops, a large square-cut ruby that was framed by tiny pearls and a pure amber pendant that dangled from a gold chain.

A small smile touched his lips as he was assaulted by the image of Raine lying on his bed draped in nothing more than the sparkling jewels.

Now that would be a sight worthy of a fortune.

There was the sound of a door shutting behind him and then the click of a lock. Philippe turned in time to discover Belfleur moving forward to slap him on the shoulder.

Although the man was attired in a tailored black jacket and crisp cravat, there was no mistaking the years he had spent on the streets as a common cutthroat. It was etched in his battered, scarred features and the shrewd hardness in his pale eyes.

"I had heard rumors you had made an appearance in Paris, but I could hardly believe them to be true. You usually have the sense to keep that ugly countenance of yours hidden."

Philippe smiled. For all his rough, and some would claim illicit, habits Belfleur was a man who possessed an unwavering loyalty to those he counted as his friends.

"On this occasion it suited my purpose to travel openly."

"Then this is not official business?"

"No, it is personal, but I hope that I can still count upon your assistance."

"But, of course." The shaggy brows lifted in surprise that Philippe would even pose the question. "You know that you have only to ask."

"Thank you, old friend, I know how valuable your time is."

Belfleur grimaced. "Not so valuable these days. To be blunt, I have grown bored with our political games. We seek to make changes only to discover that the greed and corruption remains no matter who sits upon the throne."

Philippe gave his friend a pat on the shoulder. "It is always the way with power."

"So it would seem." Belfleur shook his head in disgust before he sucked in a deep breath. "Now, what can I do for you?"

In concise words, Philippe explained Jean-Pierre's arrest and his futile chase for Seurat. He touched only lightly on his father's part in Seurat's crazed need for revenge. Despite Raine's outrage, he felt no particular remorse for the man who was determined to ruin his family. Louis Gautier was without doubt a selfish, self-absorbed creature who would stoop to any level to achieve glory, but he was still his father and Philippe would do whatever necessary to protect him.

"A difficult task, but not impossible," Belfleur said as Philippe finished. "I will call in my lads and discover if they have any information on this Seurat. It might be that they can tell us precisely where he resides."

Philippe smiled sardonically. "With my current streak of luck it is not bloody likely."

Belfleur shrugged with a Gallic wave of his hands. "We shall see. Is there anything else I can do?"

Philippe paused, his gaze shifting back to the elegant necklaces. The image of them resting against Raine's ivory skin remained a potent force. So why battle it? Raine was surely born to be drenched in his jewels.

"Actually, I did not entirely lie about needing a gift," he murmured.

"Ah." Belfleur smiled, his shrewd eyes glinting as he calculated just how much money he could squeeze from his friend. "Is she beautiful?"

"Astonishingly, breathtakingly beautiful."

The glint in the pale eyes brightened. "Then you will desire my most exclusive wares." Belfleur moved to run a pudgy finger over the sparkling ruby. "Is there anything that catches your eye?"

"I will take them all."

Belfleur gave a startled blink. "All?"

Philippe smiled. "Is that a problem?"

"Not at all." With a swift, efficient motion Belfleur wrapped the necklaces in the large swath of black velvet before folding them into a neat package and laying them in a carved, satinwood box. "*Mon Dieu,* she must be quite a wench."

Philippe's smile disappeared as he regarded his companion with a cold, dangerous expression.

"Do not ever refer to her as a *wench,*" he commanded icily. "She is a lady."

Realizing his error, Belfleur hastily thrust the box into Philippe's hands. "*Oui,* of course. Forgive me, Philippe, I meant no offense."

Philippe battled back his anger with an effort. A gentleman could not go about flogging everyone who presumed his mistress was a common tart. Even if it was precisely what he longed to do.

"Do not forget to send word the moment you learn of anything." He headed toward the door with Belfleur scurrying in his wake.

"Most certainly," the older man promised. "The very minute I have word, you shall know."

RAINE SMILED AS THE YOUNG maid seated next to her in the drawing room managed to struggle through the last of the words that Raine had written on a piece of parchment.

"*Très bien, Nanette,*" she said with genuine pleasure. "You have been practicing."

A blush of pleasure touched the round cheeks. Nanette

was a simple girl with a frizz of brown hair and plain features, who hoped someday to become a lady's maid in Paris. A dream that would be far more attainable if she possessed the ability to read and write.

"Oui."

Raine patted the girl's work-roughened hand. "If you continue to study I do not doubt that you will soon be reading and writing anything you desire."

"Merci, mademoiselle," Nanette breathed. "You are so very kind."

"Nonsense."

Raine waved aside the maid's gratitude even as her heart filled with warmth. Oddly, she had discovered during her brief hours of helping the maids with their reading that she experienced the same thrill of excitement as she had when she had taken the role of the Knave of Knightsbridge.

During her nightly escapades she had assumed that it was the daring risk and illicit danger that made her pulse race and her heart fill with pleasure. Now she was beginning to realize that at least a portion of her excitement came from the knowledge she was helping others.

She needed to be…needed.

Perhaps not so surprising when she considered the fact that she had lost her mother when she was very young, and her father had never known precisely what to do with his daughter. She had always known she was loved, but she had never felt as if she truly mattered. As if there was someone who depended upon her to fulfill their life.

Raine swallowed a small sigh at the same moment that Nanette abruptly jumped to her feet and glanced toward the nearby window.

"The master has come back. I must return to my duties," the maid muttered before rushing from the room.

For a brief, insane moment, Raine was nearly overwhelmed with a sense of relief.

Since the moment Philippe had left the cottage she had been fretting and stewing in the fear that he had collapsed on the streets of Paris. The stubborn fool would never admit he was too weak to be dashing about.

And, of course, there had been the unmistakable knowledge that Seurat was still lurking about with the desire to see Philippe dead.

As her muscles unknotted, however, a sense of annoyance replaced her anxiety. Why should she spend her time worrying when it was obvious that Philippe would do what he pleased, when he pleased and how he pleased? Let him risk his stupid neck. After all, the devil did take care of his own.

Clearing away the bits of parchment and quill that lay on the table, Raine was still standing beside the rather hideously ornate desk when Philippe swept into the room and crossed directly toward the fireplace. He placed a small wooden box on the mantel before pulling off his gloves and tossing his greatcoat onto a nearby chair.

Covertly, she watched as he held his slender fingers toward the leaping flames, her gaze skimming over the aristocratic profile and tousled curls. There was no mistaking the pallor of his countenance and the lines of pain that framed his sensuous mouth, but even wounded he managed to fill the room with his commanding presence.

Raine shivered as a heat prickled over her skin. It was grossly unfair that he should manage to disturb her with such ease. Especially when she was quite certain that he could dismiss her from his mind without the least effort.

Her vague annoyance deepened as Philippe turned his head and quirked a brow in her direction. Almost as if he were daring her to lecture him on his ridiculous refusal to take proper care of himself.

Which, of course, ensured that the chiding words died on her lips. Damn his blasted soul.

Once confident that he had managed to avoid the well-deserved lecture, Philippe leaned casually against the mantel.

"Is it my imagination or does my presence launch the servants into a quake?"

With a small sniff, Raine settled on the delicate sofa and smoothed the skirt of her rose satin gown.

"You frighten them."

"How the devil could I possible frighten them? I have yet to actually catch sight of more than a fleeting glimpse of most of them."

Raine shrugged. "No doubt your brother spoke of you upon occasion."

"No doubt." His lips twisted. "'Tis no wonder they regard me as an ogre. Jean-Pierre has always taken great delight in convincing others that I am just a breath away from Beelzebub himself."

"And you take great delight in convincing others your brother is absolutely right," she pointed out dryly.

The devil possessed the audacity to give a low chuckle. "It is true that I rarely concern myself with the opinion of others."

"You enjoy causing others to fear you."

"It does have its uses."

Her lips thinned. "So does simple human kindness. The servants would not flee if you took a few moments to assure them that you are pleased with their efforts."

He regarded her for a long moment, as if wondering if she had lost her senses. "If I was not pleased, they would be seeking new employment."

Raine rolled her eyes. The man's aloof arrogance never failed to astonish her.

"And you cannot take a few moments to offer words of praise?" she demanded.

"I pay their salary. I assure you that is far more important than any words of praise."

Without thinking, Raine was on her feet and crossing to regard him with a small frown.

"What do you fear, Philippe?"

His green eyes narrowed. "Fear?"

"Do you believe you will be thought weak if you lower your guard for even a moment?" she demanded. "Or is it that you merely prefer to keep everyone at a distance?"

"Not everyone." Without warning his arms whipped around her and Raine discovered herself hauled against the hard contours of his body. The ice melted from his expression and a dangerous heat smoldered in his eyes. "The less distance between us the better."

Her breath tangled in her throat. "Philippe...your arm."

With a groan he buried his face in her neck. "My arm is not what is currently aching."

There was no mistaking the stirring of his body as he pressed her tightly against him. Even worse, there was no mistaking her own response as his lips skated down the line of her throat.

"For God's sake, Philippe. Do you never think of anything clse?" she protested.

Philippe nipped sharply at the lobe of her ear. "Not when you are near."

Her already raw nerves rebelled at the blatant confession that she was nothing more than a warm body he currently desired. Stupid, really. He had never pretended that he had any other interest in her.

Still, the realization that he remained impervious, while every day she was growing more deeply ensnared with the vexing man, made her struggle from his clinging grasp.

"That is hardly flattering," she muttered, stepping back before he could halt her retreat.

A smile twitched at his lips. "It does not please you to know that I cannot keep my hands from you? That you plague me with thoughts of your satin skin and plum-ripe lips even when we are miles apart?"

"It takes little accomplishment to stir a man's lust," she said tartly. "As a rule one need only be a female."

"Ah, but I am a gentleman of discerning taste," he drawled. "Only the most beautiful of women is capable of stirring my lust."

"That is still no compliment. I had nothing to do with the way I was born."

He gave a sharp laugh. "You wish me to tell you that I am fascinated by your brilliant wit and astonishing intelligence?"

Raine flinched as he struck far too close to the truth. She did possess wit and intelligence. Why should she not be admired for such things?

All too aware of his searching gaze watching the play of emotions that flitted over her face, Raine abruptly turned to study the blazing fire.

"I suppose it does not matter."

She thought she heard him stifle a sigh before he reached out to lightly stroke her cheek.

"You are very difficult to please, *meu amor*. Since it is obvious my mere words cannot convince you of my utter bewitchment, perhaps I should express my admiration with a more tangible means."

Philippe shifted, and without warning Raine discovered that he was pressing the box he had brought back from Paris into her hands.

A chill settled in the pit of her stomach as she studied the elegantly carved box.

"What is this?"

"Open it and discover for yourself," he softly challenged.

With hesitant motions she pulled the lid off the box and gently tugged aside the black velvet within. She caught a brilliant flash of absurdly large diamonds and what appeared to be a ruby, as well as a golden glint of amber before she was shoving the box back into Philippe's hand.

"No," she breathed.

For once she managed to catch him utterly off guard. His brows drew together as he regarded her with a hint of wariness.

"Raine?"

There might have been a measure of satisfaction in Philippe's uncertainty if Raine had not been battling a sudden flood of tears. As it was, all she could think of was escaping before he could witness her distress.

"Excuse me," she muttered, sweeping past him to head directly for the door.

Once out of the stifling room, Raine picked up her skirts and dashed up the stairs to her chambers. Within moments she had the door shut and locked behind her.

Still in the drawing room, Philippe paced the cramped space as he struggled to comprehend what had just occurred.

Raine usually managed to surprise him. Which, of course, only added to her fascination. But this…this was completely daft.

He had just offered the chit an entire treasure chest of flawless jewels. The sort of jewels that a mere mistress could rarely hope to acquire. So why was she not overcome with joy? Why was she not tossing herself in his arms and rewarding him as she should?

Hell and damnation.

A wave of fury washed through him as he reached into the box and pulled out the necklaces. Stuffing them into his pocket, he headed for the upstairs chambers. He deserved an explanation.

And then he deserved the hours of sensuous gratitude that he had been anticipating.

His fury was not improved when he reached Raine's door and discovered she had thrown the lock. Lifting his fist, he hit the oak door with enough force to make the pictures rattle on the hall paneling.

"Dammit, open the door, Raine."

There was a long silence before Raine's voice at last floated through the air.

"Can I not have even a few moments of privacy?"

He hit the door again, indifferent to the knowledge that the entire household must be capable of hearing him, and fact that he was not behaving at all like himself.

That cold, remote part of him that allowed him to always be in complete command of his emotions was decidedly absent. Raine's fault, of course. Now she could suffer the consequences.

"Open the door or I will break it down."

There was another pause, and then clearly realizing that he was perfectly capable of breaking down the door, Raine pulled back the bolt and yanked the door open.

Standing on the threshold, she folded her arms over her chest. "There. Are you satisfied?"

Philippe narrowed his gaze as he took in her damp cheeks and reddened eyes. Lord. She had been crying. The knowledge made his chest tighten in an uncomfortable manner.

"No, I am not bloody well satisfied. What the devil is the matter with you?"

Stepping back, Raine paced toward the center of the room. "I am tired. I wish to rest before dinner."

Philippe slammed the door behind him as he followed in

her path. Reaching out, he scooped her off her feet and cradled her in his arms. There would be no more running. Not even if he had to tie her to the damn bed.

"Do not walk away from me, *menina pequena*," he growled. "Not ever."

There was no fear on the pale face as Raine met him glare for glare. "Philippe, let me down."

A hard smile touched his lips. "Very well."

While she eyed him with open suspicion, Philippe strode the short distance to dump her onto the four-posted bed. Before she could move he had pursued her downward and trapped her beneath his body.

"No." She pressed ineffectively against his chest, squirming beneath him.

Philippe gritted his teeth as his muscles stirred. Raine had never looked more beautiful with her golden curls spilling across the pillows and her face flushed with anger. Just like an exotic angel that begged for his kisses.

He fully intended to ease his frustrated desire, but not until she properly regretted her ungrateful behavior.

Planting his hands on either side of her shoulders, he regarded her with a grim expression.

"Tell me, Raine."

Her chin tilted. "Tell you what?"

"Why did you just toss a fortune in jewels back into my face?"

"I did not toss them."

His breath hissed between his teeth. "Do not fence with me. Not now."

For a moment their gazes tangled in a silent battle of wills. Then, with a frustrated sigh, Raine turned her head to one side.

"I never asked for jewels," she said stiffly.

"I am well aware you never asked for them. They were a gift."

"A gift is a pretty fan or a book of poetry. A diamond necklace is…"

He studied her pale profile, his body tensing. "Do not halt now. What is a diamond necklace?"

Raine slowly turned her head to meet his searching gaze. "Payment."

Philippe growled deep in his throat. "You dare to suggest that I am purchasing your favors?"

"Are you not?"

His gaze took an insolent survey of her slender body stretched beneath him.

"I have no need to purchase something that I already own."

A faint heat touched her cheeks, but her gaze never wavered. "Then why did you give them to me?"

"Because I thought they would please you, you irritating minx."

"And because you always buy jewels for your mistresses?" she challenged.

He stilled at her accusation. "Is that what this is about? You are jealous at the knowledge I have known other women?"

Her dark eyes smoldered with a fierce emotion. "I do not like being reminded that I am a kept woman. You have taken everything but my pride. I will not allow you to have that, as well."

Philippe found himself hesitating. He was a man who possessed strict rules when it came to the women who shared his bed. He did not endure jealous clinging, manipulation or tedious lectures. And he most certainly did not endure temper tantrums. Why should he? There were always lovely ladies anxious to offer him companionship.

On this occasion, however, the thought of tossing Raine from his bed did not even flit through his mind. Instead, his clever brain was churning through the best means of dealing with the provoking woman.

"And what have I taken?" he demanded. "Your innocence? You hardly battled me. In fact, as I recall you nearly ripped off my clothes."

His blunt honesty did nothing to ease her strange mood. If anything the pale features only hardened with displeasure.

"I suppose you will also claim you did not take my freedom? Or force me to leave my father and my home?" she charged.

Philippe shoved himself off the bed and paced across the small room. Damn the woman. He had given her a life of untold ease and luxury. More luxury than any woman in her position could have ever dreamed possible. He would not be painted as the villain.

"You would prefer to be trapped in that shabby village with a father who is destined to lure you to the gallows?"

She pressed into the bank of pillows, her expression oddly vulnerable. "You can mock all you like, but it was my life and you stole it from me. You wanted me so you took me, and you did not give a thought to who you might hurt."

Just for a moment his heart twisted with something remarkably akin to guilt. It was true he had stolen her from the life she had known. And that he had done so without thought of anything beyond his own desires.

Then he was thrusting the ridiculous notion aside. Of course he took her. She had readily placed herself at his mercy, and he was not a man who was stupid enough to toss aside what fate offered.

Whether she wished to acknowledge the truth or not, she belonged to him.

"Perhaps you should consider a career on the stage, *querida*," he drawled. "I have never seen a more convincing damsel in distress."

She closed her eyes as she covered her face with her hands. "Would you please just go away?"

With a few long strides he was standing beside the bed and grasping her wrists in a tight grip. Tugging her hands downward, he glared into her wide eyes.

"No, not until you stop this nonsense. I want the truth of what is troubling you."

CHAPTER SEVENTEEN

RAINE DID NOT STRUGGLE against his near-painful grip. Why bother? They both knew that he possessed the strength to do whatever he wished with her.

Instead, she put all her shimmering frustration into the stubborn tilt of her chin. He could manhandle her all he liked, but he could not force her to accept being his mere toy. It simply was not in her nature.

"You seem to have little interest in truth," she accused, refusing to think about the warm, male scent that was wrapping about her, or the slender fingers that had loosened their grip on her wrists to lightly stroke her sensitive skin. "Not unless it suits your purpose."

He sat on the edge of the bed, his fingers continuing their insistent caresses. "And what would you know of my purpose?"

"I know that you are obsessed with capturing Seurat and rescuing your brother."

"Hardly surprising. You would do the same for your father."

"I also know that for the moment I have captured your interest, but once this is all settled and you return to your estate in Madeira I will be tossed aside."

He stilled, his expression impossible to read. "What makes you so certain?"

Did he truly believe she was that naive? Or just stupid? She may have been raised in a convent, but she understood that while a mistress might be readily indulged by her protector, she could never expect to be more than a naughty secret that was hidden from society.

A man's home, his loyalty and his heart would be reserved solely for the woman he would make his wife.

A pain threatened to clench her heart, but Raine was ruthless to squash it. No. She was not going to allow Philippe Gautier to hurt her. He had already disrupted her life quite enough, thank you.

Which was why it was so imperative that she convince him to let her go.

"Gentlemen do not house their mistresses beneath their own roof," she said, her tone more tart than she intended. "Not unless they desire to create a scandal."

He gazed down the length of his aquiline nose, clearly indifferent to the threat of scandal.

"Do you truly imagine I care what others might say of me? My life is not ruled by the gossipmongers. And I assure you, if I decide that I want you beneath my roof that is precisely where you will be."

Her breath caught in her throat. Dear God, no. It was bad enough to remain here in Paris. It would be nothing short of a disaster if she were to be secluded alone with him at his estate in Madeira.

"You are being ridiculous. Your father and brother would never tolerate such a thing."

"The estate may belong to my father, but it is my fortune that keeps it profitable," he said with a magnificent lack of modesty. "He has no say in who I may choose to keep in my care."

"My God, your arrogance is beyond belief."

"Yes, you have mentioned that before."

"Then allow me to mention this—I have no intention of going to Madeira with you."

His brows slowly lifted. "Are you deliberately attempting to be contrary, *meu amor?* Just a moment ago you were complaining because I was going to toss you aside rather than take you to my estate, now you claim you will not go."

"I was not complaining…" She heaved an irritating sigh. "I was pointing out that I am merely a distraction that you will soon grow weary of. When that day comes, what do you suppose will happen to me?"

He paused, studying her tight expression with a strange intensity. "What do you desire to happen?"

"What?"

"What is it you want for your future?" he demanded. "Do you truly want to return to your father and that remote village?"

She lowered her gaze to where his fingers lightly stroked her wrists. Carlos had asked the same question. Unfortunately, she still had no answer. None beyond the obvious.

"It is my home."

Not surprisingly he shrugged aside her response. "A home is not a prison. At least it should not be. Your father is content with his tiny cottage and role of notorious highwayman. You were meant for much more."

She gave a short, humorless laugh. "To be some man's mistress?"

"Surely that is better than ending up as a wife to some dreary farmer?" he demanded, stubbornly refusing to accept responsibility for having stolen away the life that might have been hers.

Her lips thinned with annoyance. "It would at least be respectable."

"Respectable? A highly overrated virtue, I have always thought."

"You would."

The elegant male features tightened, as if he was being harassed beyond bearing. And perhaps he did feel harassed, she acknowledged wryly. Thus far she had yet to meet anyone that would actually dare to stand firm in the face of his considerable will. Well, perhaps Carlos, she amended. But it seemed that most of the world devoted itself to pampering to his outrageous conceit.

"Do you know how many women long to be given the opportunity to be rescued from the tedious bonds of matrimony?" His gaze slid deliberately down to the low scoop of her bodice. "You would be choking on boredom within a fortnight."

Her chin tilted another notch. "Not if I happened to love the farmer."

Expecting derision at her words, Raine was puzzled by the flare of emotion that darkened his green eyes.

"Love?" he said harshly. "Do you even know the meaning of the word?"

She blinked at his odd reaction. "I daresay I know better than you."

"Have you ever been in love, *querida?*"

"Of course." She licked her dry lips, sharply conscious of his gaze lingering on the unwitting gesture. "I love my father, and our housekeeper, Mrs. Stone, and Foster..."

"That is not at all the same, as you well know," he interrupted, his hands sliding up her bare arms to grasp her shoulders. "Have you ever given yourself entirely to another? Have you ever allowed a man to truly know the woman beneath that astonishing beauty?"

Raine shivered, as much from his fierce words as from the searing heat of his touch. Lud, what did he want from her? Was he so cruel that he would not be satisfied until he had managed to break her heart? Did his vanity demand absolute possession?

The thought was enough to chill her blood.

"What does it matter to you?" she demanded.

His lips twisted with a hint of self-mockery. "That is a question I have asked myself too often."

Raine gave an unconscious shake of her head. She was not sophisticated enough to play this particular game. Her emotions were too vulnerable, too easily manipulated by Philippe. He could wound her with very little effort.

"I think that we have strayed rather far from the point," she muttered.

"True enough." His fingers absently skimmed along the plunging line of her bodice, almost as if he were not even aware of his intimate caress. Raine, on the other hand, was vibrantly aware of the sparks of pleasure his touch was arousing. She might battle to protect her ridiculous heart, but her body had long ago declared defeat. "You still have yet to explain why you rewarded my very generous gift with a tantrum worthy of a spoiled child."

"God almighty, have you listened to a word that I have said?"

"You have said a great number of words, none of which have made the least amount of sense." His fingers tugged at the ribbons that held her bodice together. "Perhaps the trouble is that I bothered with a conversation at all. We seem to communicate much more effectively without words."

Before she could protest he was tugging her bodice downward, ripping aside the light shift and exposing her breasts to his avid gaze. She clenched her teeth as her nipples tightened and a familiar ache bloomed in the pit of her stomach. Raine might resent the manner that Philippe could arouse her with the merest touch, but there seemed no means to resist.

"You think you can seduce me to your will?" she demanded even as her body softened beneath the heated kisses he scattered over the curve of her breasts.

Philippe pulled back as he slid his hand beneath the hem

of her skirts. A smile touched his lips as his probing fingers brushed over the sensitive skin of her inner thigh.

"I think that I don't give a damn about anything but sinking myself deep into your body," he replied huskily, his eyes dark with hunger. "If I cannot please you with jewels, then I will please you with this."

Her lips parted to protest, but before the words could be uttered Philippe had bent down to replace his fingers with his mouth. She moaned softly as he nibbled his way up her inner thigh, and then his tongue was tracing through her damp heat.

A brief warning that she should refuse flitted through the back of her mind. This was hardly the way to convince him that she was genuinely opposed to being his mistress.

But a larger part of her was already sinking in the sensuous delight. What was the point in fighting? They both knew that she found his touch irresistible.

Her fingers tangled in his hair as her body began to arch. "This changes nothing," she gasped.

"You're wrong, *meu amor.*" Philippe tugged her legs even farther apart as he settled between them. "This changes everything."

RAINE AWOKE TO DISCOVER herself alone in the bed. She had not intended to fall asleep. It was, after all, only midafternoon. But the combination of her restless night and the insatiable demands of Philippe's lovemaking had taken their toll.

Feeling slightly sore and utterly sated, Raine forced herself to a seated position. There was something rather decadent about waking completely naked with her hair tumbling down her back, she decided as she glanced toward the mirror in the corner.

She stiffened as she caught sight of her reflection. Not because she looked like a thoroughly ravished gypsy with her tousled blond curls and flushed cheeks. Or because her pale skin still carried the marks of Philippe's touch.

It was the brilliant sparkle of diamonds that encircled her neck that made her muscles tense and her eyes flash.

Of all the unmitigated nerve.

Philippe had waited until she had fallen asleep to place his leash of ownership about her neck.

With a sense of premonition, she turned her head to discover the flawless ruby necklace, along with the amber pendant, had been carefully placed on the pillow.

Well, if he thought he could have the last word on that subject he was very much mistaken, she decided as she flounced from the bed and wrapped herself in a robe. Without bothering to brush her hair or pull on her slippers, she headed out of her chambers and down the hall.

No doubt most women would consider her a fool. Bloody hell, she *was* a fool. The necklaces that Philippe offered her were worth a small fortune. With them she could live the rest of her days without the least concern for money. She could travel far away from Knightsbridge. She could enjoy the delights of London or Paris or Rome. She could be truly independent in a manner she could never have dared hope for.

Even if she decided to remain in the village she could always use the outlandish jewels to rescue every widow, orphan and aging soldier that might need assistance.

However foolish, she was not keeping the necklaces. Not when they made her feel as if she had sold her soul to the devil.

Entering the drawing room, Raine came to an abrupt halt as she realized that the tall, male form standing beside the window was not Philippe. Instead, it was Carlos who slowly turned and regarded her with a slow, very thorough survey.

A blush rushed to her cheeks as she realized what he must

be seeing. A young, half-naked woman who had clearly just climbed from her bed.

"Forgive me..." she breathed, her hands clutching the robe tightly around her body. "I did not realize you were here."

An unmistakable heat entered his eyes as Carlos strolled forward. "I am happy you did not. I sense you would never have agreed to join me," he said, firmly clasping her elbow to steer her toward the fire. "Come, you must be cold."

Despite the voice of decency that warned she should return to her chambers, Raine allowed herself to be seated in one of the leather wing chairs. Over the past days she had discovered that beneath Carlos's wicked charm there was an unexpected strength in his character. He was a man who could be depended upon in times of trouble.

"I was searching for Philippe," she said in a tone that revealed her displeasure.

A dark brow quirked as Carlos leaned against the mantel, his arms folded across the considerable width of his chest.

"He said something of enjoying a hot bath and short nap before returning to Paris."

Her eyes widened. "He intends to return today?"

"*Sim.*"

"Of all the idiotic notions. Obviously he will not be satisfied until he has made himself ill."

A smile played around Carlos's full, devilish lips. Even at ease there was a hint of passionate energy that shimmered about the man. In his own way he was as ruthlessly dangerous as Philippe.

"Once Philippe sets his eye on a task he rarely allows anything or anyone to interfere in his quest," he said.

Raine rolled her eyes. "Certainly he does not allow simple common sense to interfere in his quest. The man could give lessons to a mule."

"He does have some similar qualities," Carlos readily agreed, his dark gaze lowering to the long curve of her throat exposed by the gaping robe. "*Meu Deus*. I presume that is a gift from Philippe? It is quite…ah…"

"Gaudy?" Raine interrupted sharply, a blush staining her cheeks. Gads, she had never been so mortified. To be known as Philippe's lover was one thing. It implied the consent of two willing partners. To be a mistress…well, that made her nothing more than a possession. And the payment for that possession currently hung about her neck like the heaviest of yokes. "Outrageous? Ludicrous?"

With a fluid motion, Carlos crouched beside the chair, his hand reaching out to lightly stroke the gems about her neck.

"I was about to say, exquisite. Not all women could carry the jewels with such elegance. You were clearly born to wear diamonds."

Startled by the intimate gesture, Raine abruptly rose to her feet and paced toward the center of the room. It was not that she found Carlos's touch distasteful. No woman in her right mind could deny the man was a lethal temptation. But at the moment she had enough to cope with. Adding yet another arrogant, predatory, impossible male to her life was nothing short of madness.

"You are wrong, you know," she muttered. "I was born to live in a small cottage with my father."

There was not the slightest sound, but suddenly Carlos was gently turning her to meet his narrowed gaze.

"Not even you could believe that, Raine. Such beauty would be wasted among the savages. You were meant to captivate the world."

She heaved an exasperated sigh. Did every man presume if a woman possessed passable looks she was anxious to sell herself to the highest bidder?

Or was it just something about her that made men assume that she had nothing but her body to offer? Perhaps there was a wanton wickedness inside her that they could sense.

The thought made her heart sink with despair.

"I do not wish to captivate the world. I only wish…"

"What?" With careful movements, as if afraid he might startle her into flight, Carlos cupped her face in his hands. "What do you wish?"

"What every woman wishes," she said simply. "To have the love of a good and decent man. To have a home and a family to call my own."

Thankfully the dark, handsome features held no mockery as he continued to study her pale face. Instead there was nothing more than an amused curiosity.

"And there was no man in that village of yours willing to make you his wife? I find that difficult to believe, *anjo*."

"It is not difficult to believe at all." Her lips twisted. "My birth is not of high-enough station to tempt the local aristocrats, and yet my standing and education make the local citizens uneasy. I seem to have no true place in the world."

"Ah." Something that might have been sympathy flashed through his eyes. "You are not alone, you know, *anjo*. Not all of us are born with our destinies written in the stars. Which, I have come to discover, is not always a bad thing. We are given the liberty to choose our own paths."

"That is easy for you to say. You are a man while I am a mere woman."

He chuckled softly. "You have no need to remind me. It is something I have become painfully aware of."

"What I mean is that you possess the ability to do what you will without censure from society," she said with a hint of impatience. "What choices do I have?"

"You persist in thinking of yourself as a meaningless chit

in a small village. A woman with your beauty and intelligence could have society bending to your will." His thumbs caressed the line of her cheekbones. "The world could be yours if only you would have the courage to grasp it."

Raine pulled back as it became impossible to ignore the less-than-subtle seduction.

"Carlos?"

With a wry smile, Carlos reluctantly allowed his hands to drop. "Tell me, Raine, do you love Philippe?"

She gave a small jerk at the unexpected question. "He kidnapped me."

His gaze never wavered. "That is no answer."

Raine turned to pace back to the fire. She feared what might be revealed in her expression.

"Only a fool would love a man like Philippe," she muttered, "and I am no fool."

The heat of Carlos's body flared over her as he came to stand directly at her back. Ever so lightly his hands skimmed over her shoulders.

"As much as I dislike admitting it, Philippe does claim a few redeeming qualities."

"Does he?"

"*Sim.*" He toyed with the golden curls that lay against her robe. "Philippe is fiercely devoted to his family despite the knowledge that they are utterly unworthy of his loyalty. He has retrieved his father's estates from the brink of ruin and built them into a vast empire." There was a short pause. "He also cares for you."

Raine's breath caught in her throat at Carlos's ridiculous claim. "No, he desires me," she corrected.

"It is more than that." His hand shifted to stroke the heavy necklace that bound her neck. "You cannot imagine that he lavishes all women with such stunning trinkets?"

"If he truly cared, then he would have known that buying me these jewels would only embarrass me."

She could sense Carlos stiffen in surprise. "Why would you be embarrassed?"

"I do not trade my body for wealth."

He gently tugged a gleaming curl. "Many gentlemen feel more comfortable revealing their affections with such gifts. That does not mean they are paying for your services."

She gave a shake of her head. "Philippe has no affection to reveal. He…" She was forced to suck in a sharp breath as Carlos trailed his fingers down the opening of her robe. Whatever her complicated feelings for Philippe, it did not prevent her body from reacting to the practiced touch. "He does not want to care for another," she struggled to continue. "I think his mother's death when he was so young frightened him."

Carlos pressed even closer. "Frightened him?"

"He is afraid of being hurt and left alone again."

"Perhaps, but that does not mean a determined woman could not teach him to trust again."

His warm breath brushed over Raine's ear, and with a choked sound Raine abruptly turned to regard her companion with wide eyes.

"Why do you defend Philippe?" she demanded in a voice that wasn't quite steady.

Carlos shrugged. "Philippe is as close as any brother to me."

"Yes, but…" A blush touched her cheeks. She was surely not misreading the man's intentions? He had, after all, had his hands beneath her robe. "I mean, you seem to want…"

"You in my bed?" He cut off her awkward stumbling with a wicked smile. "You spread beneath me as I find paradise?"

Raine licked her dry lips. "Do you?"

"Desperately."

He did not even bother to try to hide the slumberous heat

in his eyes as he lowered his head to brush his mouth lightly over her lips.

She gave a bewildered blink. "I do not understand."

Carlos paused, his dark male features fiercely striking in the flickering candlelight.

"I want you, *anjo,* but I am not so desperate for a woman that I would seduce one who is in love with another man." His inherent arrogance edged his words. "If you come to my arms I want you thinking of me, not Philippe."

Raine's brows drew together. "You want me to be your mistress?"

A small, mysterious smile played about his mouth. "Who can say what the future might hold?"

She gave a shake of her head. "Carlos…"

"No." He touched a finger to her lips to halt her impetuous words. "This is not the time. But know that I am near if you have need of me."

He claimed a brief, searing kiss before he turned to walk from the room, leaving behind a decidedly bemused Raine.

Good heavens. Men were truly the oddest of creatures.

Still, she could not deny there was a measure of comfort to be found in Carlos's promise.

Someday, no doubt someday very soon, Philippe would grow bored with her, or just as likely, discover another woman more beautiful and more tempting. He would have no more use for her and she would have need of assistance to return to her father.

On that day she sensed she would be turning to Carlos.

CHAPTER EIGHTEEN

PHILIPPE SMILED WRYLY as he locked the glittering necklaces in the bottom drawer of the desk located in the corner of his bedchamber.

He had not been surprised to discover the priceless gems tossed on the bed when he had awakened from his nap. A part of him might even have been disappointed if he had not found them there.

The Lord knew he might never comprehend the tangled reasoning that led to Raine's burst of outrage, but he had to admire her unwavering sense of honor. By God, what other woman would turn up her nose at a fortune in jewels just because her pride had been wounded? Especially a woman who had never been allowed to enjoy such pretty baubles in her entire life?

Miss Raine Wimbourne was without a doubt the most exasperating, annoying female he had ever encountered, but she was also the most unique. Even if he had her at his side for a lifetime, he was convinced he would never discover all the fascinating complexities to her character. She would intrigue him for an eternity.

He was not quite certain why the thought pleased him, or why the smile on his lips refused to be dismissed as he left his bedchamber and went in search of Raine.

Dammit all, he should still be furious with the maddening

wench. She had not only treated his generous gifts with disdain, but she had branded him nothing less than a blackguard.

A notion that he could not in full honesty deny.

Philippe was not a man who often searched his heart. He did not concern himself with what others might think of him, or bother to consider the feelings of another. He took what he wanted, and damn the consequences. If that made him a selfish beast, then so be it.

Now Raine was forcing him to ponder how his decisions were affecting her. And perhaps for the first time in his life he found himself wondering how to please another.

Searching through the cottage, Philippe at last managed to track down his elusive prey in the dark garden. For a moment he paused in the shadows as he studied the delicate woman. The pure, perfect features were drenched in silver moonlight, her thick curls shimmering like the finest amber. And even wrapped in the velvet cape, she managed to give the impression of fragility. As if the slightest breeze might steal her away.

His lungs squeezed with something close to pain before he was sternly thrusting it aside and moving to stand at Raine's side. He breathed in deeply of her feminine scent as he took her chilled hands and gently rubbed them between his own.

"You should not be out here alone, *querida*," he said quietly.

Raine became rigid beneath his touch, but she made no effort to pull away. "I can hardly come to harm in the garden."

"Seurat knows of this cottage and has proved he is willing to approach it without fear. He could be lurking anywhere."

"He has no reason to bother me. I have done nothing to him."

"The man is demented," he reminded her. "It is enough that you are—"

His words broke off as he silently cursed. The woman was his mistress. An exclusive position that ladies around the world longed to fill. Unfortunately, Raine stubbornly refused to be appropriately appreciative of the honor he bestowed upon her, and her dark eyes were already flashing with temper.

"I am what?"

"No, my sweet. I am not stupid enough to walk into that trap." He heaved a faint sigh. "It is enough that Seurat knows that by harming you he would harm me."

Her brows drew together at his soft words. "You cannot expect me to remain cloistered in the cottage day and night, Philippe. I will go mad."

"It will only be for a few days, *meu amor.* Once I have Seurat captured he will no longer be a threat."

She tugged her hands from his grasp, her lips thinning with annoyance. "So now I am not only to be your captive, but I am to be imprisoned, as well?"

"Hell and damnation, woman," he muttered. "Would you prefer that I not care if Seurat puts a bullet through your heart?"

"I would prefer that you had not put me in danger in the first place," she retorted. "After all, you did condemn my father for supposedly risking my neck, did you not? That, at least was my choice."

"My God, you would try the patience of a saint," Philippe growled in frustration, jamming his fingers through his hair. He was beginning to suspect that the woman had been put into this world to be a constant torment. "Will you not be satisfied until I admit that I thought of no one but myself when I kidnapped you? That I wanted you so desperately that I was willing to commit any sin, break any law to have you? Is that what you desire to hear?"

Her eyes widened in surprise at his unexpected confession. She should damn well be surprised. Philippe did not easily admit he might be in the wrong.

"Why?" she at last demanded.

Philippe frowned in confusion. "Why?"

"Why me? You could have any woman you desire."

His lips twisted. God, he had not even thought of another woman since Raine had blazed into his life.

"They are not you."

"But…"

Philippe pressed a finger to her lips. "I have no explanation, Raine. I only know that it has to be you. Just you." He lowered his head to press a lingering kiss to her satin mouth. "Now, come inside. Dinner is waiting."

She wrapped her arms around her waist. "I am not hungry."

"Neither am I, at least not for food." His gaze lowered down her tiny body. "But you are the one who is always chiding me to display more concern for my servants. Do you truly wish to hurt Madame LaSalle's delicate sensibilities by refusing the feast she has spent the entire day preparing?"

Her dark eyes flashed. "Your concern seems to conveniently appear when it suits your purpose."

"It is at least a beginning, is it not?"

She ducked her head to hide her expressive face. "If you say so."

Philippe swallowed his impatience with an effort. Gripping her chin, he gently forced her countenance upward. "Raine, please look at me."

Grudgingly, she met his searching gaze. "What?"

"Must you battle me every moment of every day?" he demanded. "Can we not for once enjoy a peaceful dinner?"

"Our battles are not always my fault. It is not as if you are a particularly congenial gentleman," she accused.

"We have already established that I am arrogant and boorish and utterly without redeeming qualities. That does not mean, however, I cannot be a charming dinner companion when I choose," he said dryly. "I have even been known to dine with kings and queens without being tossed into the nearest dungeon."

In the shimmering moonlight a reluctant smile tugged at her lips. "That is rather difficult to believe."

Something that was dangerously close to relief rushed through Philippe. It was absurd, but he could not deny he had harbored a fear that he had wounded Raine beyond forgiveness.

Threading her arm through his, Philippe tugged her firmly back toward the cottage.

"Why do you not allow me the opportunity to prove my claim?"

She heaved a small sigh as they stepped through a side door and made their way to the dining room.

"You really are impossible, you know."

Philippe flashed a devilish smile. "Without a doubt."

They entered a room that was nearly overwhelmed by an ornate walnut table and matching sideboard. Jean-Pierre's taste in furnishings was nearly as hideous as his taste in art. Hiding his grimace, Philippe forced himself to spare a smile for the hovering housekeeper.

For whatever ridiculous reason Raine found it important that the servants feel as if they were properly appreciated. On this night Philippe was willing to indulge her wishes.

"Ah. Madame LaSalle, it smells delicious," he murmured. "Roasted lamb?"

A startled blush of pleasure touched the woman's round cheeks. "*Oui,* with my own rosemary sauce."

"How did you possibly know it was my favorite?"

"Is it?" The woman fussed with her apron, attempting to hide her smile. "Well, I believe that a gentleman should always have a hearty dinner, and there is nothing tastier than lamb on a cold winter night."

"Yes, indeed." Philippe ignored Raine's startled glance as he escorted her to the table and seated her. Taking his own seat next to her, he glanced toward the servant. "I think that will be all for now, Madame LaSalle."

"Yes, of course." With a hasty curtsy the woman scurried from the room and Philippe smiled smugly as he filled Raine's plate with the various dishes spread across the table. "There, you see? I am not entirely without charm."

She rolled her eyes. "When it suits your purpose."

Philippe filled his own plate before pouring them both a glass of the rich burgundy. At least Jean-Pierre could always be depended upon to keep a respectable cellar.

"It has been my experience that most people employ charm when it suits their purpose, which is why I prefer a more direct approach." He deliberately held her gaze as he took a bite of the lamb. "And why I prefer others who speak their mind."

"Are you implying that I have no charm?"

Philippe gave a short laugh. "You have charms enough to bring men to their knees, as you well know, *meu amor*." He studied the pale features that should only belong to an angel. "It is little wonder your father felt compelled to keep you hidden behind the walls of a convent. You would have created chaos in that tiny village."

Tasting of the delicate soufflé, Raine gave a small shrug. She was remarkably indifferent to her astonishing beauty.

"My father sent me to the convent because it was my mother's dying wish."

"Did you enjoy your days among the good sisters?"

A small, reminiscent smile curved her lips. "Yes, I did. It could be stifling at times, but I took pleasure in being surrounded by friends." Her smile widened. "I even enjoyed my studies."

Philippe watched the play of emotion cross her pale face.

There was a softening to her features that revealed her memories were pleasant ones. For once her guard was entirely lowered and Philippe forgot his dinner as he savored the small glimpse into her heart.

"I suppose you tormented your hapless teachers beyond bearing?" he prodded her to continue.

"Not at all. I wanted to learn." She sipped her burgundy. "Unlike most of my companions I understood that I was being offered a gift rarely given to girls in my position. I never took my education for granted."

Philippe could easily imagine her as an eager student. She possessed an innate intelligence and natural curiosity. The perfect combination for any scholar.

"So you were wise even at a young age." He raised his glass in a small toast. "I commend you."

She shrugged as she nibbled a stuffed mushroom. "I do not know if I was particularly wise, but I did consider the possibility of becoming a teacher."

Philippe swallowed his instinctive denial. This woman wasted teaching a pack of ungrateful brats? It would have been a sin against nature.

Instead he regarded her with a faint curiosity. His experience had taught him that Miss Raine Wimbourne rarely allowed herself to be distracted when she set upon a goal. If she had truly desired to teach, then it was surprising that she had allowed anything to stand in her path.

"Why did you not?" he demanded.

"I thought—" she paused as if struggling against an unwelcome surge of emotion "—I thought my father would have need of me."

Philippe frowned at the hint of sadness in her voice.

"Which he obviously did," he said softly.

The thick sweep of her lashes lowered over her eyes. "Yes,

well, not precisely in the manner I had expected. You see, he had become accustomed to living without me."

"What do you mean?"

"He has Mrs. Stone to tend to his home and friends to keep him entertained." Her lips thinned. "He is not quite certain what to do with me."

Philippe's fingers tightened on the stem of his glass until the fragile crystal threatened to break. By God, some day he was going to get his hands on Josiah Wimbourne and thrash him within an inch of his life.

His eyes narrowed. "And yet you desire to return to your father."

"He is the only family that I have."

"Is family so terribly important?"

Her lashes abruptly lifted to reveal a startled glance. "Of course. Without my father I would be utterly alone in the world."

Philippe reached out to grasp her slender fingers, holding her gaze. "No, not alone."

He heard her breath catch before she was tugging her fingers from his grasp and hiding her hands in her lap. Almost as if she feared his touch.

"Perhaps when I return home I shall consider teaching," she said in a sudden rush. "The local vicar instructs a handful of boys in the area, I could do the same for the young girls. They have as much right as anyone to learn how to read and write."

Philippe ground his teeth at her sharp retreat. Damn the woman. She would readily allow him to perform the most intimate caresses upon her body. He had taken her in every position possible. But the moment he threatened to slip past her defensive walls, she was scurrying away.

It should not trouble him. After all, he had what he wanted.

Her willing body in his bed. But, it was not enough. Hell and damnation, it was never enough.

Rattled by the realization, Philippe instinctively slid behind his own aloof arrogance. If she wished to continue with the charade that she was his unwilling captive…then so be it.

"A worthy goal, but not one that will occur for some time, *meu amor.* At least not in England," he said smoothly. "If you wish to share your knowledge with my servants, however, I will not stand in your path."

She gave a small jerk, as if she had been slapped. "Not stand in my path?"

"No."

Her eyes narrowed to dangerous slits. "How very gracious of you."

Philippe offered a casual shrug. "You wish to be of service to others and many of my staff are no doubt eager to learn. It seems a reasonable exchange."

"Good Lord, Philippe, I was not requesting your permission. You have no authority over me."

He leaned forward, his expression hard. "You are mistaken, *menina pequena,* I have already told you that you are mine."

"I am not yours." With a surge she was on her feet and glaring down at his relentless countenance. "I am a grown woman who is perfectly capable of making her own decisions."

"Ah, yes. Decisions that very nearly led you to the gallows."

"Instead they led me to your bed."

He slowly rose to his feet. "A place you have more than enjoyed."

"How dare you…"

"I fear you will have to continue your sulking alone, *meu amor.*" Philippe interrupted the angry words, his thin smile not reaching his eyes. "Carlos will be expecting me. There is no need to wait up for me. I shall no doubt be late."

Without waiting for her response, he turned and headed toward the small foyer, where he gathered his coat and gloves before leaving the cottage.

Stepping into the garden, Philippe gave a small shiver as the icy breeze swirled through the darkness. He slowed his steps, sucking in a deep breath of the chilled air.

What the devil was the matter with him? He had promised himself he would not be goaded. That he would be in complete command of the situation. But he had only to be in the same room with Raine for his renowned composure to be crushed into dust.

It truly made no sense. His skill with the fairer sex was beyond question. They fulfilled a necessary purpose in his life and in return he kept them well satisfied. Not only in his bed, but with the sort of expensive trifles that always pleased a woman.

Well, every woman except for the damnable woman he had left in the cottage.

Of course, he had never asked so much from other women, a small voice whispered in the back of his mind.

Until Raine his lovers were no more than passing distractions that were forgotten the moment he left their beds. They were never allowed beneath his roof. And never allowed to disrupt his life.

Certainly he had never sought to capture their mercenary hearts. Or to brand himself so deeply, so thoroughly, that they would never be allowed to forget him.

Gads, he was surely losing his mind.

Entering the stables, Philippe was unsurprised to discover Carlos there before him. He was, however, startled to find that his friend had already saddled the horses and was awaiting him with obvious impatience.

His instincts prickled with anticipation. Taking the reins of his black, ill-tempered mount, Philippe easily swung himself into the saddle.

"Has there been any word from Belfleur?"

"A message arrived an hour ago." Carlos mounted his own horse and led the way from the stables. "Belfleur will be waiting for us in the back rooms of Frascati's."

Philippe nodded, inwardly relieved he already had the prerequisite white cravat tied about his neck. The gambling house was one of the most elegant in Paris and demanded that its guests be properly attired.

"He must have information," Philippe muttered as they cautiously made their way down the icy streets. "Perhaps there will be some good news at bloody last."

Easily sensing the edge in his voice, Carlos sent him a curious glance. "Troubles?"

"I am beginning to believe that females were put on this earth for the sole purpose of creating chaos in man's well-ordered existence."

"I never noticed you having any particular difficulty with women," Carlos mocked. "At least not until our carriage was halted by the Knave of Knightsbridge."

Philippe's breath condensed in the cold air as he blew out a heavy sigh. "Had I any sense I would have turned the wench over to the magistrate that night and been done with her."

"There is nothing forcing you to keep her. If she is bothersome to you, then simply release her."

Philippe frowned in warning. "Turn your attentions to another woman, Carlos. You shall never have Raine."

The younger man shrugged, but thankfully kept his mouth shut as they continued through the silent streets.

Their pace was by necessity slower than Philippe desired, but not even his impatience would allow him to risk breaking the leg of his mount on the ice. At least the traffic was light until they hit the streets of Paris. And even then the cold night had driven most of the citizens to the warmth of the nearby coffeehouses.

They arrived in the rue Richelieu and dismounted before the gambling club. Walking to the door, Philippe was brought to a halt as Carlos put a hand on his shoulder.

"You go and meet Belfleur," his friend commanded. "I wish to keep watch out here."

Philippe studied the dark countenance, sensing the tension. "You do not trust Belfleur?"

Carlos's lips twisted. "I trust no one, but on this night it is the streets that have me concerned. There is a smell of violence in the air."

Philippe had to agree. Although the wealthier citizens had crowded into the shops and gambling houses, there were still clusters of drunken revelers who roamed the streets in search of entertainment. Should they be foolish enough to clash with the King's Guard, the powder keg could blow up in all their faces.

"A sound notion." He paused, his expression somber. "If there should be trouble I want you to return to the cottage and ensure that Raine is taken to safety. Is that understood?"

"*Meu Deus,* when have I ever left your side in a fight?"

Their gazes locked and held before Philippe was giving a wry shake of his head. The bond that had been forged over years surged to the surface and once again they were brothers.

"I am asking as your friend, Carlos," he said softly. "I brought Raine to this godforsaken city, and if something were to happen to her I…I could not bear it. I would trust no other with her. Will you swear?"

The dark features tightened before Carlos sucked in a deep breath and gave a slow nod. "*Sim.* I give you my word."

Satisfied, Philippe turned and entered the antechamber of the gambling house. A dignified servant hurried forward to take his coat and gloves, his covert gaze lingering upon Philippe's distinctive ebony curls as he offered a bow.

"Monsieur Gautier?"

"Oui."

"If you will follow me?"

The servant led him into the main parlor, which was discreetly hushed despite the number of patrons who gazed avidly at the long table with its green baize. At each end of the table a manager kept a close guard on the various fortunes being tossed into the hands of fate.

His passing was barely noted as the gamblers breathlessly awaited the smooth spin of the roulette wheel, which was why such an establishment was always such a convenient location for secret meetings. He could be in plain sight and yet utterly inconspicuous. Far simpler than sneaking about.

They turned into a hall that led past smaller chambers that were similarly filled. At last the servant halted before the last door, and after a discreet knock pushed it open and waved Philippe within.

Stepping over the threshold, Philippe heard the door close behind him and he glanced around the small but elegantly furnished office. A sturdy desk with a chair was set near the row of bookshelves beneath the bay window. Across the room was a brick fireplace with twin leather chairs on either side. The familiar pudgy form was seated in one of the chairs and Philippe moved forward to join him.

"Belfleur."

"Gautier." The man waved a hand toward the matching chair without bothering to rise. "Have a seat."

"You have use of a private office?" Philippe demanded as he settled into the soft leather. "You never fail to amaze me, old friend."

Belfleur shrugged, but a smug smile played about his lips. "People owe me favors and from time to time I call them in. I thought it best that we not be seen together. No one will know of this meeting."

"You have information?"

"I believe you will find it of interest." Belfleur paused as he glanced toward a silver tray that had been set on a nearby table. "Wine?"

"Thank you, no." Philippe leaned forward, his entire body humming with a coiled tension. "What have you discovered?"

Clearly sensing that Philippe was in no mood for casual chatter, Belfleur crossed his hands over his stomach and regarded his companion from beneath his half-lowered lashes.

"One of my boys claims that he has worked for a man calling himself Seurat."

"Did he say what he looked like?"

"A small, twitchy man with a limp and a scar on one cheek. He also mentioned that the man had a strange habit of muttering to himself."

"That is him." Philippe's fingers bit into the leather arms of the chair. "What sort of work did the boy do for him?"

"He was paid over the past few years to keep an occasional eye on a cottage in Montmartre."

"Jean-Pierre." Philippe's breath caught in his throat. The bastard had been stalking his brother. Hunting him like a predator until he had at last moved in for the kill.

It was little wonder Seurat had known when Jean-Pierre would be traveling to England. And how he had so easily set the trap that had landed the young, foolish man in jail.

Holy hell, it made his blood run cold just to think of how easily the madman could have killed Jean-Pierre. If not for his deranged lust for revenge, Philippe would be visiting his brother in the family crypt.

With a sudden surge, Philippe was on his feet and pacing the small Oriental rug.

"Damn the bloody bastard. I will see him in hell."

"A charming notion."

"Where do I find him?"

"A difficult question." Belfleur toyed with the heavy gold ring on his finger. "This Seurat would approach Georges on the street and offer little information beyond telling the boy where to go and when to meet him for payment."

Philippe clenched his jaw in disappointment. Of course it could not be simple. Chasing Seurat was like stumbling through a maze.

His only consolation was the unwavering certainty that he would have his hands on the man. And on that day he would take out his frustration in blood.

He came to a halt in the center of the room. "Georges is a pickpocket?"

There was the faintest pause before Belfleur gave a nod. "Among other things."

"What street does he work?"

"The one just outside my shop."

Which meant that he had been plying his trade long enough to have worked his way up the criminal network. And that he was wise enough to not try to sell Belfleur counterfeit information. It was an unhealthy occupation.

"When was the last time he caught sight of Seurat?"

"Not for several weeks, I fear."

Not surprising. Seurat must have traveled to England before Jean-Pierre arrived there.

"Could he tell you anything else?"

Belfleur pressed his considerable bulk from the chair. "*Non,* but I believe he must have rooms close to my shop. There are boys to be hired on every street—why would he go there unless it was convenient?"

"All evidence does come back to that particular neighborhood," Philippe agreed, recalling the clothing they had found abandoned in the alley. "Still, it will take time to search through every building."

"I will have my boys keep a close eye on the cafés and markets. He must get his food from somewhere."

Philippe moved forward to clap his hand on his companion's shoulder. "You have done well, Belfleur. I am in your debt."

"Do not worry, Gautier, I will call in my marker when it is convenient," Belfleur promised. "Ah, before I forget, I hope your woman properly rewarded you for your generous gifts?"

"Oh, yes, I was certainly rewarded." Philippe gave a short laugh as he turned and headed for the door. "I assure you, it was a lesson I shall not soon forget."

CHAPTER NINETEEN

RAINE RESTLESSLY PACED the cottage after Philippe's abrupt departure. Lud, the man was without doubt the most arrogant, unreasonable, perverse…jackass ever to walk the earth.

Would he ever accept that she might be more than a pretty bauble that he could keep or toss aside on a whim? That she might possess hopes and dreams of her own?

Of course not.

Philippe might be prepared to pacify her with gaudy jewelry and pretty gowns. After all, it took no more than handing over a wad of bank drafts. There was no danger he might have to actually offer something of himself.

Only a gentleman who cared would concern himself with her true happiness.

And Philippe did not want to care. Not for anyone.

Ridiculously depressed by her dark thoughts, Raine entered the drawing room and stood before the fire. She needed something to distract her, but the cottage was empty of diversions. There were no books to tempt her, no needlework, no duties that needed to be attended.

It was really rather ironic, she acknowledged. She had escaped the confines of one tedious cottage only to be confined to another.

Although the cottage in Knightsbridge did not possess an irritating, ruthless, thoroughly delectable lover who filled her nights with sinful pleasure.

Heat tingled over her skin and her lower body clenched in anticipation. Just the thought of being in Philippe's arms was enough to make her heart flutter.

Because she was a weak, ridiculous idiot, she told herself sternly.

She was swallowing a sigh when the faint scrape of the door being pushed open had her spinning around. Expecting Philippe, Raine froze at the sight of the stranger who slipped into the room.

He was not a large man. Indeed, he stood only a few inches taller than her, and despite the heavy black coat it was obvious his body was far too thin. With a knit hat pulled low and a muffler wrapped around the lower portion of his face, it was impossible to determine more than a thin countenance with a pair of pale eyes and a pointed nose. At a glance he did not appear remarkably dangerous. Not unless one noted the hectic glitter in his small eyes.

Or the heavy pistol he took from his pocket to point directly at Raine's heart.

"If you scream for help I will shoot whoever comes through the door to rescue you," he warned in heavily accented English.

Panic flared through Raine before she was grimly thrusting it aside. This had to be Seurat. Who else would be so daring as to break into the cottage while the household was still awake? And if he was as truly demented as they suspected, she would need her every wit clear and sharp.

She licked her dry lips, just for a moment desperately wishing that Philippe was near enough to come rushing to her rescue. This tiny, emaciated man would be no match for Philippe's lean, fluid strength.

Then she was giving an unconscious shake of her head.

What was she thinking? Having Philippe here would be nothing short of a disaster. No matter what his strength he was not capable of dodging a bullet. And he was just stubborn enough to try to capture the desperate man regardless of the danger.

Striving for calm, Raine folded her hands before her and squarely met the disturbing intensity of the man's glare.

"I presume you must be the mysterious Seurat?" she said in conversational tones.

The man appeared caught off guard, but whether it was her lack of terror at his sudden appearance or the fact that she had recognized him, was impossible to say.

"Who I am is of no importance," he at last growled.

Raine kept her gaze deliberately from straying to the gun still pointed at her heart, as if by ignoring the lethal object it had no power to hurt her. Foolish, perhaps, but it was the only means to keep her dubious courage intact.

"If you are searching for Philippe, I fear he is not here."

"I know, I watched him leave."

Her heart gave a painful squeeze. He knew that Philippe was not here and yet he still had entered. Which meant he had deliberately desired to find her alone.

"What…?" She was forced to take a deep breath before she could continue. "What do you want?"

A violent tremor wrenched through his small body. "I want what has been taken from me, but for now you will do."

"Me?" Her voice was thick but thankfully steady. "I have nothing to offer you."

"On the contrary, you can offer me more than I dared to hope for."

"And what is that?"

"With you my revenge shall be one step closer."

Raine covertly backed nearer to the fireplace. There was a heavy candlestick on the mantel that she could use as a weapon. Not that it would halt a bullet if he decided to shoot her, but if he had other ghastly plans on his mind she could at least put up a decent fight.

"What could I possibly have to do with your revenge?" she demanded. "From my understanding, your quarrel is with the elder Monsieur Gautier, a gentleman I have never even met."

His pale eyes flashed with a dangerous fury. "My revenge will be visited upon the entire Gautier family, beginning with Jean-Pierre and ending with Louis."

Raine shivered at the shrill edge to his voice. Madness, indeed.

"I still do not understand what I have to do with this nasty business. I am not a member of the family."

"Perhaps not, but Philippe is besotted with you."

Even terrified Raine could not stop the sharp laugh. "You are mistaken, sir. I am just a woman who is currently sharing Philippe's house. Soon enough I will be replaced by another."

He gave a jerky shake of his head. "No, I have seen you together. I have seen how he looks at you."

"And how does he look at me?"

"As if you are a precious treasure that he fears might slip from his grasp. To lose you would wound him more deeply than any reprisal I can devise."

Bloody hell, the man truly was delusional if he thought Philippe looked at her as anything beyond a temporary convenience.

"I still do not understand what you want from me."

Seurat gave a dangerous wave of the gun. "I need you to come with me."

Her eyes widened in horror. Allow herself to be carried off by this madman to God knew where? Oh, no. She might be naive, but she possessed enough sense to know that was a very bad notion.

"I will not."

With a low hiss he moved to stand directly before her, the sour smell of his desperation hitting Raine with a sickening force.

"You are in no position to argue with me."

"Do you intend to shoot me?"

"If necessary."

"Then shoot." Her chin tilted. She would rather a clean death as opposed to whatever evil the man was plotting. "I will not go with you."

"I had hoped we could be civilized, but…"

Her heart lodged in her throat as the hand holding the gun slowly lifted higher. Bloody hell, he was going to shoot her in the head. The thought had barely registered when his hand astonishingly flashed forward and the butt of the weapon connected with her chin.

Darkness engulfed her and, without so much as a sigh, she slid to the ground.

AN ICY RAIN HAD BEGUN to fall by the time Philippe and Carlos arrived at the cottage. In silence they rubbed down their mounts before handing them over to the sleepy stable boy. They had already discussed what Philippe had discovered from Belfleur and made their plans for continuing their hunt when dawn arrived. Now, as they left the stables and entered the garden, Carlos found his feet slowing to a halt.

The cottage slumbered silently before them, the windows glowing with the promise of warmth. The thought of a hot bath and bottle of brandy was tempting. The night had started off cold and was becoming steadily more miserable. To remove his wet clothing and warm his chilled body seemed nothing short of paradise.

But even as he shivered at the cutting wind, a flare of restlessness was smoldering in the pit of his stomach.

He did not want to return to his solitary chambers. Not with the knowledge that just down the hall Philippe would be climbing into bed next to Raine.

Meu Deus. The thought was enough to make his jaws clench and his chest tight. The golden-haired beauty was crawling beneath his skin in a manner he never before experienced. Perhaps it was the mere knowledge that she was forbidden fruit. Or perhaps it was something more. Something he did not even want to consider. Whatever the cause, he knew that he was in dire need of a distraction.

It was that or doing something that he might very well regret the rest of his days.

"Carlos?"

Realizing that Philippe had stopped to regard him with a frown, Carlos gave a sharp shake of his head.

"Go in without me."

"Is something the matter?"

"I intend to have a smoke and then perhaps I will wander down to the local pub."

Philippe tensed, his expression impossible to read in the darkness. "It is a cold night for a walk."

Carlos pulled a cheroot from his pocket. "I have endured worse."

"The citizens are bound to be a tedious lot."

"There is always some amusement to be found."

Philippe instinctively reached out his hand. "Carlos…"

Stepping swiftly backward, Carlos avoided the gesture of what could only be pity.

"Just go, Philippe," he growled in a rough tone.

There was a pause before Philippe at last gave a nod of his head. "As you wish."

Carlos watched his friend disappear into the cottage before he sought the protection of the nearby grotto and searched for his flint. It took several tries before he had the cheroot lit, but at last he breathed in deeply of the rich tobacco.

Slowly, ever so slowly, he felt his tense muscles begin to ease. A sardonic smile even tugged at the edges of his mouth.

This might all be brilliantly amusing if he were not the one standing in the freezing rain, he acknowledged wryly. After all, he was a near legend for his smooth ability to seduce a pretty maid, regardless of whether or not she was attached to another. He had crawled through the windows of countless wives, stolen away nights with betrothed maidens and dodged more than one bullet from a jealous lover.

Hell, he had bedded a bride the night before her wedding.

Perhaps this was all poetic justice.

He dropped the cheroot and ground it beneath his heel before he gathered his coat about him. It was time to find a warm, willing female and rid himself of the aching frustration.

He had managed to take a step toward the side gate when there was an unmistakable roar from the cottage, followed by a loud crash.

Without missing a beat, Carlos had pulled his pistol from his pocket and was sprinting to the cottage. He charged through the back door and headed directly up the stairs, where he could still hear the sounds of destruction.

Had Philippe walked into a clever trap? Or had he stumbled across some villain who had not expected them to return so swiftly?

Carlos was prepared for any sort of danger as he vaulted into the drawing room, only to skid to a stop at the sight of Philippe prowling through the room tossing vases, dishes and figurines. For a moment, Carlos stared at his friend in amazement, wondering if he had lost his wits, and then with a shake of his head he moved forward to grasp the crazed man by his shoulders.

"Philippe, what is it?" With a growl Philippe attempted to

wrench himself from Carlos's grim hold and Carlos gave him a sharp shake. "Tell me. What has happened?"

For a moment Philippe continued to struggle, and then without warning he grasped Carlos by the lapels of his coat and nearly lifted him off the floor.

"I will kill him," he swore, his face dangerously pale. "I will squeeze the life from him. I will rip out his heart and shove it down his throat."

A cold dread clenched Carlos's heart. "Is it Seurat? Has he done something? Dammit, Philippe, talk to me."

Half expecting the distracted Philippe to throw him across the room, Carlos was unprepared when the man abruptly released him and sank to his knees, his hands covering his face.

"He has taken her," he said in a harsh voice.

The coldness spread through Carlos as his gaze caught sight of the crumpled note in the center of the carpet. Feeling almost numb, he moved to pluck it from the floor and smoothed it open.

The woman is payment for what is owed.
　　Seurat

Fury, black and unrelenting, raced through Carlos's veins. Raine. *Meu Deus.* She was so tiny, so fragile. To be at the mercy of some demented monster…

"Bastardo," he hissed, his thoughts a tangled mess as he paced the room and imagined the numerous and bloody ways he intended to murder Seurat.

He was still pacing when there was a faint noise near the door and Madame LaSalle stepped into the room with a hand pressed to her heart.

"Monsieur?" Her eyes widened with fear as she took in the shattered room and then the sight of Philippe kneeling on the floor, his head still cradled in his hands. "Blessed Mary, has there been a robbery?"

There was a tense silence before Philippe was slowly rising to his feet, his features set in pure ice. The raging emotions had been replaced by a cruel ruthlessness. The man had become a lethal predator who would hunt down and destroy his prey.

"Gather the servants in the kitchen," Philippe ordered the fluttering woman. "*All* the servants. If any of them are out I want them back at once. I will be down in a few moments to question them."

The woman responded instinctively to the command, her back straightening and the panic easing from her round countenance.

"*Oui, monsieur.* I will have them gathered at once."

Madame LaSalle rushed from the room and Philippe paced toward the fireplace.

"Carlos."

"*Sim?*"

"I want you to go to Belfleur's and begin searching the stables in the neighborhood. I want to know every person who rented a carriage and if they have all been returned."

"They are bound to be closed at this hour."

"Then wake them."

Carlos gave a nod, struggling with his own near-blinding anger. Unlike Philippe, he did not possess the means of locking away his seething emotions. He needed to hurt something or someone. And he needed to do it soon.

"Of course, but you do realize that he might have come on horseback?"

"No." Philippe gripped the edge of the mantel, his knuckles turning white from the force of his grip. "He arrived here intending to kidnap Raine. He could not risk being seen on horseback with a struggling woman, or worse, one that was bound and gagged."

Carlos restlessly paced around the room. He could not allow himself to think of Raine being helplessly bound.

"A dangerous risk," he rasped. "If he did come with the intention of taking Raine, then he would have to keep a watch on the cottage until we left. A carriage sitting in the street for such a length of time would have attracted notice."

"Unless he was wise enough to leave it near the pub."

Carlos gave a grudging nod. Seurat had proved he possessed at least some cunning. Too often he remained one step ahead of them.

"What do you want of the servants?"

"I intend to have them search the house and grounds. Seurat might have left behind something that will be of assistance in tracking him."

"A beginning, but it is not enough," Carlos said.

Philippe turned to his friend with a frigid glare. "Do you have a better scheme?"

"*Meu Deus.*" Carlos shoved his fingers through his hair. "We should have taken greater care. Raine should never have been left here alone. We failed her."

Philippe turned back to gaze sightlessly at the fire. "No, Carlos, *I* failed her. I was the one to take her from her home and to put her in danger, not you. But I will get her back. Even if I have to take Paris apart brick by brick." He gave a sharp shake of his head. "Go to Belfleur's. I will join you—"

Carlos frowned as the clipped words were abruptly broken off and Philippe bent down to touch the floor.

"What is it?" Moving forward, he impatiently bent beside his friend, wondering if he had discovered something that Seurat had left behind. "Philippe?"

Wordlessly, Philippe lifted his hand and held it toward the

fire. Carlos's heart slammed to a halt as he caught sight of the unmistakable red stain at the tip of his finger.

Blood.

Carlos muttered a string of curses as he rose to his feet and then slammed his fist into the wall. The fierce blow knocked a small vase from the mantel and rattled paintings. Unfortunately it did nothing to ease his choking fury.

Clenching and unclenching his throbbing hand, Carlos turned back to Philippe. He was still kneeling before the fire, his face disturbingly pale as he stared at the sticky redness on his finger.

He appeared frozen in place, as if he might shatter if he so much as breathed. Carlos gripped his shoulder.

"It is no more than a drop, Philippe," he said softly.

Philippe's expression remained cold and distant, but Carlos could feel the fine tremor beneath his hand.

"She was hurt."

"Do not leap to conclusions." He gave the shoulder a rough shake. "You know Raine well enough to realize she would not go without a fight. That blood more than likely belongs to Seurat."

There was a thick, choking silence before Philippe gave a nod and straightened.

"We will find her," he swore in low tones. "And then Seurat is dead."

RAINE STRUGGLED OUT OF the clinging sleep with a sense of dread. A part of her warned that she would be far better off to remain unconscious. In the thick darkness the heavy pounding in her temples was no more than a distant throb and she could pretend she was safely tucked in her bed at the cottage with no madman in sight.

Unfortunately, a larger part of her was far too sensible to

allow her to remain so terribly vulnerable when she was in the power of a desperate villain.

She was no spineless coward. Whatever she had to face she would do so with her eyes open and her shoulders squared.

Her flare of courage allowed her to wrench open her heavy lids and to glance cautiously around the room dimly lit by the early morning sunlight. There was not much to see.

She was lying upon a cramped sofa that was set beneath a covered window. There was a matching chair in a distant corner and a wooden table that held a cracked vase. The floors were bare and the paneled walls were faded and stained.

There was an adjoining room that she suspected was a bedchamber, and from the rustling noises coming from the room she could only suppose her captor was busily preparing for the day.

They were precisely the sort of low-rent rooms that could be had throughout the city of Paris.

The knowledge briefly made her heart sink.

How was Philippe possibly to find her if there was nothing to indicate that this was the home of a man crazed by a lust for revenge?

Raine pressed her fingers to her throbbing temple before she was thrusting aside the pessimistic thoughts. Bloody hell. She did not need Philippe Gautier to rush to her rescue. She was no spineless coward!

No. She had saved her father from the gallows. She had ridden through the dark roads as the Knave of Knightsbridge without a qualm.

She was a woman who was perfectly capable of saving herself.

Of course, saving herself would be considerably easier if her head was not pounding and her stomach threatening an open revolt, she acknowledged wryly.

With a tentative motion she struggled to sit upright, clutching the ragged blanket that had been draped over her as if it might ease the shivers racking her body.

It was not a great feat, but she felt decidedly drained as her head fell on the back cushion of the sofa. So drained she could not even muster the appropriate fear when Seurat abruptly entered the room from the side chamber.

Perhaps it was because he appeared so remarkably harmless. On this morning his thin body was covered by a shabby gray coat and loose breeches. Without the hat and muffler she could see his face was painfully thin with a scar that marred one cheek and a thinning thatch of gray hair. His nose was long, his lips thin and his jaw a weak line.

There was something very ferretlike about the countenance, and a disturbing glitter in the pale eyes. But astonishingly, Raine realized there was also something rather pathetic. As if he were shrouded in a darkness that imprisoned him.

"So you are awake," he muttered as he crossed to stand directly before her. He shoved out a hand holding a teacup. "Drink this."

Pain or no pain, Raine managed to sink back in the cushions with an expression of horror.

"No, get it away from me."

Her captor slowly blinked, as if offended by her distrust. "If I wanted to poison you I would not have waited until you woke up. This is water with feverfew leaves. It will help your headache."

"Considering you are the one who gave me the headache to begin with, I do not know why you would be concerned now."

Expecting an angry retort, Raine was caught off guard when his hollow cheeks flushed with embarrassment.

"I…regret having hit you. I am not a man who is violent toward women."

Raine gently touched her chin, which was still raw and aching. "Rather late now, is it not?"

"You did not give me a choice," he protested, his expression tightening. "I asked that you come with me. If you had obeyed I would never have been forced to hurt you. Now, drink."

With reluctance Raine accepted the glass that he thrust into her hands and took a sip. The water had a bitter taste from the herbs, but it did help to ease the pounding in her temple.

Lowering her gaze as she sipped the medicine, she considered her various options. Although Seurat was not a large man, she doubted she could manage to overpower him. And he was jittery enough that if she were to try screaming he might very well knock her senseless again.

Her best means of escape seemed to be luring him into a false sense of ease. If she could distract him, perhaps even charm him, he might lower his guard enough to allow her a moment to escape.

Now, she just needed to discover precisely how a woman set about charming a lunatic.

CHAPTER TWENTY

FORCING HERSELF TO DRINK the last of the water, Raine deliberately glanced around the barren chamber with what she hoped was casual interest.

"Where are we?"

"In my rooms." Seurat grimaced sourly. "I apologize that they are not more comfortable, but under my present circumstances they are all that I can afford."

She offered a faint smile, surprised to discover it was not as difficult as it should be. There was no doubt the man was dangerous and capable of striking out without warning, but he seemed determined to be polite to his captive.

"They are simple, but quite nice."

Taking her empty glass, Seurat deposited it on the low table. His movements were quick but jerky, revealing one leg was partially lame.

"They are fit for nothing more than the peasants who infest this neighborhood. I am a gentleman."

"Yes, yes, of course you are," she was swift to agree.

He turned back to regard her with a remarkably shrewd gaze. "You do not believe me, and why should you? No one else does. But I tell you, I have done great things in my life."

"Have you?" Raine tugged the blanket closer about her. "What sort of things?"

"I have traveled the world, for one thing."

"Traveled the world? You are, indeed, fortunate."

"More than fortunate." He began an unsteady pacing as his gaunt hands waved about with wild gestures. "I have been to the most exotic and remote places a gentleman could dare to travel. I have lived with natives and was allowed to see sights that no white man has ever seen. I have uncovered treasures that would make your heart weep with joy, and learned secrets that have been hidden for centuries." His hands abruptly lifted to clutch at his head, as if were being tortured by a sudden pain. Or perhaps it was the sudden voice of the demons that obviously plagued him. "And it was taken away from me. Destroyed by Gautier."

Raine wrapped the blanket more tightly around her chilled body. She could tangibly feel the overwhelming fervor that was like a poison searing through his body. He was a zealot. A man consumed with his dreams.

It was no wonder he had devoted the past thirty years to his need for revenge.

Louis Gautier had taken his life.

Or at least that was how Seurat would consider the betrayal.

"Surely Monsieur Gautier cannot keep you from continuing your travels?" she softly demanded.

Seurat's hands curled at his sides as his brows drew together into a dark frown. "Are you blind? How can I be a guide if I am crippled? There is no one who would hire me, and even if they did, I would be incapable of performing my duties. Gautier left me nothing."

A horrible notion made Raine's heart give an unpleasant lurch. "It was Monsieur Gautier who…hurt your leg?"

He gave a short, wild laugh. "Not personally, of course. He would never soil his lily-white hands upon a mere servant. *Non,* he hired others to do his dirty work."

"But why?"

"Because I would not allow him to steal what was rightfully mine. I discovered the tomb, I spent my nights digging through the sand, I was the one to be blessed by the gods."

"So you threatened Monsieur Gautier?"

"I was not going to be robbed of what I earned."

Raine hesitated, a warning voice in the back of her mind urging her to halt her prying. After all, whatever happened in Egypt two decades ago had nothing to do with her, did it? She was nothing more than a hapless pawn in this ridiculous game. And all that mattered was finding the means to escape.

Deep in her heart, however, she knew that her growing unease had more to do with Louis Gautier and just what she might discover.

Swallowing heavily, Raine found her gaze straying toward the malformed leg.

"What did they do to you?" she forced herself to ask.

A muscle in Seurat's jaw twitched as he met her wary gaze. "Three men took me far from the tent. I suppose Gautier did not wish to be disturbed by my screams. He need not have bothered. I fainted after they had broken my legs."

A wave of sickness rolled through her stomach. "You were beaten?"

"Non, ma petite, I was murdered. When Gautier left Egypt he thought I was dead and left buried in the sand. As did I until I was discovered by a wandering tribe three days later."

Raine pressed a hand to her mouth. "Dear God."

"Not God." The lean features twisted with an expression of pure hatred. "This is the work of a devil. And his devil spawn must pay."

PHILIPPE AWOKE TO DISCOVER himself stretched upon the small sofa in the drawing room. He was not certain how long he had been out. An hour? Two hours? Ever since he

had ended the hellish search for Raine through the dark
streets of Paris.

Or more precisely, ever since Carlos had ended their search.

Despite their best efforts they had managed to uncover
precious little. Carlos had found the stables that confessed that
they had rented a carriage to a gentleman that fit Seurat's description. He had also discovered that Seurat had returned it
only an hour before Carlos arrived. But none of the employees had been able to reveal anything more of the man than that
he occasionally used their stables and that he frequented the
local markets.

Philippe had been grimly set to remain in the shabby neighborhood and begin searching each building. He did not give
a bloody hell if the local citizens were all tucked in their beds
and that his intrusion might very well have him hauled away
by the King's Guard. Raine was missing and he would do
whatever necessary to bring her home.

Carlos had attempted to argue with him, but Philippe had
been wrapped in a frigid numbness that had refused to listen
to reason. That cold, ruthless sensation was a familiar one to
Philippe. It was how he had lived most of his life. Until Raine.

She was the one who had warmed him. The one who released him from his prison of ice.

Without her he could feel nothing.

Not until she was once again in his arms.

Carlos had at last brought an end to the argument by the
simple process of knocking Philippe unconscious.

Forcing himself to a seated position, Philippe gingerly
rubbed his aching jaw. He had never even seen the blow coming. Not until the pain was exploding through his mind.

At his movement Carlos slowly straightened from a chair
beside the fireplace and crossed to hover over him. Philippe
grimaced at the sight of his friend's haggard countenance and

shadowed eyes. He was not the only one suffering at Raine's disappearance.

Oddly the thought did not make him long to have Carlos horsewhipped.

For the moment they were two men connected by the same driving force, and everything else was a distraction they could not afford.

Philippe scrubbed his hands through his hair. "What is the time?"

"Near half past seven." There was a short pause as Carlos regarded him with a weary smile. "How are you feeling?"

Philippe smiled wryly. How did he feel? His jaw ached, his entire body was so weary the smallest movement was an effort and his eyes felt as if they had been filled with sand. But overall he felt…frozen. Frozen to his very bones.

"Fortunately for you I am not feeling quite well enough to repay you for your nasty surprise." He deliberately touched the growing bruise on his jaw. "Give me a few minutes, however, and I am fully confident that I will be capable of returning the favor."

Carlos shrugged. "I did it for your own good, you know. You cannot rescue Raine if you are chained in a damp cell."

"The king has more sense than to toss his wealthy visitors into jail."

"The king's justice can move very slowly, especially a king who fears the mobs more than he fears the aristocracy."

Philippe could not deny the truth of Carlos's words. Although his wealth and power ensured he was offered the sort of privileges reserved for the most elite, the current king was barely capable of keeping the pretense he was in command of the country.

"Perhaps."

Carlos folded his arms over his chest. "You know, you

could show at least a modest amount of gratitude for my having rescued you from a very unpleasant stay in the local prison."

"I might have more gratitude if I did not suspect that you took a decided pleasure in knocking me senseless."

Carlos gave a bark of laughter. "I will admit that it did not break my heart, but I have no desire to repeat the performance." He shifted his hand to rub the muscles of his neck. "At least not at the moment."

Philippe frowned. "Have you slept at all?"

"There will be time enough for sleep later."

"You will do Raine no good if you collapse from exhaustion."

"I have no intention of collapsing," Carlos said, his expression set in stubborn lines.

Philippe swallowed the words on the tip of his tongue. He did not have the energy to battle Carlos, even if it was for the man's own good. Instead he concentrated on forcing himself to his feet.

A task that took a great deal more effort than it should have, he acknowledged as he briefly swayed and a pain shot through his head.

"Damn," he muttered. "I think you might have broken my jaw."

Carlos appeared remarkably unrepentant. "Be happy that I did not truly intend to hurt you. You would not have awoken for three days."

Philippe made a rude sound as he attempted to loosen the muscles of his shoulders. "You have ensured that I have wasted enough time." He moved to pour himself a large shot of brandy. "I am returning to Paris."

"Not until you have had your breakfast." Carlos tilted his head toward the low table that held a silver tray. "Madame LaSalle brought that earlier and refused to leave until I had cleaned my plate. She also badgered me to swear on my mother's grave that I would force you to eat before I could rid myself of the woman."

Philippe drained the brandy in one long swallow, sighing as the heat exploded in the pit of his stomach and rushed through his veins. It did little to ease the pain in his jaw, but it helped to clear the cobwebs from his mind.

"This is all that I need," he said as he reached to refill his glass.

"Then you can explain to the woman why the tray is not empty," Carlos complained.

"Surely you do not fear a mere housekeeper?"

"I fear any woman who is bent on coddling a man." Carlos gave a dramatic shudder. "They are ruthless. Besides, she is upset enough."

Philippe heaved a sigh as he recalled the staff's horrified distress when he had revealed Raine's kidnapping. The wailing and screaming could have been heard blocks away.

"Yes. Raine has become a favorite of the entire staff."

Carlos's expression abruptly softened. "Hardly surprising. What other lady in her position would take such an interest in mere servants?"

"She takes an interest in everyone she encounters," Philippe said dryly. "Hell and damnation, she gave my best pair of gloves to the coalman when he confessed he did not possess any, and a pair of her own boots to that meddlesome old tartar across the road."

"She has not yet learned to disguise her kind heart."

Philippe stiffened, sensing a subtle implication that he would somehow steal away that sweet nature. Dammit, he might be an arrogant, selfish bastard, but he would never harm Raine. Certainly he would never destroy something so precious as her generous spirit.

"That is a lesson she will never have to learn. At least not while she is in my care," he said as his gaze clashed with that of Carlos's. There was a moment of silent antagonism before the chime of the clock on the mantel intruded. Philippe gave a shake of his head before he drained his glass and thumped it onto a table. Christ, he needed to get out of this cottage. He had to feel as if he were doing *something*. "We should have some word from Belfleur by now."

Carlos sucked in a deep breath, deliberately easing his tight muscles. They were both on the sort of dagger's edge that could lead to a nasty confrontation if they did not take care.

"He has his lads searching through every building in the neighborhood, as well as keeping guard on the streets. It is only a matter of time before we have Seurat cornered."

Philippe paced toward the window, only absently noting that the rain had stopped and a frozen sunlight was brushing over the village.

Logically he knew that the cunning lads that Belfleur employed were best suited to sneak through the various buildings. Not only were they familiar with the neighborhood, but they could move about without attracting undue notice.

Although he was perfectly capable of picking locks and slipping through windows, there was always the risk he might be spotted by Seurat. If the man took fright he might very well try and escape with Raine. Or worse…hurt her in retaliation.

He could not risk it.

Even if it was tearing him apart to wait about like a worthless bit of rubbish.

"Ah, *monsieur,* you are awake." Madame LaSalle bustled into the room and Philippe turned to watch as she placed a ceramic pot on the tray. Her round face was pale and her eyes reddened by tears. "I have made you a fresh pot of coffee."

"*Merci,* Madame LaSalle, but I have no time this morning. I want to make sure that my associates are keeping a careful watch on the roads and coaching inns in case Seurat attempts to flee. Then I intend to return to Paris."

The older woman lifted a plump hand to her bosom. "You have received word of Mademoiselle?"

"Not yet."

"But you will find her?" she demanded. "You will bring her back?"

Philippe met her anxious gaze, his lips curling into a ruthless smile.

"I will bring her home," he swore. "You have my word."

THE DAY PASSED SLOWLY for Raine. Not only because the rooms were cold, cramped and reeked of stale cabbage, but Seurat proved an unnerving companion. Hour upon hour he would pace the small floor and mutter beneath his breath, seeming to forget her very existence as he succumbed to the delusions of his mind.

More than once she considered making a dash across the room when he was lost in his madness. Surely she could at least get the door open far enough to scream for help before he could stop her?

A tantalizing temptation, and yet one she continued to resist. However desperate she might be to escape from the growingly dark room, she had not forgotten the pistol that he carried in the pocket of his jacket. It was difficult to forget when he had a habit of pulling the nasty thing out and rubbing his hand over it as if to remind himself it was always handy.

Seurat might be a lunatic, but he was still quite capable of pulling a trigger.

And so the day passed, with only a handful of embarrassing journeys to the adjoining room to use the chamber pot, with Seurat hovering on the other side of the screen, to provide an interruption.

Raine forced herself to remain patient. The man had to sleep eventually, did he not? She need only make sure that she could stay awake long enough to make her escape.

Not a difficult task when her nerves were so tightly wound she jumped at the slightest noise.

Wrapped tightly in the blanket, Raine watched as Seurat paced toward a wooden cabinet in the corner of the room. There was a flare of light as he struck a match to a candle and then a faint rattle of crockery. Several moments later he turned and crossed the room to shove a plate in her hand.

Raine blinked in surprise at the thick slices of bread that had been spread with butter and honey. It was odd, but she sensed that despite the fact that Seurat held her against her will, the man still considered her some sort of guest.

Thank God. She was well aware that for all her discomfort, her state of affairs could be much, much worse.

And in truth, she could not deny that deep in her susceptible heart she felt a measure of sympathy for the strange, demented man.

He had been treated shamefully by Louis Gautier, and while she could never condone his dreadful deeds, she did understand why he felt the savage need to lash out.

As she continued to stare rather stupidly at the plate in her hand, Seurat gave an impatient click of his tongue.

"You must eat."

"Thank you, but I am not hungry at the moment."

A flush stung his cheeks as he plucked the plate from her hand and set it on the wooden table. Almost as if she had offended him.

"I suppose you are accustomed to fancier fare?" he rasped in derision.

"Not at all." She met his gaze squarely. "I have spent most of my life in a convent where our meals were kept sparse to teach us to be grateful for what we did receive. And even when I returned to my father's cottage we had to be frugal with our funds. I am…accustomed to a simple life."

His expression was wary. "You live with Gautier. They toss about their money the way a whore tosses about her favors."

Raine flinched at the crude comparison but refused to be provoked. She sensed any emotional outburst would send the poor man tumbling over the edge.

"I have only been with Philippe a short time and soon enough I will be back in England." She gave a small shrug. "Then I'll be just another sailor's daughter who does not even have her pride left."

He studied her intently, seeing the truth of her words written on her face. Slowly the brittle wariness melted like dew beneath the early morning sun. For the moment she had become a sympathetic companion to his misery rather than a possession of his enemy.

"Then you know what it is like to suffer. To watch others who are so less worthy have everything, while we are given nothing."

She smiled wryly. "I have some notion."

"I should have better. I deserve better." His hands trembled as he ran them over his silver hair. "If not for the Gautier family I would be living in luxury. But they will pay. They will all pay."

"Why his family?" she asked cautiously. "Philippe and Jean-Pierre are innocent. They had nothing to do with what happened in Egypt."

The pale eyes flared with a wild hatred. "The sons carry the sins of the father. They must be punished."

"You believe this is some Greek tragedy?"

"It is justice," he rasped.

Raine licked her dry lips, searching for the means of somehow convincing the man that there was better way of achieving his goals. Not only for her own sake, but because it troubled her to think that once Philippe managed to get his hands on Seurat the unstable man would be crushed beyond salvation. Louis Gautier might strike out when cornered, but Philippe was a lethal predator who would not be satisfied until his foe was destroyed.

"Unfortunately, life is rarely fair and dwelling on the injustices do nothing to alter the ways of the world," she said softly.

He regarded her as if she were speaking a foreign language before his lips thinned in annoyance.

"Ah, I see."

"What?"

"You are attempting to convince me that I should forget what was done to me."

"Perhaps not forget, but…" She gave a lift of her hands.

His awkward pacing resumed and he shivered beneath his threadbare jacket. "You want me to abandon my plot for revenge so that I will allow you to return to your lover. Well, I am too clever for such tricks. I will not be charmed by a woman, even one so beautiful as you."

"Certainly I would prefer not to remain your prisoner, but I did not mean to imply that you should forget the past," she claimed with perfect honesty. "You were grievously treated by Louis Gautier."

A hint of bafflement touched the thin countenance. He did not trust her, but he possessed a near overwhelming need for someone to commiserate with his plight.

"Which is why I must have my revenge."

"It does not seem to have brought you much happiness."

Seurat gave a short, shrill laugh. "You do not care about my happiness."

"Actually, I do." With care not to startle the wary man, Raine slowly rose to her feet. She was forced to bite back a groan as her legs tingled in protest. She had been on the sofa for hours and her body had become uncomfortably stiff. Thank goodness she had not given in to her urge to make a mad dash to the door, she acknowledged. She would no doubt have ended up flat on her face. "I believe you have been treated unfairly."

Seurat gave a slow shake of his head. "Is this a trick?"

"No, as I said, I feel sorry for you, but I do not understand what you think to accomplish by imprisoning Jean-Pierre or kidnapping me. Neither will restore the treasure that was stolen from you, nor give you the luxurious lifestyle that you deserve."

His features tightened with remembered humiliation. "I have already attempted to gain my rightful reward from Monsieur Gautier. I traveled to his estate in Madeira after I had at last recovered from my injuries and was capable of leaving Egypt. Louis greeted me by slashing my face with a dagger and warning that if I returned he would have me killed. I had no difficulty believing his threat."

"No, I do not suppose you did." Raine grimaced, wondering if Louis Gautier possessed any semblance of conscience. He had stolen a prince's treasure, attempted to have a man murdered and had willingly put his entire family in danger rather than confess his sins. "Is that when you started to plot your revenge?"

"Oui." His thin hand curled into claws. Almost as if he was imagining gouging out the eyes of his enemy. "I intend to make Louis Gautier suffer as I have suffered."

"That would no doubt offer some satisfaction, but it will not take you from these rooms or provide the sort of comfort you desire."

"I have told you that Gautier would give me nothing."

She sucked in a deep breath. The hatred still shimmered in his pale eyes, but beneath the predictable emotion was a haunting, heart-wrenching pain.

Gad, but he was such a pathetic creature. And deep in her soul she knew that he was doomed for some horrible end. Even now Philippe was scouring the streets in search of her. And when he discovered these chambers he would not rest until Seurat had been utterly destroyed.

She felt as if she were watching the unstable man stumble toward a cliff edge, knowing each step was leading toward his death.

But what could be done to avert disaster?

Philippe might not possess his father's selfish weaknesses, but he most certainly was not a gentleman who willingly turned the other cheek. Especially not when it came to those who threatened his family.

From a young age Philippe had taken on the role of patriarch, and he possessed a grim determination to protect the Gautier clan. No doubt because he feared deep inside that he had somehow failed to protect his mother. It was precisely the sort of illogical reasoning a young boy would harbor.

He would never negotiate a peace with Seurat. Only blood would satisfy his need for punishment.

If there was to be an end to this ridiculous tragedy, it was clearly up to her to provide it.

Raine stilled as she was struck by a sudden, perhaps outrageous, notion.

"There might be a means of offering you the fortune you were denied." The words tumbled from her lips before she could halt them.

Seurat's pale eyes narrowed. "What did you say?"

Raine swallowed the lump that threatened to lodge in her throat. The past few weeks should have taught her a sharp lesson in allowing her impetuous heart to lead her. After all, if she had used the least amount of common sense she would even now be safely tucked in her father's cottage. Instead she was in France, the reluctant mistress of Philippe Gautier, and being held prisoner by a lunatic.

Being impulsive was too often a very bad notion.

Unfortunately, her heart was unruly and rarely listened to reason. It demanded that she do whatever was in her power to bring peace.

"Perhaps you could have at least a portion of the money you desire if you were willing to agree to bring an end to your vendetta."

Seurat backed away, his thin hands trembling as he scrubbed them over his face. "You seek to confuse me. Gautier will never give me the fortune I have been denied."

"Perhaps not, but I would be willing to offer you the funds."

"You?" His hands lowered so that he could regard her with open suspicion. "You claim to be a mere sailor's daughter."

"True enough, but Philippe has been quite generous." Her lips twisted at the thought of the glittering jewels. Oddly the notion of handing them over to Seurat made her feel nothing but relief, and yet she would not part with the tiny locket that currently hung about her neck for any fortune. The small bit of gold had belonged to Philippe's mother and held a sentimental worth that was priceless. "I have jewelry that would keep you in a comfortable style for years to come."

Seurat's suspicion only deepened. "You would give me your jewels?"

"Yes."

"Why?"

She gave a vague lift of her hands. "Because I believe that you have been ill-used and are due some sort of compensation. And because my father has taught me that it is my duty to assist others in need. You have greater want of the jewels than I."

Seurat gave an unconscious shake of his head as he attempted to sort through the tangled confusion in his mind.

"There is more than that," he at last muttered. "You do not do this simply because you wish to help me."

She opened her lips to deny his claim, only to hesitate. Seurat was unhinged, but he possessed a certain amount of cunning. Who could blame him for doubting that a strange woman was willing to assist him out of the goodness of her heart?

"Not entirely," she grudgingly confessed.

"Tell me why."

Raine turned from the burning gaze, wrapping her arms about her waist. It was not a simple matter for her to confess her concern for Philippe Gautier. The man considered her no more than a pretty bauble that he could enjoy for a time before tossing it away. She should detest him. And still she found herself incapable of denying she possessed an overwhelming need to protect him. Even from himself.

"Philippe is not at all like his father or brother," she at last said.

The man behind her made a rude noise. "He is a Gautier."

"By blood, yes, but not by deed. He has no interest in devoting his days to pursuing frivolous diversions or squandering his wealth on his own pleasure. Quite the contrary. He is the one who has retrieved their estates from ruin and carries the burdens of the numerous tenants and servants who depend upon him. He is—" Raine abruptly broke off her words as she realized that she was revealing far more than she had intended. Sucking in a deep breath, she turned to meet Seurat's narrowed gaze. "He is certainly not a saint, indeed, he can claim any number of sins, but he is undeserving of your revenge."

The wariness slowly eased as Seurat stepped forward and peered into her pale face. Whatever he read there seemed to satisfy his suspicions.

"You are in love with the man."

CHAPTER TWENTY-ONE

PANIC CLUTCHED AT RAINE'S heart. In love with Philippe? No. Perhaps she had reluctantly come to care for him. And certainly she desired him. There might even be a renegade part of her that occasionally craved his companionship.

But love?

Good God, only the most idiotic female would willingly give her heart to a man who was not only destined to break it in two, but one who would readily use such a weakness to trap her in his silken web. She would never be free of him. Even after he had moved on to another woman she would still be haunted and plagued by the irritating wretch.

She could not be in love. She would not allow it.

Ignoring just how ridiculous such a notion might be, Raine sternly thrust the thoughts from her mind. Now was not the time to be dwelling on such nonsense.

Actually, she preferred never to dwell on the dangerous thoughts.

Sucking in a deep breath, Raine squared her shoulders and prepared to barter as she had never bartered in her life.

"Are you willing to accept my bargain?"

Seurat gave a restless shrug. "What do you demand of me for these jewels?"

She regarded him with a steely expression. The years she had spent at the convent had not been wasted. There were few in the world who could match a nun for quelling others without ever having to speak a word.

"I will not give them to you until I have your word that you will halt your attempts to harm the Gautier family. Indeed, I do not want you to come near any of them again."

"That is all?" Seurat asked.

"No." She folded her arms over her chest, ignoring the realization that she must appear more like a grubby waif than an imposing woman capable of enforcing her will. "I also demand that you write out a confession that you forged the treasonous documents that you hid in Jean-Pierre's rooms, and I want the confession witnessed by a priest. Once you give me the paper, I will give you the jewels."

Seurat paced toward the window as he gnawed his thumbnail in unease. Raine remained patient as she carefully watched his tense profile.

She did not expect it to be an easy matter for him. He desperately desired the money. It would, after all, provide a comfortable existence and the sort of dignity that was denied him. And yet, the lust for revenge burned fierce in his heart.

He could not easily turn aside his thirst to punish the man who had stolen his glory and then tried to put an end to his life. It had been the reason he had survived, skulking in the shadows and desperately concocting his schemes for so many years.

The poison had gone so deep, and had devoured him for so long, it would no doubt be like cutting off one of his limbs to accept peace.

At last he turned back, licking his lips with a nervous motion. "And how do I know that these jewels are not paste?" he demanded.

Raine gave a lift of her brows. "Do you truly believe that Philippe Gautier would ever give his mistress fake jewels?"

Seurat grimaced as he realized how ridiculous his accusation had been. A Gautier might be many things, but frugal was not one of them.

"Even if they are real I would be arrested the moment I attempted to sell them. No one would believe that they were given to me as a gift," he challenged. "If we are to make a bargain, then you must give me coin."

Raine hated to admit it, but there was some truth to his words. Although there were always the sort of criminals willing to buy goods without tedious questions, they would hardly offer more than a pittance of what the necklaces were worth. And any legitimate jeweler would presume that Seurat had come by them in some illegal fashion.

Bloody hell. It would be up to her to somehow find the means of selling the blasted things. A task she did not have the faintest notion of how to accomplish. Certainly not without Philippe becoming suspicious.

"It will take a few days to have the jewels appraised and sold," she grudgingly agreed. "I can deliver the money here when…"

"No," Seurat growled, stepping close enough for that sour smell to assault Raine's senses. "I am not a fool."

Covertly she took a step backward. "What do you mean?"

He gave a short, humorless laugh. "Do you believe that I will remain here if I allow you to leave? *Sacrebleu.* I might as well invite Philippe to come and murder me in my sleep."

Raine stiffened as a rather ridiculous flare of annoyance raced through her. She did not like having her honor questioned. Even by a madman.

"I assure you that once I give my word it is to be trusted," she said stiffly. "I will not tell Philippe where to find you."

"I trust no one," he rasped, his breath coming in short, nervous puffs as he dared to consider the tantalizing offer. How could he not consider it? He clearly lived a miserly existence that would only become worse in the years to come. Revenge would be a cold comfort as he struggled just to survive. "I will contact you with a place for us to meet in three days. A place that I can be certain that you will come alone."

Raine reached out a hand, only to drop it when he flinched from her touch. "Then we have a bargain?"

"I do not know," he muttered, rubbing his temples as if his head was aching. "I must think."

"What is it that troubles you?" she demanded softly.

"I…"

They both froze as the sound of a tap on the door echoed through the room. It was so utterly unexpected that for a moment they merely stared at each other in surprise. Then there was the unmistakable scrape of metal as someone attempted to pick the lock. Seurat gave a soft hiss before his hand clamped on her wrist and he hauled her across the room and into the small bedchamber with startling strength.

Pulling the gun from his pocket, he regarded her with a fierce glare. "Stay in here and do not make a sound. If you try to call out I will kill whoever is on the other side of that door. Do you understand?"

Raine lifted her hands in a gesture of peace. "I will be as silent as a mouse."

He gave one last threatening wave of his gun before he was moving out of the chamber and across the outer room. Raine held her breath as she heard the door being yanked open, silently praying that it was not Philippe on the other side.

Dear God, she was so close to convincing Seurat to bring an end to this madness, but if he were to be confronted in this fragile moment by the blood of his hated enemy, Raine had no doubt he would pull the trigger without thought, without remorse.

Pressing her hands to her mouth, she battled back the fierce urge to run screaming into the other room. For the moment she could only do more harm than good by attempting to interfere.

There was the sound of Seurat's harsh voice, and then strangely the high-pitched tones of a young boy. Her prayers became more frantic at the mere thought that some innocent child might be harmed. She did not believe Seurat was a heartless killer, but if he felt as if he were threatened he would not hesitate to strike out.

An eternity seemed to pass as Seurat barked out sharp questions and the lad responded in quick, soothing words. Raine could tangibly feel the tension that filled the small rooms, but thankfully there was no hideous sound of a firing pistol or a screaming child.

Her knees were feeling decidedly weak when at last the door was slammed shut and Seurat was charging into the room, his thin face flushed with emotion. Without a word to her, Seurat brushed past her frozen form and tugged a shabby bag from beneath the bed. Once it was open, he began tossing in his handful of belongings.

Raine gave a lift of her brows as she watched his frantic motions. "What are you doing?"

"I must go."

"Go?" She frowned in surprise. "Where are you going?"

He closed the bag and grasped the threadbare coat from a nearby chair. "Someplace where I will not be found," he said as he shrugged into the coat.

"You are leaving this moment?"

He turned to her. "That boy was looking for me. Even now he is rushing back to tell your precious Philippe Gautier where I can be found. I do not intend to be here when he arrives."

Raine balled her hands in frustration. No, she could not allow him to flee until she was certain he would agree to her bargain.

"You cannot be certain that the boy has anything to do with Philippe."

He gave a short laugh. "I have not survived so long without knowing when a trap is about to close upon me."

"But what of our bargain? How can I contact you?"

With his belongings in order, Seurat once again reached beneath the bed and pulled out a length of rope.

"If I decide to agree to any bargain, I will be the one to contact you," he warned as he slowly advanced with the rope. "Until then I need to find a place where I cannot be found."

Raine abruptly began to back away. "What are you doing?"

He shrugged as he reached out to grab her arms in a biting clasp. "I am leaving and I need to make sure that you do not call unnecessary attention to my escape."

"I have already told you…" Her words broke off in a small cry as she found herself facedown on the filthy mattress with her arms wrenched behind her back. "Damn you, you cannot leave me here like this," she growled as she felt the ropes being tightly tied about her wrists and then attached to the bedpost. "I could die before someone finds me."

"Your lover will soon be rushing to the rescue," he said without the least hint of sympathy, shoving a rag into her mouth and fastening the ends behind her head. "Until then I need time to make my escape."

She heard him leave the bed and gather the bag from the floor. With a flare of panic she kicked her feet, futilely attempting to loosen the bonds that held her. Blast it all. It was all very well for Seurat to assume that Philippe would soon be charging to the rescue. He was crazy, after all. Not to mention the fact that he was not the one gagged and tied to the bed.

What if the lad had nothing to do with Philippe? What if no one came and she was left to rot in this ghastly place? Or worse, what if she were discovered by some ruffian and…

"I shall send you word if I decide to take your offer, *mademoiselle*." He gave a sudden, wild laugh. "Or perhaps I shall simply shoot Philippe Gautier and toss his body in the Seine. In either event you will have your answer."

Anger and fear raged through Raine as she struggled against the damnable rope, not stopping until she felt the blood dripping down her arms.

Why the devil had she thought she wanted an adventure? If she managed to return to her father's small cottage she swore that she would never, ever begrudge the peace and quiet again.

PHILIPPE WAS STANDING in the alley behind Belfleur's shop when the sun settled behind the horizon. The surrounding buildings protected him from the frigid breeze, but it was still painfully cold as he restlessly paced the filthy cobblestones.

He could, of course, be within the shop, warming himself beside the fire and sipping the excellent cognac that Belfleur always kept close at hand. A far more sensible choice than standing in the cold while his blood turned to ice in his veins.

More sensible but impossible, he acknowledged as a shiver racked his body.

Within the confines of the shop he found it oddly difficult to breathe. As if his lungs were too tight to capture the elusive air. And worse were the nervous glances of his companions, who eyed him with a wary fear. Clearly they thought that he might begin a mad rampage on the streets of Paris at any moment.

Not that he hadn't felt the urge to do a bit of rampaging, he ruefully acknowledged. As the hours passed with no sign of Seurat or Raine, his entire being trembled with the need to strike out.

Instead he was forced to wait in the cold, dank alley as the various boys trotted up to make their reports.

It had been Belfleur's notion to make each of the lads return to the shop every two hours and inform them where they had been and where they intended to go next. That would make certain that if one was captured by Seurat they would know swiftly to set out a search and, more important, precisely where to start looking.

A wise notion, but it did slow the amount of ground that could be covered.

Philippe pulled a silver flask from his coat pocket and took a deep drink of the brandy. As he returned it to his pocket there was the scrape of approaching footsteps and he hastily turned, expecting one of the numerous boys to appear.

Instead it was a small woman wrapped in a thin cloak who slipped from the shadows to stand directly before him. In the flickering light of his lantern it was easy to determine that she was a pretty wench with a halo of blond curls and blue eyes. He could also determine that she was astonishingly young.

At least in age, he amended silently, as she reached up to smooth a hand over his chest. There was a weary knowledge in the depths of her eyes that revealed she had already experienced far too much of the world.

"You are a fine sight on such a miserable night. Such a gentleman should not be alone," she murmured in inviting tones. "Come with me and I'll warm the chill from your body."

Philippe grimaced as he stepped sharply from her clinging hand. He held no taste for common whores. Especially not those who looked young enough to be in the nursery.

"Not on this night, child."

"I am no child." She pouted as she pulled open the cloak to reveal a gown that was cut to fully reveal her small curves. "Shall I prove that I am a grown woman?"

Philippe was startled to discover something very close to sympathy for the girl as she shivered beneath the chilled air. Dammit all. He did not want to notice that she looked cold, and vulnerable and so horribly young.

It was entirely Raine's fault, of course. Before the irritating woman had charged into his life he had never been bothered by the great horde of unfortunates who were forever crossing his path. Now he found himself actually considering what Raine would expect of him. As if he feared the notion of disappointing her.

Hell and damnation.

He heaved a deep, resigned sigh. "Close your cloak, child, I have no need of your wares."

"Every man has need of my wares," she persisted, grimly attempting to keep her teeth from chattering. "Unless you have peculiar tastes?"

Philippe gave a low laugh as the image of Raine's beauty flared through his mind. "Not peculiar, just…particular."

Her smile faltered as she sensed that a potential customer was slipping from her grasp.

"I can be anything you want," she coaxed.

"No." He gave a firm shake of his head. "I have interest in only one woman."

"A man who is capable of being faithful?" the whore scoffed in disbelief. "She must be a most intriguing woman."

An agonizing pain threatened to pierce the ice that protected him from sheer madness. "She is…perfect."

The blue eyes flickered with a hint of envy. "Then why do you stand alone in the cold?"

"I am waiting to take her home," he said simply.

"A fortunate woman."

Philippe shrugged. "I am uncertain she would agree, at least not at the moment, but I intend to change her mind."

The chit heaved a sigh as she grudgingly tugged the cloak around her thin body. "If you cannot convince her, then you need only return to this street and ask for Jeanette. I can help to ease a broken heart."

"I shall keep that in mind."

"Such a pity." A small smile tugged at her lips as she ran a knowing gaze over his large body. "I should not have minded having a man such as you beneath my skirts."

The woman moved away and began to disappear back into the shadows. Philippe growled beneath his breath as he experienced that unwelcome surge of pity once again.

Raine would expect him to do more than send the pathetic whore on her way. She would expect...bloody hell, she would expect him to rescue the wench from the cold, filthy streets.

"Jeanette," he called out wearily.

She halted and turned with an expectant expression. *"Oui?"*

Philippe reached beneath his coat to withdraw a small leather bag. "Take this."

She took the bag with a puzzled frown. "What is it?"

"A gift."

"You've changed your mind?"

"No."

The puzzlement deepened as she gave a slow shake of her head. She was not the sort of woman that received gifts without being expected to offer her body in return.

"Then why would you offer me anything?"

Philippe smiled with a trace of self-mockery. "Because I have been told by someone I admire that it is what I should do."

With stiff fingers, Jeanette tugged at the strings that held the bag shut and peered within. Her loud gasp echoed through the alley as she slowly lifted her gaze to regard him in a stunned disbelief.

"Sacrebleu. This is a blessed fortune," she said in an unsteady voice. "What do you want from me?"

Philippe did not blame her for her suspicion. Hell, he would be suspicious himself. Those who possessed generous hearts were as rare as the crown jewels.

"I want you to eat a warm meal and find safe shelter for the night. It is far too cold to be upon the streets."

She gave a choked laugh that was closer to a sob. "I can live upon this for a year."

"Perhaps it will give you an opportunity to discover a less-dangerous career."

The blue eyes filled with tears as she reached up to touch his cheek with frozen fingers. "Are you an angel?"

"An angel?" Philippe gave a harsh bark of laughter. "Not bloody likely. Anyone who knows me will attest to the fact that I long ago sold my soul to the devil."

"I do not believe it," she whispered. "You have been sent by God and I will hold you in my prayers every night. Bless you, *monsieur*." With a cry she reached up to place a kiss on his cheek. "Bless you."

Philippe grasped her shoulders and gently tugged her away. He did not desire flamboyant gratitude. At least not from this woman. He had done this for Raine, and it was her approval that he sought. Rather pathetic, but what was a man to do?

"Be on your way, child."

With a last sob the girl turned and scurried down the alley, as if she feared he might suddenly change his mind and demand back her treasure.

Philippe gave a rueful shake of his head as he wondered what his acquaintances would think of his peculiar behavior. No doubt they would presume that he had taken the last step to lunacy. And perhaps they would be right.

"Well, Gautier," a familiar voice whispered from the doorway behind him. "Are you attempting to be canonized for sainthood or do you intend to join the lovely Jeanette later and allow her to earn that rather tidy fortune?"

Philippe did not bother to turn his head as Belfleur moved to stand beside him.

"Neither," he said in clipped tones. "I simply wished to be rid of her."

"You could have accomplished that task with a mere wave of your hand. There was no need for such generosity. Especially if you are not planning to enjoy the sweet rewards of that charity."

Philippe heaved a sigh as he turned to regard his friend with a lift of his brows.

"Did you seek me out with a purpose?"

Belfleur hesitated before he at last gave a lift of his pudgy hands. "Carlos has commanded that you are not to be allowed alone for any length of time."

Philippe stiffened, disliking the notion that he was being discussed behind his back as if he were a babbling idiot.

"A rather presumptuous command from a mere servant."

Belfleur frowned in disapproval at Philippe's cold words. "Carlos is your friend, and as your friend he is worried."

With an effort Philippe eased his tense muscles. Belfleur was right, of course. He might find the concern of others chafing, but he would be a fool to take offense. There were few in this world he truly trusted. He could not afford to lose those that he did.

"And you have been chosen to become my nanny?" he teased in an effort to lighten the mood.

Belfleur readily followed his lead as he gave a loud laugh. "A daunting task, I will admit."

"Do not fear. I have not yet taken leave of my senses. The city of Paris is safe from my wrath for the moment."

"I must admit to some relief." Belfleur cast a glance about the pale ivory buildings. "I am rather fond of 'Cara Lutetia,' as the Emperor Julian once called Paris."

Philippe flashed his companion a startled glance. "*Meu Deus,* do not tell me that you have actually read a book?"

"Do not spread that ghastly tale about. I should hate to lose my reputation as an uneducated brute."

Philippe made a rude sound. "No one who knows you, Belfleur, would ever think you were anything but shrewd, ruthless and as lethal as a snake hiding in the grass."

"Here, now. You shall make me blush."

"I doubt if you have blushed since you left the nursery."

"True enough."

They both fell silent as they stared into the shadows. Philippe paid little heed to the sounds just beyond the alley. He had no interest in the screeching vendors or drunken revelers or brawling street thugs. His entire attention was trained upon listening for the soft sound of footsteps that would portend one of the pickpockets returning to offer his report.

For long moments they remained standing side by side, and then Belfleur reached up to lay a hand on Philippe's arm.

"You do know that you cannot stand out here the entire night? You will freeze what few wits you have remaining."

"I will come in later."

The older man heaved a faint sigh. "This woman…she must mean a great deal to you."

Philippe grimaced. "I seem to be hearing that oft of late."

"Can you deny it?"

He could not, of course. Over the past hours he had been forced to accept that the thought of his life without Raine was a bleak destiny that he could not bear to contemplate.

Until she had arrived he had merely gone through his days with a single-minded determination to build his business, and on occasion, to assist the king. There had been nothing beyond his duty and responsibility.

He had been cold and alone without ever realizing that such warmth could be found in the companionship of a woman.

The knowledge should have been terrifying. After all, he

had always taken pride in his ruthless independence. He never wanted to share his life with another. The past had taught him that he was bound to be disappointed when he depended on anyone for his happiness.

At the moment, however, his only terror was that Raine had disappeared from him forever.

The grim thought barely had time to form when Philippe was distracted by the soft fall of footsteps. He instantly straightened and glanced toward the corner of the alley.

"Someone is approaching," he murmured softly.

Belfleur peered into the dark, his round face easing as he recognized the skinny urchin hurrying in their direction.

"Ah...it is Victor. And he is early." Belfleur stepped forward, his brows lifting as the boy with a shock of black hair and grubby face skidded to a halt before them. "Have you news?"

The boy narrowed his eyes as he glanced toward Philippe. "Did you mean it about the reward, *monsieur?*"

Belfleur gave a low growl as he grasped Victor by the collar of his shirt and gave him a sharp shake. "You try my patience at your peril, boy. Tell me what you know."

Victor smiled with a sly arrogance. "I found the man. Now, where's my money?"

CHAPTER TWENTY-TWO

THE NEXT HOUR PASSED WITH a blur of frantic urgency.

With Carlos and Belfleur at his side, Philippe followed Victor to the shabby building where Seurat had held Raine captive. Philippe would never forget the first sight of her lying upon the filthy bed with her hands tied behind her back and her arms smeared with blood. Fury had seared through him at the knowledge that she had endured such brutal treatment, and an unexpected flare of guilt at the thought that this, at least in some small portion, was his fault.

Somewhere in the back of his mind he had been aware of Carlos searching the rooms for the absent Seurat and then organizing Belfleur and his gang of pickpockets into a web of eyes and ears to keep a watch upon the neighborhood.

The fact that it should be his position to be taking the lead in the capture of Seurat was buried beneath his fierce concern for Raine. At the moment all he cared about was taking the woman from the ghastly hovel and returning her to his home so that he could properly tend to her.

After gently untying her bonds, he had cradled her in his arms and carried her down to the waiting carriage. Even as they were rattling their way to Montmartre he refused to allow her to leave his grasp, instead settling her on his lap and covering her with a heavy blanket.

Raine, of course, protested against his tender care. She

was not the sort to easily cast herself in the role of feeble victim and disliked being fussed over. Trapped in his arms, she continued to assure him that she was perfectly well and that she had been treated as a respected guest by Seurat. Even as he carried her through the cottage she was pleading with the servants to halt their tears of joy and to be about their duties.

Philippe easily ignored her objections to being carried like a child and hauled her to his chambers. Within a short time he had her stripped of her rumpled gown and soaking in a hot tub as he gently washed her clean of the clinging dust.

Beneath his tender touch her muscles slowly relaxed and she leaned her head against the back of the tub.

"Oh, this is heavenly," she murmured softly, her eyes closed. "I did not believe I would ever be warm again."

Philippe knelt beside the tub, stripped down to his breeches. Until this moment he would have laughed at anyone who suggested he would ever play lady's maid for a woman. Such a thing was disturbingly intimate. Far more intimate than mere sex. But in this moment he could not deny that he found himself reveling in performing such a service for Raine. Indeed, he was unable to stop himself.

He had to touch her. He had to feel the satin heat of her skin, smooth his hands from the top of her curls to the very tip of her toes. He had to assure himself that she was alive and unharmed.

He studied the delicate profile as a peculiar surge of emotion shot through his heart. With her heavy swath of lashes sweeping her cheeks and the stubborn line of her jaw softened, she looked unbearably young and innocent.

"Perhaps you will take more care on the next occasion you run off with another man, *meu amor*," he murmured as his fingers trailed down her arm. "Not all gentlemen are so concerned with your comfort as I am."

She chuckled softly. "I shall bear that in mind."

His entire body stiffened as his fingers reached her wrist and the flesh that was rubbed raw from the ropes. The fury he had battled to keep at bay while he cared for her slashed through him with a brutal force.

"We should send for a doctor," he rasped. "These wounds need to be tended."

She reluctantly opened her eyes to regard him in puzzlement.

"They are merely scraped, Philippe. They will heal in a few days."

"Seurat shall pay for every moment he held you captive, do not fear."

Her brows snapped together at his solemn promise. "No."

Philippe sat back on his heels. "I beg your pardon?"

"If I desired revenge upon Seurat, I would seek it for myself. I do not need or want you to punish anyone on my behalf," she informed him sternly.

His gaze slowly narrowed. "I was not asking for your permission."

"Of course you were not." She did her own bit of eye narrowing. "Why should you concern yourself with what I might want?"

Angry words were poised on Philippe's lips before he forced himself to swallow them. Raine could claim an astonishing collection of skills, not the least of which was the ability to rouse the temper he had not even known he possessed.

"Oh, no, not tonight, Miss Wimbourne. You are not going to provoke me into an argument," he informed her as he scooped her from the tub and wrapped her in a thick robe. Once she was warmly garbed he carried her to the bed and tucked her beneath the covers. He stretched out next to her and firmly tugged her into his arms. "On this night I intend to hold you close and assure myself that you are truly back where you belong."

She tilted her head to give him a wry glance. "In your bed?"

"In my bed, in my home, at my side. Where I am, is where you belong." He tucked another pillow beneath her head. "Are you warm enough? Do you need more blankets?"

Her brows slowly lifted at his solicitous concern. "Philippe?"

"Yes?"

"Are you feeling quite well?"

"No." His arms tightened about her slender body. "In truth, I am not entirely certain I shall ever feel quite well again."

She reached up to lightly touch his cheek. "I am safe and unharmed. There is no need to worry."

"Perhaps you are right, *meu amor.*" He grasped her fingers and brought them to his lips, his gaze holding her own with a steady promise. "I shall not have to worry because I shall never allow you to be left without a guard again."

She heaved a faint sigh. "You are being absurd."

Just a few weeks ago Philippe would have entirely agreed with her opinion. He had always held absolute confidence in his own ability to conquer any enemy, whoever or whatever it might be. Now, however, he was absolutely determined to make sure that there were at least three burly servants keeping constant watch on the cottage. There would be no more surprises. For once he possessed something too precious to risk.

Breathing deeply of her enticing scent, Philippe allowed the warmth of her small body to chase away the last of the lingering chill.

Raine was home. She was where she belonged.

Tucking her head beneath his chin, Philippe simply held her until there was a soft knock on the door and Madame LaSalle bustled in with a heavy tray.

Crossing the room, the older woman offered a rare smile, as if pleased to discover that Philippe was capable of taking proper care of her beloved mistress.

"Here we are," she said briskly, settling the tray on the bed. "A nice cup of broth and bread still warm from the oven."

Struggling to sit upright against the mass of pillows, Raine breathed deeply of the enticing scents.

"Madame LaSalle, it smells wonderful."

"It is precisely what you need to recover your strength. So be warned that I am not leaving this room until you have eaten every bite," the housekeeper said sternly.

Accepting that he would be allowed no privacy with Raine until the staff had finished their fussing, Philippe reluctantly lifted himself off the bed and wrapped a robe about his half-naked body.

"Has Carlos returned?" he demanded.

"*Oui.* He returned only a few moments ago. He is eating in the kitchen."

He bent down to brush his lips over Raine's brow before straightening to regard the housekeeper with a warning gaze.

"Do not allow her to stir from that bed."

Madame LaSalle gave a nod, her hands on her hips as if quite prepared to use brute force to keep Raine abed.

Certain that Raine was out of harm's way for the moment, Philippe left the chamber and made his way to the narrow kitchen. As Madame LaSalle had promised he found Carlos at the table eating a large bowl of stew.

"Did you discover anything?" he asked as he leaned against the wall.

"Very little." Carlos took a deep drink of his wine. "The rooms held few possessions. Certainly none that would lead us to where Seurat has fled."

Philippe had not dared to hope that Seurat would be so careless as to lead them to his latest lair. And in truth, it was not his swift disappearance that was currently troubling him.

"He could not have gone far. Belfleur's lads are searching

every street and alley. I have offered enough reward to make sure they do not allow so much as a mouse to slip past them."

Carlos polished off the last of his stew and leaned back in his chair. "I do not believe he intends to try to slip past them. For the moment I sense he intends to find a dark corner to hide in while he plots how to punish you. He will not be pleased you interfered in his revenge."

"I hope you are right, my friend." Philippe smiled with cold anticipation. "On this occasion I intend to be prepared."

Carlos nodded, his fingers tapping restlessly on the table. "How is Raine?"

"Remarkably well and already lecturing me on my wish to punish her captor," he said dryly.

"She was not—" the muscles in Carlos's neck worked as he struggled against a blaze of emotion "—harmed?"

Philippe had no need to inquire to his companion's meaning. Neither had spoken of their appalling fear that Seurat might force himself on the vulnerable woman, but it had been a heavy burden that they had both endured. A woman could recover from bruises and scrapes. To be raped was a wound that did not heal.

"No," he said in emphatic tones. "She assures me that Seurat behaved as a perfect gentleman."

Carlos released a shaky sigh. "Thank God."

"Indeed."

There was a startled silence as Carlos narrowed his gaze. He had not missed Philippe's distracted tone.

"Should you not be pleased Seurat did not harm her?"

"Of course I am relieved." Philippe pushed from the wall to prowl across the flagstone floor. "Had he so much as laid a hand upon her…I would have pursued him to the gates of hell to destroy him."

"Then what troubles you?"

Philippe came to an abrupt halt and shoved his fingers through his hair. "Why did Seurat release Raine?"

"He did not precisely release her. He merely left her behind."

"But why? He could have forced her to go with him when he fled."

Carlos shrugged. "Perhaps he feared she might endanger his escape. Hauling around a screaming woman does tend to attract attention."

"Taking her from his rooms would have offered considerably less risk than taking her from this cottage. Once he had her in his grasp, she would be compelled to obey his commands," Philippe pointed out.

Carlos gave a startled laugh. "Raine obeying commands? That would be a sight worth seeing."

Philippe's lips briefly twitched. It was true that Raine had an uncanny habit of ignoring even the most direct commands. Still, not even his stubborn beauty was proof against a gun pointed at her heart.

"Why did he not force her to go with him?" he repeated.

"It could be he thought that she had served her purpose," Carlos suggested. "He proved he could slip beneath your nose and steal away something you value."

Philippe frowned. If he had discovered nothing else about Seurat over the past few weeks it was that he was determined to have his full pound of flesh from the Gautier clan.

"But he must have realized she was the perfect means of gaining whatever he desired from my family," he argued. "I would have done anything, given anything to have her returned."

Carlos gave a lift of his brows. "Actually, Philippe, I doubt he suspected any such thing."

"Seurat might be unhinged, *amigo,* but he has proved he is not a fool."

"Yes, but as far as Seurat was concerned, Raine was your

current mistress, nothing more." Carlos slowly rose to his feet and crossed to stand directly in front of Philippe. "What would you have done if he had taken any of your other lovers?"

Philippe blinked at the unexpected question. "I would not have left them at the mercy of a madman."

"You would, of course, have attempted to rescue them, but you would not have bartered your soul for their release."

A wry smile touched his lips. He could hardly argue the truth of his friend's words. "Perhaps not."

"I still am uncertain what is bothering you."

"I am not entirely certain myself." Philippe gave a restless shake of his head. He had no explanation for the irritating sensation that he was looking at a puzzle with a vital piece missing. "I only know that Seurat is obsessed with his need to hurt my family. It does not make sense that he would have the means to harm me within his grasp and simply allow her to escape with no more than a few scrapes."

Carlos pondered for a long moment, his dark features lined with weariness. Like Philippe, the younger man had refused to rest until Raine was returned. A knowledge that both pleased and troubled Philippe.

"There seems to be only two possibilities," Carlos at last muttered. "Either Seurat panicked and fled without completing his revenge, or he has conjured another means of punishing you."

"I will not allow him to have another opportunity. He must be found."

Carlos gave a slow nod, his dark eyes hard with determination and he moved toward the door. "I can assure you there will be no stone left unturned."

IT WAS TWO DAYS AFTER her return to the cottage before Raine at last had the opportunity to request a private meeting with Carlos.

Philippe had proved to be remarkably persistent in keeping her under his constant surveillance. Not a difficult task since they had rarely left his chambers, she wryly acknowledged. Philippe was always a demanding lover, but since her return he had been insatiable. If she were a fanciful woman she would have thought his clinging arms and tender kisses were a sign that he had realized during her absence that he held an affection for her. That just perhaps she meant more to him than a warm body in his bed.

As it was, she was wise enough to realize that his fierce, relentless passion was no more than some primitive male need to mark his possession.

Not that the knowledge had diminished her pleasure in his lovemaking, she was forced to concede. When Philippe was trembling from the force of his desire and whispering soft words in her ear, she felt as if she were the most cherished, most treasured woman ever to have been born. In those moments she belonged utterly and completely to him.

Dangerous sensations that warned her to complete her plans for dealing with Seurat, and to complete them without delay.

Once Philippe could be assured that Jean-Pierre was no longer in danger, he would be anxious to return to his estates in Madeira and Raine would be sent back to England.

This afternoon, at last, Philippe had announced his intention to return to Paris and seek out further acquaintances to assist in the search for Seurat. She had watched from the window as he had ridden down the cobblestone streets toward the city before sending one of the maids in search of Carlos. She was quite certain Philippe would not leave her at the cottage without his trusted companion to keep an eye upon her.

Her faith was not misplaced, and she was just finishing her luncheon when Carlos strolled into the drawing room. As always he was attired in rough woolen clothing that molded to his large body, and he brought with him a warm, spicy scent that uniquely suited his exotic looks.

He also brought with him a fierce, smoldering power that swept through the room like a force of nature.

It was that power she was in need of on this day.

Carlos halted in the center of the room and regarded her with a hooded gaze. "You do know that if you leave one morsel upon that tray poor Madame LaSalle will spend the entire afternoon fretting on what special treat she can create to tempt your fickle appetite?"

Raine rose to her feet with a small grimace. "An entire regiment could not consume the amount of food that Madame LaSalle sends to me."

"It is her method of revealing how much you have come to mean to her." A smile curved his lips. "Quite a remarkable feat considering she is a dragon who terrifies the entire village from the poor coalman to the local priest. Perhaps you have some relationship to St. George?"

"Nonsense." She gave a click of her tongue. "Beneath her gruff manners Madame LaSalle is a very kind woman."

"If you say so." His dark gaze swept over her with an unnerving intensity. "How are you faring?"

Raine stifled a sigh. It was a question that was put to her at least a dozen times a day, and while she appreciated the concern she felt like a fraud. Her brief stay with Seurat had not been nearly the terrifying ordeal that others insisted on believing.

"I am truly fine. Seurat is not entirely sane, but he treated me well enough." She smiled wryly. "I wish that everyone would not treat me as if I suffered some Shakespearean tragedy."

His brows lifted. "Not many women would view being kidnapped by a lunatic and bound to the bed so lightly."

"There were moments when I was frightened," she confessed. "But in truth Seurat is such a pathetic creature it is difficult to feel anything but pity when in his company."

"He may be pathetic, but he is also dangerous and extremely cunning."

"Yes, I know. I have not forgotten what he has done to Jean-Pierre." She wrapped her arms about her waist, her stomach giving a sudden twist of unease. It had been a simple matter to consider asking Carlos for his assistance when she was in the privacy of her room. Now that he was standing before her, Raine discovered her nerves tightening. He was not the sort of man who could be led about by a charming smile and flutter of her lashes. If she confessed her plans and he decided they were outlandish he would not hesitate to put a swift, brutal end to them. She sucked in a deep breath and gave an unconscious tilt of her chin. "That is why I asked you to join me."

He gave a short, mirthless laugh as he turned to stroll toward the fireplace. "I did not dare to hope it was for the mere pleasure of my company."

Raine frowned as she studied his harsh profile. "You must know that I always enjoy your company. I consider you a very dear friend."

He seemed to flinch as he briefly closed his eyes. "*Meu Deus,* why do you not stab me with a dagger and be done with it?"

Truly alarmed, Raine crossed the room to lay a hand on his arm. "Carlos? Did I say something wrong?"

There was a long, tense silence before he gave a sharp shake of his head and squared his shoulders. Whatever emotion had been gripping him was hidden behind a tight smile.

"Why did you wish to see me?"

Sensing his muscles flex beneath her lingering touch, Raine dropped her hand and regarded him with a wary expression.

"I...need your assistance."

"You know I am ever at your service." The dark features slowly eased as he sensed her apprehension. "Raine?"

"First I must have your word that you will say nothing to Philippe about what I am to tell you."

Carlos leaned against the mantel. "That is a difficult promise to give, Raine. Philippe has been my friend since I was a mere child. I would not deceive him lightly."

"Of course you would not and I appreciate your loyalty," she said sincerely. "I would not ask this of you if I did not believe it was in Philippe's best interest."

A sardonic smile touched his lips. "Philippe may not agree with your notion of what is in his best interest. In fact, I am fairly certain he would not, considering you came to plead your case with me rather than him."

"He is simply unable to be reasonable when it comes to Seurat."

"Do you blame him?"

Raine twisted her hands together as she turned and walked toward the window. Over the past two days she had pondered her rash promise to Seurat on a hundred occasions. She well knew that her susceptible heart could be easily manipulated. Especially if she thought that some poor soul was being abused by a man of privilege. It offended everything she held dear. But while she had told herself Seurat might very well be playing her for a fool, she could not convince herself that he had been lying. His wounds were all too real.

"I do not blame Philippe, but I do blame his father," she said as she turned back to meet Carlos's steady gaze. "Louis Gautier is responsible for this entire mess."

"I presume that Seurat managed to sway your sympathy with his well-rehearsed tale of how he was wronged?"

Her chin lifted at the hint of derision in his tone. "I think that having ruffians hired to murder you is a bit more than being merely wronged."

The dark eyes narrowed. "Is that what he claimed?"

"It is, and I believe him."

His lips abruptly twitched, his large body moving with startling grace as he crossed to lightly brush his finger down the line of her jaw.

"There is no need to poke out your chin at me, *anjo*. I am well enough acquainted with Louis Gautier to believe him capable of murder if it would further his dreams of glory."

"Then you will help me?"

"That still depends upon what you want of me."

"I have…" Words failed her beneath his intense gaze. Bloody hell. He was going to believe she had lost her mind. And she could not blame him.

"Raine?" he urged gently.

"I have made a bargain with Seurat," she abruptly announced.

His fingers tightened on her face. "So Philippe was wise to question why you would have been released unharmed."

Raine frowned at his strange words, but she refused to be distracted. "I do not believe Seurat would have harmed me regardless of our bargain."

His brooding gaze followed the path of his fingers as he brushed them over the cut still obvious on her lip.

"This says otherwise."

"It does not matter," she said impatiently. "All that is important is that Seurat is willing to put aside his desire for revenge for a price."

"And what is that price?"

"I have promised to sell the necklaces that Philippe gave to me and offer the profits to Seurat."

Carlos dropped his hand and stepped away from the bewitching minx. Not just in shock, although he was certainly stunned by her outrageous suggestion, but because he wanted to do so much more than brush her lips with his finger. He wanted to crush that rosebud mouth in a kiss that would reveal the hunger that pulsed through his body. He wanted to tug off that delicate ivory gown and reveal the slender beauty that was hidden beneath. He wanted to plunge himself so deeply inside her that she could think of no other man but him.

Instead he turned away and struggled to think clearly. "*Meu Deus.* Do you have any notion what those necklaces are worth?" he rasped.

"Their worth is nothing in comparison to having Jean-Pierre freed and Philippe spared from the constant threat of Seurat plotting some devious revenge."

He gave a disbelieving shake of his head. Surely there was no other woman who would so easily dismiss such priceless jewels? Certainly none of his acquaintances.

"The same thing will be accomplished when we capture Seurat and haul him to an English prison."

"*If* you capture him."

He instinctively turned, astonished she would even question the inevitable fact. He and Philippe had spent years tracking down the most cunning traitors. Men who had power and position and enough supporters to make it a dangerous proposition to spy upon them. The thought that they could not capture a stray lunatic was absurd.

"Never doubt he will be cornered like the rat he is, Raine."

She waved aside his arrogant confidence. "Then Philippe will see that he is punished."

Carlos shrugged. "Of course."

"And so Seurat will suffer as Jean-Pierre and Philippe have already suffered." Her beautiful features tightened with a fierce emotion. "And Louis, the actual villain, will remain unscathed."

"Such is the nature of scoundrels."

"It is…immoral, and deep within Philippe he will know that he is protecting his family at the cost of true justice," she said, her voice throbbing with genuine outrage.

Carlos smiled wryly, resisting the urge to reach out and stroke the soft heat that flooded her cheeks. She was so frighteningly innocent. So pure.

"Perhaps that is how you would feel, Raine, but I do not believe that Philippe possesses your tender heart," he said.

She heaved a deep sigh, her arms wrapping about her tiny waist. "You are wrong, you know. Philippe does not readily reveal his emotions, but he feels deeply."

Carlos hastily swallowed his laugh. "You are the first to accuse him of that sin."

Her dark eyes became pleading as she stepped close enough to cloak him in her sweet scent.

"Carlos, you know as well as I that Philippe bears the weight of far too many burdens," she murmured. "And that he holds himself responsible even when it is others who fail."

He sucked in a sharp breath, struggling against the sensation he was tumbling into those wide, impossibly beautiful eyes.

"Holds himself responsible?" he demanded in bemusement.

"Yes." Her hand reached out to touch his arm, sending a blaze of need roaring through his body. "He blames himself for his mother's death, for Jean-Pierre being imprisoned, and if he is forced to destroy Seurat because his father is too weak-willed to return what he has stolen, then he will hold himself to blame for that, as well."

Carlos ground his teeth, resisting the urge to inform the gullible woman that Philippe was very far from the saint she desired to paint him. It was not loyalty toward his friend that stayed his tongue. All was fair in love and war. No, he would quite willingly do whatever necessary to turn her from Philippe, but not at the cost of tarnishing that delicate purity.

That was something he would protect with his very life.

"Philippe's desire to destroy Seurat no longer has anything to do with his family," he said cautiously. "Seurat sealed his own fate when he kidnapped you."

Her face paled, her nails digging into his arm. "That would only make it worse. I could not bear to have someone harmed for my sake. How could I live with such a thing?"

Carlos gave a slow shake of his head. *Meu Deus.* Her father should have left her in that blasted convent where she belonged.

"And you think to prevent this dreadful fate by bribing Seurat?"

"Yes."

"Could it be, *anjo,* beyond wishing to keep Philippe from sacrificing what remains of his soul, that a part of you wishes to rescue the madman from his well-deserved fate?" he demanded softly.

A wistful smile curved her lips. "Is that so wrong?"

"No." Carlos heaved a sigh, knowing he was lost. "It might be foolish, but it is not wrong."

"Then you will help me?"

CHAPTER TWENTY-THREE

AFTER WINNING CARLOS'S reluctant agreement to assist with her daring scheme, Raine did not give herself an opportunity to enjoy her victory. There was still any number of obstacles to overcome. The first of which was discovering where Philippe had hidden away the necklaces that she had tossed back in his face.

It had taken the rest of the afternoon to locate them locked in the bottom drawer of his desk. Thanking the heavens that one of her father's scandalous friends had taught her the art of picking a lock, she at last had the jewels hidden at the bottom of her armoire.

On the morrow Carlos would travel to Paris and sell the gems. Once they had the money she would be prepared to meet with Seurat. Always presuming he did agree to meet with her.

With her task completed, she had taken a long bath and dressed for dinner. Oddly she still did not feel the relief she had been expecting.

Raine tugged her curls into a simple knot as she attempted to determine the source of her niggling unease. It could not be the knowledge that she might very well be hastening the day Philippe would rid himself of her presence. After all, that realization was responsible for the dull ache that clutched at her heart.

It was not until she entered the drawing room to discover

Philippe awaiting her that she accepted what it was that troubled her.

Guilt.

Despite the fact that she was truly doing what she thought best for Philippe, she could not entirely dismiss the knowledge that he might not appreciate her efforts to rescue him. Especially when he discovered she had hocked the beautiful jewels he had so generously given to her.

Gentlemen were rarely reasonable when it came to their pride, and Philippe would no doubt be furious with her until he had the opportunity to accept that she had dealt with Seurat in the best means possible.

Not that it truly mattered, a voice mocked in the back of her mind. As soon as he realized that his brother was out of danger, he would be returning to his estates. Without her.

Her mouth was dry and her nerves raw as Philippe noticed her entrance and prowled toward her. He was attired in a black jacket and breeches that molded to his lean body with flawless perfection. His shirt was a crisp white and his cravat intricately tied with a diamond stickpin that shimmered with a cold fire.

In the flickering candlelight his classic beauty was near breathtaking.

Halting before her, Philippe lifted her hand to press a lingering kiss to her fingertips. A kiss that Raine felt to the tip of her toes.

"Ah, *meu amor,* you look beautiful, as always," he said, straightening as he peered deep into her eyes.

Raine felt a honey heat spread through her body and instinctively tugged her hand from his grasp and stepped back. Her nerves were wound tight enough without adding the heady force of his potent sensuality.

"Thank you, Philippe." She could only hope that her

smile was not as stiff as she suspected. "Was your afternoon productive?"

A frown flickered over his countenance before he turned to cross the room and pour himself a measure of brandy. "Not nearly so productive as I had desired. Seurat seems to possess an uncanny ability to disappear."

Her stomach churned, that ridiculous sense of guilt deepening as her gaze clung helplessly to the elegant grace of his movements.

Oh, Raine, cease this foolishness, she silently berated herself. She had made her decision, and if time proved her to be in the wrong, she at least had the comfort of knowing that she was following her heart. It was surely all that could be asked of her.

"Perhaps he has fled Paris," she managed to mutter.

Sipping his brandy, Philippe leaned against the heavy sideboard and regarded her beneath half-lowered lids. "It is a possibility, but I think it unlikely. Paris is his home. If he leaves he will have nowhere to hide."

She gave a nervous lift of her hands. "Yes, but he is not thinking clearly at the moment. He might bolt without concern that he will be sleeping in hedgerows."

"Then my men will find him." A cruel smile touched his lips. "There is no road left unguarded."

Raine swallowed the lump in her throat, desperately hoping that he had not been quite so careful as he believed. After all, Seurat needed to be capable of sending her a message, and at some point they would have to meet.

"You appear to have thought of everything."

He drained the brandy, and then, setting aside his glass he relentlessly paced toward her stiff form. Raine hastily backed away, coming against the wall with a sharp jolt.

His green eyes glittered with a strange fire as he stopped

directly before her, his hands landing on the wall on either side of her head. Her heart hammered as she realized that she was effectively trapped. She possessed an absolute certainty that Philippe would never physically harm her, but she knew enough of the stubborn man to realize that if he suspected that she was harboring a secret he would not relent until he had forced it from her lips.

"You do not seem pleased by my thoroughness."

"Of course I am."

The autocratic nose flared at her strained voice. "Raine, what is troubling you?"

"Nothing is troubling me."

He grasped her chin in a firm grip. "Do not ever attempt to lie to me, *meu amor,* you do not possess the skill for it. Tell me why you are behaving as if I have suddenly grown horns and a tail."

"That is absurd."

"Is it?" he growled, his eyes smoldering with annoyance. "Then why do you retreat from me as if you fear I might hurt you?"

"I…I suppose the thought of Seurat still manages to unsettle me." She spoke the first words that came to her mind, unprepared when his expression abruptly softened and his fingers curled gently against her cheek.

"Raine, you have told me everything, have you not?" he rasped in obvious concern.

She blinked in bemusement. "What do you mean?"

"The bastard did not…"

"No," she breathed, a blush staining her cheeks. "Philippe, I am quite unharmed. I did not mean to imply that the thought of Seurat frightened me. In fact, I feel nothing but sympathy for his madness."

The concern disappeared as he dropped his hand and

stepped back. Perversely, Raine felt a flare of disappointment as the warmth of his body was replaced by the chill in the air.

"Raine, I have attempted to indulge your tender heart, even when you blithely give away my favorite gloves, two sets of my finest boots and insist that I treat my servants as if they are my dearest acquaintances rather than my employees, but I will not allow you to waste your pity on that worthless madman," he said sternly.

She wrapped her arms about her waist to quell the urge to shiver. "It is my pity to waste."

"Not on this occasion."

"Philippe, you are being ridiculous."

"You belong to me, Raine Wimbourne." The ingrained arrogance was etched upon every line of his countenance. "And that includes your loyalty."

She pushed from the wall, her hands clenched at her sides. "I belong to no one, Philippe Gautier. And my loyalty must be earned, not commanded."

He glared at her, clearly battling the urge to throttle her. Then, astonishingly, he turned away and shoved his hands through his hair.

"Damn you, Raine Wimbourne. Are you attempting to drive me to Bedlam?" he demanded in strained tones.

Raine's heart squeezed as she belatedly noted the weary line of his shoulders and the tightness of his body. It was obvious that past weeks had taken their toll on his ruthless strength.

"I think it is best if I return to my room."

She moved to pass Philippe only to be halted as he reached out to grasp her arm and spin her about to face him.

"No, *meu amor,* you are not going anywhere until you have told me why you are behaving so strangely."

"Philippe, I…" Her words broke off as she met his burning green gaze. There was annoyance smoldering in the crystal-clear depths, and something else. Something that might have been an aching need that was echoed deep within her.

"What?" he prompted softly.

All need to flee from his presence melted beneath the haunting magic he always managed to weave about her. Soon, perhaps within days, she would be tucked safely back in her father's cottage. And she would never, ever see this man again.

How could she possibly waste a single moment?

"I do not wish to fight with you." She took a step toward him, her hand lifting to touch his face. "Not tonight."

His breath caught, his arms sliding around her waist. "What do you wish?"

Raine allowed her fingers to skim down the lean cheek, shivering at the rasp of his dark whiskers and the heat of his skin. He was so magnificently male.

"I am not entirely certain," she whispered unsteadily.

What did she wish?

To mean more to him than a passing fancy? To know that when he awoke she was his first thought, and when he went to bed it was her name he whispered? To be the very reason he lived?

Ridiculous, impossible dreams.

But, in this moment he was here. And he desired her. It was all she would ever have of him.

Vibrantly aware of the penetrating gaze that watched her every expression, Raine allowed her fingers to drift over his chiseled lips. Without warning he nipped at the tips of her fingers, his arms tightening until she was flush against the hard muscles.

"Do you know, *meu amor,* this is the first time you have willingly touched me?"

Feeling oddly light-headed she offered a faint smile. "Shall I stop?"

"Never." His voice was harsh, but the hands that stroked her back were infinitely tender. "I find I enjoy being seduced by an exotic angel. You have leave to touch me anywhere at any time."

"A rather generous offer," she teased.

His head lowered to brush his lips over her forehead and down the length of her nose. He hovered a breath above her mouth.

"I cannot claim to comprehend your odd mood, but at the moment I do not wish to question my good fortune." His lips captured hers in a kiss of stark hunger. "Come with me, Raine," he whispered against her mouth. "Let me take you to my bed."

Raine did not hesitate as she twined her arms around his neck. Time was slipping away and she would be a fool to waste a moment.

"Yes."

With a low growl of satisfaction, Philippe scooped her into his arms and carried her up the stairs. Once in his rooms he locked the door and moved to lower her gently onto the mattress.

Raine propped herself on her elbows to watch as he stripped off his elegant clothes. The flickering fire bathed his skin with a warm sheen, playing over the broad width of his chest and the ripple of muscles. His lean, finely hewed features were already tight with desire and his eyes glowed like the finest emeralds.

He looked like a god, she thought in bemusement. Apollo himself, who filled the room with his seductive power.

Joining her on the bed, his fingers easily dealt with her own clothing, his skill briefly reminding her that he must have undressed dozens of women with the same urgent talent. It was a thought that she fiercely shoved aside. For once she did not want to think of the past or the future. She only wanted to enjoy the moment.

As if sensing her hesitation, Philippe cupped her face in his hands and regarded her with that unnerving intensity.

"Do not become shy, *meu amor,*" he murmured, his thumb stroking her bottom lip. "I have devoted too many nights to thoughts of having those sweet hands stroking my body to bear for you to stop now."

His voice was soft, but Raine did not miss the hint of yearning that was threaded through the words. Her heart melted as she lifted her hands to press them to his chest. How many nights had he devoted to learning every sweep and curve of her body? How many soft cries had he wrung from her throat as he had kissed and nibbled endless paths of pleasure?

Tonight it would be her opportunity to discover the secrets of his body.

Clearing her mind of everything but the feel of his hair-roughened skin beneath her fingers, Raine explored his chest, lingering upon his nipples as a groan was wrenched from his throat. The sound only emboldened Raine as she leaned forward to replace her fingers with her lips.

Philippe arched against her, his hand curving about her neck as she flicked her tongue over his nipple.

"*Sim,* sweet angel, do not stop, I beg of you, do not stop."

Raine had no intention of stopping. There was a heady satisfaction in knowing that it was her touch that was making him shudder. Her lips that were causing his heart to race.

Her hands continued their restless search, traveling over the slope of his shoulders, the length of his arms, the hard planes of his stomach. Her blood heated and her stomach constricted at the fascinating contrast of the smooth silk of his skin layered over his rigid muscles.

"I like the feel of you," she whispered. "Your skin is so warm."

He gave a choked groan, his breath coming in great rasps. "It is on fire, *meu amor.* Your touch has set me aflame."

When her hands at last reached the large thrust of his erection she briefly paused, and then with a tentative touch she stroked down the pulsing shaft until she reached the soft pouches beneath.

Philippe's hips jerked off the mattress, his hand tugging her head toward his lips so that he could kiss her with a searing urgency. His tongue thrust between her lips just as his cock surged between her fingers. Raine tightened her grip, her head spinning beneath his devouring lips.

Beneath her touch his body trembled, a fine shimmer of perspiration coating his skin. For once he was not the practiced seducer in command of their lovemaking. Instead he was caught in the throes of her touch, of the pleasure she was capable of giving him.

An unexpected flare of satisfaction touched her heart and she wanted to please him, to know that she could make him shiver and plead for more.

She wanted the memory of her etched so deeply he would never be capable of forgetting her.

Unaware of the poignant sadness that tugged at her heart, Philippe pulled back with a rasping growl.

"Oh…God. I need to be inside you, *meu amor*," he said in thick tones. "I want to feel you riding me."

Not at all certain what he meant, Raine gave a startled gasp when he rolled onto his back, taking her with him. She braced her hands on his chest as she stared down at his flushed countenance, her legs straddling his hips. He held her gaze with ease as he used one hand to adjust his erection, his other hand on her hip as he guided her downward.

Raine's heavy lids lowered as she was slowly impaled by his rigid flesh, and when he began to roughly thrust his hips, she tilted back her head and allowed him to take control.

In this moment he belonged utterly to her.

It was a memory that would have to warm her in the lonely years ahead.

CHAPTER TWENTY-FOUR

PHILIPPE AWOKE WITH A rare sense of contentment. Not that it wasn't always pleasurable to awake beside Raine, he ruefully acknowledged. What man in his right mind would not be delighted to discover his arms filled with such a beautiful woman? But on this morning there was a new satisfaction.

Meu Deus, Raine had offered herself so sweetly last night. There had been no barriers, no conflict, no sense of grudging acceptance. Instead she had been openly wanton, giving and taking pleasure with such abandon that he had been forced more than once to plead for her to end his torment and bring him to satisfaction.

Strange to think that he would enjoy being at a woman's mercy. Certainly he would never have allowed any other female to gain the upper hand. Not in his bed and not in his life.

But with Raine...with Raine all he could comprehend during the blaze of searing pleasure was that she had at last opened herself to him. She had held nothing back as she had led him to paradise over and over.

She had accepted that she belonged to him utterly.

Reluctantly rising from the bed where Raine sprawled in naked splendor, he forced himself to ignore the urge to wake her with a kiss. He was already hard and aching. One touch and he would forget the determination to continue his hunt of Seurat.

In Raine's arms he could forget his brother's desperate

plight, his need to be done with this business and return to the duties of his estate and even the demands of the king.

Which only made it more imperative that he be done with this unpleasant task so that he could sweep Raine off to Madeira. Once there he intended to sate himself until he could at last rid himself of this obsession. Only then would he be capable of returning his attention to the endless responsibilities that awaited him.

Within the hour he was bathed and dressed. Pausing beside the bed, he leaned down to regard Raine with a faint smile. She looked so tiny upon the large bed, so fragile. With care not to wake her, Philippe reached down to touch the tiny locket that lay against her breast. The gold was tarnished, but it glowed with a surprising warmth against her ivory skin. As if his mother approved.

Giving a shake of his head at his odd fancy, Philippe turned and left the room. He truly was out of his wits, he conceded as he headed through the cottage. But on this morning he could not seem to make himself care.

He entered the kitchen to discover Carlos finishing his breakfast. The younger man glanced up at his entrance, his brows slowly lifting.

"Good morning, Philippe, you are appearing particularly pleased with yourself," he murmured. "Has there been word of Seurat?"

Philippe did not attempt to wipe the smile from his lips. It would be an impossible task when his body still ached with sweet release and the taste of Raine was still on his tongue.

With a shrug he reached for a fresh croissant and devoured it in a few bites. "Not as yet, but I intend to change that today."

Carlos rose to his feet. "You are going to Paris?"

"I am leaving now." He moved to pull on his greatcoat,

pausing as he sent his companion a searching gaze. "You will remain here to keep a guard on Raine?"

There was an unexpected pause before Carlos gave a nod of his head. "If that is your wish."

Philippe halted, a frown tugging at his brows. "You had other plans for the day?"

"Nothing that cannot be altered. When do you expect to return?"

Philippe's frown deepened. There was a stiffness to Carlos that he found odd. As if the younger man were attempting to hide something from him.

"It is difficult to say. I may remain for dinner with Frankford. I would like to have word of what is happening in the world. Soon enough I shall be able to return my attention to my neglected business, I do not wish to be entirely ignorant." He grimaced, disliking the notion of being absent from the cottage for the entire evening. "And there is the possibility that he might have some news of Jean-Pierre. Gossip travels swiftly, even across the channel."

Carlos placed his hand on his shoulder and gave a light squeeze. "The king will do nothing irrevocable without contacting you first. He owes you too much."

"The king is a selfish child who is often at the mercy of his own whims. If he should take it into his mind that Jean-Pierre is a threat to his throne he will have him executed before calmer minds can prevail."

His dark eyes narrowed with a grim determination. "We shall have Seurat captured before the king can indulge in one of his fits of madness."

"I pray you are right." Philippe smiled wryly and glanced toward the door. "Take care of Raine."

Carlos dropped his hand from his shoulder and heaved a faint sigh. "It is a heavy burden you place on my shoulders, *amigo.*"

Philippe stilled, once again sensing that his companion was troubled. "Carlos? What is it?"

Stepping back Carlos smiled with a wry amusement. "Be on your way, Philippe. Raine is safe in my hands."

DARKNESS HAD DESCENDED before Raine heard the sound of Carlos entering through the back door. At last. She had been pacing the floor for hours, terrified that he would not return in time.

Shuddering with relief, she forced herself to await him in the drawing room. The lower floor would be filled with servants bustling about to prepare dinner. What she had to say to Carlos needed absolute privacy.

Another ten minutes passed before she heard his approaching footsteps and he finally entered the room. His dark hair was rumpled and his cheeks reddened by the cold wind, but that did nothing to soften the raw power he brought with him.

With a small sound of relief she flew across the room to grasp his arm in a tight grip.

"Oh, thank God, I did not think you would ever return."

His gaze ran a restless path over her upturned face before he grimaced and pulled his arm from her grip. "I have only been gone a few hours, *anjo*. It was not a simple matter to discover someone willing to offer a suitable sum for your jewels."

She paused in astonishment at his words. "But why? You said they were worth a fortune."

"And so they are, but not if the person buying them believes them to be stolen." His smile was mocking. "There are few who would believe that the son of a Portuguese fisherman would have claim to such valuable property."

"Oh." Raine lifted a hand to her heart, stark regret flaring through her. Lud, but there were moments when she truly was stupid. She would never do anything to hurt this man. Not even if it meant assisting Philippe. "I never thought…I am sorry, Carlos."

He gave a shake of his head, his expression revealing that he had no desire to speak of the hours he spent attempting to sell the jewels.

"It does not matter, I have managed to acquire what you need."

"A good thing." She reached into her sleeve to pull out the crumpled note she had read a dozen times while she waited for Carlos's return. "A boy brought this to the door just after luncheon."

Smoothing the torn piece of vellum, Carlos swiftly read through the short note. It said nothing more than that Raine was to come alone to meet Seurat in the cemetery of Pere-Lachaise at half past nine. And to bring the money she had promised.

Carlos lifted his head, his expression grim. "The cemetery is not far, but we do not have much time."

"We?" Raine gave a wild shake of her head. "No, Carlos, you cannot go. If Seurat catches a glimpse of you he is certain to bolt."

Carlos reached out to grasp her shoulders in a tight grip, his eyes smoldering with an unreadable emotion. "I will remain out of sight, but do not think for a moment that I will allow you to go to this meeting without me. For all we know it could be a trap."

Raine swallowed her sigh. It would be pleasant to just once have a man who did not feel the compulsion to give her commands.

"That is ridiculous." She met his gaze squarely. "If Seurat desired to hurt me he could have done so while he had me in his rooms. All he desires is the ability to live his life with a bit of dignity."

"He is a madman." He gave her a slight shake. "Who can say what he might take it in his mind to do?"

"Carlos…"

"No," he growled in warning. "Either I go or I will lock you in your rooms and reveal all to Philippe when he returns. There will be no debate on this."

Raine rolled her eyes, not doubting for a moment he would lock her away. Carlos had agreed to assist her, but it would be by his rules.

"Very well, but you must not allow Seurat to catch sight of you." With her own command delivered Raine turned and gathered the cloak she had left on a nearby chair. "We must go. If I am late there is no telling what Seurat might do."

She was busily tugging the cloak around her shoulders when Carlos cupped her chin in his hand and forced her to meet his searching gaze.

"You are certain of this, *anjo?*"

She blinked in puzzlement. "Certain of what?"

His expression was oddly somber as he studied her upturned countenance. "If you meet with Seurat, if you offer him the money necessary to make his escape from Paris, Philippe might never forgive you."

Raine was startled by the sharp, wrenching pain that twisted her heart. Had she not already accepted her plan would bring an end to her fleeting relationship with Philippe? What did it matter if he walked away with indifference or disgust?

Strangely she realized it did matter. The thought that Philippe might recall their time together with anger rather than fondness made her feel as if a black cloud had settled upon her soul.

Which was absurd, she sternly chided her flare of despondency. What did it matter if Philippe cursed her from dawn to dusk? When he returned to Madeira she would never set eyes upon him again.

She was doing what was right. She could not hesitate out

of some foolish fear that Philippe might not appreciate her efforts to assist him. Someday, if there were any justice in the world, he would accept that this was the best solution for everyone involved.

"My decision is made, Carlos," she said, relieved when her voice did not quaver. "I will see it through."

She thought she heard him sigh before he squared his shoulders with determination.

"So be it, Raine." A faint smile touched his lips. "We shall go to the devil together."

THE DAY WAS A LONG and frustrating one for Philippe. Despite the numerous boys that continued to haunt the streets, there had been no sightings of Seurat. And Philippe's own discreet searches of the various buildings had provided nothing more than suspicious glances and a handful of threats to call for the guards.

As he halted before the busy café his every instinct urged him to return to his cottage and the beautiful woman awaiting him.

Once again he was cold and tired and in desperate need of a bit of comfort. Especially the sort of comfort that Raine was willing to provide.

But he had spoken honestly to Carlos. It had been too long since he had sought out information of what was occurring beyond Paris. He had too many people who depended upon him to entirely ignore what was happening in the world beyond.

On the point of dismounting, Philippe was halted as a grimy urchin dashed down the street, clearly attempting to capture his attention.

"Monsieur."

Philippe waited until the boy skidded to a stop beside his horse. *"Oui?"*

"I have a message for you."

With a flicker of surprise, Philippe reached down to take the crumpled note. *"Merci."*

The boy lingered, and with a faint smile, Philippe reached into his jacket to pull out a handful of coins. He dropped them into the messenger's outstretched hand, then waited until the lad disappeared into the shifting crowd before reading the note.

Philippe's heart gave a sharp leap at the short demand to meet with Belfleur at his shop. It could mean only one thing. Seurat had been found.

Without hesitation he urged his horse into motion and swiftly made his way through the heavy traffic. He was wise enough to keep an eye out for the numerous thugs and cutthroats that plagued the city, but his mind was churning with the fierce satisfaction that soon he would be returning to England and Jean-Pierre would be released from his filthy cell. Just as important, he would be done with this unpleasant task and he could return to his estates.

An unwitting smile touched his lips at the thought of watching Raine as she caught her first sight of Madeira. He knew in his heart she would be captivated by the rugged beauty of his home. How could she not be? There was nothing so magnificent as the craggy cliffs and small coves filled with fishing boats. Or the rolling hills that were covered by his precious vineyards. Even his house was splendid. A sprawling villa that was situated to offer a breathtaking view of the scenery.

And of course, there would be plenty of nearby villagers who would be grateful for her incessant need to be of service to others. She would be pleased to discover that his tenants were a warm and generous people who would readily show her the affection she had lacked in her life until now.

Philippe's thoughts were still wrapped about the image of Raine filling his home with her unique spirit when he realized he had reached his destination.

With a shake of his head to clear his thoughts, Philippe dismounted and tossed the reins to a nearby pickpocket who lurked near the door. The lad would know better than to try to take off with the stallion. Belfleur could be a harsh taskmaster.

Philippe entered the shop, frowning as he found the front shop empty. "Belfleur?"

The rotund Frenchman appeared from the back door, waving his plump hand for Philippe to follow him. "Come in, Philippe. We will speak in the back."

With a shrug, Philippe allowed himself to be led to an office that held a small desk and dozens of cabinets that were convenient for hiding ill-gotten goods. Crossing to the desk, Belfleur poured them both a measure of brandy and pressed a glass into Philippe's hand. Then, with oddly jerky motions, he turned to stir the dying embers of the fire.

Philippe drained the welcome heat of the brandy and set aside the glass. He was impatient to be done with the business.

"Where is the bastard?" he demanded. "Do you have him trapped?"

Belfleur slowly straightened and turned to regard Philippe with a guarded expression. "*Non*, this has nothing to do with Seurat."

Philippe clenched his fists as disappointment flared through him. What the devil was Belfleur thinking? He had to know that his note would send Philippe rushing to his establishment with the conclusion that his enemy was within his grasp.

"Your message said it was urgent that you speak with me," he said, his cold tone warning that he was not pleased.

Belfleur grimaced, but he offered no apology. "I have discovered information that I believe you would wish to know."

Philippe took a step forward, not at all in the mood to play games. His entire evening had been thrown into disarray by this ridiculous diversion.

"Hell and damnation, Belfleur. If you have something to tell me, then get on with it. I have matters to attend to."

Still, the man hesitated, sipping at his brandy before heaving a sigh and squaring his shoulders. Rather like the proverbial messenger bearing bad tidings.

"I have just come from dinner with an old friend who told me of a peculiar encounter he had with a customer today," he at last confessed.

Philippe stiffened. "Peculiar in what manner?"

"A foreign gentleman entered his establishment with the wish to sell a near fortune in jewels."

"And what interest should I have in this?"

"He was certain that the jewels were recently purchased from my own modest shop only days ago. Naturally it piqued his interest that they would be so swiftly sold."

The air was squeezed from Philippe's lungs as he abruptly began to pace the room. "What sort of jewels were these?"

"Three rather beautiful necklaces."

"The necklaces I purchased?"

"Oui."

Philippe reached the small desk and placed his hands flat on the surface. A cold dread was forming in the pit of his stomach. A horrid sense that he was being steadily led to the guillotine.

"A foreign gentleman, you said?"

"Spanish, my friend claimed. Or perhaps Portuguese."

The coldness spread even further as Philippe straightened with a shake of his head. "Carlos? No. It is impossible."

Belfleur sighed as he drained the last of his brandy. "I fear my friend was quite clear in his description of the gentleman and it fit Carlos remarkably well."

"I have known Carlos most of my life. He would never steal from me," Philippe growled even as a traitorous voice began to whisper in the back of his mind.

Carlos was fascinated with Raine. Even if he had not openly admitted his interest it would have been obvious in every lingering glance, every smile that touched his lips when she entered the room and every frantic hour he had been tortured when she had been missing.

How far would he go to have her as his own?

And more important, did Raine prefer the handsome, passionate young man who might very well be willing to offer her the honor of marriage? She had made it clear that she was shamed by the thought of being a mistress. Perhaps the hope of retrieving her tarnished reputation was too great a temptation.

Was that why she had been so sweetly giving last night? Was she saying goodbye to him?

The mere thought was enough to make him growl with a low, lethal fury.

Easily sensing the violence that now prickled the air, Belfleur held up his hands, eager to remind Philippe that he was innocent of any crime.

"There is nothing certain, Philippe. However, I would suggest that you discover if someone has managed to steal your treasure."

Philippe was already headed for the door.

No one would steal his treasure.

No matter what he had to do to keep it.

To keep her.

CARLOS GRUDGINGLY LINGERED in the depths of the church as he watched Raine pick her way over the uneven ground of the cemetery. It was not his nature to skulk in shadows while a fragile female went to confront the enemy. Especially when that female was Raine.

But somehow the bewitching minx had managed to wrestle a promise from him. He was not to take a step from the church unless he was convinced that Seurat meant her harm. She was determined to see this desperate plot through, and he discovered he did not possess the will to oppose her.

Which only proved that he was an idiot, Carlos acknowledged with a heavy sigh. He knew all too well that her willingness to place herself in such risk revealed just how deeply she had become attached to Philippe. A realization that made him smolder with an aching frustration.

Had he any sense at all he would have gotten on his horse and ridden from Raine Wimbourne the moment he suspected the truth of his feelings. Someplace far enough that he could ease his passions in a willing woman. Perhaps several willing women. None of whom had a taste for coldhearted, arrogant aristocrats.

His wandering thoughts were abruptly shoved aside as Raine came to a halt in the middle of the cemetery. From behind a crypt a limping form stepped forward to confront the startled woman and Carlos stiffened. Damn, they were too far away. If Seurat intended her harm...

Distracted by the fear that surged through his body, Carlos was uncharacteristically oblivious to his surroundings. A painful mistake, he discovered when he was grasped by the shoulder and spun about to encounter a descending fist.

The blow cracked his jaw and blinded his vision, and it was only his years of training that enabled him to instinctively jerk his head backward to avoid the second jab. Keeping his head low, Carlos used his considerable strength to shove his shoulder into his attacker's stomach, sending them both onto the dusty stone floor.

He managed to land on top, but it was a short-lived victory. Even as he pulled back his arm to punish his brazen opponent, his sight cleared enough to realize that this was no accomplice of Seurat, or even a random thug. The moonlight slanting through the open door revealed the unmistakable features of Philippe Gautier.

Astonishment made him falter for only a heartbeat, but it was long enough to give Philippe the advantage. With a low curse, the man had flipped Carlos onto his back and held him in place with a threatening hand wrapped around his throat.

"Did you truly believe you could take her from me, *amigo?*" Philippe growled, his face a deadly mask of intent. "Did you think I would not hunt you down and kill you?"

Carlos grasped Philippe's wrist and managed to loosen his hand enough to prevent himself from being strangled. How the hell had Philippe managed to track them to this cemetery? Had he suspected that they were plotting behind his back and waited for them to expose their hand?

Struggling to breathe, Carlos realized that it did not matter how he had found them. For the moment it was far more important that Philippe had convinced himself that Carlos was attempting to steal away the woman he considered as his own.

"If I had intended to take Raine away from you, Philippe, you would never have found us," he rasped. "And my choice certainly would not have been a damp, frigid church in sight of your cottage."

"You think I am a fool?" The green eyes flashed with a hectic fire, revealing the terrifying depths of his fury. Carlos had never seen his friend in the grip of such emotion. Not even when they had discovered Jean-Pierre was rotting in an English prison. It spoke to his desperation at the thought of losing Raine. "I know you stole the necklaces that I bought for Raine," he continued. "I also know you took them to Paris and sold them."

"How did you—" His startled question was choked off as Philippe's fingers tightened on his throat. "Damn you, Philippe, I cannot breathe."

"I do not care."

"I am not a thief," Carlos protested, relieved when the fingers eased. He had no desire to hurt Philippe, but he would not meekly allow himself to be throttled. "Raine gave the necklaces to me of her own will and requested that I sell them."

Philippe stiffened, a muscle in his jaw throbbing as he struggled to control his fierce response.

"You claim that this betrayal was Raine's notion?"

"There is no betrayal, but yes, it was your mistress who approached me and pleaded for my assistance," Carlos said.

"You lie."

"No, Philippe, not in this. I tell you the truth."

There was a frozen silence as Philippe accepted that Carlos was not lying. A brief flash of something that might have been sorrow burned in his eyes before he was narrowing them with anger.

"She asked you to take her from me?"

"That…was not her intent," he said cautiously.

Philippe sucked in a sharp breath. "Damn you, I will not endure riddles. Why did you take the jewels?"

"Because Raine desired the money they would bring," Carlos grudgingly revealed. Despite his pledge to Raine, they needed to be done with this nonsense. She was out there alone with Seurat. If something happened to her it would be entirely his fault.

"If she wanted money she need only have asked me for it," Philippe said, his voice raw.

"She did not wish you to know of her plans."

"Her plans to leave me?"

"No."

"Damn you, Carlos, I saw the two of you leaving the cottage. Together." Those slender fingers once again pressed into

Carlos's throat, bruising his skin and choking off his air. "Where is she? Tell me."

"Bloody hell, Philippe."

"Tell me."

"She is in the cemetery."

"Why?"

Carlos closed his eyes and accepted that his promise to Raine was at an end. He would not risk her welfare even to keep his word.

"She is meeting with Seurat."

"Seurat?" With a smooth motion, Philippe was on his feet, his expression harsh with disbelief. "He is here?"

"Sim." Carlos struggled to his feet, his hand rubbing his abused throat. "As you suspected the bastard did not simply release Raine. She negotiated her own escape. This meeting was a part of that bargain."

Philippe gave a slow shake of his head, as if having difficulty in accepting that he might have been mistaken in his furious assumptions. At last he turned and headed for the nearby door.

"Come with me."

With a swift motion, Carlos was hurrying to place himself in front of the charging Philippe.

"What do you intend to do?"

Eyes narrowed, he said, "First I intend to capture the man I have been hunting for too long, and then I intend to teach Raine just how dangerous it is to cross my will."

Carlos grasped his friend by the shoulders, his expression grim. "No."

The finely carved features hardened to a cold, aloof mask. "Carlos, if you value your life you will release me this instant."

"I will not allow you to hurt Raine."

"She is not yours to protect."

Carlos flinched at the stark truth of his words, but he refused to relent. "Nevertheless, I will do so."

"Damn you, Carlos, I do not harm women, no matter how much they might deserve it."

"I have your word?" Carlos persisted.

A growl rumbled deep in his chest. "Release me or discover that while I do not harm women, I am quite willing to harm any man who stands in my way. Including you."

CHAPTER TWENTY-FIVE

RAINE COULD NOT DENY an edge of unease as she cautiously made her way through the cemetery. It was not that she feared Seurat would harm her. Or at least that was only part of her unease. Instead it was a nagging sensation that thus far it was all going too smoothly.

Since the night that she had crept down the stairs to discover that her father was the infamous Knave of Knightsbridge she had managed to stumble from one disaster to another. She was coming to expect trouble.

The fact that there had yet to be any was making her skin prickle and her palms itch.

Swallowing the nervous urge to chuckle at her absurdity, Raine skirted the edge of an ancient crypt. In the same moment a dark form suddenly appeared before her.

Raine pressed a hand to her heart as she recognized the painfully thin form of Seurat.

"Good Lord, you startled me," she breathed as she came to a halt.

Despite the shadows it was obvious that Seurat had suffered over the past few days. Not surprising considering it must have been a difficult task to remain hidden from Philippe's numerous spies.

His hair stuck out in a bristle of gray and his face was filthy and unshaven. There was also a rather foul stench about him that made Raine wonder if he had been hiding in the sewers.

The hectic glitter in his eyes, however, had not altered. He was a man who was rapidly reaching the end of his sanity.

"You brought the money you promised me?" he demanded with a wary glance about the empty cemetery.

"Of course." She clutched the carefully wrapped package beneath her cloak more tightly to her chest. "You have your confession?"

Seurat gave a low hiss, his hand reaching into his pocket to pull out a folded parchment. "I am a man of my word, unlike your lover. Now, my reward."

Raine held out her hand. She could not afford to be duped. Jean-Pierre's life might very well hang in the balance.

"I wish to see the papers first."

Seurat took an awkward step forward, his features twisted in anger. "You doubt my honor?"

Raine did not flinch, her hand still held out. "I wish to make certain that it has been witnessed by a priest."

The man muttered a string of curses, but at last he shoved the parchment into Raine's hand. "There. Are you satisfied?"

Raine shifted so that the moonlight spilled on the paper in her hand. She was briefly startled by the elegant script, until she realized Seurat's duties in Egypt would have also included keeping records for his employees. Turning her attention to the actual words, she read through the confession and then studied the wax seal at the bottom.

It did appear that all was in order and she lifted her head to meet his glittering gaze.

"And I have your promise not to trouble the Gautier family any further?" she insisted.

"*Sacrebleu,* I have given you my word," he groused, and

then his gaze shifted over her shoulder, his eyes widening in horror. "Damn you."

"What?"

"You have tricked me."

Uncertain what the blazes was troubling the man, Raine slowly turned her head, her heart lodging in her throat as she watched Carlos bounding past her to tackle Seurat to the ground.

"No," she screamed.

Seurat futilely battled the far larger man, his head turning to give Raine a wounded glare.

"May your soul rot in hell," he rasped.

"Halt," she cried. "Carlos, what are you doing? You gave me your pledge that you would not interfere."

Arms, as hard as granite, suddenly wrapped around her from behind, jerking her painfully against a male body.

"Ah, but I gave you no such pledge," a voice whispered in her ear with a lethal softness, a hand reaching beneath her cloak and wrenching the bundle of money from her grasp.

Raine knew immediately whose arms imprisoned her. There was only one man who could make her heart leap and her blood run hot with a mere touch.

Turning her head, she glared at her captor. "Philippe. What are you doing here?"

His expression was grim, his eyes as hard as emeralds. "Do not say a word, *meu amor.*"

"But…"

His arms tightened until they threatened to cut off her breath. "Not a word if you value your soft hide."

Philippe waited until he was certain that Raine would heed his warning, then, ignoring the urge to shake the exasperating woman until her teeth rattled, he loosened his grip and stepped past her.

In silence he watched as Carlos at last subdued the struggling Seurat and hauled him to his feet by the cuff of his coat.

The man who had been his family's nemesis for years was smaller than he expected. His head would barely reach Philippe's chin and he was thin enough that it appeared a stiff breeze would send him tumbling. Hardly the fearsome opponent of Philippe's imagination.

At the moment, however, he was indifferent to the realization that such a tiny, pathetic creature could have caused him such grief. He was even astonishingly indifferent to the fact that Seurat was captured and his troubles had seemingly come to an end.

For the past half hour he had been consumed with the driving fear that Raine was about to slip from his grasp. It had burned through him with a searing fury that refused to be dismissed, even now that he was forced to accept that he might have been mistaken in her purpose.

Perhaps Raine had not intended to leave him. At least not on this night. But what of tomorrow? Or the next day? She had already proved that she was capable of deceit, of plotting behind his back and accomplishing the impossible feat of luring Seurat from his well-hidden lair. She had even managed to seduce Carlos into her web. Who was to say that she might not use those talents to escape him the next occasion he was forced to leave her side?

The thought was intolerable. Beyond intolerable.

Raine was *his*. Every silken inch of her belonged to him.

And he was sharply aware that the time had come to take the necessary steps to make sure that she was firmly and irrevocably bound to him.

But first he had to put an end to Seurat.

Concealing his burning awareness of the vexing female standing directly behind him, Philippe regarded Seurat with a frigid expression of disgust.

"Carlos, take our prisoner and return to England with him."
With a flick of his wrist he tossed the packet of money toward
the younger man. "Hire as many men as necessary to make
sure he does not escape."

Carlos easily caught the bundle and tucked it beneath his
jacket. Just for a moment he narrowed his gaze, as if he were
contemplating the notion of refusing the command. After all,
traveling to England would take him far from Raine.

Philippe took a step forward, his hard gaze warning his
friend that it would not matter how near he might be to Raine.
She would never be his.

With a grimace, Carlos gave his captive a sour glance.
"And once I am in England?"

"Take him to my town house," Philippe said, his thoughts
sorting through the swiftest means of having his brother released. "I will send a message to Windsor so that the king is
aware of your arrival."

Carlos gave a choked cough. "Not the most comforting
thought. I have no desire to awaken one morning to discover
the king waiting in the foyer."

Philippe smiled wryly, ignoring the various curses that
Seurat was spewing. "Do not fear, the king will not bestir himself to such an effort. He will command that you bring your
guest to the palace to make his confession."

Carlos gave the small man a shake. "And if he will not
confess?"

Philippe did not hesitate. "Kill him."

Seurat gave a shrill moan, but neither gentleman paid him
any heed. Instead they locked gazes in the silver moonlight.

"While I am rescuing Jean-Pierre what do you intend to
do?" Carlos demanded.

"That, *amigo,* is none of your concern," Philippe said softly.

Carlos narrowed his gaze. "Philippe."

"Return your favors to those women who are forever tossing up their skirts for you." Philippe allowed a smile of anticipation to touch his lips. "Raine will soon be beyond yours, and every other man's, touch."

RAINE WAS FORCED TO BITE her tongue as Carlos hauled poor Seurat across the cemetery and toward the carriage that was waiting behind the church.

Damn and blast. Had she not suspected that something was bound to come along and spoil her excellent plan?

Unfortunately, not even her darkest imaginings had envisioned Philippe Gautier arriving like an avenging angel and destroying all that she had attempted to achieve.

Which was foolish. When was Philippe *not* charging in and making a muck of her life? It was beginning to seem as if that was his sole duty in this world.

As if sensing her brooding thoughts, Philippe turned to her and held out an imperious hand.

"Come."

She took a step back, her brows drawn together in annoyance. "No, Philippe, you must listen to me."

He growled low in his throat, moving forward until he loomed over her with intimidating force. "I have told you not to speak."

"I will bloody well speak whenever I wish, and I am not going anywhere until you hear me out," she retorted.

His expression was cold and edged with a dangerous intent. "I have obviously coddled you too well, Miss Wimbourne. You believe you can flaunt my commands without danger of reprisal. That assumption is about to come to an end."

Her lips parted to demand his meaning when his hands were encircling her waist, and before she knew what was occurring, she found herself tossed over his shoulder as he headed toward the nearby road.

Caught off guard, it took Raine a moment to gather her rattled wits. Had the man lost his mind? She was no sack of potatoes to be toted about in such a manner.

With her legs firmly trapped by his arms, she could do nothing but pound her fists against his solid back.

"What are you doing? Put me down."

Her efforts were rewarded by an unexpected smack to her backside. "If you do not cease your struggles I will bind and gag you, do you understand?"

"Of course I do not understand." She gave his back another blow. "Have you taken leave of your senses?"

"Without a doubt," he muttered, halting before the horse that he had hidden in the nearby trees.

With an ease that revealed the coiled strength in his lean body, Philippe tossed her into the saddle and vaulted behind her. Once settled, he wrapped a binding arm about her waist and urged the stallion into a brisk pace.

Raine was jerked against his chest and instinctively grasped his arm as the mount slipped on the precarious ice.

"Are you attempting to break our necks?"

"You are right," he whispered next to her ear, slowing the horse to a more cautious pace. "I might be willing to risk your pretty neck, but I am rather fond of my own."

She tilted back her head to glare into his forbidding countenance. "If you intend to be in such a foul mood for the duration of our journey, I would prefer to walk."

His arm tightened. "If you are wise you will not press me at this moment, *meu amor.* My honor prohibits me from striking you, but there are any number of satisfying means of punishing you."

She opened her lips to inform him precisely what she thought of his dire threats, only to snap them shut again as the horse once again slipped on the ice. For the moment it seemed preferable to allow Philippe to keep his attention on the treacherous road.

Besides, she could not deny the faintest hint of fear that clutched at her stomach. She had seen Philippe in a fury before. Indeed, she seemed to possess a talent for riling his temper. But there was something…implacable about his fierce mood. A remote starkness. As if she had unwittingly crossed some line that had altered their relationship forever.

The thought made her heart clench with a raw pain.

She had known that it was a possibility that Philippe might not understand her desire to assist Seurat. That he might be angry until he realized that this solution was best for all involved. But she had not expected this impregnable barrier that made her wonder if he intended to toss her from the cottage the moment they returned.

The thought plagued her as they climbed the steep hill and at last reached the gardens of the cottage. Philippe was swiftly off the horse and plucking Raine from the saddle when one of the large men that Philippe had hired to keep guard on the cottage stepped from the stables.

Keeping Raine cradled in his arms, Philippe gave a jerk of his head toward his horse.

"Take care of my horse and then come to the kitchen. I will join you there."

The man did not so much as lift a brow at the sight of Raine being held so intimately by his employer as he gave a nod of his head. Perhaps it was a common sight for hired thugs.

"Oui, monsieur."

Striding toward the cottage, Philippe did not spare even a glance toward the woman he held in his arms. It was as if he had forgotten her altogether, Raine acknowledged with a jaundiced glare at his perfect countenance. And perhaps it was for the best. It was better to be forgotten than to be dumped in the rose bushes.

They reached the cottage and, lifting his leg, Philippe kicked open the back door to carry Raine over the threshold.

With a squeak of surprise Madame LaSalle rushed forward, her hands pressed to her ample breasts as she regarded Raine clutched to Philippe's chest.

"Blessed Mary, has there been an accident?"

"We are both well, Madame LaSalle," Philippe assured the fluttering woman, moving past her with a tight smile. "All we need is a measure of privacy."

The woman flushed as she gave a small chuckle. "Oh. *Très bien.*"

"Does it please you to embarrass me?" she muttered as they headed out of the kitchen and up the stairs.

His cold green gaze lowered to meet her mutinous expression. "The only thing that would please me at the moment is to place you over my knee and acquaint your backside with my hand."

She flinched at his biting tone. "You said you did not strike women."

"Then I shall have to find some other means of pleasing myself." He stepped into his rooms and without warning Raine found herself set roughly on her feet. She was still attempting to regain her balance when Philippe moved to the connecting door that led to her chambers and turned the key in the lock. Slipping the key into his pocket, he turned and regarded her with an aloof, unreadable expression. "Take off your clothes."

Whatever Raine had been expecting it was not this. Pressing her hands to her heaving stomach, she backed toward the center of the room.

"What?"

He put his hands on his hips, his expression icy. "I spoke quite clearly. Take off your clothing."

"No." She gave a wild shake of her head. "I will not."

"Then I will do it for you."

Her eyes widened in disbelief, but before she could do more than take a few hasty steps backward, he had his arms around her and easily tossed her onto the large bed.

Raine fought him, of course, kicking and scratching as each piece of clothing was roughly ripped from her body. She could not accept that Philippe would force himself on her. Not that it would be force for long, a tiny voice whispered in the back of her mind. He had only to touch her to make her melt in need. But, to be coerced against her will was no better.

"Brute," she muttered futilely struggling as he tugged off the last of her garments to leave her stark naked. "Arrogant, loathsome beast."

Astonishingly he did not join her on the bed. Instead he stood looming over her, a satisfied smile on his lips.

"Now attempt to escape me, Miss Wimbourne," he challenged.

Raine frowned in puzzlement, a puzzlement that only deepened as he smoothly gathered her clothing from the floor and headed for the door. Without a backward glance he stepped out of the room and closed the door firmly behind him. In the silence Raine heard the key tumble the lock.

He had effectively trapped her in the room, she realized with a vague sense of confusion. With both doors locked her only hope of escape would be the window, and no matter how desperate she might be, she was not about to risk her neck by leaping from such a height. Especially not when she was stuck without a stitch of clothing.

But why?

Did he think she might flee from him in terror? Did he truly believe her to be that cowardly?

Absently, Raine wrapped the covers over her shivering

body. Despite the fire that burned with cheery persistence in the grate, she felt chilled to the bone. Only to be expected, she supposed after standing in the damp cemetery for so long. But more than that, she realized that the cold had seeped into her heart.

She had failed. Miserably.

Seurat was captured and convinced that she had betrayed him. Carlos was being commanded to England and obviously in Philippe's bad graces.

And she…

Well, truth be told, she did not know what Philippe intended for her. All she knew was that she had made a mess of the entire situation and she had no one to blame but herself.

Brooding on the disastrous night, Raine felt her heart leap as the lock was turned and Philippe stepped through the door. Closing it behind him, he placed the tray that he held on a low table and then calmly began peeling off his elegant garments.

Raine scooted to a sitting position on the bed, the covers pulled to her chin.

"What are you doing?"

He did not falter as he dealt with the last of his clothing and then strolled across the room with complete indifference to his nudity. Raine did not want to watch, but how could she resist? The play of firelight over the sculpted lines of his body was enough to steal the wits of any woman.

Seemingly unaware of her lingering gaze, he reached to pull on a thick robe and tied it firmly about his waist as he returned to the table and plucked the napkin from the tray.

"First I intend to enjoy the dinner that you so rudely interrupted."

Raine gritted her teeth, telling herself that she was not the least disappointed that he had was not eagerly leaping into the bed beside her.

"If your dinner was interrupted, the blame is your own," she said, her tone peevish even to her own ears. "I certainly did not seek your presence."

He held her gaze as he ate a portion of the ham. "No, I do not suppose you did. Tell me, *meu amor,* what did you hope to accomplish with your little ploy?"

Her lips thinned as she pointed to the parchment that had fallen to the floor while he had so efficiently stripped her of her clothing.

"That."

He gave a lift of his brows as he continued to consume the large amount of food piled on his plate.

"What is it?"

Her temper stirred at his obvious indifference. "It is a confession from Seurat that is signed by a priest. If you had not interfered, my *little ploy* would have rescued Jean-Pierre without all this fuss."

He wiped his hands on a napkin and reached for his glass of wine. "By this fuss I presume you mean Seurat's well-deserved punishment?"

"I believe he has been punished enough."

The green eyes darkened to reveal he was not as composed as he would have her believe.

"But it was not your decision to make," he reminded her in a cold voice. "You knew that I would not approve of your absurd plan. That is, after all, why you chose to turn to Carlos for assistance, is it not?"

She unconsciously dampened her dry lips. "I thought it best for everyone involved."

"Best?" He moved to tower over the bed. Instinctively, Raine burrowed deeper into the pillows behind her. "You thought it for the best to offer the enemy that I have sought for months my own fortune to allow him to escape?"

"It was not your fortune." She clutched the blankets even tighter. "The money came from the necklaces that you gave to me."

"Necklaces that you refused to accept, if you will recall, *meu amor,*" he drawled with a humorless smile.

She bit her bottom lip, eying him warily. It was unnerving to realize that she had not the least notion of what was going on behind that aloof expression.

"Is that why you are angry? Because I sold the necklaces?"

His body stiffened, but his expression did not alter. His command was strangely frightening.

"It no longer matters. Seurat will soon be in the king's hands and Jean-Pierre will be released. Your betrayal has at least brought an end to the bastard."

Her eyes widened. Not only at his callous dismissal of Seurat, but at his blunt accusation.

"I did not betray you."

"No?"

"No." She forced herself to meet his searing gaze. "I told you that I was hoping to halt Seurat's revenge and bring an end to your need to destroy him. Even if you will not admit the truth, you must know deep in your heart that the blame of this horrid situation belongs on your father's shoulders. You seek to punish the wrong man."

"I shall punish whomever I desire," he warned.

"Even if it is wrong?"

He made a sound deep in his throat as he turned and paced toward the fireplace. She did not need to read his mind to realize he was annoyed by her refusal to meekly accept his verdict of Seurat's guilt.

"You seek to be my conscience?" he demanded.

"It would seem that someone needs to be."

"Enough, Raine," he growled. "I have no desire to speak

of Seurat. Instead we shall concentrate on what I am to do with you."

Her mouth was suddenly dry as she realized what was coming. This was it. He was going to inform her that he was done with her.

She told herself that she was relieved. At last she could return to her father and the life he had stolen from her. These brief days of madness would soon become nothing more than a distant dream.

Somehow the words did not lighten the heaviness that tugged at her heart, but she managed a stiff smile as she swallowed the lump in her throat.

"You have accomplished what you desired in Paris," she said in a voice that thankfully did not shake. "I assume that you will be returning to Madeira."

"On the morrow."

Her fingers clutched the covers. "So soon?"

"There is no need to delay, and I will admit that I am anxious to be home."

"Then it is perfectly obvious what is to be done with me."

A strange smile touched his lips as he moved back to the bed. "I am relieved that you agree, *meu amor.* I feared that you might foolishly attempt to battle the inevitable."

She smiled wryly. He would, of course, be arrogant enough to assume she would plead to stay at his side. Had he ever possessed a mistress who was not anxious to keep him as a lover?

Well, if he expected such nonsense from her, he was destined to be disappointed.

She managed to tilt her chin to a proud angle. "I only ask one favor of you."

He quirked a dark brow. "And what is that?

"I ask that you offer me sufficient funds so that I can return to England in at least some comfort."

"Ah." With an unexpected motion he shifted to sit on the bed next to her. "I fear that will not be possible."

Raine glared into the impossibly handsome features.

"You promised that you would see that I was returned to England in safety."

"And so you shall be…in time," he drawled sardonically. "My business demands that I spend at least part of the Season in London. And no doubt you will wish to visit your father while we are there."

"Visit?" Her frown only deepened. "I do not understand."

He shrugged, his expression revealing nothing of his inner thoughts. "I cannot imagine why. It all seems rather straight-forward to me."

"You said you were going to Madeira."

"And so we are, *meu amor*. Indeed, we will travel straight to the island in just a few hours. I have already spoken to my groom to assure we have a carriage awaiting us at first light."

She straightened from the pillows, her jaw clenched. He intended to take her to his home? No. As painful as it might be to have Philippe walk away from her, it was preferable to being dragged to Madeira.

Gad, did he not realize how humiliating it would be to en-dure the disdain of the servants and villagers who had known him since he was a small lad? To live in the home that would someday be filled with his children?

"No, Philippe, I will not go to your estate," she said, her expression set in determined lines. "It is not proper."

He slowly shifted, his arms landing on each side of her body to trap her beneath the covers. He was close enough that his breath brushed her cheek and the scent of his warm body wrapped her in its potent force.

"You are wrong. Nothing could be more proper. It is where you belong."

"A mistress does not reside beneath her lover's roof."

"No," he whispered, his eyes watching her with a strange intensity, "but a wife most certainly resides with her husband."

Shocked silence filled the room as Raine struggled to accept that she had not misheard the low words.

"Good Lord," she rasped, pressing herself into the pillows, "you've gone mad."

His lips twisted as he stroked a finger down her flushed cheek. "We have already established that is a distinct possibility, but that does not alter the fact that I intend to make you my bride as soon as we return to Madeira."

"Why?"

"Why Madeira?" He gave a lift of one broad shoulder. "I have always desired to be wed in my own chapel. However, if you prefer to marry before we leave Paris I do not suppose there is anything to stop the marriage from taking place before the local priest, since you were raised Catholic."

She sucked in a shuddering breath. He must be teasing her. This had to be a cruel joke intended to punish her for having dared to go against his will.

"Do not jest, Philippe, it is not kind."

His green eyes narrowed, his expression relentless. "This is no jest, Raine. You will be my wife."

"But…you do not want to marry me."

"You are a very clever woman, *meu amor,* but not even you are capable of reading my mind. I have devoted years to avoiding the most determined attempts to trap me into matrimony. If I did not wish to marry you then I would most certainly not do so."

Raine gave a slow shake of her head, her body cold with shocked disbelief. She felt as if she had been hit by a racing carriage, or tossed off the edge of a cliff. Either of which seemed more likely than Philippe Gautier proposing marriage to her.

"I am your mistress, for goodness' sake," she breathed in a strangled voice.

His hard lips quirked. "Yes, I do recall spending a number of delicious hours between your soft thighs."

A rush of heat stained her cheeks. "Gentlemen do *not* wed their mistresses. Not unless they are determined to court scandal."

He gripped her chin, forcing her to meet his fierce expression. He did not look like a man who had taken leave of his senses. Indeed, he appeared in frightening control of himself and the situation.

A far cry from her own numb bewilderment.

"There are few who know that we have lived together in this remote cottage." He shrugged, his arrogance on full display. "When we arrive at my estate we will simply say that I have brought you from England so that we could exchange our vows in the family church. No one will question my word."

She gave a choked laugh that was closer to a sob. "Even if we were capable of performing such a charade, not even your word can alter the fact that I am the daughter of a simple sailor, not to mention the Knave of Knightsbridge."

"There will be no mention of your father's illegal activities," he warned, easily dismissing any concern at the inevitable gossip. "And while your birth may be humble, it is respectable. Any whispers will be swiftly forgotten once you have given me a son or two."

Raine's breath caught as a savage longing ripped through her. To have this man's children. To hold them against her breast and offer them all the love that burned in her heart.

But at what price?

She could not begin to fathom the reasons for Philippe's abrupt proposal, but she did know that it had nothing to do with affection. He had long ago buried his more tender emotions, if he had ever possessed them at all. He could never offer her more than passion. And even that would no doubt be shared with dozens of mistresses.

No. She would slowly die being tied to a man that she loved who could never return that love.

Far better for a swift end that offered no hope for a future together. How else could she forge a new life for herself?

Dropping her face into her hands, she cowardly hid her tears from his probing gaze.

"No…no more, Philippe. This is madness. I cannot be your wife."

His hands gripped her wrists, and with a sharp tug he had them pulled away from her face and pressed against his chest. Without their protection she was forced to meet the blazing green gaze.

"Make no mistake, Raine, you most certainly will be my wife," he swore coldly. "The sooner the better."

Her heart halted as she sensed the grim determination that smoldered beneath his icy composure.

"But why? Why me?"

"I have told you." He leaned forward until his lips were brushing her own. "You belong to me, *meu amor*. This simply makes it official."

CHAPTER TWENTY-SIX

RAINE WOULD LATER RECALL very little of the trip from Paris to Madeira. Not that there was much to recall. Once upon Philippe's yacht, she had been virtually held prisoner in her cabin as Philippe had set his crew on a grueling pace. She had been allowed topside for a brief morning stroll and another at sunset, always with a grim Philippe at her side, as if he feared she might fling herself overboard. But otherwise she had been trapped alone in the cramped cabin, taking her meals on a tray and sleeping in the narrow bunk alone.

Through the long days she had nothing to do but brood on her strange, terrifying twist of fate. Over and over she had wrestled to understand what the devil was happening.

She could not believe that Philippe truly intended to wed her. Why would he? He could have any woman he desired. Women who were beautiful, and wealthy, and sleekly sophisticated. Women who came from the same world as he did, with the ability to stand at his side with pride.

What could he possibly want with a female such as her?

She could bring him no dowry, no social connections, no skills beyond playing the role of highwayman. A skill that did not seem entirely suitable for his wife.

And since he had already seduced her into his bed, it could not be an overwhelming passion that would prompt such a desperate offer.

Her hours of contemplation brought no answers. In truth, they did nothing more than leave her with a pounding head by the end of the day.

Crawling beneath the covers, Raine once again settled in for another lonely night. She had long ago stopped fretting over the fact that Philippe did not join her in the cramped bunk when darkness fell. What did it matter if he no longer sought her out? If his desire had already waned then perhaps he would come to see sense. It was, after all, the only thing that they held in common.

She shivered as she drifted off to sleep. A sleep that lasted only a few moments as a hand gripped her shoulder and abruptly shook her awake.

"Raine." Philippe's voice whispered directly next to her ear. "You must wake."

"What?" Wrenching her eyes open, she blinked in confusion. "What is it?"

"We have arrived."

The fog was seared from her mind at his soft words and with a small gasp she scooted upright.

"So soon? I...I thought the trip would be longer."

There was the scrape of a flint and then candlelight bloomed, revealing Philippe's aristocratic features and the tousled raven curls. Shifting, he turned to stare down at her with that aloof expression that reminded her of the first night they met.

"My ship is built for speed," he informed her. "A fortunate circumstance, considering the number of times I have been pursued over the years."

"Somehow I am not at all surprised."

He shrugged aside her tart words, holding out a slender hand with obvious impatience. "Come, Raine. It is late and I am weary."

Raine felt her stomach clench as she struggled to breathe. "Please, Philippe, I do not want this. Return me to England, I beg of you."

Expecting a sharp retort, or even to be hauled from the bed and shoved into her clothes, Raine was startled when his cold features softened and he perched his large body on the edge of the mattress.

"Why do you cower in your bed, *querida?*" he demanded. His voice was rough, but at least the ice had melted. "You have braved the gallows to rescue your father, you entered my bed with the boldness of a trained courtesan and bartered your freedom from a madman. Why does the thought of becoming my wife make you tremble?"

"Because…" *Because I love you and living with you day after day with no hope of having you ever return my love would slowly destroy me.* "Because I will only make a fool of myself, and you, as well. I am not trained to live among nobility."

His lips twitched. "Trained? Like a thoroughbred?"

Her eyes narrowed as she experienced a spurt of anger. "Precisely as a thoroughbred. Young ladies do not possess some natural instinct to understand how to run a vast household or to move in society. They have governesses who devote years to teaching them the skills they need."

He grasped her chin, his brows drawing together. "Raine, you are beautiful, finely educated and intelligent enough to learn whatever skills you believe are necessary for my wife. If you have need of assistance we can easily send for one of my far-flung relatives to come and live with us until you feel confident in your abilities."

"Even if I could learn, I still will not be accepted by society," she said with a small sniff.

"You worry over nothing, *meu amor,* you will be accepted."

"Why? Because you say so?"

"Yes."

She rolled her eyes. "Not even you can force a horde of nobles to look upon a sailor's daughter with anything but contempt."

"But you will no longer be a sailor's daughter," he said, a smug smile touching his lips. "You will be the wife of Philippe Gautier, and I possess enough wealth and power to make sure even the haughtiest dowager is forced to treat you with the utmost respect."

"My God, you are arrogant."

"And you are a liar."

She tugged her chin from his grasp. "Liar?"

"Whatever is troubling you has nothing to do with what you fear society may think of you. At least not entirely." The green eyes flared with warning. "Do not try to deceive me, Raine. I can read it upon your face."

Raine glared in frustration. "Does it matter why?"

The elegant features tightened, almost as if she had managed to wound him, before he was gracefully rising to his feet, and then, reaching down, he scooped her off the bed, her shivering body still wrapped in the blankets.

"Not at the moment," he said blandly, carrying her with ease out of the cabin and up the narrow passage. "I have an eternity to discover what secrets lurk deep in your soul."

Raine gave a choked gasp as she hastily tucked the blanket to her chin. "Philippe…what are you doing?"

His features might have been carved from granite as he carried her onto the deck and headed straight for the railing.

"Taking you home."

"You…you cannot force me to marry you, you know."

"Never underestimate me, *meu amor,*" he growled softly.

She heaved an exasperated sigh, avidly aware of the

crew watching them with broad smiles before they hastily set about lowering the narrow boats that would take them ashore.

"You may put me down, I am not going to leap overboard," she muttered.

In answer his arms tightened about her, his gaze lowering to tangle with her own.

"I have not forgotten your dislike for small boats, *meu amor.* Close your eyes and hold on tight. I will keep you safe."

RAINE AWOKE WITH DAWN and crawled from the vast bed that Philippe had carried her to the night before. It had been too dark to take much note of her surroundings, and in truth, she had been far too vexed by his high-handed behavior to care. Now, however, she was anxious to catch a glimpse of the home that held Philippe's heart.

Pulling a blanket around her light shift, Raine moved to open the French doors that led to the long balcony running the length of the elegant villa. She leaned against the iron-scrolled railing and allowed her gaze to drink in the beauty before her.

A thrill of pleasure raced down her spine as she realized they were perched upon a rolling hill that offered a stunning view of the lush landscape. No, it was more than stunning, she silently mused. It was…breathtaking.

She sucked in the scent of lavender and camellia as her gaze skimmed the valleys and distant cliffs. Accustomed to England's gentle countryside, Raine found the dramatic scenery enough to make her sigh in delight.

She was leaning forward to admire the elegant garden located just below the balcony when a pair of strong, familiar arms encircled her waist and pulled her against a warm body.

"You have awoken early, *meu amor,*" Philippe whispered,

his lips brushing her ear. "I hope you find your new home to your liking?"

Pure, searing desire poured through her body at the feel of his hands pressed intimately against her lower stomach. It had been so terribly long since she had known the heat of his kisses and magic of his touch.

She swallowed a groan as she resisted the urge to turn in his arms and put an end to her torment.

"It is…astonishing," she at last managed to breathe, her gaze blindly locking on the distant waves. "There is something very untamed about its beauty."

"I could not agree more." His lips slid down the curve of her face so he could lightly nibble at her neck. "In truth, it is a miracle that the island was even discovered by the Portuguese.

She struggled to make sense of his words. "Why do you say that?"

"Henry the Navigator sent his best navigators to explore the coast of West Africa, but two of them were blown off course and landed upon Porto Santo. From there it was another year before they dared the dangerous waters to claim Madeira for Henry."

She shivered beneath his caress. "I suppose all this land now belongs to you?"

His lips and teeth continued their assault upon her neck, his hands pulling her sharply against his hardening arousal.

"Not all, but certainly as far as your eye can see. Upon those distant hills are my vineyards," he murmured.

Her eyes slid closed as her hands clung helplessly to the arms that surrounded her. "Ah, the famous Madeira wines?"

"Precisely." He trailed his tongue up her neck. "Although Prince Henry no doubt introduced the first vineyards, it was the Jesuit priests who began the wine-trading industry. They once held large tracts of land and their power was quite formidable upon the island."

"As yours is now?"

"True enough," he admittedly absently, his mouth now exploring the line of her jaw.

Against her will her head dropped back onto his chest, her body clenching with aching need. Gad, but she wanted him to tug off the blanket and run his warm hands over her quivering body. She wanted him to spread her legs and enter her with a slow, powerful thrust.

She sucked in a deep breath as her entire body shuddered with longing. "I have never understood why the wine is so sought-after," she said, her voice thick with need.

Philippe chuckled softly, perfectly aware of the havoc he was creating. "It begins with the grapes, of course. The climate and richness of the soil provide the finest vineyards. And then the wines are fortified with brandy and the casks of wine are heated to help preserve them during the long voyages. The process gives the wine a unique flavor. Later I will show you the wine houses, but for this morning I believe you would prefer to prepare for our guest."

Raine stiffened, the haze of sensual delight disrupted as a chill inched down her spine.

"Guest?"

Easily sensing her abrupt tension, Philippe grudgingly removed his arms and stepped back so she could turn to regard him with a wary gaze.

"The local priest, Father Tomas, will be taking luncheon with us," he said carefully.

Raine clutched the blanket about her as she glared into his impassive expression. "Do you often share luncheon with your priest?"

"As a matter of fact, I do." He met her gaze squarely. "However, he was invited today to begin planning our wedding."

Her heart lodged in her throat as she gave a shake of her head. "No, Philippe."

His hand reached out with an impatient motion, sending Raine hastily stepping back to avoid his touch. Unfortunately, she had forgotten the trailing blanket and with a small cry she felt herself plunging back toward the low railing.

With a curse, Philippe moved to sweep her into his arms, carrying her back into the bedchamber and dumping her onto the vast bed.

"Damn you, Raine, I will endure no more of your impulsive foolishness," he growled as he stood glaring down at her, his face pale as if she had truly frightened him.

She cringed against the force of his furious tone, her eyes wide. "It was an accident."

His harsh expression did not ease. "An accident that nearly broke your bloody neck. When you are my wife you will exercise a good deal more self-control to overcome your rash habits, is that understood?"

Her own temper snapped as she lifted herself to a seated position and thrust out her chin.

"Perhaps the thought of breaking my bloody neck is preferable to that of marriage to you."

A dangerous silence entered the room as he slowly bent down until they were nose to nose.

"As soon as your trunks are brought to the room, Miss Wimbourne, you will attire yourself as befits the mistress of this house and present yourself in the drawing room." His hand lifted to cup the back of her neck, yanking her to meet his lips in a brief, possessive kiss. "Do not even *think* of keeping me waiting."

With his threat delivered, Philippe stormed from the room, slamming the door behind him.

Left on her own, Raine buried her face in her hands.

Dear God, she had to stop this.

PHILIPPE RESTLESSLY PROWLED the drawing room, his temper still frayed and his mood foul. For once the elegant room with its satinwood furnishings and long row of windows that offered a view of the distant cove failed to soothe him. Not even his collection of rare Roman coins offered a distraction.

Instead he paced from one end of the polished floorboards to the other, his hands clenched at his sides.

Damn Raine Wimbourne. It had been nothing short of hell to keep his hands off her during the interminable trip from Paris. Night after night he had lain awake, tormented with the need to seek out her cabin and relieve his aching hunger. But he had forced himself to remain away, ridiculously believing that he owed her the respect of waiting until their wedding night before he once again tasted of her sweet body.

The frustration had taken its toll on his sadly strained nerves. Was it any wonder that he had snapped when she had nearly killed herself attempting to avoid his mere touch?

"Perhaps the thought of breaking my bloody neck is preferable to that of marriage to you."

He clenched his jaws as he recalled the sight of her pale face surrounded by the halo of golden curls. Her expression had been...what? Fear? Desperation?

Certainly not joy.

Reaching the far wall, he slammed his hand against the paneling before turning to pour a healthy measure of wine.

Damn the vexing wench. There was not a woman throughout Europe who would not faint with delight at the thought of wedding him. Including more than a few with royal connections.

Now a mere sailor's daughter with a tattered reputation and

no hope for a future beyond seclusion in a damp cottage was refusing to even contemplate all he could offer her.

It was enough to make any man long to howl in fury.

He was sipping his way through his third glass of wine when the sound of footsteps had him spinning about to regard the large, heavy-set priest with a thatch of silver hair who entered the room with a wide smile. As always Father Tomas brought with him an air of good cheer and robust energy. It was an energy that he devoted to caring for his flock with uncommon good sense, as well as uncommon kindness.

"Philippe, welcome home," he boomed as he moved across the room to shake Philippe's hand with a firm grip.

Forcing a smile to his lips, Philippe regarded the man who had been as much a friend as spiritual adviser for the past ten years.

"Thank you, Father. You are looking well," he said smoothly.

"A bit too well, I fear." With a chuckle the priest patted his expanding stomach. "My besetting weakness for *bolo de mel* is beginning to show for all the world to see."

Philippe could not prevent a small chuckle. The entire village knew of the priest's weakness for the sweet honey cakes, and in their love for him they ensured that he was never without his favorite treat.

"Ah, well, we all possess our weaknesses, do we not?"

The shrewd brown eyes studied Philippe's countenance for a long moment, his smile fading as he seemed to sense the tension that gripped Philippe.

"Is all well, my son?"

"Perfectly well." With a shrug Philippe set aside his wine. "Carlos is in England releasing Jean-Pierre from his prison cell, and the man who was responsible is in the hands of the king. Our family is once again safe from evil-doers. At least for the moment."

Tomas gave a slow nod, his expression pensive. "I did not doubt for a moment you would be victorious, Philippe. Never in my long life have I known a gentleman who is more capable of setting a path and seeing it to the end. Some may claim that you were born with the Midas touch, but I know 'tis your own stubborn will that has given you such success."

"Should I take that as a compliment or an insult?"

Thomas shrugged. "God helps those who help themselves."

Philippe wryly thought of the woman who had yet to make an appearance despite his command. He was beginning to doubt that even divine intervention could assist him in comprehending the bewildering minx.

"A nice notion, but not always accurate," he said, the faintest hint of bitterness darkening his low tone.

Tomas tilted his head to the side, studying Philippe with a mixture of curiosity and concern. At last he delicately cleared his throat.

"There have been rumors swirling through the village all morning."

Philippe gave a humorless laugh as he moved to pour himself another glass of the rich wine. He had known that by announcing to his housekeeper that the woman he had carried into his home was destined to be her mistress, word would spread as swiftly as wildfire. At the time, however, he had merely been intent on making sure that the staff understood that Raine was to be treated with utmost respect. Now he had to wonder why he bothered.

Downing the wine, he slowly turned to meet the priest's searching gaze.

"Surely a man of the cloth does not lower himself to listening to common gossip?"

Tomas lifted his pudgy hands. "Honey cakes are not my only weakness."

Philippe gave a short, humorless laugh. "I presume that this gossip must have something to do with my return?"

"It is said that you have brought back an English bride from your travels. I dismissed the rumors as idle chatter until I received your invitation to luncheon."

Philippe gave a lift of his brows. "You have received an invitation to dine at my home on several occasions without presuming I have towed back a bride."

"Ah, but those invitations were more a matter of a polite request, not a royal command that I present myself at an appointed hour."

Philippe blinked in surprise. He had been weary when he had arrived home and dashed off the note to the priest, but he was certain he had not written it as a royal command.

"Surely I was not that ungracious?" he protested.

"Not ungracious, simply abrupt," Tomas corrected. "Not surprising if you are, indeed, contemplating marriage. Such an important occasion tends to make the most sensible of men rather volatile." He gave a faint shake of his head. "Rather strange considering they put themselves in such a predicament of their own free will. You would think they would be at peace with their decision."

Philippe gave a shake of his head and tossed back his wine. "Only a priest would speak such nonsense."

Tomas blinked in surprise. "And why would you say that?"

"Because if you had any dealings at all with women you would understand perfectly how they can make a man behave as a babbling idiot."

"Ah." The large man strolled forward, his brows lowered in concern. "Philippe, why do you not confess to me what is troubling you?"

"I doubt you could be of assistance with my current troubles, Father."

Not surprising, Tomas was undeterred by Philippe's sharp tone. He was a man who believed it his duty to assist any of his flock in need, no matter how unworthy they might be.

"It is true that you have brought a woman to be your wife?" he persisted. "An Englishwoman?"

"Yes." Philippe absently rubbed the tense muscles of his neck. "Miss Raine Wimbourne."

"I suppose she is beautiful?"

"Beautiful enough to make angels cry with envy."

"But you are no longer certain that you wish to wed her? Do not torment yourself, Philippe. It is far better to acknowledge your mistake now than for the both of you to live in regret for the rest of your lives. If it troubles you to have to wound the young lady, I shall be happy to speak to her for you."

"No," Philippe rasped, desperately wishing it was all that simple. It would be an easy matter to walk away. It was a good deal more difficult to hold on to what he wanted. "I have not changed my mind."

"Then…"

"It is Miss Wimbourne who has doubts about our marital bliss," Philippe interrupted.

"Oh." Tomas blinked several times. "Oh."

Philippe smiled wryly. "Precisely."

"Well, I must admit that is a surprise," Tomas said, gathering his composure. "I may not be a worldly man, but I do know that you are considered quite a catch on the marriage market."

"Obviously not the catch I had once presumed myself to be."

"I see." Tomas frowned in confusion. "Has the young lady revealed the reasons for her objection to the marriage?"

"She claims that she does not believe she is of suitable birth to become my wife."

"She is not a…" Tomas cleared his throat. "A lady?"

Philippe slammed his glass onto the table, the delicate crystal nearly splintering beneath the force.

"Yes, she damn well is a lady, and anyone who dares to say otherwise will answer to me."

Tomas held up his hand in swift apology. "Of course."

"Her birth might have been humble, but it is perfectly respectable."

"Still, it might be a bit overwhelming to be thrust into an entirely different sort of life. It could be she just needs time to adjust to her new circumstances," he pointed out softly.

Philippe made a sound of impatience as he resumed his pacing. Raine Wimbourne feared nothing. Not the magistrate, not the ill temper of a powerful nobleman, not the threat of a madman. No, Raine did not make her decisions out of cowardice. She charged through life with a reckless abandon, far too often allowing her heart to lead her.

"That is not why she hesitates," he muttered.

"Are you certain?"

"No man with a bit of sense could claim to be certain when it comes to a female," he said dryly. "But I am convinced that there is more bothering Raine than the thought of a luxurious life."

There was a short silence as Tomas watched his impatient trek across the room. "Forgive me if I am overbold, but could it be that she is in love with another?"

Philippe stiffened as he turned around with a sharp motion. During the long trip home he had brooded for hours upon whether Raine had been swayed by Carlos's obvious attentions. It would not be surprising. Carlos was young, passionate and possessed an easy charm that Philippe could not hope to compete against.

But, while the possessive need to bind Raine irrevocably to him still roared with stunning force, his more logical self had slowly come to accept that Raine did not consider Carlos as more than a friend.

If she truly loved Carlos, then she would not have allowed Philippe to send him to England without her. At least not without a fierce battle. And certainly she would not still shiver with awareness whenever he was near. Raine's loyalty to her unworthy father revealed that she would not stray once her heart was given.

"No." Philippe gave a firm shake of his head. "She would never respond to my touch if she loved another."

Tomas abruptly lifted his thick brows, as if struck by inspiration. "Ah."

"What?"

"She cares for you, Philippe," he said simply. "What are your feelings for her?"

Philippe instinctively shied from the blunt question. "I have offered to make her my wife."

"Men take wives for any number of reasons, many of which do not take into account the needs and desires of the women that they wed."

Philippe frowned at the implication that he intended to be some sort of ogre to Raine once they were wed. He may have many faults, but he knew how to care for those who belonged to him.

"What could Raine possibly desire that I cannot give her?"

Tomas met his gaze squarely. "Love."

CHAPTER TWENTY-SEVEN

RAINE REMAINED IN HER ROOMS until dusk began to paint the sky with a spray of soft lavender and pink. She had not been precisely hiding. In fact, she had spent every moment awaiting Philippe to arrive and haul her downstairs for his luncheon with the priest. It was not at all like Philippe Gautier to issue commands and then not insist that they be followed through.

But much to her surprise he had not so much as strayed near her door. And even more surprising, a delicious luncheon that included fresh tuna and fried corn meal had been delivered by a smiling maid.

Of course, there had been no real need to join the two gentlemen, she acknowledged wryly. Philippe was perfectly capable of arranging the wedding without her presence. God knew he had been arranging her life for weeks without consulting her.

Settling on a marble bench, Raine allowed her gaze to roam over the exotic garden and then toward the magnificent villa. It was truly beautiful here. A small glimpse of paradise.

This was a place that she could be happy, she thought with a small sigh. There was such a sense of ease and peace about the estate. Even the servants had openly welcomed her presence, as if they were genuinely pleased at the thought that she would soon be their mistress.

A pity that it was never going to happen.

Ridiculous tears pricked her eyes and trailed down her cheeks. Bloody hell. She had promised herself she would not cry.

"If you do not approve of the gardens, *meu amor,* you are at liberty to alter them in any manner you desire," a soft voice whispered from behind her.

With a tiny gasp, Raine spun about, her hand pressed to her pounding heart. "Philippe. I did not hear you approach."

In the fading light he looked as handsome as ever. He was dressed casually in a blue jacket and buff breeches with his cravat loosened to reveal the strong column of his neck. As he stepped closer, however, Raine was startled to note that there were unmistakable lines of weariness marring his countenance.

Perhaps understandable considering what he had endured over the past months, but it still came as something of a shock. He always seemed…invulnerable to the normal human weaknesses.

Unaware of her inane thoughts, Philippe studied the unmistakable dampness of her cheeks, his arms crossed over his chest and his eyes hooded.

"No, you appeared quite occupied with your thoughts. Would you care to reveal what are you thinking of?" he demanded.

She turned her head to regard the sweeping beauty before her. "I was thinking that you have a lovely home. It is little wonder you were so anxious to return."

"Lovely, but not lovely enough to tempt you, eh, Raine?"

Raine turned back at the unexpected edge of bitterness in his tone. "Would you truly desire me to marry you simply to gain a lovely estate and garden?"

His expression was inscrutable in the fading light. "Women often marry for such things."

They did, of course. A woman had little choice but to offer herself to the highest bidder to gain a measure of security. Thankfully, she had her father and his small cottage until she managed to discover a means of supporting herself. She would have no need to sell herself to a man certain to break her heart.

"You are no doubt right, but I am not interested in bartering my future for a comfortable home," she said.

"Then what do you desire for your future?"

A wistful smile touched her lips. She knew precisely what she desired, what would offer her the happiness she sought.

"I want to find a place where I can feel needed," she said softly. "Truly needed."

The green eyes smoldered with a dark emotion. "You believe I do not need you?"

She swallowed the urge to laugh at the thought of this man ever making himself so vulnerable.

"Of course you do not. You are completely independent and certain of yourself. You are not a man who allows yourself to need anyone."

Without warning he grabbed her hand and yanked her to her feet. Raine stumbled in surprise, unable to halt him from wrapping his arms about her waist and pulling her against the length of his body.

"You are wrong, you know, *meu amor.* I need you," he rasped, his face buried in her golden curls. "I need you quite desperately at this moment."

The manner that he needed her was rapidly evident as she felt the stir of his erection. For a mad, crazed moment Raine arched against his hard, deliciously warm body. They were all alone in the garden, surrounded by the lush perfume of the night. She ached to be close to him. To lie beneath him as he made her feel as if she were the most important woman in the world to him.

It was only the knowledge that the illusion would be all too fleeting that made her lift her hands to press against his chest in denial.

"No, Philippe."

His brows snapped together at her rejection. "No?"

She sucked in a deep breath, ignoring the fierce heat that flowed through her blood. "What you need is a physical release that could be provided by any woman."

"Not, I trust, *any* woman," he mocked, clenching his jaw.

She shrugged her shoulders, wrapping her arms about her waist. "Any woman who happens to capture your fancy."

"Dammit," he ground out, shoving his fingers through his hair as he stared at her in stark frustration. "I do not want any woman but you."

"For now." She resisted the temptation to step back from the danger that smoldered in his eyes. "Once we are wed, however, you will swiftly tire of me."

"So you are capable of reading the future?"

She lowered her head as the tears once again threatened. "Perhaps not, but I am capable of being a realist when I need to be."

"Raine…"

"Let me finish, Philippe," she whispered softly.

There was a moment of silence before he released an explosive sigh. "If you insist."

"Eventually you will tire of me, it is inevitable. And then you will still have your busy life to keep you occupied and no doubt a series of mistresses, while I will be left here alone."

"Hardly alone," he growled. "If you would bother to take the time to become acquainted with the estate you will realize that there are a great number of servants and villagers who have need of your generous heart. You could alter their lives in any number of ways." There was a short pause before his hand reached out to lightly touch her curls. "And, of course, you will have our children to keep you occupied. They most certainly will have need of their mother."

Pain seared through her at his casual words. Gad, did he have no shame? Did he believe that he could dangle the temptation of children before her and make her forget he had not denied the fact he would abandon her while he enjoyed his life and mistresses far away?

She jerked from his touch, her eyes wide with distress. "Please...do not."

Philippe allowed his hand to fall, his face tight as he easily read her battered emotions.

"Damn you, Raine, what do you want of me?"

"I have told you what I want of you," she replied, too overwrought to notice the strange hint of torment in his eyes. "I want you to send me home."

Dashing past his frozen form, Raine did not look back as she headed for her room and slammed the door.

She might be Philippe's prisoner, but she would be damned if she would allow him to see her cry.

RAINE WAS NOT CERTAIN what she had expected after her emotional outburst in the garden, but it was not to be abandoned for the next week.

As day after day passed without a glimpse of the irritating man, Raine began to wonder if he had actually left the island. It was either that or he had barricaded himself in his rooms, she decided as she ate her meals alone in the vast dining room and wandered the corridors of the villa late at night.

She told herself that she was relieved that he had gone away to sulk. At least he was not bullying her into a marriage that clearly would be a disaster for both of them.

Ridiculously, however, she found her spirits slowly sinking. Not even in the cottage in Montmartre had she felt quite so lonely, so isolated. The servants were all perfectly kind, but it was obvious that they considered her the mistress of the house and any effort to treat them as friends rather than mere staff was met with an awkward unease.

With nothing to do but brood, Raine found herself spending more and more time in the gardens, seeking a peace to soothe her troubled heart.

On this morning the beauty surrounding her failed to offer the distraction she sought. It did not seem to matter how hard she tried, she could not pull her thoughts from Philippe Gautier. Where was he? Was he truly attempting to avoid her?

Or could it be that he already had a lover here that was keeping him fully occupied?

The last thought was enough to make her heart clench with agony and sent her charging back to the house with a hurried step. She would not dwell on such a terrible notion, she told herself sternly. It would do no good to torment herself with the thought of Philippe in the arms of another woman.

Moving through the seemingly empty villa, Raine made her way to her room and entered with a flurry of muslin skirts. She had barely crossed the threshold, however, when she came to a halt at the sight of the young maid who had been attending to her since her arrival, bustling about the room with a harassed expression on her pretty face.

"Good morning, Maria," she said, her brows lowered in confusion.

Scooping a handful of gowns from the armoire, Maria moved to place them on the bed and proceeded to fold them with swift hands.

"Good morning to you, Miss Wimbourne," she said in a distracted tone. "I have brought you your breakfast."

Raine glanced toward the tray on the bedside table. As always there was a tempting array of fresh fruit and spiced pork that was a favorite among the people of the island. At the moment, however, she had no interest in food.

"Thank you, it looks delicious." She turned her attention back to the maid. "May I ask what you are doing?"

Maria glanced up in puzzlement. "Doing?"

"With my clothes?"

The puzzlement only deepened. "Am I not folding them to please you?"

Raine gave a slow shake of her head, a cold dread settling in the pit of her stomach. "I have no real preference for how you fold them, but why are you doing so?"

For a moment Maria regarded her as if she thought Raine might have taken leave of her senses, and then a nervous smile touched her lips.

"Ah, you tease me." She wagged a finger in Raine's direction. "Very naughty of you when we have so much work to be done. How we shall ever be prepared in time is beyond me."

Raine pressed a hand to her spinning head. "Maria, please stop for a moment."

With obvious reluctance the maid dropped the pretty walking gown onto the bed and regarded Raine with an expectant expression.

"Yes?"

Raine licked her lips, wishing her heart were not pounding so loudly in her ears. It made it difficult to concentrate.

"Tell me precisely what you are doing."

"I am packing your bags as the master requested," she explained.

Raine stepped backward, leaning against the door as her knees threatened to give way. "Monsieur Gautier requested you pack my bags?"

"Of course." Maria blinked in bafflement. "We have little time if we are to meet the boat before luncheon."

Feeling as if she must be in the midst of some strange dream, Raine pressed a hand to her chest. "The boat?"

"Have you forgotten we are to leave for England today?"

"We?"

"Oh." The maid's troubled expression cleared. "You did not know that I am to travel with you?"

"No, I did not."

With a chuckle Maria returned to folding the numerous gowns. "Well, the master said you could not travel alone, even if it is aboard his own ship. It would not be right."

"I see."

"You need not worry about me once we arrive. The master has given me plenty of coin to stay at an inn until the ship returns. He even gave me some extra coins so that I can enjoy whatever sights I like while I am in England."

England? She was returning to England with Maria?

What of Philippe? Was he joining them? Or was she to be shipped off alone?

"That—" she hesitated and cleared her throat "—that was very generous of him."

"*Sim*. It is all very exciting. I have never been so far from home."

"Will you excuse me, Maria?"

Without waiting for the maid to glance up, Raine was slipping through the door and hurrying down the hall. She had to have a few moments alone.

Reaching the staircase, she leaned against the scrolled balustrade as she struggled to make sense of her tangled thoughts. A difficult task, she discovered as she sucked in deep gulps of air.

Inanely her mind turned back to her last moments with Philippe in the garden.

"Damn you, Raine, what do you want of me?"

"I want you to send me home."

Had Philippe at last come to his senses? Had he realized

that a marriage between them was a terrible mistake? It seemed the only possible explanation.

Raine waited for the surge of relief that should surely be coming. This was what she wanted. What she had pleaded and begged for. There was no earthly reason not to feel overjoyed that soon she would be on her way home.

But what she felt was not relief.

In truth, she felt nothing at all. As if her heart had become suddenly and inexplicably numb.

Unaware of the passing time, Raine was at last startled out of her daze of shock by the approach of the gray-haired butler, who regarded her pale countenance with a hint of concern.

"May I assist you, Miss Wimbourne?"

Raine was about to send the servant on his way when she paused. She had to speak with Philippe. She had to know if he was, indeed, intent on setting her free. And if so...why.

He had been so adamant that she was to be his wife. So determined that she would belong to him. What could possibly have made him change his mind?

Conscious that the servant was patiently awaiting her response, Raine cleared her throat.

"Yes, I was seeking Mr. Gautier."

"I fear he left early this morning to inspect his vineyards. He will not be returning until late."

The breath was squeezed from her lungs at the casual words. Philippe intended to pack her off without even saying goodbye? Was he truly so indifferent to what had passed between them?

Hating herself for the horrid sense of loss that abruptly flowed though her, Raine clenched her hands together and swallowed the lump in her throat.

"Did he leave a message for me?"

"He requested that I give you this, miss."

The butler reached beneath his jacket to remove a carefully folded parchment. With trembling hands Raine took the offered letter and opened it to discover that it was no message. Instead there was a bank draft for three thousand pounds tucked in the folds.

A hot surge of color stained her cheeks as she ducked her head to hide her shamed expression from the butler. It was bad enough to realize she had been callously given her parting payment like a common mistress, but Philippe could not even be bothered to deal with the trifling matter himself. Oh, no, he had left the embarrassing task to a servant to further humiliate her.

Just for a crazed moment, Raine trembled on the edge of shredding the filthy bank draft into a dozen pieces. She was not a whore and had no intention of being treated like one. Only common sense came to her rescue.

As much as she disliked the thought of giving in to Philippe's attempt to shame her, she realized that she would have need of funds once she reached England. She could not simply return home on foot, no matter how her pride might rebel.

Keeping her head lowered, she clenched the bank draft in her trembling fingers and silently damned Philippe to the netherworld.

If he had desired revenge for her refusal to wed him, then he had certainly succeeded. She felt as soiled as any tart, and was wishing to God she had never, ever crossed paths with Philippe Gautier.

"Thank you," she managed to choke out.

"Will that be all, miss?"

"No…wait," she breathed in shattered tones, her hands reaching to fumble with the clasp of the necklace about her neck. The golden locket fell into her hand and she briefly gripped it tightly before forcing herself to hand it to the impassive servant. "This belongs to Philippe."

The servant bowed. "I will see that it is returned to him."

"And would you tell him…"

Her words trailed away as the servant gave a lift of his brows. "Yes?"

"Nothing." She gave a shake of her head. "Nothing at all."

UPSTAIRS IN HIS PRIVATE chambers, Philippe stood at his window and watched the carriage sweep down the tree-lined drive. Within the hour Raine would be safely stowed upon his ship bound for England. She would be out of his home out of his life and out of his thoughts.

Or at least that was the promise he had made to himself when he had reached the decision to return Raine to England.

He clenched his mother's locket tightly in his hand as his entire body trembled with the urge to dash after the retreating carriage. It had seemed a simple matter in the middle of yet another sleepless night to concede defeat. Why the devil should he attempt to lure an unwilling bride to the altar?

God knew that he had only to crook his finger to have hundreds of eager debutantes flocking to the island to claim him as their husband.

If Raine wished to rot in a damp, isolated cottage, then so be it. He had enjoyed her delectable body for weeks. Soon enough another woman would catch his eye and ease the frustrated ache lodged deep in his body. It was inevitable, was it not?

Now, however, in the cold light of day and with his wits unclouded by brandy, he found the sight of Raine being carried away from his home far from satisfying.

Hell and damnation. Why had he arranged for her to depart so swiftly? Even if his pride had refused to allow him to be in Raine's company for fear he might actually beg her to become his wife, he at least had the pleasure of watching her from afar as she drifted through the gardens or sat in the drawing room gazing at the sea. Or catching the sweet scent of her lilac perfume when he passed by her chamber.

Or most important, knowing that she was always safe.

Who would take care of her in England? Her worthless wastrel of a father? Philippe gave a short, humorless laugh. Josiah Wimbourne was as likely to toss the reckless chit into some disaster as to keep her from harm. Certainly he would not trouble himself to find the means to make his daughter happy.

Realizing the direction of his thoughts, Philippe abruptly turned from the window and paced toward the large portrait of his mother that hung above his fireplace.

He had done the only thing possible, he told himself sternly. It had been sheer torture to have Raine so near and not have her in his arms.

His gaze lifted to study the strong, determined line of his mother's face. Oddly, in the slanting light she appeared vaguely disapproving. Almost as if she were aware of what was occurring and was not at all pleased.

Ridiculous, of course.

His mother had died years ago in her futile attempt to rescue her family. She had made her decision and left behind her son to forge his own path in this life.

But was she truly gone? a voice whispered in the back of his mind. Slowly, his gaze lowered to the locket in his hand. Did he not continue to allow the memory of her loss to haunt him?

Raine had accused him of never depending upon anyone and he had not argued. Why should he? He took pride in his self-sufficiency. It had made him strong enough to care for his family and to build a financial empire.

When a man was foolish enough to depend on others he was only doomed to disappointment.

Besides which, he had never encountered anyone who wanted him to have need of them. To be vulnerable.

Not until Raine.

A sharp pain struck like lightning through his body, nearly sending him to his knees. Whirling about he tossed the locket across the room.

Damn the woman.

What the devil had she done to him?

CHAPTER TWENTY-EIGHT

RAINE AWOKE TO ANOTHER morning of heavy clouds with the threat of chilled rain in the air. It was the same as every other morning since she had arrived back in England a fortnight ago.

Resisting the urge to remain in her narrow bed with the covers pulled over her head, Raine forced herself to dress in a warm wool gown and made her way to the small drawing room. If she lingered in her bed it would only cause her father to fret.

Although Josiah had accepted her return without a painful inquisition of what had happened during her absence, he could not completely hide his concern.

He at least suspected that Raine had possessed the poor judgment to fall in love with her captor, and that she still suffered from the pain of leaving him.

This morning, however, she was determined to be done with the ridiculous sense of grief that shrouded her like a dark cloud and get on with her life. She owed it to her father.

After all, he had taken great pains to convince the neighbors that her disappearance from the cottage had been nothing more scandalous than an extended trip to London. She would not undo his good work by continually moping about like some figure from a tragic opera.

Busying herself with lighting a fire and pulling open the heavy drapes, Raine did not hear the sound of footsteps until the door was pushed open and her father stepped into the room.

As always he studied her with that anxious, searching gaze before he forced a smile to his lips.

"I thought I might find you here, pet," he said as he walked to join her upon the window seat.

"Good morning, Father." Her brows arched at the sight of the new gray jacket and breeches she had ordered from the local tailor. "You are looking very smart. Are you going to the village?"

"I do have a few errands that I must deal with this morning and then I am joining the magistrate for luncheon. We often meet at the pub for a game of chess and a few pints."

She leaned back, her eyes wide with surprise. "The magistrate?"

Josiah smiled wryly at her shock. "Since you've been gone I have discovered that Harper is not a bad sort. Certainly he is the only one in the village capable of giving me a decent game of chess. And since I have given up my career as the Knave of Knightsbridge, I no longer have need to consider him my enemy."

"Good heavens. You have retired your role as highwayman?"

His smile slowly faded, his pale countenance showing every one of his years as he gave a nod of his head.

"Yes."

Raine reached out to lay a hand on his arm. "Why? You were doing such good."

"But at what cost?"

"I do not know what you mean."

"I mean, that I was blinded by my own arrogance," he said with a sigh. "Even if I did manage to offer a bit of assistance to my friends, I was an idiot to risk my neck when I knew that I was all you have left in the world. And even more an idiot to ever allow you to put yourself in danger."

Raine abruptly realized how her father must have tormented himself after her disappearance. The lingering pain was etched in the lines of his face and in the depths of his eyes. He clearly blamed himself for all that had happened.

"You did nothing," she said firmly, her fingers squeezing his arm. "It was my decision to become the Knave of Knightsbridge."

"Only because I left you no choice. You could hardly stand aside and watch me hang. No. I have not been a good father to you, pet."

Raine's heart twisted at his words. "Do not say that."

"It is true." His expression hardened as he covered her fingers with his own. "After you were taken from me I swore an oath I would do better. And I intend to keep that oath."

"Oh, Father," she breathed, reaching up to lay a soft kiss on his cheek.

"I do love you, Raine."

She smiled at his gentle words, a portion of her aching heart easing as she gazed tenderly at her father. Perhaps Philippe would never return her feelings, but she had a home and a family who cared for her.

It was more than many women had.

"And I love you, Father."

His hand tightened on her fingers. "You must know that there is nothing I desire more than to see you happy."

She gave a small jerk as she tugged her fingers from his grasp. "I am happy," she muttered.

Josiah gave a click of his tongue. "Raine, I may be old, but I am not completely blind. I see the shadows that lurk in your eyes. That bastard hurt you and you are still hurting."

Her lips parted to deny the claim, only to close at her father's steady gaze. What was the point in lying? She was not nearly a skilled enough actress to conceal her aching heart. All she could do was assure him that she did not intend to become a tedious companion.

"I cannot deny that he broke my heart. Or that I miss him," she said, her voice carefully bland. "But, I am not silly enough to devote my life to pining for a gentleman who has no doubt forgotten my existence."

"Good." Her father's smile returned, a sly glint in his eyes. "Then perhaps you will join me in the village. The magistrate always manages to casually inquire when you might return. You made quite an impression on him."

Raine resisted the urge to shudder. The magistrate had been a perfectly nice gentleman, but she had no romantic interest in him. She had no romantic interest in any man.

"A tempting offer, but I am not yet ready to encourage the attentions of Mr. Harper."

"Raine, you cannot hide yourself in this cottage forever," her father chided.

Raine shrugged. "I have no intention of doing so."

"Then, what are your plans?"

Raine rose to her feet as she gazed out the window, her expression pensive. "I have been thinking that I might begin classes for a few of the girls in the village. It would take some time to start a proper school, but for now I could at least make sure they learn to read and write."

A silence filled the room, broken only by the crackle of the fire. At last she heard her father stir and rise to his feet. Stepping behind her, he laid a gentle hand on her shoulder.

"Raine."

Turning, she studied the odd expression on her father's face. "What?"

"You are—" he hesitated and cleared his throat "—you are a remarkable young woman."

A ridiculous blush touched her cheeks. "Hardly that."

"Yes, you are." Josiah's smile held a hint of sadness. "And so much like your mother it makes my heart ache. She was always thinking of others."

"Just as you do," she said softly.

Josiah flinched. "No, I am not nearly so noble."

"But you risked your life."

He gave a firm shake of his head, his expression one of self-disgust. "There are any number of ways I could have assisted those who had need of me. Certainly, your own desire to educate the poor young girls will give them opportunities far beyond a few coins. I merely chose the one that offered the opportunity to dash about like a hero from some Gothic novel."

Raine gave a click of her tongue. "You are far too hard on yourself, Father. You are a wonderful man who is most certainly a hero among the villagers."

His hand gently cupped her face. "From now on, my dear, I intend to be a hero only to you. I allowed myself to be distracted, but no more. You are the most important thing in my world."

PHILIPPE WAS CHILLED to the bone by the time he arrived at his London town house. He had never found winter in England particularly pleasant, certainly not when he could be enjoying the pleasant warmth of Madeira.

His mood, however, was startlingly light considering his voyage had been rough enough to shake the nerves of the most hardened sailor, and he had arrived to an icy drizzle that had made the trip to London a misery.

From the moment he had made his decision to return to England and fight for Raine, he had felt a peace he had never before experienced settle in his heart.

All those endless days of roaming through his empty house, unable to concentrate on work, unable to eat or sleep, unable to even find an interest in the numerous women upon the island who made it obvious they would be more than willing to offer him comfort was at an end.

It was as if he had simply been going through the motions, waiting for his mind to at last reach the conclusion his heart had made the moment he had encountered Miss Raine Wimbourne on that dark road.

The mighty had, indeed, fallen, he acknowledged as he entered the back door to the kitchen. And he did not even have the sense to care.

Leaving his heavy coat and hat beside the door, he pulled off his gloves as he moved into the kitchen and discovered his faithful groom seated at a long wooden table eating a bowl of stew.

Perhaps sensing he was no longer alone, Swann abruptly lifted his head, nearly falling backward as he leaped to his feet.

"Bloody hell, sir, you startled me." Gaining his balance, he gave a tug on his jacket and discreetly wiped his hands on his pants. "Welcome home."

"Thank you, Swann."

"We were not expecting you." Swann regarded him with a narrowed gaze. "Is there trouble?"

Philippe smiled wryly as he rubbed the aching muscles of his neck. Gads, it had been a long journey.

"You could certainly say that."

The servant instantly squared his shoulders and jutted his chin in an aggressive gesture. Swann enjoyed a good fight as well as the next man.

"You know I am prepared to stand at your side."

"A generous offer, but I fear that I must muddle through this mess on my own." He tilted his head to the side, noting the thick silence that cloaked the house. "Is my brother at home?"

Swann's battered countenance hardened with distaste. He rarely bothered to hide his lack of respect for Jean-Pierre.

"No. His valet said something of the fool trying his luck at the local halls before visiting his fancy whore."

"I am relieved to discover that his brief imprisonment did not impair his spirits."

"Bah." Swann turned his head to spit on the ground. "The boy does not have the wits to be grateful you saved his worthless neck. He was back to his whoring and gambling the moment he walked out of the prison."

Philippe shrugged. He had done what he could for his brother, but from this day forward Jean-Pierre would have to solve his troubles himself. Philippe intended to concentrate on his own future.

"I possessed little hope that Jean-Pierre would actually change his ways. He has far too much fondness for his life as a hardened rake."

"Fool."

"I suppose we are all fools in our own ways," Philippe said, considering his own hectic flight to England. Then, with a shrug he turned his attention to more important matters. "Has Carlos remained?"

"Aye. He is in your library."

"We shall speak later."

With a nod toward his faithful servant, Philippe made his way from the kitchen and up the stairs. Within moments he was entering the library to discover Carlos seated at a chair beside the fireplace with a nearly empty bottle of brandy at his side.

Philippe gave an unconscious grimace as he studied his friend's brooding expression.

Soon enough, Carlos would have a beautiful woman in his arms that would help him to forget Raine. But in the meantime, Philippe could sympathize with his dark mood.

"Are you attempting to empty my cellars in my absence?" he demanded as he strolled across the Persian carpet.

With a small jerk of surprise, Carlos rose to his feet, his brows lifted in surprise.

"Philippe. What the devil are you doing in London?"

Heaving a sigh, Philippe lowered himself in the seat opposite his friend. His entire body ached with weariness.

"I have hopes that I am merely passing through."

Carlos's dark countenance was wary as he resumed his own seat. "Have you brought Raine with you?"

Philippe abruptly turned his head to study the fire. So, Raine had not contacted Carlos to tell him of her return to England. A fierce relief ran through him. She might not yet be his, but she belonged to no one else.

"She is in Knightsbridge with her father," he at last admitted.

Carlos gave a choked cough. "In Knightsbridge? I did not believe when I left Paris that you intended to ever let her out of your sight again."

"I did not." Philippe forced himself to meet his friend's searching gaze. "After you left I took Raine to Madeira with every intention of making her my wife."

"Your wife? *Meu Deus.*" Carlos did not bother to hide his shock. "What happened?"

Philippe's lips twisted in a humorless smile. "Raine made it clear that she would not wed me."

There was a moment of silence before Carlos slowly smiled. Damn the bastard. He clearly found it quite amusing that Raine was leading Philippe on such a merry chase.

"Ah."

"You do not seem especially surprised," Philippe said sardonically. He could not truly blame his friend for being pleased that he was being punished for his sins. It was no doubt a long-overdue punishment.

Carlos shrugged. "Raine is not like most women."

"I am well aware of that." Philippe settled deeper in the leather chair. "If she were like most women, then she would have committed murder for the opportunity to land a wealthy husband."

"She might have been content to wed you for the sake of your wealth if you had not had the bad taste to make her fall in love with you."

Philippe flinched. The thought of Raine loving him brought with it a confusion of emotions. Elation that he had managed to win her heart, and an agonizing realization that he had treated her with such a selfish lack of concern for her tender emotions that she might never forgive him.

Dark, biting pain clenched his heart before he was firmly thrusting aside his defeatist thoughts. No. It could not be too late. He would not allow it to be too late.

"Then obviously I must discover another means to tempt her to become my wife," he said softly.

"And what would that be?"

"If she will not have my wealth, then perhaps she will have my heart."

"Meu Deus." With a jerky motion, Carlos reached for the nearby brandy and drained the bottle in one large swallow.

Philippe could not halt a small laugh at his friend's astonishment. "My thoughts precisely."

Carlos's dark features momentarily hardened. His own feelings for Raine were still raw enough for him to resent the thought of Philippe taking the woman as his bride. Then with an obvious effort, he forced a smile to his lips.

"I suppose I have nothing left to do but offer my congratulations."

With an effort, Philippe pushed himself to his feet and held his hands toward the fire. As weary as his body might be, his mind was restless and anxious to complete his tasks in London. The sooner he was done, the sooner he could leave for Knightsbridge.

"Ah, if only it were that simple."

"What do you mean?"

"I possess an uncomfortable feeling that Raine will not be as willing as you to believe my love for her." He gave a shake of his head. "She has convinced herself that I consider her as no more than a possession that I intend to stow away on Madeira while I supposedly enjoy a string of mistresses around the world."

"Was that not what you intended to do?" Carlos demanded.

Philippe sighed. "In truth, I gave little thought to the future beyond ensuring that Raine was irrevocably mine. I suppose I assumed that once she was my wife she would suddenly be content with whatever I was willing to offer her. It was not until she was gone that I accepted just what a bastard I had been."

"Yes."

With a short, humorless laugh, Philippe turned to meet Carlos's accusing gaze. "You cannot make me feel worse than I already do, *amigo.* I kidnapped her, seduced her and treated her as a meaningless courtesan that I intended to toss aside when I tired of her. The only thing she ever asked of me was that I open my heart to her, and it was the one thing I refused to offer. If there were justice in the world then I would no doubt be forced to spend the rest of my days alone, longing for the one woman I can never have."

Carlos's stark expression faintly eased at Philippe's obvious pain. "I have noted that there is rarely justice in this world," he said wryly.

"Thank God, because I have no intention of allowing Raine to slip away from me," he said, his voice rough.

Crossing his arms over his chest, Carlos paced toward the heavy walnut desk. He perched on a corner as he regarded Philippe with a hint of curiosity.

"You still have not explained why you are in London rather than Knightsbridge."

"First I must know what happened to Seurat."

"Did you not receive my letter?"

Philippe gave an impatient wave of his hand. "Yes, I know that Seurat was forced to confess and that Jean-Pierre was released from prison, but where is Seurat now?"

Carlos's curiosity deepened as a faint smile played about his lips. "I requested that the king hold him captive until you could arrive and personally punish him for his sins against your family."

"He is at Windsor?"

"No, I believe he is being held in the same prison cell that your brother so recently occupied. The king thought it a nice jest."

"Good." Philippe planted his hands on his hips. With any luck at all he would be on his way to Knightsbridge before luncheon tomorrow. "In the morning I want you to go to the prison and have Seurat brought here."

Carlos sucked in a sharp breath. "You surely do not intend to hang the poor man in your drawing room?"

"Nothing so dramatic," Philippe assured him.

"Then what do you intend to do with him?"

"I intend to release him."

Carlos muttered a curse as he straightened to cross the room and stand directly before Philippe.

"Have you taken leave of your senses?" he demanded. "A few weeks in a damp cell will not have eased Seurat's crazed lust for revenge on your father. If anything he is no doubt even more anxious for blood."

Philippe shrugged, his once-fierce need to exact payment from the pathetic creature overwhelmed by his need to prove to Raine that he could change.

"Perhaps, but I no longer intend to protect my father, or even my brother, from their own sins. I have far more important matters to attend to. From now on they shall have to fend for themselves."

"And if Seurat decides to make *you* the focus of his retribution?"

A slow smile curved Philippe's lips. "He will not."

"How can you be so certain?"

"Because he will know that his life is being spared solely because Raine pleaded his cause, and that she will soon be my wife."

Carlos gave a slow shake of his head, regarding Philippe as if he had never truly seen him before. And, in truth, he hadn't, Philippe acknowledged. Until Raine had tumbled into his life, he had closely guarded himself from others. He was determined she would never be hurt by another even at the cost of his own happiness.

"This makes no sense," Carlos growled. "You have devoted months, not to mention a near fortune, to capturing Seurat. Why would you simply release him?"

"Because it is what Raine desires," he said simply. "And I intend to prove that from this day forward her happiness is all that I care about."

CHAPTER TWENTY-NINE

FOR ONCE RAINE BARELY noticed the chilled breeze as she turned the cart onto the narrow path and urged her ancient horse to a pace just above a slow crawl.

When she had left her cottage earlier in the day, she had no notion of what to expect when she arrived at the local vicarage. Certainly the vicar had been encouraging when she had spoken with him about the possibility of holding classes for the girls. But she had no real notion of whether or not there would be any genuine interest from the villagers.

After all, many households needed their daughters to begin earning a wage when they were still very young. The girls might very well be forbidden from using an entire afternoon on something that would bring in no coin.

Much to her surprise, however, when she had walked into the vicarage she had discovered the drawing room nearly overwhelmed by the numerous children. Even more surprising, they had all been avidly eager to learn.

Her heart held a decided glow of warmth that battled the falling gloom of the late afternoon as she rattled down the road. She might not be about to alter the world, but at least she could make a difference in this small village.

For now, that was enough.

Lost in thoughts of the numerous supplies that she would need to order from London, Raine paid little heed to the shadows that lined the narrow path. Why should she? Since her father had given up his role as the Knave of Knightsbridge the roads were once again safe.

Or at least they should have been safe.

As she pondered how many slate boards and boxes of chalk she would need for the upcoming months, there was a rustle in the hedgerow that made her stiffen with the first flare of alarm. A tingle inched down her spine as she realized just how alone and isolated she was on the barren stretch of path.

Telling herself it was no more than a stray dog, or perhaps a grouse settling for the night, Raine futilely urged her poor horse to a faster pace. She was less than a mile from her cottage, she reassured herself. In just a few minutes she would be safely in the stables and…

A shriek of fear was wrenched from her throat as the hedges parted and a large stallion burst onto the road. On top of the saddle was a caped form that seemed terrifyingly huge in the fading light.

Raine's heart beat frantically against her chest as she wrenched the cart to a sudden halt. Oh, God. She had been a fool not to accept the vicar's offer to accompany her home.

Perhaps sensing her frozen fear, the man urged his large steed forward, his face nearly hidden behind a thick muffler.

"Stand and deliver," he at last growled.

Raine's heart skipped and then plummeted to her stomach. Not in fear on this occasion. No. She recognized that voice.

"Philippe?" she rasped, her stunned astonishment turning to fury as he tugged down the muffler to reveal the painfully handsome features she had never thought to see again. "God Almighty, you nearly made my heart stop beating," she said, her voice harsh.

His green eyes glinted with an indecipherable emotion as

he moved forward. "Oddly, you have the same effect on my heart, *meu amor.*"

Her hands tightened on the reins, making the poor beast toss her head in protest. Bloody hell. She could not think, she could barely breathe, as she struggled to accept that Philippe was not some figment of a nightmare.

"What are you doing in Knightsbridge?"

"You are not a fool." His lips twisted as he studied her pale face with a hungry gaze. "You know precisely what I am doing in Knightsbridge."

Wounded pride came to her rescue as she gave a tilt of her chin. Just weeks ago this man had tossed her off his estate like a bit of rubbish. She would not fall beneath his potent spell again.

"Actually, I cannot imagine. You made it clear when you commanded me to leave Madeira that you were done with me." She forced a stiff smile to her lips. "Is there another maiden in the village you have come to kidnap?"

Philippe lifted his brows in mild surprise. "Surely you cannot be angry with me, *querida?* It was you that refused my offer of marriage, and you that demanded to be returned to your father's care. It is rather unfair of you to punish me for obeying your commands."

"I am not attempting to punish you," she snapped. "I simply do not believe we have anything further to say to each other."

"We shall see about that."

His bland tone gave her no warning of his intentions, and it was not until he had leaned forward to snatch her from the cart that she realized her danger.

"Philippe, stop this at once," she squawked, finding herself settled on the saddle in front of Philippe with his arm wrapped tightly around her before she could even begin to struggle.

"No," he retorted, urging his horse to turn about and head down the narrow path.

Raine clutched at his arm, fiercely aware of the hard strength of his body and the scent of his skin that cloaked about her with a tangible force.

Dear heavens. Even after he had shattered her heart, she still responded to him with a searing awareness that was making her heart pound and her blood race with excitement.

Blast the irritating man.

She might be furious with him, but a part of her still trembled with joy at his unexpected arrival.

"You cannot leave my horse in the middle of the road," she charged, desperate to distract herself from her treacherous reaction.

"That nag will not stray far." Philippe urged his mount to a faster pace. "I will send Swann back to collect her, although it would be kinder to cut her reins and let the poor beast free."

"Kinder for me, as well," she muttered.

He leaned down until his lips brushed her ear. "And what is that cryptic remark supposed to mean?"

Her breath caught as she closed her eyes against the heat spreading through her body.

"It means that you devote a great deal of time to carrying me off to one place or another. Usually without my consent."

"If I were ever so foolish as to await your consent, *meu amor*, then I would never be able to carry you off." His arm tightened about her, his fingers tantalizingly close to the curve of her breast. "An appalling thought that does not bear contemplating."

Instinctively, she attempted to twist away from the seductive touch. "Philippe."

"Do not squirm, Raine." His voice was suddenly thick with his own need. "Not unless you deliberately wish to torment me."

"The notion has some appeal."

He chuckled softly, but he made no response as they crossed the yard of her father's cottage and within a few minutes entered the shadows of the stable. The horse had barely come to a halt when Philippe was leaping to the floor and crossing to speak with the elderly groom who was absently whittling in a corner.

Raine narrowed her eyes in suspicion as Philippe spoke briefly to the servant, who promptly strolled from the stable, shutting the door behind him.

Her suspicion only deepened when Philippe returned to the horse and easily plucked her from the saddle. With a deliberate motion, he slid her body down his own before she was back on her feet.

Raine swallowed a groan of pleasure as she forced herself to step away from his lingering touch and glared into the face that had haunted her nights since her return to England.

"What are you doing?"

Philippe shrugged as he casually tossed aside his hat and gloves. "It is warm enough in here to keep us from freezing and we at least have a measure of privacy."

Raine shivered in fear. The stables suddenly seemed small and dark and far too intimate with the sweet smell of hay in the air. Dear God, she did not want to be alone with this man. Not when her body was already aching to be crushed in his arms.

"I do not want privacy. I want you to return to Madeira and leave me in peace."

His hooded gaze regarded her in the shrouded darkness. "Is that what you have found here, peace?"

"Yes, I have," she said, thinking of the eager girls she had just left.

"Your father said that you had spent the day at the vicarage with your students."

Her eyes widened in horror. "You spoke with my father?"

"Our meeting was long overdue." Something that might have been regret clouded the perfect features. "I owed your father my deepest apologies, as well as the assurance that I would make sure your future was properly secure."

So that was it, she thought as she abruptly turned away to hide her hurt expression. He was here out of a sense of guilt.

"You have already secured my future. Or do you not recall the three thousand pounds you requested your servant offer me before having me escorted off your estate?"

There was a long pause, as if she had managed to strike a nerve, then she heard him heave a deep sigh.

"That was ill-done."

"Why?" She gave a faint shrug, relieved when her voice came out cool and dismissive. "It is the method that most gentlemen use to rid themselves of unwanted mistresses."

"Damn you," he growled, his hands landing on her shoulders to turn her to meet his burning gaze.

"What?"

"Do you wish to know why I sent you away?"

"It was obvious that you had tired of me. Just as I warned you would."

"I will never tire of you." His hands shifted to cup her face in his hands. "There has not been a moment that you have not haunted my thoughts."

Her heart slammed against her ribs. "Rubbish."

The lean, heartbreakingly handsome features twisted with anguish. "My God, Raine, there is not a room in my house that is not filled with your delicate scent, or where I cannot recall the sound of your voice. And my garden…" He slowly shook his head. "It is now no more than a bleak reminder of all I have lost. You are branded on my heart. And that is why I was forced to send you away."

Her knees went weak as his soft words slammed into her with ruthless force. He seemed so…sincere. As if he truly was in pain.

Was it possible that Philippe really had missed her? That he regretted allowing her to leave? Had he come to...

No, oh, no, Raine Wimbourne. She could not be so gullible. Philippe could never give her what she needed. And she could not endure being hurt again.

"Is that supposed to make sense?" she demanded.

He smiled wryly. "When does a gentleman in love ever make sense?"

"My God. No, Philippe." With an agonized gasp she jerked from his touch and headed toward the door.

He caught her within a handful of steps, his arms wrapping about her waist as he buried his face in her neck.

"Do not run from me, Raine, I beg of you."

Tears filled her eyes as she gave a frantic shake of her head. "I cannot do this."

"Please, *meu amor,* you claimed that I had no need for another in my life, but you are wrong, just as I have been wrong for so long. I thought that being alone made me strong, but that was only an excuse." He shifted his head to press his cheek against hers. "I was quite simply a coward."

Raine was forced to grasp the lapels of his coat to keep from sinking to the ground. "You were afraid of me? Ridiculous."

"I was afraid to allow you into my heart." He made a sound deep in his throat. "No, that is not true. I had no choice about whether or not you entered my heart. You charged in without invitation. What I feared was acknowledging just how much you had become a part of my life. That was why I was so desperate to convince myself that you were no more than a passing fancy."

The memory of his extravagant gifts returned with a sharp pain. "Your mistress," she said in flat tones.

"Yes. A mistress does not break a gentleman's heart. Or so I believed until you." He grimaced. "But even as I was attempting to deceive myself, a part of me knew the truth. Why else was I frantic to find you after you disappeared from London? Why else did I force you to travel with me to Paris? Why else did I spend every moment attempting to bind you to me so tightly that you could never escape? Either I am truly a madman, or I already knew that you were the one woman who was destined to be my future."

Raine's eyes filled with tears. "Pretty words, but that does not alter the reason I left you, Philippe."

"I know, *meu amor.* You asked nothing more of me than to accept that I need you. And I am here to tell you that I do. I need you so desperately that I will do anything." Without warning Philippe slowly kneeled before her, his darkened gaze never leaving her face. "Even get down on my knees if that is what you desire, to prove I am empty and lost without you."

"What are you doing?" she breathed in surprise. Never in her life had she expected to see Philippe Gautier on his knees. Not for any reason.

"I have something for you. Actually, I have two gifts."

Her brief bemusement was shattered with a flare of annoyance.

"Good God, Philippe. Do you still think I can be purchased like a piece of goods?"

"No, you will want these gifts, I assure you," he interrupted, reaching beneath his greatcoat to pull out a folded piece of parchment.

Raine stiffened, painfully reminded of her last day on Madeira. If this parchment held another three thousand pounds she swore that she would blacken his eye. And perhaps break that perfect nose.

With shaking fingers she unfolded the paper, her brows drawing together as realized there were no unpleasant surprises.

"A letter?" she muttered, her eyes widening as her gaze

drifted over the elaborate, sprawling handwriting at the bottom of the page. "Good heavens, it is signed by the king of England."

Still on his knees, Philippe flashed a heart-rending smile. "I requested that he assure you that Seurat has been released."

Raine sucked in deep breaths of the hay-scented air. She was accustomed to Philippe charging into her life and creating chaos, but this made no sense.

"You have had him released?" She gave a shake of her head. "But why?"

"Because it was what you desired," he said simply. "And from this day forward I intend to prove that I will do whatever necessary to make you happy."

She licked her dry lips as she struggled to accept that he truly had made such a sacrifice for her. And it was a sacrifice. Seurat had threatened his family, and for Philippe there could be no greater sin. His need to punish the man was an overwhelming force in his life.

And he had given it up. For her.

"I...I do not know what to say," she whispered.

With elegant ease Philippe rose to his feet, once again reaching beneath his coat.

"Here is my other gift," he said softly.

Glancing down, Raine watched as Philippe pressed the golden necklace into her hand. Her eyes filled with tears at the sight of the precious locket. She knew it meant more to this man than all the jewels in Europe.

Slowly her eyes lifted to meet his searching gaze. "Your mother's locket."

A slow smile curved his lips. "She would want you to have it. You are the only female I have ever met that is worthy of her."

She became lost in his smoldering gaze. "But I am not, Philippe. I am nothing more than a sailor's daughter."

"You are Raine Wimbourne." He carefully reached to pull her into his arms, as if he feared she might recoil from his touch. "A woman of honor and dignity. A woman with a sweet, generous nature who brings happiness to all those whom she encounters. A woman who would rather live in poverty than to accept the blundering proposal of a man who is undeserving of her."

Raine leaned back to regard him in startled horror. "I have never thought you undeserving, Philippe."

"Then you should have." He pulled her tightly to his body, his expression dark with regret. "I wanted you to love me. I wanted to you to offer me your very soul without having to risk returning that precious gift. I was a fool. And I have paid a dear price." He leaned forward to press his lips to her forehead. "I love you, Raine. Please tell me that I am not too late. Tell me that you can forgive me."

Raine felt a small smile begin to tug at her lips. Philippe had swallowed his pride to follow her to Knightsbridge. Even more he had released Seurat simply because he knew it would make her happy.

And he had said the magic words.

I love you.

Her heart sang with joy as she lifted her hand to lightly touch his cheek.

"I will forgive you if you make me one promise."

Pulling back, he regarded her with a desperate gaze. "Anything. Anything at all."

"From this day forward you must promise that you will stop your appalling habit of kidnapping poor, unsuspecting females."

There was a moment's pause, and then, giving a loud shout of laughter, Philippe swept her off her feet and held her tightly against his chest.

"Oh, *meu amor,* I can safely promise that the only woman

I will ever bother to kidnap will be my beautiful, daring, passionate wife." His eyes darkened with a smoldering heat. "And I intend to hold her hostage for all eternity."

CHAPTER THIRTY

Madeira, One Year Later

AS WAS HER HABIT, RAINE SPENT the morning enjoying her breakfast in the beauty of the garden. It not only offered a few moments of solitude before her busy day of overseeing the household and meeting with the numerous villagers who now turned to her for assistance, but over the past weeks she had discovered that the crisp air helped to counter the morning sickness that plagued her.

Rising to her feet, Raine absently touched the faint swell of her stomach that was the only indication she would soon have an addition to her family.

Philippe was delighted, of course. At least when he was not worrying himself into a state of near panic. Since their wedding he had proved to be an astonishingly protective husband. He was forever fussing over her to ensure that she did not overtire herself, or take the slightest risk. Now that she was pregnant he was nearly insufferable. If he had his way she would remain tucked in her bed with a dozen servants hovering about to tend to her every need.

Not that she truly minded, she acknowledged as she entered the sprawling villa. It seemed unbelievable, but over the past year, Raine had tumbled even more deeply in love with her husband. Her marriage was not always easy; they were both far too stubborn not to have their occasional spats. But over the passing days they had developed a relationship that offered far more than mere passion. They were friends, and companions and partners as they worked side by side to keep Philippe's numerous companies profitable, and to oversee the charities that Raine had already established.

It was a hectic, wonderful life that Raine could never have dreamed possible.

As she was climbing the stairs, Raine's happy musings were interrupted by the unmistakable sound of Philippe's low cursing coming from his study.

Startled as much by the realization that her husband had returned so swiftly from his daily inspection of his vineyards as by his obviously foul mood, Raine altered her path and entered the study.

As always her heart gave a tiny leap at the sight of the man who had changed her life. Even casually attired in buff breeches and a worn jade jacket he appeared more a god than a mere human.

For a moment she simply allowed herself the pleasure of watching him pace across the room with short, jerky steps. A warm, delicious desire swirled in the pit of her stomach. Good heavens. She would never, ever tire of walking into a room and finding Philippe awaiting her.

With a happy sigh, she forced herself to move forward. She hoped whatever was troubling her husband would not take long to soothe. They had a few hours to spare before the local children would arrive for their English lessons. Hours that could be nicely spent upstairs in their private chambers.

"Good Lord, Philippe, whatever is the matter?" she teased.

Philippe held up the sheet of paper he had gripped in his hand.

"I have just received word from Mr. Boland. That ridiculous buffoon has the audacity to refuse my request to come to the estate and remain until the baby is born."

Raine gave a shake of her head. She had been adamantly against Philippe's determination to bring London's most celebrated surgeon to the island. She far preferred the local doctor, who was not only a sensible man, but one who had delivered hundreds of babies over the years.

"I did warn you that a doctor of his reputation would hardly be willing to give up his practice for weeks merely to have the honor of bringing your child into the world," she said.

"*Our* child," he corrected as he moved to stand directly before her, his hand reaching out to lightly touch her stomach. It was a habit he had developed from the moment he had discovered she had conceived. "And, as I offered him a bloody fortune, he should damn well be grateful."

Gently she lay her hand over his. "Obviously he is not nearly so intelligent as you thought him to be."

He offered a sour grimace. "Obviously not."

"Do not fret, love. I have told you over and over I am perfectly satisfied with our local doctor."

His expression darkened, his eyes shimmering with concern. "Perhaps we should return to London until after the babe is born."

Raine stiffened in alarm. It would take a bloody battalion to force her from her home.

"Absolutely not," she said in a tone that defied argument. "I would be miserable waddling about in that cold, damp air. Besides, I want our baby to be born here. This is our home. The place where we will raise our family, surrounded by people we love."

"But if something were to go wrong…" His features softened with the adoration he now revealed without hesitation. "I could not bear to lose you, Raine."

She reached up to lay her hand on his cheek, her heart nearly bursting with happiness. "Nothing will go wrong, but even if it should, I would trust someone I know rather than a stranger. I will not budge on this, Philippe."

Her tone was soft, but Philippe knew her well enough to realize when he had been beaten. Heaving a sigh, he wrapped his arms about her waist.

"Have I ever told you just how remarkably stubborn you are?"

"At least once every day." She sent him a coy glance. "But, I shall forgive you as long as you also tell me you love me every day."

An intelligent man, Philippe was not slow in responding to her subtle hint.

"Every day? You are a greedy little thing. Still, I suppose for the sake of our children I can be forced to give in to your demands." With a smooth motion he had her swept off her feet and was carrying her swiftly toward the door. "Of course, I do have a few demands of my own."

Raine chuckled as her body readily melted with need. "It was your demands that made this situation, if you will recall."

"Hmm." His head lowered to nuzzle at her neck. "I am not certain if I entirely recall. I think perhaps you should remind me."

She wrapped her arms about his neck. "Do you know, Philippe, I truly do believe this must be paradise."

He smiled with a tender warmth. "Until you arrived it was merely another house on a pretty island. You have made my home a paradise, *meu amor.* And you are my very own angel."

On sale 6th March 2009

BECKET'S LAST STAND
by Kasey Michaels

For years, Courtland Becket denied himself the only woman who stirred his blood, yet he could no longer ignore the lovely Cassandra. For gone was the girl he had once teased – replaced by a fully grown woman, adamant that they act on their long-denied feelings. It was time for him to allow himself a taste of the forbidden!

But passion's price could prove too high when an age-old enemy returns to wreak revenge against the entire Becket clan, leaving Courtland torn between his new-found love and his duty to the family that means everything to him…

"Kasey Michaels aims for the heart and never misses"
—New York Times bestselling author Nora Roberts

Love is the most tempting betrayal of all…

Scotland, 1561

By trying to help the reckless, defiant Mary, Queen of Scots take her rightful place on the throne, Lady Gwenyth Macleod is at perilous odds with Rowan Graham, a laird accomplished in both passion and affairs of state.

The more Gwenyth challenges his intentions, the less he can resist the desire igniting between them. But will Gwenyth's last daring gamble lead her to the ultimate betrayal – or a destiny greater than she could ever imagine?

Available 16th January 2009

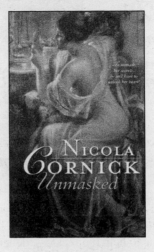

Regency

High Society
Affairs

Rakes and rogues in the ballrooms – and the bedrooms – of Regency England!

6th March 2009
A Hasty Betrothal by Dorothy Elbury &
A Scandalous Marriage by Mary Brendan

3rd April 2009
Desire My Love by Miranda Jarrett &
The Rake and the Rebel by Mary Brendan

1st May 2009
Sparhawk's Lady by Miranda Jarrett &
The Earl's Intended Wife by Louise Allen

5th June 2009
Lord Calthorpe's Promise by Sylvia Andrew &
The Society Catch by Louise Allen

8 VOLUMES IN ALL TO COLLECT!

www.millsandboon.co.uk

M&B

MILLS & BOON

Historical

On sale 6th March 2009

Regency

THE RAKE'S DEFIANT MISTRESS
by Mary Brendan

Snowbound with notorious rake Sir Clayton Powell, defiant
Ruth Hayden manages to resist falling into his arms.
But Clayton hides the pain of betrayal behind his charm,
and even Ruth, no stranger to scandal, is shocked by the
vicious gossip about him. Recklessly, she seeks to silence
his critics – by announcing their engagement!

Regency

THE VISCOUNT CLAIMS HIS BRIDE
by Bronwyn Scott

For years Valerian Inglemoore, Viscount St Just, was a secret
agent on the war-torn Continent. Returning home, he
knows exactly what he wants – Philippa Stratten, the
woman he left for the sake of her family… But Philippa
won't risk her heart again. Valerian realises he must fight
a fiercer battle to win her as his bride…

Secrets always find a place to hide…

When DEA agent Rodrigo Ramirez finds undercover work at Gloryanne Barnes's nearby farm, Gloryanne's sweet innocence is too much temptation for him. Confused and bitter about love, Rodrigo's not sure if his reckless offer of marriage is just a means to completing his mission – or something more.

But as Gloryanne's bittersweet miracle and Rodrigo's double life collide, two people must decide if there's a chance for the future they both secretly desire.

Available 6th February 2009